Kurt Tommyrot, author of *Subliminal Messages You Can't Refuse*, "Read this book."

"I want to dearly know how did I live so long and not learn this stuff? I demand a refund." Stephen Queen Nader III, author of *It Keeps Getting Worse*, and *Chewbacca Didn't Smoke For a Reason*

"I really didn't want to like this book. Gave it my best to snigger it, but it just stirred up so many trainwreck memories that I couldn't put it down any more than I could forgo an opportunity to pose for a selfie with Peter Pan." Samuel Bassinet, host of multiple podcasts and nimby garage sales coming soon to your neighborhood

"Wear a straight jacket or you're bound to break a rib. But I know a great chiropractor. His name is Doctor Gary." J.P.G13 Johnson of the Atlanta Declarative Sentence

INSURRECT ME

BY WILLIAM KIRK

Insurrect Me

Copyright © 2024 by William Kirk

All rights reserved. No part of this publication may be reproduced, stored in a retrieval system, or transmitted, in any form or by any means without the prior written permission of the publisher, nor be otherwise circulated in any form of binding or cover other than that in which it is published and without a similar condition being imposed on the subsequent purchaser.

First Printing, 2024

ISBN : 9798326563088

Published by William Kirk
Cover design by: PJ Kirk

Book Interior and E-book Design by Amit Dey (amitdey2528@gmail.com)

To the Paul Girls of Wilder, Vermont
the Farley Boys of Nicasio, California
the forests of Anniston, Alabama
& to home fires
Illuminating the channel

ACKNOWLEDGEMENTS

I'm thanking you, because all of you have participated in getting this book to the bookshelves. You probably don't remember the times your quick thinking kept me out of jail. Yeah, that was me. With special appreciation to Don Swaim, who has run the Bucks County Writers Workshop for twenty-five years; Marina Pruna and her Writers in Paradise Experience at Eckerd College; with a special thanks to Anja Delgato, tutor extraordinaire. And not to leave out Rosemont College that has gone out of its way to put up with my trespasses. Double plus my copyeditor, Emily Gorsky. She knows her commas, I on the other hand, thought they were synonyms for sleep, something to avoid so as to not miss the show. And Amit Dey who cut the book down to size so POD would stop rejecting it. And most importantly, sister Peg @ Visual One, who drew the perfect cover and likely why you opened it.

TABLE OF CONTENTS

Chapter 1: That's One Way Out 1

Chapter 2: One Way In. 19

Chapter 3: Two Way Street. 29

Chapter 4: Some Circles Are Rounder 35

Chapter 5: One Way Street. 41

Chapter 6: Annuity Potholes. 49

Chapter 7: Sinkhole. 59

Chapter 8: Round Tube. 63

Chapter 9: Ferris Wheel on Fentanyl 69

Chapter 10: Circle in a Box. 75

Chapter 11: Inside Midlight, Outside Night. 87

Chapter 12: Going Where One Has Always Been 93

Chapter 13: Nowhere To Go, Nowhere to Be. 97

Chapter 14: Roller Coaster Jig 113

Chapter 15: Port of High School 127

Chapter 16: 359 degrees 149

Chapter 17: Pizzas Are Round 153

Chapter 18: Forward to Back 159

Chapter 19: No Pins Nor Needles. 167

Chapter 20: Bemusement Ride 177

Chapter 21: Applicant Highways 187

Chapter 22: Tire Marks. 197

Chapter 23: Roadkill 203

Chapter 24: Homeless Pothole 207

Chapter 25: First Invention Was the Trail. 219

Chapter 26: Labyrinth Unfurled 225

Chapter 27: Highway Get-Away. 233

Chapter 28: Encircling the Wagons 245

Chapter 29: Parking Lot Upper Mobility 263

Chapter 30: Monitor Circuit. 267

Chapter 31: Speeding in Park 269

Chapter 32: Babbling En Route 273

Chapter 33: Split-Step Labyrinth 283

Chapter 34: Another Parking Lot 285

Chapter 35: 80-Year-Old Cycle. 289

Chapter 36: RV Avenue 293

TABLE OF CONTENTS

Chapter 37: Convoy to the Capitol 299

Chapter 38: Four Wall Pace Track 305

Chapter 39: Melody's Joy Ride 315

Chapter 40: Hurrah Rush 319

Chapter 41: One RV On the Loose 323

Chapter 42: Bullying Along on the Interstate 327

Chapter 43: A Million Miles an Hour at Home 331

Chapter 44: Buy the Way 335

Chapter 45: Bathtub Ring 341

Chapter 46: Jose's Bike Ride 345

Chapter 47: Keypad Rodeo 349

Chapter 48: Back From the Store 351

Chapter 49: In and Out 361

Chapter 50: Parked In a Park 371

Chapter 51: No Hitching 373

Chapter 52: Last Call 379

Chapter 53: Circling Down the Drain 399

Chapter 54: Insurrection Epiphany 403

Chapter 55: Film Noir 409

Chapter 56: Speed Up in a Turn 415

Chapter 57: The Stakes and Cake 419

CHAPTER ONE

THAT'S ONE WAY OUT

It's Christmas Eve everywhere but in the home of Andy and Melody MacClean. No decorated tree stands inside. No stockings are nailed to the mantle. And it's no telling how long that mistletoe has dangled from the pots-and-pans rack hanging above the cooktop. Surely, it would take an agile couple to maneuver under it for a quick peck. Nearly impossible without suffering third degree burns if Andy was cooking. But, not so long ago, the impossible was their favorite hunting ground. What's a little charred flesh?

The current activity is not going on in the kitchen, but in the basement where their Christmas ornaments lie undisturbed inside plastic bins. Andy MacClean shaves another band of walnut from the Hiroshima plaque. He puts down the diamond sharp chisel and blows off the sawdust to better eye the work in progress. Progress is tricky to measure through a full-face respirator mask. Andy has to feel where he's going by the shiver of the lathe and hear it in the patient resistance of cellulose leaving its ancestral home. The plaque has to be completed by the Epiphany to make the deadline. That's less than two weeks away.

The phone rings.

He steps away from his lathe to read the phone number. It's the bank loan officer. What can Andy tell him? Andy lets it ring out and is thankful the guy doesn't leave a message. If Melody was home, she would have picked up. "Confronting beats hiding," is her motto. "It's also the best way to try out my latest and improved evasion tactic."

Andy is pretty sure the way out of their predicament is not words but cash in hand. He takes off his mask and gloves and dials Mrs. Watanabe's number. Maybe he can move up the delivery date and, with it, the payment for the plaque. The phone rings on when there's a buzz from an incoming call. The phone ID number is the hospital's. He cancels Watanabe, presses the new call button, and says, "MacClean here," no more sure he wants to hear from the hospital than he does from the bank.

"Melody MacClean's husband?" the voice on the other line asks.

"Yes."

"Pick her up today before six o'clock or she stays here until next year. Got that?"

"What the hell? Is this a ransom notice?"

"Whatever would make you think that? I'm Doctor Howard Driscoll, adjunct assistant chief psychiatrist at Sheppard Pratt Psychiatric Hospital. And all of us doctors are going home to our families for the holidays at six. Sorry for the short notice. I have to go. Lots of calls to make."

The name sounds familiar but wrong too. Hadn't he spoken to every doctor at Sheppard Pratt by now? Howard Driscoll sounds like an actor in a sitcom. He has to finish the plaque. He can't afford to lose another day.

"And Mr. MacClean, one other thing," says the voice on the other line. "She insists that you bring her a Cinnamon Dolce Latte when you pick her up." Click.

It's after four and Sheppard Pratt is a good hour and a half drive in good traffic. And on Christmas Eve? While fantasizing living another week absent Melody minding, he unties his apron and calls, "Benedict Arnold." Then he tosses his apron into the hamper and switches his thoughts to navigating Baltimore's back streets, in case Christmas drivers get religious about sticking to the speed limit. Unlike the ever-recalcitrant Melody MacClean, Benedict Arnold, leash in mouth, is already whipping Andy's calves with his tail.

Andy makes it to Sheppard Pratt with three minutes until six. No time for a latte. He parks their Buick in the emergency lane and waves at the valet, who waves back and doesn't leave his podium. By now they're friends.

He takes the stairs to her room on the fifth floor but finds an elderly man in her bed, his wife sitting beside him. They're holding hands as if saying their final goodbyes. He apologizes and walks over to the nurse station. No one is there. He doesn't pass anyone in the halls. Is it Christmas Eve or the end of the earth? He goes down one floor: no difference. So, he races down to the first floor and approaches the help desk.

He doesn't recognize the woman behind the glass panel. Surely, she will tell him which room Melody is in now.

"I'm sorry," says the woman, name tag 'Prudence,' in smaller lettering 'volunteer'. Andy wonders why a multi-billion-dollar hospital can't afford receptionists and why the volunteers always had first names from some other century. "I don't see that we have your wife registered. Could she be under a different name, maybe her maiden name? Melody…"

"Call Doctor Howard Driscoll," says Andy. "He's the guy who called me. Told me to come and get her."

Prudence checks one of her binders. Then another. "No, we have neither a patient nor a doctor named Howard Driscoll. Perhaps you're at the wrong hospital. Sinai? Med Star? Johns Hopkins?"

"Look, Miss Prudence, I'm not at the wrong hospital. I've visited my wife here half a dozen times. Probably twice that."

"What can I tell you? She's not here now."

"Tell me when she left then," asks Andy.

"I'm sorry," Prudence says. She points to the binders in front of her. "I only have access to these. The hospital prints them out every morning."

"How about Doctor Rosenberg? Doctor Whitton? Doctor Horst?"

Prudence flips through her binders. Three times, she points with her thin, white index finger at the large, red, stamped block letters in the binder stating that the requested doctor is off duty. "It is Christmas Eve, Mr. MacClean, after all."

Anger clamps Andy's jaws shut. Enough talk. He wants to grab this woman by the throat and… What? This isn't him. He didn't come here to hurt anyone. He came here to take Melody home. His car is outside, engine running, keys and Benedict Arnold inside. What's he going to do now?

Andy tries to take a deep breath, but the air already in his lung lobes refuses to abandon its recently hard-won sanctuary, triggering a coughing fit. When he takes a step back to not hack all over Prudence, he finds there's a woman standing barely an inch behind him. Excuse me? She's sucking an inhaler and holding an overflowing paper grocery bag. A bribe? Why hadn't he thought of that.

Andy looks up at the clock hanging over Prudence's head. It's sixteen after six. It's too late. The doctors are gone. This is his life. So close to the finish point before everything collapses around him. The world has it in for him.

Between coughing spasms, he says, "Thank you," to Prudence, adding under his breath 'for nothing,' and stands aside for the woman who's here, she says too loudly, to pick up her son. He walks away as her complaints about the traffic and drug side effects fades.

Why can't he be more assertive? What is he afraid of? Why does he back down in front of women? He needs an espresso, double. Anything stronger and he'd be the one under a psychiatric hold.

Andy drives to the Starbucks a mile south. Benedict Arnold prowls the backseat. The sun is gone, the sky practically lying on the Buick's roof. He parks. His breathing returns to normal.

He takes Benedict Arnold for a walk. The dog nips his palm when Andy ties him to the bike rack. His palm is barely bleeding, but still. When he tries to see what is bugging Benedict Arnold, the dog backs up against the bike rack and assumes his most ferocious defensive pose. Andy remembers tying him to this bike rack many times before. Had some thug pestered the dog here? Vowing to just get a coffee, drink it in the car, and flee home, Andy walks into the store. What is he going to do when he gets home? At this point he really doesn't care. How could it matter?

When he enters, he has to wave his hands in front of him to fan away aromas' assault— pumpkin, spice, cinnamon. Please. He orders coffee. No, he doesn't need room for milk. While the cashier counts Andy's change, a tray laden with drinks and microwaved meals bursts through the kitchen's swinging doors. Behind the tray marches a woman who, except for the stilettos, must have been dressed by her teenage son—low hanging cargo pants, purple Ravens sweatshirt, and red floppy Santa hat. Instead of continuing to the drive-in window, she looks right at him, "You're late."

Melody MacClean places her tray at the drive-in window, winks at the ear-budded barista sitting there, shakes her apron off, hops onto and swings over the cashier counter, and takes Andy's arm. Commandeering his coffee, she says, "If you were a gentleman, you would have ordered two."

When they walk out, they find that Benedict Arnold has dragged the bike rack three feet closer to Starbuck's front door. Andy unties the dog, and he leaps hip high into Melody's one-armed hug while she territorially protects the coffee from spilling. The MacCleans have always equated spilling anything with a mortal sin. She takes a sip and says, "Always scalding hot." Then she chugs it, tossing the cup in the trash bin, and the three make it to the Buick after Andy returns the bike rack to its starting gate.

Andy lets Melody in the passenger side. Benedict Arnold quickly jumps in her lap, and Andy goes around the car to sit in the driver's seat. Before starting the car, Andy asks, "Who is Doctor Howard Driscoll?"

"He's a new friend of mine," says Melody, "He's studying to be a ventriloquist."

"I guess I worry myself about you for no good purpose," Andy says as he drives out of the parking lot and heads home.

"You're smarter than that, Handsome," says Melody. "I never worry about you. See what I got?" As she says this, he hears the rattle of pills in a bottle near his ear.

"A rattlesnake?"

"Of course. The snake comes with a six-month supply of Xanax. We are the beneficiary of hospitals' soft spots for releasing psychiatric patients in time to celebrate Christmas at home and, not uncoincidentally, out of their over-shampooed hair. Not to discredit my matriculating from five-point suicide watch in a padded cell to compliant patient being a personal best. My third inspired performance in four years. I'm offering the movie rights to the highest bidder on eBay."

Andy half-listens to Melody as he drives home, north up Interstate 95. Cars and trucks whiz by, everybody vying with everyone else to reach home in time for opening Christmas presents. Not a draw for the MacCleans. She's his Christmas present; not the gift kind.

"After each electric shock, I backtrack from the womb," Melody says. "I'm reborn. Until I insert a filter, I react to every sensation equally, a lazy Susan, hogtied to the next stimuli. Every sound, feeling, and sight redirects me from the one before. Once I insert the filter, I have a platform to rank them."

Andy asks, "And that's important because?"

"Without ranking values, we have no reason to get out of bed. The onslaught of sensations overwhelms every defense coping mechanism. Our brain logically concludes that if we don't get out of bed, we will avoid all of this trauma. Better yet, don't wake up at all. Welcome to the eternal oxymoron imperative—We are wide awake."

Normally, this time of year, a driver would see a foot of snow on both sides of the road and, farther out, bleak, leafless trees, icy gray farmland, and a hodgepodge of tract home roofs. In 2020, a driver sees a blight of stark red and blue campaign signs.

The signs are for the immediate past presidential candidates, Trump and Biden. A contest that naggingly holds half the nation in suspense. The reason for planting so many opposing signs is unclear, unless their bright contrasting colors are to remind everyone how ugly the campaign has been. All of it. Andy mumbles, "Bring back the dirty white snow."

Waving her hands at the campaign signage Melody asks, "When's the election?"

"It's over," Andy says. "We voted at our precinct on November 3."

"Before my latest admittance at Sheppard Pratt?"

"Yeah, the day before."

"Certainly was propitious of us," says Melody. "What a wonderful sound, pro pi shush of us. As long as no one shushes me. Who won?"

"I forgot. Your room didn't have a TV, did it?"

"I was busy. Besides, psycho wards only show reruns of Andy Griffith. Even *I Love Lucy* is deemed too contentious."

"That's crazy. I mean, that sucks," says Andy. "Trump won, but the elites won't let him take office. Trump is organizing a rally so we can make sure he stays in office. I'm going to be there. Armed."

"Armed with what, stapler and scissors?" asks Melody. "You told me all my handguns were stolen."

"I'll find something."

"If he won the election, how can the elites keep him from staying in office?" asks Melody. "I don't remember it working that way."

"Widespread voter fraud," says Andy. "Voting irregularities, dead people voting, hacked voting machines, immigrants stuffing ballots, buses going across states, you name it," says Andy.

"I don't get it," says Melody. "So, the elites, whoever in the hell they are, they don't seem to have an address, claim the vote was rigged? In America?"

"Land of the free, if you're simple enough to believe that," says Andy.

"How'd Trump do it?"

"No, no, no," says Andy. "Biden did it."

"Sleepy Joe? The guy who only knows how to go along? His idea of a novelty is ice cream?"

"Yes."

"So, when he woke, pun intended," says Melody, "he manipulated the vote count in fifty states? Republicans let him? We have to give Joe more credit than we ever had. Heck of a guy. Move over Andy Griffin, I gotta learn about this."

Melody turns on the radio and scans through the stations. She listens to snippets from a dozen until she settles on NPR. After about thirty minutes, she switches to a rock station and turns the volume down. Rafferty's "Baker Street" plays. She says, "Not a peep about Trump winning. Your hearing aid needs new batteries?"

"I hear fine," Andy says. "It's just that Trump's losing doesn't make any sense. He was far ahead then all of a sudden… I'm not buying it."

"You always have had a skill for detecting the least likely alternative and being blind to what is right in front of your nose. Your glasses need new batteries?"

"My vision is twenty-twenty, just like the year."

"Then you're the one who should be taking Xanax. We could split 'em. I'll take them on odd numbered days. You swallow them on even numbered days. We could just skip leap year. How about that? This is a leap year, except it's over on New Year's. What an unlucky break."

Suddenly Melody points out the window. "Look over there. Isn't that the same silver Mercedes SUV we saw the day we drove here?"

"Where?" Andy asks.

"It just passed us, you had to have seen it."

"Hard to say Melody, there are hundreds of silver SUVs on the road."

"I recognize the driver," says Melody. "He's wearing the same smirk on his face. Statistically rare that we would see him again. He must be following us."

"By passing us?"

"Correction," says Melody. "Repassing us."

"Well then, it does seem odd."

Then Melody yells, "There he is again, same smirk, but now he's driving a royal blue Jaguar."

Andy asks, "What would you like to do when we get home, Melody?"

"I thought we were going somewhere. Aren't we going somewhere? I'm so tired of being in the same place. It's Christmas. Isn't there anyone we can visit? I saw a sign for a Hess gas station. Could we stop there? Buy a toy truck for our imaginary grandson. Buy some gas, pass some gas. Open a window, will ya?"

"It wasn't me," Andy says, as he pushes down the button that rolls down the back windows. "I think it was Benedict Arnold. Tell me where you want us to go, and I'll take you there." "End of the Line" plays on the radio.

"Petaluma," says Melody. "We'll pop in on Bob and Susan."

"Susan and Bob divorced. Bob lives in Sebastopol with Sheri."

"Same difference."

"Melody, that's three thousand miles away," Andy says.

Melody pulls her seat belt from her waist and asks, "Why is this belt so tight? You afraid of me jumping out?"

"It's the same belt in the same car we've had for years, Melody."

"How come you didn't mention how far away it was when I asked?" Melody says. "I can still count. I'm just so tired of being asked to count backwards by sevens from one hundred. Medical science is stuck in a rut. And this seat belt is going to have to suffocate someone else today. I'm releasing it of its obligation. There, I can breathe again."

"I'm sorry."

"You're always sorry," says Melody. "If I could deposit your sorries in a Swiss bank account, we'd be in a Mercedes or a Jaguar, not a Buick. Where can we go? Can't we visit our parents? How about our kids? A traveler needs a destination. That's part of the word's definition. Unless maybe you're the Traveling Wilburys. They never went anywhere."

"My mom and dad are deceased," says Andy, "Liver failure. And your mom and dad live three thousand miles away also. Jeremy comes by our home all the time, mostly to ask for a loan, but…"

"Jeremy? Remind me again, which one is Jeremy?"

"We adopted Jeremy after Sam was born, remember? You insisted Sam have a playmate when you couldn't have another baby."

"Uterine sarcoma," says Melody.

"That's right."

"So, you performed a hysterectomy."

"What are you talking about? I'm not a doctor," says Andy.

"You didn't get my permission."

"No, I didn't," says Andy. "I wasn't going to wait for you to come out of sedation so I could ask you if it was okay and then have them rip you open again. The doctors said that surgery was the safest course. I couldn't lose you. And I wasn't going to. Every time we go over this you tell me you would have done the same thing. Melody, we've been over this a million…"

"A million is a finite number. What happened to Sam? Died?"

"Yes," says Andy.

"Something I religiously choose not to remember."

Melody switches the music off, and they continue in silence until she says, "You know murder-suicide wouldn't require much explaining to the authorities. Ironclad on both our parts."

"You start that talk, and I turn around and take you back to the hospital. Maybe I'll check myself in with you this time. Sometimes…"

"I'm just talking. What else is there to talk about, how the Ravens are doing? Prognosticating on the weather would be as effective. And those weather people, they stopped forecasting. Now, they hawk the weather as if it were listed on the stock exchange. Buy SKY, sell SNOW. Always spouting some fresh hyperbole for why they were wrong yesterday. Last chance before the cumulus clearance. It's enough to make me puke. Can I say that?"

"Yes, you can. Disgust of others is fair game, disgust of yourself is not."

"Let's go home then. I like it there, just not when you're there. We need to do something about that, but not right now. Tomorrow, maybe. Right now, I want to be with Benedict Arnold and drink beer."

"He's really missed you," says Andy.

"What about you Mr. MacClean?"

"What about me?"

"Did you miss me?"

"Of course I did," says Andy. And he had, but it was more a continuum of crazy anxiety dribbling into a scary grief. Before her memory started to fail, every single day was a gasp-inducing amusement ride, worth twice the price of admittance, even when the wounds were slow to heal. Now she was a half-submerged crocodile. On top, polite and funny, underneath harboring an undisguised desire to drag and drown the two of them in the nearest swamp.

"So, what's on the agenda camp director?" asks Melody. "Jet skiing up the Matterhorn, delivering meals to the homeless in gated communities, shoveling rain off the driveway?"

"Is it clear on the right?" Andy asks. "I need to switch lanes and take Highway Forty."

"No."

"That's funny, I don't see anyone in my rear mirror," says Andy.

"There's a rise full of tract homes," says Melody. "Plus four or five buzzards circling overhead. They all look dangerous."

"I'm betting they stay off the macadam," says Andy as he switches into the exit only lane. "You have your infusions. Doctor Wiseman promised me if you showed up before the end of the year, you could keep your spot on the drug trial. He said things had dropped off some, so there would be room for an appointment."

Through research and persistence, Melody had been accepted into the one drug trial that showed promise in slowing the rate of memory decline. Taking a pill would not work, not even drug cocktails. The chemicals had to be infused directly into the bloodstream in order to bypass the digestive system which, when detected, would swat the drug into the liver. The drug had to make its way to the hippocampus, memory's gatekeeper. Once she was in the Alzheimer's study, his new primary occupation became seeing that she got her there. The infusion took two hours, the drive each way another hour. Then, there was a four-hour wait afterwards to make sure she did not suffer from brain swelling and total paralysis, one of the known serious side effects. Every two weeks, he lost a full day of work.

"You can close the windows now, Snowman," says Melody. "I'm freezing up here."

Andy does.

"What is the point of attending a rally for the loser?" asks Melody. "Distressed sale of sour grape flavored Chapstick? Pick me up a tube or two at one of Trump's merch tables, will ya? They're guaranteed to become collectibles."

"It's not over until it's over," says Andy. "We'll see how those elites react after the rally. The Electoral Count hasn't been certified yet. We have a chance to stop it from happening."

"Enough of what we can do nothing about. Do something that can make our lives better, less grim, less, I don't know, less criminal maybe? Beer sounds good."

"There's the Hiroshima plaque."

"Aren't you finished with that yet? You started the Hiroshima plaque when the cops took me to Sheppard Pratt."

"Just about done except for the staining. I called the Watanabes this afternoon. Called them twice before that. They're not picking up. Buyer's remorse maybe. We need that dough. The mortgage is past due."

"It's nice to know that some things don't change."

If the Watanabes didn't come up with the five grand, Andy would have to do some fancy dancing to keep their home. Work at Walmart on weekends maybe. Beg. "We're not losing our home, Melody."

"It's just studs and sheetrock, pipes and electrical wiring for Christ's sake," says Melody. "I can live out of a cardboard house.

Duct tape is cheap. I know we haven't any money, just can't seem to attach numbers to it anymore. It's as if the numbers are children who have forgotten how to play well together. Calculus used to be my best friend. Now, even negative numbers refuse to behave, and I can no longer recite the first hundred numbers after 3.14 in pi like I used to. One four, one five, nineufferous…"

"I like being around people who think like me."

"Everybody wants to be around people who think like they do. But at a rally, you only learn what you already know. It's like watching a Hollywood movie. Nothing is revealed."

"That's not true. You learn how inflation will go through the roof, the national debt will spiral out of control, and illegal immigrants will replace us in the cover of night."

"I see you've been listening to ultra-right news while I've been gone. Fear mongering for kids. I thought we'd put that angry monster to bed."

"You weren't around," says Andy. "And you're always telling me to learn both sides of an argument." Andy's going to the Stop the Steal Rally. He's not going to let anyone talk him out of it, even Melody.

"You sure I'm well enough for you to leave me all alone?" asks Melody. "Can't you go last year instead?"

"You'll be fine, Melody," says Andy. He looks over at her and takes an exaggerated breath. He smiles and says, "We are going to be fine."

Melody asks, "Sam isn't fine, is he?"

"No, he died."

"How did he die?"

"He killed himself."

"I mean how did he kill himself?"

"Hung himself."

"Just like what got me into Sheppard Pratt?"

"Yes."

"How could I have done that? You threw away every chain and rope and string and wire we had in the house after the time before. You even threw out all our cellophane tape. I had to string a series of Post-its to seal cereal bags closed. What did I use, spider webs?"

"A bra."

"It better not have been one of my good ones!"

CHAPTER TWO

ONE WAY IN

At noon the next day, Christmas, an old car with out-of-state license plates parks in front of a two-story colonial home. It matches the architecture of all other homes in the subdivision except for paint color. The home belongs to Damascus's Chief of Police. The driveway is empty. The driver walks up to the front porch and pushes the doorbell. The Chief's stepdaughter opens the door, sees the visitor through the glass and steel screen door, and asks her, "May I help you?" Out of the visitor's sight, the stepdaughter's fingers linger on a bright red alarm button.

"You got my letter?" the visitor asks. "You know I'm your momma, right?"

The stepdaughter assumes the confused visage that works well with her teachers in high school and examines this very thin woman standing before her. To the stepdaughter, the woman looks about thirty. She wears too much makeup, jangly jewelry, flowery perfume, and not enough clothing—loose top, hot pants, and heavy nylons down to her flats. It's not more than forty degrees outside.

The stepdaughter shakes her head.

"I'm Donna Kind. I'm your momma. You're Theresa Elizabeth Kind, right? I recognize you from when you was three."

"My name is Telly," the stepdaughter says.

"Well, Telly's short for Theresa. I like that. Sauce to it. You know your daddy made it so your initials would remind everyone of technology. He was very big on technology. T E K. Everyone calls you Telly because you've earned it. It's nice."

Telly has long fantasized about her real mother suddenly showing up, but she looks past the woman. She doesn't see anyone behind her. She whispers, "Is my Daddy here too?"

"Oh, no. That effer's never going to show his face. Believe me."

"I'm afraid you should come back when Chief is here," Telly says, "Okay?"

"Chief? Like in Chief of the Commanches?" says Donna.

"My stepfather, Chief of Police Lutz Delorean."

"You call your stepdad Chief?" asks Donna. "Of all the…"

"It's a sign of respect, Mrs. Kind," says Telly, reassuming her confused visage, but this time it's not for show.

"Momma's a sign of respect, too," says Donna. "Making your child call you 'Chief' is criminal."

"I have to go now," says Telly.

"I understand. You almost an adult and surprise, here's your mother on your doorstep, after fifteen years. Fifteen years gone. This is not so infrequent where I come from! You lucky these days to see your real parent for the first time in a casket smelling funny. This fentanyl business reeling us in like catfish on a hot summer morning. Dumber and dumber, we get."

Telly looks the woman over again. She doesn't look much like her. Telly is built like a football tackle. And only one of their facial features matches: pronounced *Dudley Do-Right* chins. They're also the same height, so at least they stand eye level. Telly won't be intimidated by this woman. She's going to be eighteen in a month.

"I did not get a letter."

Tree roots, sown by Chief's admonition to not let anyone into the house unless he was there, pierce the foyer fake hardwood flooring and anchor her feet. But at the same time, dozens of tiny mice squeak, *this is your mother, your mother, your mother.*

"You think your stepfather maybe didn't want you to know about me?" says Donna.

Donna knows there is plenty she doesn't want her daughter to know about her. Like how Donna had given her up for adoption when the daycare costs ate too deeply into her cocaine and wine budgets. Or her present employment, but who knows, her daughter might take to the calling.

She recalls what Telly's doctors had said about Prader Willi Syndrome, another example of males promoting themselves over the people who have to live with it. Impaired cognition, intellectual disability, and deficits in social awareness. These should work in Donna's favor.

The girl was no longer a toddler. No nose and rear end to constantly tend. No reading mindless children's stories to put her to sleep at night. The hard labor and numbing monotony were over. What mattered was that disability check, which doubled when her daughter hit eighteen. Until death do us part, baby.

"So, Telly, why you living in this suburban cemetery?" The set-up. "Where you can't even read your own mail." The hook. "You should be living in the city, where the action is, not where comparing your lawn with the neighbor's is the week's highlight. How do you spell yawn?" The free gift.

Telly is weakening. She has imagined meeting her mother a thousand different times and ways. This doesn't match one of them. But the mice are unrelenting. Chief could be stealing her mail. And she has been badgering him about where she would live when she became an adult. What is this about living in the City? No one else seems to be around.

Telly drops her hand from the alarm and opens the screen door. She finds herself in a too-tight hug. She's expecting bad things are going to happen, but when Donna releases her and no bad things happen, she returns Donna's hug, equal in length and intensity. Hugging has never been integrated into the DeLorean household. All that's missing is dessert.

Donna walks in and says, "I was getting parched out there. Something to drink?"

"I'll get you some water," Telly says and disappears into the kitchen.

Donna follows Telly while casing the place. The teakwood furniture speaks cash. The wall hangings show good taste. The lack of clutter and dust betrays a housekeeper, weekly. This is going to work out nicely; yes, it is. A short dumb young girl, easy to lead. The check is in the mail. But watch out, stepdaddy's a policeman. Don't count those chickens just yet.

Donna stares at the glass of water in her hand. Let's see where this goes. "Water is all you got for your momma?"

"The water is very good here."

"You got juice, some soda, something stronger? Morning is past us, Telly."

"Milk, juice, and Kefir are in the fridge," says Telly, "but Chief is gone, and he has the key."

"The refrigerator has a lock?"

"Yes, for my protection," says Telly, narrating her scripted summary of Prader Willi. "PWS is a NIH-recognized neurodevelopmental genetic disorder caused by the deletion of chromosome fifteen from the father. It's incurable. Comorbid with Prader Willi is a lack of intelligence. We often develop hyperphagia, hypertonia, temper outbursts, and/or OCD. We can be identified by our almond shaped eyes and narrowing skull at the temples. Our dominant symptom is hunger. I am never not hungry, no matter if I just ate. Most people with Prader Willi become obese. I am not yet, but almost." Then she adds in a sudden burst as if she expects someone to immediately pin a medal on her chest for remembering, "The average lifespan of someone with Prader Willi is thirty-two. I am seventeen, so I have fifteen years left to live."

Donna tries to do the math but feels like she has to break out of a full nelson hold of information first. This is not going to be easy.

"You must have read all about it," adds Telly.

"Yeah, I did," Donna says, "but that was a long time ago." She points to the refrigerator, "Ain't never gonna be a lock on my refrigerator door." Another hook.

"You must live in heaven," says Telly.

"You come live with me, and there'll be no locks on the refrigerator, and no calling me by a title. My name is Donna. But you'll call me Momma."

Telly rolodexes through the other kitchens she had been in and realizes none had locks on their refrigerators. The light switch toggles on. "You want me to live with you? You're my Christmas present!"

"Call me Momma."

"Momma," Telly yells and gives Donna another hug, same as the last one. She's dialing in a newfound skill. Donna spills water from her glass. It puddles on the hardwood floor. When Donna disengages, Telly sees the water and screams. She pulls a volley of paper towels from its dispenser and wipes away every drop as competent as if she was covering up a crime. "I'm sorry Momma, I just got so excited."

"That's okay, Telly," says Donna. "I'll be your Christmas present. What do you think? A girl should live with her momma, right?"

"Right, let's go. Wow," says Telly, "I have to pack." She heads for her bedroom.

"Hold on, okay?" says Donna, "Not today. I have to prep, you understand? Move some furniture around, fluff up the sheets, that kinda stuff. Had to make sure you wanted to come first, but now that we're sure…You sure you didn't receive no letter?"

She says it knowing she never mailed a letter and that she has been scouting Telly's house out for some time to spring this trap. It's always best to keep repeating the lie until no one doubts it. She's feeling this is going too well. Life's a master at throwing in a monkey wrench at the most inopportune time. She peeks down the hall. No one is walking down it to destroy her conquest.

Telly chants, "No locks, no locks, no locks," while visualizing milk shakes, pizzas, and fries. She starts to give Donna another hug, but she stops when Donna asks, "Ready for the big day little girl?"

"I thought *you* said not today."

"I mean when you are eighteen, when you are officially an adult."

"February sixteenth, though they won't let me graduate for two more years."

"We do things different in the City, better and quicker," says Donna. "I can't remember, but do you still get Social Security on the third of every month?"

"I get a check every month. The actual day it arrives varies."

"And may I ask how much is that, Telly?"

Telly tells her. Donna feels clean sheets and central air. "One thing though, one thing, you gotta keep this a secret. Our secret. Our surprise. You can keep a secret, can't you? When we move into my place then you can tell the world. If not, this house of cards will all fall down like Humpty Dumpty."

"You live in a house made of cards. Playing cards? How does it stay standing? Does it leak?"

"Just an expression kid. But keep *my coming here* a secret."

"I'm good at keeping quiet," says Telly. "I don't talk much. I don't even have a BFF. We kinda quit being BFFs. Chief says keeping secrets keeps other people from stealing your money. But today is special, isn't it? It's Christmas. I can talk all I want. And you're my Christmas present."

"Golden," says Donna. "By the way, speaking of money, you have a few dollars? Say a twenty? I need to replace the gas in the car that I borrowed to get here."

"I have money. I have a job," says Telly. "I'm training to be a nurse."

"My momma was a nurse," says Donna. "She never made enough, and she was always too tired to cook dinner. She always smelled of fast food. How much they pay you?"

"I get seven dollars and fifty-six cents an hour."

"They pay you sixty dollars a day for emptying bedpans and wiping shit off of ancient asses?" says Donna.

"I do more than that. I give shots, take blood, and help with physical therapy."

"Don't get me wrong," says Donna. "I'm fine with that. The sooner you learn to live with what you got, the better off you'll be. If I learned that earlier, I would live in a better place."

Telly asks, "Where am I going to live?"

"Baltimer."

"What street?"

"Jamestown."

"What number?"

"Seven Four Three, apartment forty-five," says Donna, enjoying this rapid-fire Q and A.

"Who do you live with?" asks Telly.

"I live by myself right now," Donna says. "But I'm looking for a roommate. Know anybody?"

"Yes, me. Me. Me."

"You?" says Donna. "H'm, well, not sure if I have enough money to pay all the moving vans, we gonna need to get your things over to my place."

"I think I can fit everything in my van," says Telly.

"You have your own car?"

"My step-grandparents bought it for me," says Telly. "It's old, but I souped it up with a new carburetor and fuel ignition. I'm saving for new struts. I've won six junior race car championships."

"I bet you have," says Donn. "Why don't you drive that souped van over to my place on the first?"

"Eight o'clock?"

"Make it noon, okay?" says Donna.

"I can't believe this is happening to me," says Telly.

"Remember not to tell anyone. Not even your former BFF," says Donna. "I have to be going, got a lotta cleaning to do. And about that twenty…"

CHAPTER THREE

TWO WAY STREET

When Andy gets up on Christmas morning, he finds Melody watching TV. "Melody, Merry Christmas. You never came to bed last night?"

"It's one of the side benefits of Xanax," says Melody. "Another side benefit is fire breathing. Keep your distance, Cave Man. Be a shame to spoil that five-dollar haircut."

"Melody, you got to sleep."

"I will. Right now. Now that you're up. Don't wait for me." Melody doesn't go to the master bedroom. Instead, she picks up a magazine, pulls out a coffee cup, and sits at the kitchen counter. She positions the cup directly in front of her, a silent command, and directs her attention to the magazine's tiny print.

Andy says to himself, "situation normal...," and out loud, "Benedict Arnold." He takes Benedict Arnold for a walk. He'll make coffee when he gets back. See if she hasn't gone to bed.

When he returns, Melody is gone. He walks in the direction of the bedroom only to hear light snoring. He backs out.

Christmas h'm. Andy makes coffee, pours some into the cup Melody left on the counter, and sips from it as he makes then eats breakfast—poached eggs on toast with link sausage. Sated, he figures he should call Jeremy and wish him a Merry Christmas, father to son, that kind of thing, before he works on the plaque. Pours himself another cup. He had squawked when Melody told him how much Yellow Mountain Coffee costs, but it's damn good.

"So, Dad, nice of you to call. How's Mom?" asks Jeremy. "Put her on the phone, will ya?"

"She's asleep, I think," says Andy.

"Wake her up then. It's almost nine o'clock. I need to talk to her. I was just about to call you guys anyway. I went to the hospital a couple of days ago. They said Mom checked out last week. How come nobody told me?"

"Yeah, how do you know anything, especially if it's about Melody?" says Andy. "And Merry Christmas to you, Young Man. Did you like our present?"

"What present?"

"I sent you a check."

"Oh yes, fifty bucks," says Jeremy. "Forgot all about it, thanks."

"What did you get your mother?"

"I left it at the hospital. They told me they expected her back soon."

"I went to the hospital yesterday. Found her working at Starbucks down the street. How did you know she was released last week? The hospital wouldn't tell me anything."

"Amazing what flashing a badge will get you," says Jeremy. "So, will you wake her up for me?"

"She just went to bed a few minutes ago. Was up all night. What's so important that you have to talk to her?"

"My business."

"What you up to young man?" asks Andy, again.

"Figuring everything out is all," says Jeremy.

"When you do, please let me know. It always seemed to me everyone did that in high school. It was like butter melting atop pancakes. Somehow the butter refused to melt on mine."

"What I learned in high school was that everyone is really your enemy," says Jeremy. "No matter what they say or do. Everyone is competing against you for the goods."

"Yeah," says Andy. "The secret is to keep that to yourself and go along with what everyone wants, stay out of the crosshairs."

"You didn't do that very well, Handcream MacClean."

"I had dyshidrotic eczema,' says Andy. "Granddad had it too. My hands were a mess in high school. If you'd seen them, even you would have looked away."

"I have a strong stomach, Dad."

"You do."

"I've never seen any pictures," says Jeremy.

"Didn't take any," says Andy. "My hands looked like open wounds. Yellow-orange scabs were constantly flaking off. As bad as they looked, the itch is what killed me. I used to fantasize about chewing my hands off right at the wrists, like wolves do if a paw gets caught in a trap."

"I know the story, Dad. You would rub lotion on your hands, and when a classmate saw that, he'd begin pumping at his crotch. Everybody joined in."

"But we all had nicknames back then," says Andy. "Niles Jansen became Smiling Miles, Edward Crazer became Crazy Eddie, Charles Weekes became Cactus Cheeks, and Regina Webster became Red Lobster, both for standout acne.

"Words are real. Words hurt even worse than stones. But having to act like it wasn't humiliating was a test, right? I had to show it didn't get to me. You know what I also learned?"

"No, what?"

"No matter what," says Andy, "just smile and look people right in the eye, and by golly they'd smile back. Every time. That meant everything was fine. Even if I didn't have the slightest understanding of what had just happened."

"Weren't they really laughing at you?"

"You can tell. Laughs are different. Donald Trump never laughs at us."

"No one laughs at me," says Jeremy.

"With your build you could intimidate a five-star general."

"So, you're not bitter about being called Handcream?" asks Jeremy.

"Nope, after a few months it became a badge of honor," says Andy.

"So, that's how you handled being bullied, taking it on the chin."

"Jeremy, you talk big" says Andy. "While you are busy corralling tourists at the Capitol, we are going to save the country."

"From whom?"

"The homeless, the Democrats, the blacks, the Hispanics, the elites. They're taking over. While we are busy building this country, they're busy stealing it."

"The POCs?"

"If the shoe fits," says Andy.

"I'm a POC," says Jeremy.

"But you get it. Others don't."

"How come Mom disagrees with everything you say?"

"That's Melody," says Andy. "Only way she will agree with me is if I change sides."

"But everyone says Mom is brilliant," says Jeremy. "She served as the Atlantic Mensa chapter president for two terms. Something not to forget."

"Something else we shouldn't forget is Donald Trump's TV show. For twenty years, he ruled the air. And he's going to continue to."

"Yeah, Mom loved that show, but I always thought she was laughing at it, not with it."

"That I could tell."

"So, Dad," says Jeremy, "now that I've acquiesced to this soul-searching talk, will you please wake Mom up?"

"Okay, I'll see if I can…"

"Jeremy, she's not here."

"What are you talking about? You said she was sleeping."

"I thought she was," says Andy, "but the snoring must have been Benedict Arnold. I checked every room in the house. She's not here."

"Should I put out a BOLO?" asks Jeremy.

"What in the heck is a BOLO?"

"It's an anagram for *be on the lookout*."

"What happened to the time-honored APB?" asks Andy.

"Who knows? It probably offended someone. Either way, you want me to call the station?"

"Nope. Her purse is also missing."

CHAPTER FOUR

SOME CIRCLES ARE ROUNDER

Donna Kind drives back to her apartment. She has to circle the apartment complex four times before she finds a large enough parking space to squeeze in without banging bumpers. She walks to her building then trudges up the three flights of stairs. As her foot hits every filthy tread, she wonders whether she should hose it down before Telly arrives. On the second-floor landing, she says, 'Hi,' to Charley and drops a quarter of tribute into his waiting palm, careful not to show disgust if skin happens to meet skin. Charley, a squatter, who lives there with his shopping cart, provides needed security. And with that crippled left arm, even management, notorious for evicting families on major holidays, hasn't mustered the gumption to shoo him away.

Victor's sitting on her couch, exactly where he was when she left in his car. He's playing video games on his phone but is not so engrossed as to miss Donna's return. He signals that by stretching one long arm out and rubbing his fingers with his thumb. "Keys, Donna."

Donna fishes the keys from her purse and tosses them at him. He snatches them out of the air then coils them onto his belt and adds, "Gas money, Donna."

"Who said anything about gas money?" says Donna.

"Please, Donna."

Donna pulls a five out and says, "Change, please."

Victor gives a deep laugh and says, "Why I like you so much. You should do stand-up. Serious." He returns focusing on his video game.

Donna goes into the kitchen and returns with a glass of Port in one hand and a lit joint in the other. She plops onto the couch next to him, her light weight making no impression on the sofa's cushion. She offers him a hit. Victor waves her off and finishes his online match. Then he says, "Better not be a molecule of damage to my wheels. Not one ding."

"You care more about your car than me," Donna says.

"Not true. You are family. So, how'd it go? New money or same old story?"

"It went okay," says Donna. "She's telling me she will drive over with all her stuff on New Year's Day, like you told me."

"She got wheels?" asks Victor.

"Says she does."

"Saves me from loaning you mine. Sad though."

"Huh?" asks Donna.

"She not eighteen yet and has a car. And you pushing forty…"

"Not yet I'm not," says Donna. "Stop with that gaslighting bull."

"You could use a roommate."

"Just not you, right?" Donna asks.

"Something buggin' you?"
"Not a thing."
"You lying twat," says Victor. "Let me guess, h'm, what is her home like?"
"It's fucking immaculate, magazine cover interior. Everything is in its place."
"So, you're worried she will eye this sty and bolt?"
"It's not a sty, exactly. Just needs some sparkle." Her walls had turned funky beige from the oil burning space heaters she used to circumambulate the utility bill. Her carpets were stained from entertaining accidents, and, per the maintenance agreement, carpet cleaning was her responsibility. New carpeting wasn't scheduled until 2025.
"Where's this daughter of yours going to sleep?" asks Victor. "Has that even been on your radar?"
"Of course it has, just I haven't decided is all," says Donna.
"Better not interrupt business." says Victor.
"Of course not. With her EssEss check, I can afford a bigger place. Got three different recruiters lookin'."
"How you intend to spend it?" says Victor, his smile growing with every exchange.
"My customers would appreciate it if I did," says Donna.
"They and I would," says Victor. "You have to get Telly's check mailed here. If you do that, I can make sabotaging that delivery as impossible as it is to unsubscribe to FeedSpot.
Once FeedSpot got you, you practically have to enter witness protection to keep from paying them every month. I've learned a lot from those guys."

"I'll call you the day I get it."

"And what are you going to do with your amateur dead bug collection?" says Victor.

"What you spilling?"

"All those spiderwebs at the corner of every ceiling, Baby," says Victor. "They're eye-level to me. I'm six' four, remember?"

"She's no taller than I am, and she wears thick glasses. She won't see that."

"The place could use some air freshening too," says Victor. "It stinks."

"That's from burning incense to mask the aroma of cannabis and freebasing," says Donna.

"Do some coke and get to it, Girl. Just be sure you're sparkling for Karl at eight tonight and Henry tomorrow at noon. I'll be by tomorrow night, earlier if things pick up."

"Isn't today Christmas?" asks Donna. "I thought Christmas was a work holiday?"

"Stand-up again. You know what holidays are for?"

"Big tips," says Donna. "Where's your Christmas present for me?"

"Smells like you're smoking it right now."

"Am," says Donna. She inhales exaggeratedly and coughs out, "Good shit too."

"You're welcome, bye bye," says Victor, "And thanks for the tie." He leaves.

Donna goes into the kitchen, rests her joint in a butter dish, and puts that in the refrigerator. She examines the refrigerator's insides for comfort and nourishment. Her best shoes don't count, and the oldish looking milk and Styrofoam takeout boxes of mystery fast food don't appeal. She settles on the gallon jug of Port. Pours herself another glass.

Once she finishes the Port, Donna traipses down to the Dollar Store with the remnants of Telly's twenty. She buys liquid bleach, soap, and vinegar. Bleach leaves a scent that people associate with health, which she thought was ironic since bleach kills everything it touches, even color.

She drops the cleansers off in her bathroom, checks the medicine cabinet, and does two lines. Girls are supposed to purr before a clean bathroom. At least, that's what Donna's been told. She's never felt that way. This was where the dirty work was done. Sooner be out of it than in it, and hers showed.

She assaults the toilet, tub, and sink in circular motion. She rubs the cleansers on, massages them onto the ceramics, moves to the next fixture, repeats, and repeats again, all the time thrashing her hands and arms as frantically as a drowning child. But the calcium scale deposits are glued to the ancient cheap ceramics as tight as barnacles to a commercial steamer hull.

The sun is dying outside, and her strength follows suit. She's bone tired, muscle sore, and near despair. When she examines her achievement, she doesn't notice much improvement, though the floor looks shiny from what she can see through the entire roll of wadded up paper towels covering it.

She feels woozy and sees sparkles in the air as if she were at a carnival and fireworks were drizzling down from the sky. She sits down in the bathtub and naps. When she wakes, it's true dark, and she needs a few minutes to orient herself. She pulls herself out of the tub and pours herself another glass of Port. She feels wet and decides to shower. When she re-enters the bathroom and turns on the lights, she says to herself, "Be real, it's hopeless."

What had she been thinking? Fantasy had driven her all her life, and fantasy had always failed her. She's consistent if nothing else. She laughs. Telly will have to accept her as she is. Hasn't everyone else? Actually, most had moved on. She could be tough. There's always an offramp if you stay in your lane long enough. And she'd have more energy tomorrow, after Karl and Glenn, or was it Henry. Besides, she had until the First. That's a full week away, a double lifetime for the fentanyl crowd. Would Telly keep quiet that long? Maybe she'd throw up some curtains. Then Telly wouldn't see how rundown the neighborhood is. How pathetic is that?

CHAPTER FIVE

ONE WAY STREET

Andy sips from a coffee mug in his right hand. He holds the Buick's car keys in his left and watches the sun's creep highlight the calendar tacked on the kitchen wall—Tuesday, December 29. He had once loved her, and her Audrey Hepburn looks until her illness turned her against him and practically everyone else. She has evolved from the woman he worshiped to his adversary child. Now, everything he says is an accusation, even if he says, 'it's a wonderful day.' He recommends nothing. That way, they argue less, and he can buy the groceries, cook the food, and take the remains out to the curb on Tuesdays. He gives in to each of her demands, in words. Having learned that if what she wants from him is wrong, she will forget what it was, come a minute or two.

On Christmas morning, he had found her two blocks from home. He had driven up to her in the Buick and asked, "You need a lift young lady?"

"You look familiar," Melody said, slowly examining the car as if it was an entirely foreign means of transportation. "I prefer riding with strangers."

"Where you headed?"

"The beer store."

"Beer is heavy. You going to carry it back home yourself?" That got her into the car, and he drove them home. Today, he isn't having any luck getting her into the car.

Regardless of how often he reminded her of an appointment or how many wrong days she showed up before him fully dressed, pestering him that they had to leave, when it was finally and really time to go, she would complain he hadn't given her enough notice. So, they were either inexcusably late or entire no shows.

"I am going to take a shower. I don't like you," says Melody. She walks from the kitchen into the adjoining TV room. Andy thinks the dark blue floral blouse and black nylon pants she has on are what she slept in. Besides doing all the shopping and cooking, he does the laundry. He sniff-tests her clothes before he washes them because she's as likely to put the clothes he just washed in the dirty laundry basket as to put her soiled ones in the chest of drawers.

"The bathroom is the other way, Melody," says Andy.

"Go to Petaluma. You'll like it there," she says, and sits down on a sofa facing him. She sips her coffee. He also makes their coffee every morning.

Raising his voice so she can hear him from the kitchen, Andy says, "Where we need to go right now is Johns Hopkins. We have an infusion appointment at one o'clock." He doesn't ask her if she remembers. He knows that Melody treats all questions as if he's testing her. That is guaranteed to start an argument.

"It's either too early or too late. Pick one," says Melody. "Just go away, leave, terminate your residence here, goodbye."

And then, just as quickly as he remembers not to ask her anything, he forgets and asks her, "Who would take care of you then, Melody?"

"I don't need any *taking care of*."

Andy goes for the jugular and regrets it almost before he gets the words out, "Who's going to buy you your beer?"

"Now that *you* have brought beer up, where's mine?"

"Melody, it's eleven o'clock in the morning."

"How can I tell? The right looks light. Phone!" she yells.

Andy pockets his keys, walks over to the phone and eyes the call identifier. "It's Johns Hopkins. I'll put it on speaker.

"Hello, Andy MacClean here."

"This is Linda. I see you haven't left yet. Is Melody coming today?"

Melody stays in the TV room, close enough to hear the speaker phone. She turns the TV on and says loudly, "Tell Linda the cloudshine through the skylight didn't align with my Lucky Charms cereal today." Then she whispers, "Where are you hiding the beer, where is Benedict Arnold, and while we're wearing out the wheres, where did you put my bras? I can't find one, and I've surveyed every room of the house twice, including the attic."

"We have to go, Melody," Andy says through gritted teeth. "Just get in the car. We can buy you new bras and cold beer on the way there. Kill two birds with one stone, right?" She doesn't move, looking at Andy as if he's just too dense to understand. Andy shakes the phone receiver at her and says, "Melody, take the phone, you tell Linda whether or not you are coming today."

She waves him off.

"Melody," says Andy, "if you miss an infusion your memory may get worse. I can't remember the word, but stopping a drug can hurt its effectiveness later." Then he adds, "Do you know where your purse is? You'll need that."

"The word is *irrelecant*," replies Melody, "though you won't find it in the dictionary. Yesterday isn't here anymore, but the memory of my missing an appointment I intend to forget right this second? There, done! Achievement absolutely accomplished, and assiduously at that." Then she points at the TV and says, "Bannon is threatening Armageddon and Whatshisface, the Prez, will not attend the inauguration. And here's Benedict Arnollld."

Melody welcomes their dog and begins scratching him just behind the ears. "Oh, he's so beautiful I could cry. I am crying. Want a rub, you wonderful guy? Of course you do."

"I'm sorry Linda," says Andy, "I can't even get her to the phone much less in the car."

"We may have to scratch her if she doesn't make it in here today," Linda says.

Then a male voice comes over the line, "Andy, this is Doctor Wiseman."

"Hi, Doctor Wiseman. I really don't know what to do, she's... Maybe it's time to drop her from the drug trial?" Maybe this is the opportunity Andy's been waiting for.

"There's no second chance, Andy," says Dr. Wiseman. "She's already seven weeks behind. One more and… Once she stops taking it, there's no medical evidence her brain can catch up. Patients are practically bribing us to be included in this study. You absolutely sure? You might be signing her death sentence."

Andy's breathing slows. This conversation reminds him of one he had with a car mechanic over replacing his brake pads. "I can't get her…"

Melody yells from the TV room, "Give them our telephone number. Tell them I provide therapy for victims of serial drug trial abuse, first and second degree. Five consultations free. After that half price."

"I heard that," says Dr. Wiseman. "Okay, Andy, you're entitled to one follow up consultation. I have a few open dates in January."

"We've reached the last switchback on this hike, doncha' think? Thanks for all you have tried to do. Goodbye, and thanks again."

"And goodbye to you Andy. You two have been coming here every two weeks for three years. Melody's a hero for volunteering on this pilot drug study. I want to personally thank you. I know it was a hardship. We know the battles you must have been waging to get her here."

Melody yells out, "I just want to live while I'm here."

"So, Andy," says Dr. Wiseman, "how are you holding up? Health statisticians warn us that the life expectancy of a family caregiver drops one hundred days for every year."

An odd remark from the medical establishment. The longer she lived the sooner he would die. Isn't the drug designed to keep Melody and her memory intact longer? Lose-lose with a lurid twist.

"Oh look, it's starting to snow," says Dr. Wiseman.

"So, where's all the climate warming business?" asks Andy, laughing.

"I did the math, Andy. It took me three whole months. Climate change is inevitable based on the temperature readings."

"I thought it was hydrocarbons?"

"They're what is making the earth hotter," says Dr. Wiseman.

"President Trump thinks it's hogwash," says Andy. "If the earth is warming, why is it snowing now?"

"You are comparing apples to oranges. Have you done the math?"

"No."

"Then you are not qualified to have an opinion," says Dr. Wiseman.

"I can still have an opinion."

"I wonder how much better the world would be if people who refused to look at the facts resolved to at least not express an opinion on the matter."

"That would eliminate entrepreneurism," says Andy. "Our country is based on entrepreneurism."

"That's a fair point!" says Dr. Wiseman. "Where would we be indeed if we couldn't bet on hunches? We'd be a completely different species."

Melody walks into the kitchen and says, "I read in the papers that the FBI just busted a chimpanzee bookie ring at the zoo."

Andy says, "I've read enough. Reading about stuff usually sends me down rabbit holes. I prefer to live above ground. It's not a hunch when it's snowing, for god's sake. No offense, but ka'ching, Doctor done-the-math."

"Good luck Andy. I'll miss you," says Dr. Wiseman. "You've been a worthy sport through all this."

Andy hangs up the phone. Melody walks away to fill her coffee cup. Andy says to himself, "What made this country great was our ignoring threats. Full speed ahead. Remember Y2K? Another strike out from the elites. They don't know that much."

The TV is still on. Andy goes to turn it off, and instead he is hypnotized. A voice that a funeral director would covet says, "You know what it is and it's bothering you, but you don't really know what to do about it, right? You've heard some scary reports at the same time the government is commanding you to get your shoulder punctured, to wear face masks and social distance. Who's protecting our freedom?

"You wonder where this is going to end? COVID-19 is not the issue. The issue is your anxiety over maybe getting COVID-19. A sense that something is being taken away from you, something you'll never regain. Who are you supposed to listen to? Doctors, the government, politicians, or some guru on the Internet sitting on a Zafu pillow with his hands in his lap? One thing is for sure: it's vital that you find out. There's a lot of misinformation out there. Don't wimp out. Read and do your own research. Here at Kramer Drugs..."

Melody walks in behind Andy and asks him, "What are you watching?"

"An ad I think."

"What's it for?"

"I don't know."

"Then why are you watching it?"

"I don't know; it grabbed my attention," says Andy, scrunching his shoulders. "Like I'm going to obey a TV set? How stupid do they think I am?" He turns the TV off.

"You're smarter than that, Handcream!"

"I am, and I am going to the Trump rally."

"I know, wild forces couldn't keep you away," says Melody. "Oh, I remember seeing that ad. It's for Ketamine. Tried it once and got a rash all over my body. You had to take me to the hospital."

"Yeah, I remember, we got rear ended in a snowstorm, and the guy just drove away."

"No, he didn't. He got out of his car, examined our car, came over to your car window, shouted, "No damage to either car," and then he drove away. All while snow was coming down in these ever-larger white constellations of fluff."

"Same difference. Cost us two thousand dollars to repair the bumper and the backup cameras. I don't understand how you can remember that but not that today was an infusion day. And infusions were supposed to help your memory."

"Is it today? Do I have time to dress?"

CHAPTER SIX

ANNUITY POTHOLES

Telly had aced her intern interview at Saved Angels, and why wouldn't she? Telly knew the place inside and out, having been dumped here to visit her grandparents almost every weekend for thirteen years. Esther, its director, remembered her well.

Telly's grandparents, Beth and Joe Delorean, had founded it. They knew a lot about hotel management after feasting on three sumptuous meals a day at the Lord Baltimore Hotel for fifty years, without once having to cook a meal or wash a dish themselves. When would they possibly have found the time? However, aren't there always howevers?

First, Lord Baltimore started losing staff, and the meals and maid service often fell far below its once proud five-star rating. Second, the last of their longtime hotel friends, Emma, had moved into a nursing home, the rest of their friends having preceded her to other elder care facilities or to the other side. The third and most important was the math. They had figured they were secure even after Bernie Madoff had made off with the bulk of their wealth.

They still had rental property. They owned a prison. The State always paid like clockwork, until it didn't. The DeLoreans fell victim to the State's arbitrary decision to stop incarcerating dopers and release them all instead. Lord Baltimore's fees, extended out, would exhaust their ancient annuities, spitting out at zero interest until totally sputtering out about five years before the two's internments. How untimely.

Their only other possession was Joe's collection of 1953 Hudson Hornets. Joe refused to even talk about parting with his Hudsons. Sooner kill him. Beth declined to, not without a short struggle. But their banker had a plan. He proposed profiting from the latest investment fad: timeshare reverse home mortgages for senior citizens. But here, your death canceled all ownership, fees, and liability. This was a solid advantage over timeshares, where the owners only realize the swindle when they try to sell their timeshare and discover there are no buyers. The timeshare developers had monopolized all avenues of trade. Timeshare owners, if that is what you want to call them, often have to pay the developers to take the timeshare off their hands in order to stop paying the eternal monthly fees. Timeshare owners had invested in a liability; three cheers to entrepreneurism.

Four separate but identical buildings, each four stories tall, sit on thirty acres. Elevators in the center service all four. An atrium connects them, and a cantilever balcony allows the staff to oversee the inmates when they're not locked away in their cells. This is the perfect architecture for managing mobility-challenged senior citizens. It even has razor wire fencing to discourage wandering John and Janes in the memory care unit from escaping.

The plan: make as few changes as possible, also known as spending the least amount of money, while keeping some pastiche of the former prison. The cell numbers remained, as did the barred doors. They just would have a polyester screen door behind them. Each cell had been built to accommodate six prisoners, so there would be enough room in each cell for a couple to fit in a few favorite pieces of furniture to make it homey. The lobby and meeting rooms, on the other hand, would be furnished in the latest trend of architectural invisibility—used stuffed sofas and chairs from failed banks, mahogany-looking cabinetry of vinyl wallpaper stretched and ironed on particleboard, and acoustic ceiling panels from folded K-Marts, complete with familiar water stains. No one would dare complain about the sharp resemblance to a funeral parlor. There just wasn't a polite way of bringing up your final downsize.

To make the new rest home stand out in the emerging market, Beth and Joe promoted a novel approach: everyone would be on a first name basis, and everyone would be guaranteed their cell until they died or moved out of their own volition. Its owners, Joe and Beth Delorean, after all, would be living there to guarantee service was stellar. The declarations worked. Subscriptions for residency built up an early waiting list. No elderly couple researching rest homes could resist.

Their banker had the land appraised, and, as it sometimes happens, found it was valuable, being only a forty-minute drive from Washington D.C. The loan went through; the land held for collateral. The balloon payment wouldn't come due before the two of them were angels themselves. Beth had CPT, Joe emphysema, and both were too obese for gastric bypasses. The bankers were all in. The forward-looking banker had already lined up investors for the resale when the Deloreans's time came. There was one downside. Nothing would be left for their two sons, Franklyn and Lutz. But Beth and Joe decided they had given them enough already, even buying Lutz's stepdaughter a used van on her sixteenth birthday.

The rehabilitation of old and dilapidated institutional buildings is immensely popular in Maryland, which has more than its share. Permitting and variances for the facility were streamlined, and remodeling proceeded without the usual nimby lawsuit delay tactics that often required decades to resolve. The Deloreans quickly moved from Lord Baltimore to Saved Angels, saving themselves from insolvency.

When Beth and Joe died from COVID-19, a few months apart, the reverse mortgage collided with the balloon payment coming due. Their banker put the property up for sale to cover the note. It didn't. Not the best time to sell assisted living homes. COVID-19 had landed, and assisted living developments had begun a mass salute of goodbyes in the form of crocodile-tear bankruptcies. The investors were not happy, nor were they cowed.

They created Mergency, a newly minted hedge fund, pledged to fill the gap by buying up nursing homes for a nickel on the dollar, a dime if they were feeling generous. The American way. Because as COVID-19 snuffed out a lot of old people, it unleashed mucho dinero. Wage earners no longer had to pay rest home rent for their parents, and life insurance policies coughed up their limits. The yin and the yang of financial markets now directed from the cemetery's new occupants, no longer vocal, but their wills yelled.

Cruise ship owners, sports car manufacturers, and McMansion builders were swamped with orders.

Mergency gleefully smelled the roadkill and snapped up Saved Angels. A little too snappily, it turned out.

Mergency immediately found itself in financial straits. Saved Angels's once swollen waiting list had dried up. The usual management reshuffling and promotional fanfare could not stem the income shortfall created by the death of so many customers from COVID in such a short order. And nowhere other than a senior residence center did the disease spread faster to the most vulnerable, fed by the underpaid and unvaccinated hired help who rotated through their front doors like angels of death in Edgar Allan Poe's tales. So, Mergency sold Saved Angels, but the sale was rescinded once the new buyers read Saved Angels's residence agreements.

In a reverse timeshare mortgage, the residents were king. Mergency couldn't have the building torn down until the current residents either died or were found satisfactory alternative homes at no charge. This would take time. Too much time. Mergency was not shy about facing the music. It filed for bankruptcy, annulling the lifetime promise to its residents and promoting Saved Angels's thirty acres as prime real estate for what Americans yearn for more than anything: another shopping center. Its current residents would have to fend for themselves. In the meantime, staff would be cut to just a hair above the standard for gross negligence.

Hedge funds love interns, also known as slave labor. Once trade unions caught on, businesses started paying interns—minimum wage. Telly interns at Saved Angels, assigned to the financial hardship unit. In status, she's a dozen steps above a candy striper but ten miles below a registered nurse, though she does almost everything a nurse does. She draws blood, gives shots, dispenses medication, and encourages and restrains patients. She just doesn't have a nurse's liability nor authority, a point the residents remind her of whenever they don't want to obey her commands.

Patients think twice before they cross her. Though she's not built for speed, her thin short legs motor like foxes when called on. It didn't hurt that running space quickly evaporated in a locked unit, that most residents were over seventy years old and ran out of wind quickly, and that many forgot why they were running sooner still. The patients still held the upper hand. There was no punishment you could threaten them with. They were already here for life.

Telly had been obliquely put on notice that her job was in jeopardy when told that her nurse trainer had been let go. "No worries," said Esther, the facility director. "You can work until New Year's Day. And then we will see. After all, you've been here six months, and with COVID-19, that's six years' worth of experience. You're practically a registered nurse."

"Will I be paid as one?" Telly politely asked.

"Don't be silly," said Esther. "But with the deadly speed this pandemic is traveling, we may all be dead before next New Year's Day."

Telly blamed foreigners for Saved Angels's problems. She knew this because her stepfather told her that the Chinese had created the virus in a lab and because most Saved Angels's employees spoke English with a strong foreign accent. Common salutations required a few back-and-forths, while complicated instructions stretched on until asking for help became verbal hara-kari. It was clear immigrants were planning to take over and replace her. She just couldn't understand why they were choosing the jobs everyone else was fleeing because they paid so little.

Telly was the butt of most of the nurse's eye rolls at Saved Angels. She asked too often what the time was, she stayed in the restroom too long, and she arranged her lunch out in front of her like a fort preparing for an assault, then devoured every crumb with military precision. Still, she was always on time, she could mimic what her trainer showed her with only minor intermediate corrections, and she made so little that her pay wasn't eroding theirs. She had an eating disorder; didn't they all?

Telly had never dreamed of being a nurse. Still didn't. Her stepdad had told her that with her Prader Willi Syndrome, nursing was the best job she could hope for. Even her special ed counselor told her it was a good fit.

But she dreamed of being a racecar driver. She was a natural, having the reflexes and empathy of a snapping turtle. Cutting off a driver at a tight curve was orgasmic. She had been driving since she was nine, helped by being five feet tall at that time. That was before she precipitously stopped growing at twelve years-old and five feet four inches.

Lutz Delorean regularly boasted of her skill and pitted her against other police officers, making bets on the outcome. The bets were small to match police officers' pay, but the bragging rights made the effort worth it for him.

As soon as she could legally drive, Beth and Joe had bought her the van. It was the antipathy of being souped up, but she drove like it was. When she started garnering speeding tickets and had to pay the fines out of her savings, she smartened up. She bought a radar detector, even though it was illegal, and her stepfather was a cop. Then, she started saving to buy a new Alfa Romeo.

After six months, she was starting to enjoy being thanked for her services, if not yet for actually helping people. But she had earned enough to open up an installment account for a new car. She never thought to ask what it would cost to save an angel.

Telly swipes her fob and walks into Saved Angels, passing the empty receptionist desk before going through an Employees-Only door to wash up. She finds the sink filthy, grabs some Babo from the vanity, and scrubs the sink as she soaps and rinses up to her elbows. The washroom is claustrophobic, with fake wood cabinets on every wall, cheap linoleum on the floor, and a small plastic mirror. The paper towel dispenser is empty, so she shakes her hands off as best she can on the floor. She can tell by the spots on the linoleum that everyone else is doing the same. The flashy brochures mailed out to entice residents strategically omit pictures of the employee working areas.

She checks her mailbox, the lowest tier in a plastic bin tower, and finds her list of duties, same as last shift. Actually, the exact same piece of paper. She makes out her sweat-stain thumbprint on the page's left-hand corner. Her former trainer had always listed her duties in longhand with a personal note about the most recent troublemaker.

The nurses have been instructed to dress themselves in their COVID-19 attire in pairs, so each can check the other's security. She rings for help before she starts dressing and is 90% finished before Rebecca arrives to help. Rebecca is an intern like Telly. She lives only a few blocks from Saved Angels and offers Telly her place to stay overnight in the event of inclement weather.

First on the list: check on Izzy Iceman hourly. Telly pulls her earbuds out from a zippered pocket. Protocol requires that all personal property be stored in pockets with zippers when not in use. Any dangling wire or cable seen by a patient will be snagged, like how a baby will always manage to knock your glasses off. She wears the earbuds to cancel out Izzy's serial shrieking mixed with the beeping, humming, hushing, and whirring of all the machines he's hooked up to. As a nurse intern, she's constantly reminded that every movement, every word, and even every gesture, has to be for keeping the patient alive. "It's a shame," she thinks, "that they do not think the same way about their patient's sleep. Who could possibly rest with all of this hullabaloo?" She requires a few minutes rest every time she leaves his room to regain herself.

Izzy Iceman's every musculature movement is being monitored and recorded for reasons unfathomable to Telly. The other nurses had hinted Saved Angels was having to defend itself against a lawsuit for his contracting COVID-19 there.

After making sure every appliance is operating correctly and none of the lines have lost connection, Telly records the readings on the clipboard beside his bed. She notices the last post was six hours ago. She sets her watch to beep in an hour.

Upon leaving Izzy's cell, Telly spots a posting in the corridor. Big thick black lettering. The director has been replaced. Her name is Ruth Stephopolis. There's neither mention of where Esther went, nor when staff can meet Ruth. Telly will, and shortly.

CHAPTER SEVEN

SINKHOLE

Damascus Police Chief Lutz Delorean, wearing his full-dress uniform, pops into his kitchen and finds himself face-to-face with his stepdaughter. She's standing at attention. One hand in a salute, the other holding a cereal bowl. It's empty and clean. He gives her his don't-bother-me-now frown, slaps her on the rump with his gloves, and jogs downstairs to the basement after carefully securing the door behind him with a shackleless padlock.

The basement is a testament to the unfinished. Bare concrete slab floor, concrete block walls, and wood joists, wood cross bridging and plywood overhead. No furniture, not even the traditional ping pong table. Lighting is supplied by thirty-two monitors. They hang from the joists via Battleship Gray angle-iron straps. You might have thought you had stumbled into a pirate news studio.

Lutz hums the melody to Wagner's "Flight of the Valkyries" while snapping on each monitor's volume just long enough to catch the talking heads' gist before pressing mute and moving farther along the circuit. He comes to the last screen. He stops humming. It's blank. He checks the time and date on his Rolex. He keys in his password. Still blank. Tomorrow, at the latest. He vapes Cherry Delight, turns around, and trudges upstairs, again securing the door behind him like the prison guard he used to be. Once back in the kitchen, he yells, "Telly, scan time!"

His daughter appears, a little out of breath, bowl still in one hand and gives him a high five with the other. But he doesn't slap her palm. Instead, he pulls a gun from a kitchen drawer and scans her hand. After reading whatever was on it, he tells her, "Good News, Miss Prader Willi, you are still among the living."

"My name is not Prader Willi. Prader Willi is a genetic disorder."

"Okay, okay, spare me the whole essay. I've heard it before, remember? Only physical force can dissuade a person with Prader Willi not to eat if eats are around and unguarded. I've even had to put a time lock on your lunch pail."

As soon as she leaves for school or work, her lunch pail becomes her anchor until she returns home, when she immediately surveys its insides to make sure a golden nougat of nutrition isn't hiding inside. It never is. Then her primary focus moves to the padlocked refrigerator and the pantry, as nowhere else in the house did food lodge. Except for the dining room and the kitchen counter, and then only when preparing or eating meals. Snacking is a lost memory.

"Next you're going to tell me you couldn't have Prader Willi if you were not among the living, right?" says Lutz.

"Yes. If you're dead, you won't be hungry all the time. But with Prader Willi, you can expect me to no longer be among the living when I reach thirty. I have twelve years to live. Did I lose weight?"

"Thirteen years, Miss Hangry. No, you gained two and a half pounds."

"Super, that's an improvement, isn't it?" she says. "Now can we have breakfast, Chief? I'm famished."

"When aren't you? Let me unlock the fridge first. What were you doing just now?"

"Packing my backpack."

"Didn't you get the memo? It's New Year's Day, 2021. A Maryland State public holiday. Special Order of the day: no school. Everyone has the day off except for essential services. How do burritos sound?" asks Lutz as he pushes food around in the freezer.

"What sounds do burritos make? If it's New Year's Day, why are you in your blues? I have to work. Did you fill my van with gas like you said you would? People in residence care don't take holidays off…"

"I'm making a little surprise inspection to see who actually shows up for work today and what condition they're in after New Year's Eve. Sorry, you'll have to get your own gas. I forgot. Want to come and see the fireworks at the station?"

"I saw enough fireworks last night."

"Pull down a bowl for me, will ya?" says Lutz, while he reads the instructions on the burrito's label.

"Sour cream please."

"No can do, Plump Plump Girl. But last night's fireworks were nothing compared to the firepower you are going to hear next week. On that you can bet your bottom burrito."

CHAPTER EIGHT

ROUND TUBE

When America's TV industry had run out of sitcom spin offs, it literally stole story ideas from foreign broadcast networks, starting with the closest ones. Once Canada's programming was laid waste, it honed in on Britain's, before scalping everything European then Asian. Enter reality shows. Reality shows were real, if you didn't count the jerry-rigged opening act and the behind-the-scenes popularity contest fumbling at the end. Talent became incredibly optional, and photogenicity and extremity were shoe-ins. That is until viewers got bored with bug eating, snake slithering, and tattoo-covered muscle-shirt heroes. Then, the producers, volleying hard to keep their jobs, brought viewers into the cutthroat world of business. "Bob, your team is handling ten thousand widgets a minute. What could you do to make it eleven?" For unimaginable reasons, this wasn't banal to American viewers.

Donald Trump's show theatrically brought audiences into a big business's boardroom, where real deals were cut, profits measured, and failures exposed. It turned out to be a combination of the *Gong Show* and *The Price is Right* and was wildly popular. Andy watched every episode multiple times, some so often that he would mouth the contestants' remarks before they spoke.

When Donald Trump first announced he was running for President of the United States, Andy was all in. He became a Trumper immediately. Andy put Trump bumper decals on his truck and wore a MAGA cap wherever he went. Strangers suddenly started stopping him in the street, thanking him, and shaking his hand. Andy liked that. His customers liked his new swagger and that they were having custom bowls made by a Trumper. They felt even more superior.

When a film surfaced in which Donald Trump could be heard saying that soldiers are idiots for risking their lives and complaining that the country was paying their medical bills, Melody had asked, "Handcream, time to bet on a different horse?"

"This is just a smear campaign," responded Andy. "It is orchestrated by the Democrats. Remember that film clip where a black woman admitted to denying loans to whites?"

"I do," said Melody. "It turned out to be fake, as it left out the punch line."

"That's right. This could be fake too. Trump could have been playing the part in a movie. You don't really know."

"Handcream," said Melody, "the other participants in the film are US generals, not actors."

"I'm not changing horses in midstream," replied Andy. "Loyalty is a wet knot that can only be separated with a sharp blade. Once I'm in, I'm all the way in. Didn't Joe Namath say that once? That's what loyalty is, if you haven't forgotten."

"So, you're going to follow the quote of a retired quarterback who advertises underwear on the side?" said Melody. "You're smarter than that, Handcream."

"So, I should have divorced you when you lost half our savings with Bernie Madoff, when you crashed our car into a church, or when you left Sam on the Long Island Ferry to spend a weekend with that Bohemian?"

Melody always had only a dim recollection of her megalomaniac episodes.

"The churches are saying God always chooses a flawed man to lead us," said Andy.

"Sure did this time, Handcream." said Melody. "He's filed for bankruptcy multiple times, been married multiple times, and sued or been sued over a thousand times. That works out to a flaw a week for twenty years running. There once was a king named Wenceslas. Maybe we can crown him, King Endlessflaws. There's precedent."

Donald Trump's fitness for office was his TV celebrity status. People love familiarity. He had no burning bush, no epileptic seizure revelation, and no schizophrenic voices telling him what to do. He said he had a solution for everything even if he never did tell you what it was. That would have been too simple, too easy. Like thinking banning automatic weapons would diminish school shootings, legalizing drugs would decrease fatal overdoses, and outing systemic racism would reduce hate crimes. He was the solution.

Melody, in her work as an actuary, came into contact with many big businessmen, as they like to call themselves. She found them entertaining, full of hot air, but mostly bullies, so she gave them little weight. She was Teflon to bullies. She dealt in hard facts, not threats. When Trump ran for office, she did not enter the breach. When he won the nomination, she winced. When he won the election in 2016, she was saddened, but not flabbergasted nor particularly annoyed. "Let's see what he does, maybe it's a good thing. Maybe he'll show us all his boorish behavior was just to get our attention and he really will shake things up for the better."

Andy, sitting in his Barcalounger, his butt less than a foot above the carpet, says to the TV, "You can't believe a word he says."

Melody and Andy are watching the late-night news, staying on channel to catch the ball drop at Madison Square Garden and finishing their dinner of spaghetti and salad. Andy had splurged with some grocery store champagne for the occasion. Images of losing their home to the bankers have been trumped by the absence of the sheriff paying them a visit this week.

He's remarking on a film clip, showing the president-elect, Joe Biden, listing on his fingers what he'll do the first few days after taking office.

"They're both politicians, Handcream. Biden swears that he's against fracking then opens government land for oil companies to drill on. Trump said he had a medical plan to end all medical plans. It's still hidden in its non-transparent gift wrapping."

"Biden," says Andy, "has wrapped himself up in being this honest yokel. You know he lies. He tells you the truth now just so you miss seeing his hand in the cookie jar. Everybody lies. Everybody acts in their own self-interest."

"But Handcream, if that were true, why should anyone believe what you just said?"

"That just proves my point! Logic and fancy ideas didn't stop Caesar, Alexander the Great, or Napoleon, did they? Ideas are fine for parlor games. But in the real world, might wins nine times out of nine-and-a-half. You tell me as an actuary, you are risk averse, so why bet against the king? No one beats the king! Try it at checkers, and you lose every time. What replaced the French and Russian Revolutions? After a million or so people were murdered, the people replaced them with new kings! Kings work."

Andy belches, looking at his flute of bubbly. It's getting low. He debates leaving his warm sanctuary to refill his glass but thinks better of it. Then, he looks over at Melody; her glass is empty. She's shaking it at him. He gets up, and she hands him her flute and says, "We have an *elected* president. We have had an elected president for almost two hundred and fifty years."

"Are you sure?" asks Andy. "The people in power are pulling all the strings. Democracy is a con job. What's the expression? So far, so bad." He walks into the kitchen and pours the rest of the champagne into their glasses and returns.

Melody accepts hers and, after taking a sweet sip, says, "If democracy is a con, why care who is on the throne?"

"Trump is why we are on a new road to prosperity."

"And the people in power, as you call them, didn't want that before?"

"Prosperity for them," says Andy.

"When did that change, Handcream? The poor are only getting poorer, the rich richer."

"He just needs more time."

"We gave him four years," says Melody. "Where and when was the shake-up? The only thing that changed was the calendar."

CHAPTER NINE

FERRIS WHEEL ON FENTANYL

Telly had been fantasizing about turning eighteen for years, but her dreams always broke down when she got to thinking about where she would live. Whenever she brought the subject up, Chief would shoo her away with, "There's plenty of time to discuss that," or, "let's wait until you graduate," or, "I'm looking into a nice place in Springfield for you. It has running water and an inside toilet, but the cafeteria is outside, haha." She was old enough to know Springfield was a Psychiatric Hospital, as Chief was constantly ferrying criminals to or from there.

She doesn't go to Saved Angels on New Year's Day. She isn't scheduled to. After the Chief leaves for his surprise inspection, she loads her van with the clothes and stuff and drives to Donna's. She's going to have a new life. One without locks on the fridge. One without the Chief constantly telling her what she can and cannot do. One with freedom. One with her mother, her real mother. Wow. She's an adult now. It has finally happened. And she hasn't even graduated from high school.

When she arrives at Donna's home, a plaintive patter of had-I-knowns joins her heartbeat. It doesn't let up for one second the entire nineteen hours she stays.

Like apartment number 42 equating to the fourth floor. Three flights to lug her stuff. Three flights every day, sometimes multiple times a day. Stamina is not Telly's strong suit. Her home only had one floor besides the basement, and the Chief never let her down there.

And like halfway before she even reaches Donna's apartment, Telly bumps into Henry. He hasn't shaved in forever, smells like compost, and smiles silently while he hands her a frozen dinner package from his shopping cart. Well, at least the present temperature outside should keep it frozen. "Thank you, but no, my hands are full at the moment." A situation that, by Henry's quick and surgical reinsertion of the package into his cart, he had not been unaware of.

And like when she finally rings Donna's doorbell and a man opens the door and yells out, "She's here." He wears lots of bling and is attended by a Pitbull whose bulbous eyes follow her as if she might have brought lunch or, worse, is lunch.

Donna languidly welcomes her in the foyer, if you can use that term for the twelve square feet which opens out to the living/dining room, kitchen, bathroom, and one bedroom. "Telly, how wonderful. Been waiting for you all day. This is Victor and his dog, Grief. Victor's my manager. He was just leaving, as the saying goes."

Victor offers his hand for her to shake. Grief stays by his heels, vigilant as a cat keeping a fly just out of reach in sight.

Telly asks Victor as she vigorously pumps his hand, "Where does the saying go?"

Victor laughs and smiles. He lets go of her hand and says to Donna, "This might pan out just fine, Girl."

Telly just stands in the foyer, her hands rowing her suitcase back and forth in front of her. She tells herself they must be speaking in street code. "Maybe I was supposed to have learned it in school. Now I really have to know since I'm grown up." So, first thing's first, speak your mind, girl. She giggles then asks, "Which way's my bedroom?"

Donna's quick to see apprehension in a client's face. "You got more stuff to bring up, right?"

Victor says, "Seriously?"

Donna places her palm on Victor's stomach, pushing him softly away from Telly, and says, "You can bring the rest up here like a water brigade every time you returns from outside. So, take a break. You like lemonade?"

"Yes, very much. Where's my bedroom?"

"Good, there's some frozen in the fridge. Why not make us some?"

Telly fox steps into the kitchen and swings the fridge door open wide as if it was to a treasure chest. Her expectations are instantly dashed by the bleakness inside and then immediately restored when she hears Donna say, "When you rested, we will go grocery shopping."

While Telly is making lemonade, she sees Donna lay her palm out before Victor, and he snaps out three bills from the wallet he wears in his sock.

And the had-she-known about the apartment's strange odor. It clings to everything, even the silverware. Something burnt, maybe rotting.

But the trump had-she-known card is learning she doesn't have a bedroom. She's relegated to the living room, hardly larger than her own bedroom. The couch is her bed. It doesn't even fold out and stinks of something different than exhaust, organic but old.

Donna is insistent, "I know I know, but don't worry. This is all temporary. Our new apartment is opening up in a week, maybe less. It has real heat and new paint. You'll have your own bedroom there. You'll love it."

Telly senses a flaw in Donna's enthusiasm, which brings to surface her stepfather's instructions on how to lie-detect. First, narrow the options. Telly asks, "Is it in this same building, on the same floor?"

When Donna hesitates before answering, "No, it's a few blocks away." Telly has her answer.

Telly probes further, "I'd like to see it. Let's walk there. It would make me feel better." Always end a lie detector question with emphasizing its importance to you. If the Chief was right, and Donna is lying, Donna will make an excuse for why not right now.

"Not right now, Baby. I am so busy with you moving in and everything." Telly looks around the living room. She tries to imagine all that needed to be done to make room for her. She shrinks a little inside but congratulates herself for not having brought the rest of her stuff up those stairs.

And more than all the had-she-knowns together, there is Donna herself. After Victor and Grief leave, Donna spends the bulk of her time scrolling on her laptop and asking Telly questions on how to get Telly's Social Security check delivered to Donna's address instead of the Chief's. Telly thought they were going grocery shopping together.

Telly figures, just like she left Chief, she can leave Donna. She's growing up.

At five in the morning, when she's sure Donna is asleep, she collects her belongings. It's a lot easier toting her clothes and stuff down the stairs than it was carrying them up. Even Henry is asleep. When she gets to work, she will ask Rebecca if she can stay with her for a few days. Rebecca said she lived only two blocks away. Telly had also read that some people live out of their cars. Certainly, that would be no worse than staying at Donna's. And she can return to Chief any time she wants. A father might reward his child for figuring out her mother was a grifter. A grounding was much more likely. Most important was Telly's plan for that Social Security check, an Alfa Romeo, bright red.

Her shift at Saved Angels begins at eight. She has plenty of time to stop at a diner for an omelet and pancakes a la mode.

CHAPTER TEN

CIRCLE IN A BOX

Chief Lutz Delorean canters down his basement stairs. He doesn't lock the door behind him. When he sees Telly again, he'll shoot her. And it won't be long. If it is, he'll torture her first.

He walks up to the first monitor and unmutes it. He sees a man in a muscle shirt, curly brown silver hair spilling out of it, and recognizes the gravelly voice.

"We have to protect our children, our grandchildren. The schools are stealing them from us. They're teaching our children one lie after another. Lies that make them hate us, make them hate themselves. This is why the suicide rate for teenagers has skyrocketed. Have you seen the numbers? The schools give every single child the champion's trophy. They think they can do nothing wrong. They now crave attention and, to get that, they're now demanding sexual transfer operations. It's too hard being the sex they were born into. 'Oh Grandad, stop calling me Jennifer. I'm Cagney now.' Makes me sick to my stomach..." Lutz mutes the monitor, gives the speaker a point for spreading the blame for the rise in teenage suicides on CRT instead of the real culprit—social media. Imaginations like this garner extra clicks, and clicks are the new wealth multiplier. Good for him.

Lutz walks down to the next screen. Here's a man with a wonderful tan, wearing a three-piece pin-stripe suit, standing in front of a ceiling-high stone fireplace before a sixteen-point elk head. The taxidermist, by design or default, had given the elk a look of bemusement. The man, not the elk, is saying, "We, the long suffering, we, the true and original bearers of the country's torch, are being systematically and systemically disenfranchised. Excuse the big words. How about if I just say, 'We are getting fucked.' Even our religion is being squeegeed away from us.

"We can't pray in public anymore. Not at ballgames, not in school, not even in our legislative bodies, unless we want to get arrested. Yes, that is happening. These people don't eat oatmeal or cold cereal for breakfast. They don't fry up steak and potatoes for supper. They teethe on salads, suck down kale frappes, or eat what we would insist are scraps for the dog out of a tortilla shell.

"And you better believe we are complicit. We don't sit down at the dinner table as a family anymore. We eat off marble kitchen counters while our kids play video games and listen to Taylor Swift in their bedrooms by themselves. Have you listened to her lyrics? She'd be sitting in a penal colony if she toured half the countries on the planet.

"We drive our kids away from our own neighborhood so they can dance in a dojo, meditate in a sangha, paint in an atelier. Then, there's soccer, for Chrissake. Soccer's for sissies. MRI field agents have co-opted high school football. Ever see a middle linebacker broadside a wide receiver in the flat then watch the receiver get up, shake it off, and run back into the huddle? Try watching a professional soccer game. A player will writhe in agony when he's as much as touched by an opposing player's pinkie. It's theater not sport. I'm throwing a yellow flag."

Lutz says to himself, "Socrates predicted cultural ruin two thousand years ago." He mutes Tan man and walks to the next monitor and unmutes it. A man in a white doctor's coat in front of what looks like a medical clinic examining room says, "This is a beta-vitaminum. Bita means better. This will evacuate your bowels faster than a colonoscopy mouthwash with only half the discomfort, and the fantastic part is that you can use it every day…"

Lutz bookmarks it to his laptop and moves to the next monitor. This time it's a young blonde woman, with a face rating of five plus and a voice so sexy he double-checks to make sure this isn't a porn site, saying, "The Dems, who paid for the election with all that stimulus money, have increased the cost of your basic needs by two hundred percent. Bait and switch, Baby." A baby cries in the background. Lutz wonders if the speaker is aware the audience hears that. She must have as she froze the screen for a full minute. So, it's part of the script, well done.

She goes on, "How much are you plunking down for baby formula these days? Who do you think is really to blame for this? Chipmunk Adam Illegal Shift, Nancy Pull My Trigger Finger Please, and Chuck Shoe More."

Lutz muses that Lady Daily is getting stale. He deletes the link and Facebook's algorithm switches to a bearded towhead barking out, "It was different for our parents. We didn't notice, as we were too busy trading baseball cards, cribbing off the smart kid, and chasing peeks at the girls. Everything was a straight line for our parents. They worked. They got paid. They saved and bought a home. They retired, moved to Florida, and played golf. Tra la la. You did what they expected of you. Came home for holidays, birthdays, and funerals.

"Today, life is much more complicated. Computers crushed us. Smartphones killed us. Every minute is now being split into smaller segments for have-to-dos. Before you can complete an inhale and remember what you intended, digital messages are flooding your smartphone telling what you just missed. Exhaling has now become optional."

Lutz can tell that this link comes from Moscow. He recognizes the tone and its mimicry of Lady Daily. Reminds himself that the fear-of-missing-out is big business.

Why did Telly leave? He had her cell phone and her password. Its contacts only contained medical doctors and him. Text history was limited to logistics. "Where are you? What time will you be there? Where were you?" She must have been planning this for some time. He had inspected her room. So little was out of place, she could move back tomorrow. Maybe she plans to.

He walks to the next monitor where a panel of men wearing deacon's caps are mid-debate. One is saying, "I can personally attest to never being unkind to a black person, if black is politically correct to say, that is. I can't keep up with what they want us to call them these days."

Another says, "Let's not forget, some of them are actually civil."

The first speaker continues, "Though I can't say I know any of them very well. I see a lot around, but I keep my conversation to the subject at hand, don't let it tail past what the weather's like or how the Orioles are doing. And I never bring up B-ball. Stopped watching it long ago. And somehow NASCAR never comes up in conversation with them."

Lutz mutes it. He calls them the Supremes under his breath. He walks to the next monitor. Another panel, this time sitting in separate folding chairs on a tiny stage. It's broadcast out of Reverend Joseph Jones Hillsdale College. "In a recent *Psychology Today* article, a study concluded that we decide whether we are going to like someone or not within a few seconds of meeting them, often before they have even said a single word. The Beatles were right, something in the way she moves. The study says only stern discipline can overcome this bias. Why call it a bias? We got the person right in the first seconds, no further review required."

A thin man, all in black including his beret, says, "Libs are upset because we don't like them. They're of a breed that falls over itself trying to be liked. We do not suffer from that disease, never have. We do what we do. Like or dislike us. We don't care. We don't fawn. We know everyone is corrupt. Expecting people to be honest is what makes no sense. They put on this act that they're looking down on us when, in reality, they're projecting that we're looking down on them. We're not. We're oblivious, and that's what galls them."

Lutz presses "Like" then mutes the panel discussion and steps to the next monitor which has *The Bing Stills Show*. Bing's identifying characteristics are his tactility and whispering. Lutz pumps up the volume.

"Instead of inhaling the familiar exhaust, sweat and fast food—the sweet smell of progress, our nostrils are attacked by fried chicken and curry. Instead of seeing people who dress like us, our eyes are assaulted by saris, head scarves, and hoodies. Instead of listening to music, our ears are blasted by melodies whose only rhythm is shock changes of pace and rapid-fire lyrics that are unintelligible, meant to get us all excited, not calmed."

Lutz mutes Bing and unleashes the next screen, Thucker Caligari is mid-lecture, "How can we not be outraged? We figured our children will only be with us a few years before they're off making millions, so why not buy them whatever they want? Interest payments on our debt are only temporary, right? But they're not. They're compounded. And "Lo and Behold" our children move back in and milk off us after college. They say we taught them how to sponge.

"We did. We joked about how we faked doing our job at work, remember? The angles we cut. And maybe we exaggerated a bit. We told them that the law that the riches go to those who work the hardest was a myth created by the rich to keep everyone else working. And we are not suckers. Meanwhile, we are working two jobs. Our primary job has new duties, most of them out of our wheelhouse. Our company was sold, and as soon as the new owner found out how profits were being faked, we were offered work downstairs handling customer complaints or out in the cold. We don't like the cold. So now we listen to sad sack stories about the company's miscues from nine to five then scoot over to the local golf club where a major payday awaits after we sell a golf shirt. Big time is not around the corner. It's not even in our neighborhood." Lutz mutes Thucker and switches to the podcast featuring Never-Trumpers. A gray-haired, overweight, elderly woman in a Hawaiian muumuu laments, "Now some of us are refusing to accept that Trump lost the election. Why not, you might ask. We denied climate change and 'Here's Johnnie.' We denied the pandemic and three to four thousand of us, well mostly us, die daily. We disparage LGBTQs and find they have overwhelming social support. Who knew? The Bible be damned. We rallied against immigrants then had to hear our preachers condemning us for being unchristian. Take heart. Trump cannot last forever. We can't be wrong that often. A life without immigrants, without non-heteros, and without Democrats can happen. And I'll tell you how. But first, please press the donate button."

Lutz mutes it and unmutes the next monitor. It's a labor union steward with that out-of-breath voice they manufacture to establish that they aren't professional speakers, "We can see the future, and what we don't see is a lavish retirement party, much less a pension. Human Resources promised us that becoming independent contractors would make us true entrepreneurs, opening up golden riches. Management's mission has been, and remains to be, 'how much can we get out of Joseph or Jane and not have to pay for medical benefits?' Working employees until we burn out. So, all of us now work twice as hard AKA into the hospital with no benefits. Except for HR, of course. They have to stay on to handle your lawsuits and mail out the annual birthday and condolence cards."

Lutz says to himself, "Laced with communism," before he mutes it and unmutes the next monitor. It's called *Unfiltered*.

"Gays are no longer reviled. They're adulated—make sure you take one home for dinner. I guess I meant *to* dinner. Blacks no longer have to live in their ghettos. They're given multi-million-dollar settlements for bogus pardons. Immigrants are no longer shot for crossing our borders. They're welcomed with free lifetime welfare income and medical coverage. All are the go-to for publishing books, music, and films. Everything white-inspired is anathema. Is anyone paying attention to who pays for this grand theft? Taxes. You thought that money was yours? No siree. Your hard-earned money is ever faster going to people who will never have to work a day in their lives.

"Your taxes are supporting their bad decisions. You sure didn't tell them to be born in Central America or South America, where their country's failed leadership has been overwhelmed by criminal drug lords who profit by selling drugs to your neighbor's kids. You sure didn't encourage them to be born queer when they could just buck it up and keep quiet about it like we all did for centuries. Freud promoted that, if I remember right. As far as the color of their skin, where's your reward for lightening it every chance you had? Haha. Our great and great-great grandparents sure did." Lutz calls this link the piners and the whiners.

He mutes it and turns on the next monitor. It's the Unpolitically Correct crowd. A very angry looking man is spewing, "With Jill you don't bring up climate change, with John LGBTQ, with Larry immigration, and with Mary abortion. Et cetera, et cetera. We are so beset by minefields to fire-walk that proving we are a good person is as likely as being able to thread a pinhole with the lit fuse of a dynamite stick. But tiptoeing around every issue in town builds sexy calves, right? We can now only safely talk about sports debacles and cat videos. So, what should we do? Let us talk about death. Death relentlessly stalks us. You're a day older, make no mistake about that, and another day closer to being pushed around in a wheelchair to lay flowers down at your spouse's headstone."

A voice from a professional-sounding DJ interrupts, "Please visit our survivors-estate-planning website., and press subscribe if you like this!" Lutz laughs to himself, wondering how anyone who listens to this doesn't see that it's all grift. He mutes it and switches on a libertarian website.

"You know what your problem is? Your momma. While she was supposed to be caring for you, bringing you up as an American, she was instead busy chasing the almighty dollar and running hard after the seven deadly sins, like they were goals, not paths to hell."

Lutz mutes it and starts to pace around his basement. Parents. His own mother hadn't worked, but she hadn't taken care of him either, his nanny Marsha had. Marsha had babysat Telly a couple of times. What happened to Marsha? The Eversole's hired her as their kids' nanny. Would she take Telly in? Worth a shot. He calls up the Eversoles.

An unfamiliar voice answers, "Hello, this is the Eversole residence, how can I help you?"

"Would you put Marsha on, Walter?"

"My name is Sooraj. May I ask who I am speaking to?"

"Chief of Police Lutz Delorean. What happened to Walter?"

"Walter is with Mr. and Mrs. Eversole, vacationing in Viet Nam."

"Then where's Marsha?"

"She's with them too."

"How cozy. Listen, when do you expect them back?"

"It will be a while. The weather here is almost frigid. If this is an emergency, I could ask Marsha to call you. Is this a good number?"

"No emergency, just checking in. Marsha was my nanny thirty years ago. Just tell her I was thinking of her, thanks," says Lutz. He hangs up and doesn't hear Sooraj's goodbye. What was he thinking?

Mothers. His wife Lydia, Telly's stepmother, had disappeared almost nine years ago now. She'd loved Telly. Spoiled her. Is it possible she returned? Not likely. He had it on good authority her home village had been burned to a crisp by a drug cartel. He hadn't followed up on her after ICE got wind of her illegal status and flew her home. Lutz figured she would contact him as soon as she had the chance. So far, she hasn't. Almost a decade now.

Then, there is Donna Kind. Telly's birth mother. Telly hadn't been with her since she was three. Would Telly know how to even contact her? Even remember her?

Telly had recently started locking her bedroom door. When he ordered her to let him in so he could inspect it for food, she reluctantly had. He didn't find any food, not even crumbs. When he left her room she locked it right back, reminding him a girl needs her privacy. Still, that had been new for her.

Mothers.

Mm-hmm, Donna Kind. Telly had been nagging him about living on her own. She could go anywhere she could afford. Maybe this internship had swelled her head. She's so naive. He hadn't thought she'd ever move out. Since his parents' financial fumbling, he found living off a chief's salary a tough climb in the land of hypo-opportunity. His parents had bought the home for him. It's free and clear, not that the property taxes make it feel that way. Telly will become an adult next month, so her Social Security check is about to double. Still, he doesn't think she earns enough to make rent, much less the other essentials.

According to the adoption papers, Donna was an addict with no reportable income source. So? He remembers she had been pretty good looking. She also had a community college degree in something. Those circumstances dovetail. Find Donna.

Find Telly.

CHAPTER ELEVEN

INSIDE MIDLIGHT, OUTSIDE NIGHT

Every curb on Jamestown Street is plugged with a car. The red paint by the fire hydrants is religiously disobeyed. Low-hanging tree limbs discourage any driver from finding refuge on the front lawn. Lutz double parks his unit. He leaves the engine running, flashers on. The flashers beat out red and white, competing with the Christmas lights shimmering through the apartment windows.

The building notices the intrusion by a foreign object and goes quiet despite this being the day after New Year's. The festivities may restart at any minute.

He rushes up the three flights of stairs. Surprise is the cops' favorite tool. He catches his breath at the top landing. Like many police officers and military men, their once massive, muscled shoulders and chest descend to their gut as they age. Doing three serious sets of ab exercises five times a week is too much pain for the reward, a woman's attention. Plus, both had receded along with their hairlines.

Lutz busts through Donna's apartment door. He finds that the apartment is lit only by candles and a tiny Christmas tree atop the TV. He flashes his flashlight like in all the cop shows, except he doesn't yell, "Police." He doesn't say a word. Neither does anyone else in the building.

Donna sits alone on her couch wearing only a Raven's jersey. The couch is too far from the wall. Lutz pulls the couch further back, not quite catapulting Donna out and finds a very young man on all fours. He's shaking like he has a severe fever. Lutz brandishes his badge in the man's face. After a long hesitation, the man finds poise enough to pull his pants up and refasten his belt buckle. Lutz high-armpits him out of the apartment. On the landing, Lutz tells him, "First time's a freebee, second time I find you with a ho, jail time, and I call your parents."

The shock of all this irons the inebriation out of the young man everywhere except for in his legs.

"Be careful on those stairs," says Lutz. "I'm not calling you an ambulance."

Lutz walks back inside and searches the place. He knocks over everything that is knockoverable but is careful to avoid upsetting the candles. Donna plays demure. She lights up a regular cigarette. She's confused but not nonplussed. She's been on the wrong side of a rototiller before. She goes over how she will explain this to Victor. Victor is supposed to make sure this never happens. She needs to be accurate, but she has such a bad memory for details. She reminds herself where the cash and pills are stashed. He doesn't have the look of a seasoned vice cop, and he moves too old to be new. She needs to time when she stretches out her naked legs. Is he after trade or merch?

When Lutz doesn't find anything, even in the refrigerator, that indicates Telly might have been there. He comes over to where she sits and blurts, "Where is she?" He half-scares himself at the volume of his voice, having forgotten how out-of-breath he is from the stair climb. He makes a mental note to speak softer and will his heart to slow down.

Donna giggles. Then catches herself. Of course this is about her recently departed false- savior, Telly. She had moved out without even leaving a note. Not as stupid as the doctors thought her to be. This is stepdad acting-out time. Small time law hood. Bet he doesn't know the First Law of Acquisition. When you get a pull, deny you have it. Doesn't matter if you do or don't. It only convinces the mark you do have it, and therein lies the treasure.

Donna says, "Who? I live here by myself."

"Your daughter, Miss Donna Kind. One Telly Kind," says Lutz.

Donna takes an exaggerated draw on her cigarette, catching an ash in her hand without a flinch from the heat, asks, "My daughter?"

Lutz, realizing he's on the hook now, not the reel, stays silent. So does Donna. She takes another drag, waits for more ash to fall.

Lutz breaks, "Your and my daughter. Miss Kind. Telly Kind!"

"You're Telly's adopted dad?" says Donna. "I thought you looked familiar, but boy, have you aged. Telly, Telly your stepdad wants to see you." Donna swivels her head around as if Telly might pop out of nowhere at any time. "Not here, I guess. But do stop by anytime Mr. Delorean." She hikes up her jersey a calibrated inch.

Lutz doesn't bite. "Where'd she go?"

Donna's cash antenna hums. She pulls her jersey down coquettishly and says, "You gonna clean up this mess you made here? You gonna pay for my busted front door? You out of order. You ain't vice," says Donna. "Reparations, Mr. Policeman."

"Tell me where she went!"

"The door is four hundred, housekeeping one fifty. Call it five hundred, and I don't call the county and tell them that a cop broke into my place without a warrant."

"Where is she?"

"You not getting the message, Mr. Policeman. You want me to start screaming rape? You know who I am. I know who you are. Want to find out how large my lungs are? They're under my top. Are you here for a peek? That will cost you a grand."

"Worried about that, I am not," says Lutz as he plumps down on the couch next to Donna. He assumes the humble pose that sometimes works. He makes no indication he wants to be any closer to her.

"Okay, give me a grand, and don't look at my mams," says Donna. "And I'll tell you where she is."

"I'll pay you five hundred when I find her if you tell me she is. But you only have twenty-four hours. After that, I don't need her. But if I find out you lied to me…"

"She got something you want?" Donna asks.

Lutz stares down at his hands. He says, "You not getting the message."

"Maybe I can get it for you," says Donna, as she holds her cigarette out in front of Lutz for a drag. He takes a long one and hands the cigarette back, exhaling a mountain of smoke.

Donna edges the negotiation along like the pro she is, "Two fifty now, five hundred more when you find her where I tell you she is. Final offer," says Donna. "Doors ain't cheap, and neither are reputations."

Lutz laughs and shakes his head, mumbling, "Reputations." He looks over his hands like he's going to show her a backhand. Donna's jaw tightens up, her chin now even more angular, reminding him of Telly.

Lutz reaches into his pants pocket and pulls out five crisp bills. Donna is not slow to snatch them. She snaps through the five fifties. She'll downsize them before she tells Victor about this. She authenticates the sting by looking right in Lutz's eyes and says, "Black's Shelter for Abused Women. It's on Castle Street."

"Why would she go there?"

"Said she had friends. She goes back and forth, ya know. I don't run a prison like she says you do. And sometimes, my boyfriend stays the night."

"Victor Bridge, your pimp?"

"My boyfriend."

Lutz scrunches up his eyes and says, "He put the move on Telly?"

"You serious? That girl… Truth is she's afraid of Victor's dog, Grief. Most are."

Homes for the abused are rabbit holes if you are seeking missing persons. Lutz knew their commandments. They would not give you the name on their own driver's license without a foolproof current warrant. If he printed a fake one, the home director would insist on talking to the judge who signed it at a number listed in the phone book. He'd seen it happen. He's lost, and the clock relentlessly ticks. He goes to Black's anyway, pleads mercy, cries over losing his daughter, "She's mentally ill, she's being played by others, she needs her diabetes medication." Bernadette Black, a lovey-dovey matron of the mistreated, dons her guardian robes. Asks him point blank, "Why's it the police are always asking us to break the law?"

When Lutz prattles out the matter of life and death boilerplate excuses, Bernadette says, "And you'll lock us up whenever we do. Go home unless you want to stay for a selfie of us together. It'll just take me a sec to apply my lipstick."

Lutz drives home. He's completely dependent on waiting for word from others. I wonder if any of us appreciate the anxiety cops feel being so dependent on random gossip to do their jobs. In this case of course, we are not sure what his job is.

CHAPTER TWELVE

GOING WHERE ONE HAS ALWAYS BEEN

Alzheimer's should have struck Andy, not Melody. Andy is the one with an incredibly poor memory. Pretty much why he failed school. Andy takes information in on a catch-and-release basis. Once used, he discards it. School teachers taught as if yesterday's lesson, once taught, was learned forever. Andy forgot yesterday's lesson and was summarily abandoned by school.

How was he supposed to remember yesterday's lesson when the math teacher insisted he use logic, the English teacher demanded he use rules of grammar and punctuation that held no logic, and the history teacher graded on what happened in a particular order, regardless of rules and logic?

When they married, Andy was confident that Melody would always know what to do, so he would too. All he had to do was ask Melody. But then, seven years ago, she arrived home from her Princeton glass corner office atop a skyscraper by ambulance with a full security attachment.

Melody, at forty-five-years-old, senior executive vice president of the largest reinsurance company in the world, was serendipitously Slinky-ing down Alzheimer's slide. She holds doctorates in economics, law, engineering. After passing all ten national exams, she earned a full actuary fellowship, the most respected position in the insurance industry. She had an encyclopedic knowledge of, what seemed to Andy, everything. Maybe the toll of knowing everything wore a brain out. He doesn't know. His own brain always felt tired.

When Melody was first brought home, Andy figured she was suffering a mental breakdown, so he immediately went about finding a doctor who could fix her up. Instead of fixing her up, they solidified his distrust in experts—the elites.

Depending on the psychiatrist *du jour*, Melody had bipolar, OCD, ADHD, and major depression, with schizophrenia taking practice swings in the batting circle. Each doctor had initiated a drug regimen that Melody religiously adhered to and talk therapy that she gave serious lip service through. None of it helped. After two years of this whack-a-mole mental volleyball, Andy had her see a neurologist.

Dr. Wiseman, the neurologist, explained that her brain was constipated. The waste matter produced from sense, thought, and memory interactions was not flushing out like it was supposed to. Instead, the waste matter was balling up, damning the neuron paths for later retrieval. His diagnosis: early onset Alzheimer's. His prognosis: although there is no cure, there are some promising drug trials in the pipeline. Would she submit to one?

Doctor Wiseman's conclusions made sense to Andy and Melody. She agreed to join one of Dr. Wiseman's drug trials.

———

Meanwhile, Andy's once exhilarating roller-coaster marriage evolved into a contest between his white-knuckle defense against Melody's intractable and irascible demands, only entertaining to audiences who favor dysfunctional relationship sitcoms or horror movies. Popcorn anyone?

The one blessing that saved Andy from running willy-nilly all day long was that she often couldn't remember what she had insisted on thirty seconds ago, but it all left him with little motivation to stay around for the climax. But what was he supposed to do without Melody to guide him?

When he suggested they go to the grocery, she recommended that they scout out planet Saturn. "Wasn't Jeff Bezos offering scenic tours? Why not apply for a lottery ticket? I know his broker." When he said she needs to see the podiatrist about her swollen feet, she demands that he first see a psychiatrist for his tennis elbow. "It must be mental. You keep saying it hurts. It looks fine to me." If he asked her if she needed anything, she told him to drive her off a cliff. Though tantalizing, Andy couldn't do that. She had been his leader for twenty years. He would now dedicate himself to making a soft landing for her, as soon as he could find out what that looked like.

Andy had pored through the Diagnostic Statistical Manual, the bible for discovering what mental disease you had. According to the book, everyone suffered from at least one. Evidently, most of us build up coping mechanisms to keep our mental illnesses from derailing life's major requirements of hygiene, nutrition, shelter, and relationships. When we don't, we are fitted with a mental illness hat.

After he had read the entire 800 pages, Andy wondered why the doctors hadn't included Oppositional Defiant Disorder. They hadn't because none of the psychiatrists had listened to him, and none of them had to live with her, nor was there a heavily populated queue to do so. Much less was there a queue to help Andy navigate these cascading waters.

The family caregiver gets finger-pointed to group therapy, led by fellow clueless caregivers, and gathered together to share horror stories and trainloads of complaints about the medical system. A movie only masochists would pay to see.

With his personal world crashing in on him, Donald Trump's arc to the presidency threw Andy a lifeline. Trump's rise broke Melody's fall.

The elites were at Trump's mercy. They couldn't handle him. The country was coming back to its senses. Trump's regaining the White House, after this vote count snafu, had become an obsession for Andy and millions of other Trump fans. He would go to Trump's rally. He would do whatever he could to return Trump to the presidency.

Melody had always liked Trump's TV show, if not its star.

CHAPTER THIRTEEN

NOWHERE TO GO, NOWHERE TO BE

After looking in on Izzy, Telly's list of duties is to ask each of her eight charges if they've eaten lunch and taken their afternoon medication, get confirmation from others that they indeed had, and herd all eight into occupational therapy class by four-thirty. These aspirations weren't always possible, but during her tour of duty at Saved Angels, she had learned where discarded medication and missing patients found sanctuary.

Looking in on Izzy hadn't taken long. Izzy Iceman is laid out on his hospital bed inside a closed white body bag. A bright yellow tag hangs on the bag's white handles. Ferdinand G. Ickovichny is typed out in bold black block print. COVID is ink stamped over his name in pink. Telly assumes she doesn't need to spend any time making sure all of his wiring is in place, as he isn't connected to any.

Telly is just learning to question orders that don't make sense, like having to check off whether a patient had taken their medication when the patient wasn't on the floor anymore, or comatose, or dead like Iceman. It isn't natural for her to disregard others' orders, especially Chief's, but she's starting to get the hang of it.

Patient Michael Lewis Reef confronts Telly as soon as she makes it into the quad where hallways branch out to the cells and meeting rooms. As Michael Lewis Reef rants, she's questioning whether or not she should still look in on Izzy hourly. He wouldn't mind. He wouldn't melt, for sure, but would she be criticized for not knowing better either way?

"You have to release me this minute," Michael Lewis Reef shouts. "I read the contract! Now that the business has been sold, I am entitled to a six-month grace period and the right to reject any residence that doesn't suit me, so I'm suing. You better believe that! Here are the summons and complaint for my extradition. They're my walking papers." While making a pantomime of having handcuffs removed, he says, "Let me out of here." He swishes the papers in her face. When the pages barely miss her cheek, he freezes then takes two steps backwards, ready to run forty more if Telly raises a hand to swat him.

Instead, Telly snatches the papers, which he releases as if surprised that he was holding anything. She unrolls the paperwork to find the Entertainment Section of *The Washington Post*. The headline is Bob Dylan's birthday. It's dated May 24, 2020, and damp from Michael Lewis Reef's courteously sitting on it to absorb the yellow signature of his incontinence from staining the cheap vinyl upholstery. Telly drops the paper in a trash bin and washes her hands at the nearby disinfectant station. She says, "Hi, Michael Lewis Reef. Good to see you. Did you finish your lunch and take your afternoon meds?"

"None of your business," he answers, then adds, "Ask Sue."

"Of course he did," says Sue, sitting on a sofa and never taking her eyes off the TV, streaming CBS *Late Afternoon Digest*. The panning of tourists making funny faces in order to be caught in the camera's swath is evidently newsworthy to her.

"You see, of course I did," echoes Michael Lewis Reef.

"He always does, like clockwork," says Sue. She turns to Telly and asks, "Is there any more muffins?"

"*Are* there any more muffins?" says Telly, putting a check by Michael Lewis Reef's name on her clipboard.

"I don't know," says Sue.

"Sue, did you have lunch and take your meds?" asks Telly.

"Of course she did," says Michael Lewis Reef. "Do you think she's an ignoramus?"

Telly puts a check by Sue Ireland's name and asks her, "Why not look for muffins in the dining room?"

Sue stretches her arms out in an exaggerated yoga swan pose and says, "I think I will. Which way is the dining room?"

"Take a right," says Telly pointing in that direction.

"I tried left earlier today. It didn't work out so good. Maybe I'll look for them later after I go right, or tomorrow when I haven't already gone left yet. They keep telling me I have to work on my balance."

"While you are going that way, would you look for Jane for me? Sometimes she holes up in the library. It's on your way. I don't see her around, and I have to find out if she has taken her meds."

Sue answers, "I always wanted to be a spy. I'd be a good spy. I wouldn't tell a soul."

"You'll tell me though, right?" asks Telly.
"I don't know. Can I trust you to keep a secret?"
"Yes," says Telly.
"Okay then, I'm off. But don't forget to remind me."
Telly wonders if she should ask Sue what didn't work out so good. She reviews her checklist and receives her answer at the top, 'BEFORE DOING ANYTHING NOT ON THIS LIST, COMPLETE EVERYTHING ON THIS LIST.' When reading this the first time, Telly had figured out it would be impossible to comply. But rather than pointing that out, she waited for its impossibility to make its appearance. Then she would see what happened.

Michael Lewis Reef is eighty-one-years old. He resents being in a resident care facility and relentlessly tries to worm his way out. The employees and residents of Saved Angels call him Virgil Hilts from the movie *The Great Escape*. He wears a wide leather belt. He has notched it for every failed escape attempt. So notched is it that Michael Lewis Reef weaves three large rubber bands around it so that his pants stay up. Magically, they do.

Michael Lewis Reef had been a telephone company street address guide for forty-six years. He'd known every street in the county and the points where every street intersected. Then he retired and latent paranoia emerged. Fearful his retirement earnings would be insufficient, he moved out of his home to live off the land. His wife stayed in the home, existing quite comfortably off the checks that kept coming from his pension, social security, and IRAs.

Michael Lewis Reef was a crack shot and an inveterate camper. He lived like deer. He was always moving, vigilant and wary of predators, pretending he was a trophy candidate himself.

But when the number of missing locals tumbled over the statistical norm, the news media felt obligated to alarm the citizenry. It wasn't long before paranoid homefulls fingered this homeless vagabond. Law enforcement plucked him from the one butcher shop that he frequented. It supplied restaurants with groundhog meat. Some consider it a delicacy. Michael Lewis Reef traded non-roadkill groundhog meat for meals and bait.

After intensive grilling and exhaustive DNA testing, the police found no link between Michael Lewis Reef and any of the missing persons. Now in their hands, no government entity knew what to do with him. They had no long-term facilities to hold an innocent man, but they feared if they let him go, and the number of missing persons rose again, they'd be a laughingstock. CYA is a conscientiously transmitted disease when so close to a nation's capital.

With Michael Lewis Reef in custody, the rate of missing persons returned to its mundane pre-percentage. Of course, it could all have been a matter of the reporting. Sometimes the baseline is so small, a change of one or two equates to a large enough percentage to give the media, always looking for a firestorm to ignite, fuel enough to entice another paying customer to subscribe in order to save their life. More often, the change is from new eyes inputting the data. New eyes decide what had been left off before or delete what had been erroneously included, like children late for first bell or husbands showing up mysteriously on time for their weekly henpecking session.

Meanwhile, the deputy who had put Saved Angels's invoice on auto pay took a leave of absence, and her replacement misplaced the paperwork. Then Michael Lewis Reef's wife died of lung cancer, and their children initiated the ritual fight over who got the home. So, he stayed locked up at Saved Angels—nowhere to go, nowhere to be.

While Michael Lewis Reef is always plotting to escape but a pansy if pressed, Sue Ireland is direct and violent, particularly if you get too close to her or her things. Her things were trash. She just couldn't let stuff, perfectly usable stuff, especially not-rotting-yet food, go to waste. It's unethical. It's negligent. It's even treasonous, more than likely.

When social services performed an inspection of her subsidized apartment and found enough merchandise to open up a good-sized store for customers interested in buying nicely wrapped trash, they had decided this was the last time, previous threats having made no headway. They moved her to Saved Angels. The price was right, thanks to a government grant for veterans. Sue had served multiple tours of duty in Iraq and Afghanistan.

Social services hoped that living with others might encourage her to act like the rest of us. Few of us have an urge to inspect commercial waste containers for salvageable food, secure it in plastic wrap, and give it to whoever is in the neighborhood. Sue was never into capitalism. They monitored her assimilating into the general public by taking a monthly inventory of the plastic wrap supply.

Sue has twenty-ten vision and a mean streak. She believes that pain should be inflicted liberally and often. It's a universal imperative. This is one reason she wears ankle bracelets that keep her from entering the kitchen. The kitchen staff didn't want her to see all the food they threw away. Another reason was knives. Her tableware is the opposite of paperless. Unlike Michael Lewis Reef, Sue isn't aggrieved that Saved Angels is up for sale. Management changes offer opportunities.

Jane Macom is Telly's most cooperative patient. She really doesn't belong here. She isn't elderly, she isn't physically disabled, and she doesn't bother any of the other patients. Six feet tall, portly with short beefy arms, larger beefier legs, but a model's face that you could adore if you don't mind that she always needs a shave.

She also has the agility and tenacity of a teenager, the mental phase she never grew out of, including the tendency to fabricate sensational lies about herself.

Initially, she was not expected to stay more than a month. Bedbugs had infested her apartment building. She told the other patients she had been raising them to form a circus. Her apartment management company's insurance carrier transferred her here until the pest exterminators were through. But they're taking their sweet time, with the assistance of the public adjuster, who knows the longer she stays there, the bigger his take. She's been at Saved Angels for six months.

Jane likes it here, having her meals cooked, sheets changed, floors mopped. She also never complained when she heard Saved Angels was up for sale. She told everyone, "I was a Navy rat. I've lived in Morocco, Paris, and Peoria. What's another move for me?"

In truth, Jane was born here in Montgomery County and had never left it, except for a five-year stretch up north at Springfield Hospital. Springfield Hospital treated her schizophrenia with Clozapine, which allowed her to live an independent life, if you don't count having to work for a living.

She *had* moved around a lot. The county's goals for harboring indigents evolved from building large housing projects in redevelopment neighborhoods, to buying up dilapidated apartment buildings in ethnic enclaves, to refurbishing abandoned homes in drug ghettos, before circling back to building large housing projects. The impetus for each about-face being spending less per capita, the holy grail. For optics, housing people in tents, or even caves, had not passed muster during the brainstorming sessions to find housing for indigents whose relatives either refused them or lacked the resources themselves to take in.

The sheer number of changes of address requests had motivated the postal service to shred all of her mail as a means of delivering it. The housing department had moved Jane so frequently, the DMV knew her on sight from the number of times she'd been photographed for a new license.

The county had issued her a voucher for replacement clothes, as all of hers had to be burned. But Jane never could find anything that she liked or would fit at Goodwill. So, she walks around Saved Angels in a hospital gown and is often mistaken for staff by visitors asking for directions. She sends them all to the glass windows looking out at the pretend park that extends a full ten feet past the building's walls.

None of the Saved Angels residents took offense to her. They could well see she could break them into kindling in a blink. But she never hit anyone. The voices in her head always talked her out of it. She's constantly afraid that the voices might talk too loudly, and people nearby would hear them. And people, being ever curious and cold-hearted, would exorcize the voices out of her skull.

She'd seen it done on TV. She didn't know how she'd get by if she lost her voices.

As Sue is looking for Jane in the library, Telly looks for Jane everywhere else. Jane is frequently found stuck in mid-stride, talking to herself. Telly finds her staring out one of the large windows looking out at the ten-foot-deep park. It was installed to meet the State's nature requirements.

Jane is arguing with herself. "I told you not to tell them anything!"

"There's a man wearing camouflage fatigues outside."

"No, he isn't cute!"

Telly had learned never to touch Jane. The first time she had, Telly had spent the rest of her shift apologizing. Jane's shriek is loud enough to convince a battleship armada to reverse engines. It had startled the security guards, ever half-somnolent from working two eight-hour shifts a day for an eternity, into semi-cardiac arrest.

Telly peers out the window to see what Jane is looking at. She sees a man in camouflage and a COVID-19 mask walking around the corner and out of sight. Telly thinks he's a landscaper, but something in his stride... It's cold out there. She says to Jane, "Miss Jane, Miss Jane, the man left, but do you see that hawk? It's so big. I mean so big. Do you see it? Oh, it just flew away."

Jane jerks her head around and squats low as if she might miss the most important event of her life. She whispers, "Where is it? Shush, don't let it hear you!"

"Oh, you just missed it. May I ask, what did you have for lunch?"

"Lunch? Isn't it still time for breakfast? Yes, I was on my way to lunch when I saw this guy in camouflage. You know, I used to be quite a hunter, very handy with a Browning shotgun. Daddy taught me. We used to skeet shoot all the time. *Pull!*" Three times Jane repeats the word 'pull' and each time, at lightning speed, launches her arms up like she's going to shoot down a goose or a clay pigeon or a camouflaged man flying near the ceiling. Each time, Telly jumps a little, having been taught to be very respectful of guns. Each time, Jane gives Telly a look to indicate she hadn't seen anything to shoot at, so she wouldn't fire her weapon, the professional she was. "I think you are trying to fool me. You and your tricks, always trying to distract me from what I want, and what I want is lunch. Where is lunch?"

"In the dining room. Follow the signs," says Telly. "By the way, have you taken your afternoon meds?"

"I don't take no drugs."

"Sure, you do, they help you sleep."

"Why would I take them when I'm up?"

"Because they take time to work, remember?" Noting her left hand is clenched, Telly asks, "What's in your hand?"

Three pills appear when Jane unfolds her fingers. Jane says, "How about that?"

Telly extends her arms forward to indicate they should walk together and says, "Let's go to the dining room and get you something to down those pills with."

"No coffee, remember, I do not want to be hyper."

"And hyper is not how we like you," says Telly. "It will be like a hike in order not to be hyper. You like to hike."

"I do."

"They'll have those pesky bedbugs out of your place in no time." Jane says, "You keep telling me to be patient. But I don't want to be a patient."

"That's a pun, good for you."

"It's not good for me. When the bedbugs are gone, I'll be gone."

Telly, walking and looking straight ahead under the assumption that Jane will keep up with her, remembering well to keep her distance, says, "I'll miss you when you're gone."

"You will?"

"Of course."

At this time, Sue meets them and, overhearing their conversation, greets the two of them with, "I won't miss you. You were supposed to be the other way, Jane."

"Jane got turned around," offers Telly.

"Fat chance. She did it just to annoy me," says Sue. "She knew I was looking for her. By the way, Jane, did you have lunch? Did you take your meds?"

Jane says, "Sue, can't you think of something of your own? You're not Nurse Kind. You're not even kind."

Telly interrupts, "That's not nice to say, Jane."

"Oh, forgive me for saying something that wasn't nice. It was meant to be funny," says Jane. "All you ever say is, 'have you done this,' or 'have you done that?' Don't you ever think for yourself?"

"That's true," says Sue.

"Nurse Kind," says Jane. "Why do you never talk about our souls, our real selves?"

"I haven't a clue, and nobody better tell me," Sue says as she breaks away from the two and accelerates down the hall as if running away from the cops. When she's out of sight, Telly walks Jane to the beverage dispenser in the dining room and leaves her there so Telly can locate her other charges, ask them the same two questions, and get confirmation from a witness.

Telly mimics how the regular nurses talk and act. Do this, Do that, Right now, Or Else... The nurses, however, are assigned as many as forty patients, not Telly's eight. And they're just as often covering for a nurse who had not shown up because of COVID-19, which was now in mid-stroke and haunching high to infect the entire decade. Hope was not in sight, and relief was threatening to remain permanently on the disabled list without a newly renegotiated contract.

Telly has been trying to build up that compassion thing that the nurses assured her was the real reward. This has been a hard hill to climb, living as she did with Lutz, who berated everyone indiscriminately. He seemed to hold some secret knowledge of what was really going on, that nearly everyone besides him was either an illegal alien, ignorant, or mentally ill. It is hardest for the seriously disturbed to see their own derangement. Believing that everyone should think and act just like you is its endearing trademark.

After confirming all her charges for lunch and meds, Telly corrals them into the occupational therapy room. It's four-thirty, more or less, though none of the clocks at Saved Angels are synchronized. Five & Under stores provide the clocks, batteries not included.

The occupational therapist is not there, and the room has not been prepared for them. The chairs and tables line the walls, folded up. The patients don't make a move to shake the chairs out so they can sit down for the wait. Telly doesn't either. It isn't on the checklist. The patients cling to the walls without chairs or tables to lean on. Five minutes go by. No one says anything. Another five minutes. Everyone silently stares ahead into the center of the room. A few actually look at the clock on the wall. Finally, Michael Lewis Reef turns to Telly and asks, "Do you like me, Telly?"

Telly jack rabbits out, "Yes, of course. I think of you as family."

Then Sue asks, "So, are you going to stick around? The director just left. I heard she got a better job in Seattle."

Another patient adds, "I heard she moved to Uruguay, where there isn't much COVID."

Telly notices that some of the other patients are snickering, almost lustily. She takes the questioning as a challenge. If she hedges, they will know she's just like all the rest. She says to herself that she isn't at all.

"People with Prader Willi don't live very long. When I die, I won't be here anymore. But I promise to stay around until then."

Another patient says, "That's long enough for me." The other patients give her a calm, choppy applause. Telly feels what she has seldom felt before—appreciation. The snickering doesn't diminish though.

Ruth, the new director, tall and stern looking, rushes in and cases the room. She peers up and down her clipboard, evidently taking a silent roll call. Telly expects her to tell them the therapist won't be making it. This has happened before. They would reschedule. Ruth doesn't do that.

Instead, she says, "Sorry for keeping you waiting. This is Cassie." She points to a very athletic-looking, recent college graduate-looking woman with a face very suntanned for January. "Cassie is replacing Margaret, your occupational therapist and your intern. You are getting a two-fer. I am sure you'll love her and respect her requests as much as you did Margaret and the intern. I'll leave you all to get newly acquainted."

Ruth then turns to look directly at Telly, who is stunned into stone. Ruth says, "Telly, how nice to meet you. I'll explain your new assignment in a couple of minutes. Wait in my office until I can finish my other tasks. Thank you. See you then." Then Ruth snaps out the door, leaving Telly like the last leaf on a tree in fall.

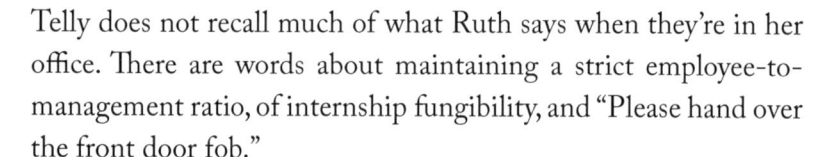

Telly does not recall much of what Ruth says when they're in her office. There are words about maintaining a strict employee-to-management ratio, of internship fungibility, and "Please hand over the front door fob."

Telly leaves Ruth's office, tears welling up. Michael Lewis Reef confronts her. He says, "So, 'until I die' means five minutes later. No, I'm exaggerating, forgive me, ten minutes. It must have been ten, right?"

Telly doesn't have an answer for Michael Lewis Reef. She heads for the changing room to unfasten all her COVID-wear. She had snuck out of Donna's this morning with everything she owned in her van. Now, she's praying she can ask Rebecca for a place to stay, but when she goes to punch out, she sees that Rebecca's name has been removed from the inboxes along with her own. It's back to Black's Shelter for another night.

CHAPTER FOURTEEN

ROLLER COASTER JIG

Melody enters the kitchen, her arms muscling a wad of Kleenex overhead. She's drying her hair. She throws the wad into the recycling bucket then walks to the refrigerator. Her head looks as if she has just come in from a blizzard. She opens the refrigerator and says, "Where's the beer?" It's seven-thirty in the morning.

She closes the refrigerator door and throws eye daggers at Andy, who is sitting at the kitchen counter eating Wheaties in Half-and-Half with raspberries. She tries to remember something different that is all-his-fault. But by the time she makes it to where Andy is sitting, she can't remember what it might be. This would incontrovertibly fluster anyone else. She asks him in a deadpan voice, "Can't you not be so mad all the time?"

Andy stops chewing his cereal and says, "I take it that my place in the universe *today* is to make sure beer is on hand and not be so mad."

"Everyday!" Melody spits out, "But beer is always first. Protecting the country from a foreign takeover is second. Keeping

Jeremy from being shot is third. He's a police officer, and cops are targets."

"How am I supposed to do all that?"

"You have so far, haven't you? Just remember to do them in ascending order of importance. By the way, when are you going to take a long trip?"

"You're getting your wish," Andy replies. "I'm leaving." He rinses his bowl out, places it in the dishwasher, and heads downstairs to his workshop.

"Be careless down there so you don't kill yourself."

"If I do, you'll be the first to know."

"Probably not," says Melody. "You know I hate down there. The glues you use smell like somebody died, and recently."

"I'll keep that in mind."

"If you do die," says Melody, "mail me a postcard, not a letter. Letter postage costs twice as much, and I might need the extra cash. What about the beer?"

"I'll pick up some after I walk Benedict Arnold," Andy lies. He stores beer in the car trunk. It's safe there from her random foraging because she has forgotten how it opens.

Melody is not a friendly drunk. Not too long ago, after Andy had gone to sleep, Jeremy dropped off a six pack of beer and a bottle of prosecco in exchange for a Venmo transaction. She polished off the beer and the prosecco. Andy was awakened by a loud crash at four in the morning and found her lying on the floor, unable to get up. While he carried her back to bed, she accused him of fucking her in the anus. The next morning, she was none the worse for it, and when he reminded her what she had told him, she said he was making it up to embarrass her. He asked himself, "If I put her in memory care, would the cops come and lock me up for sexual abuse?"

If you walked down into Andy's basement, you would feel a sense of order and peril. Three lathes of different calibers line one side, and shelves of wood blocks, sorted by age and species, line the other. In between are rows of blades sharp enough to give goosebumps to the Marquis de Sade, who would have unhesitatingly paid for the expanded tour. Although there is no shrine to the Marquis, one corner is dedicated to President Donald Trump. An emporium of caps, cups, bumper stickers, key chains, shot glasses, posters, pennants, and flyers. Andy was particularly proud of the ones from the Utah rally, where he'd earned a purple heart, COVID-19. But homage to the shrine will wait today. He's got to finish the plaque.

Freeing his mind from Melody-maneuvering, Andy focuses on what has become their livelihood, turning wood. What is wood turning? Trying to put it in a single sentence is akin to describing the Mona Lisa or mental illness in one. You go first.

Wood turning is transforming a section of a tree into something else, like a bowl, a plaque, a trophy. "Big deal," you say. You buy ceramic bowls for a few bucks, and when they chip or break, you throw them out and buy new ones, easy peasy, though having a stray shard puncture your bare heel stirs up a short, frantic, non-celebratory dance. But your view is irrelevant. Andy and a few others like him were infected with the itch to follow the grain in wood and create something never made before, never seen before, probably never even dreamed of.

He brought a tree back from the dead. Instead of rotting in some field, it became a utensil to eat with, to mix stuff in, and to have a home built around. In real time, Andy became god, immortalizing something that had died so that it could live for millennia. Wood turning is also an occupation from which one cannot allow their mind to wander, that is, if one expects to be able to walk back up the stairs with enough digits to dial 911.

He dons his apron and examines his workbench to see where he left off. He is working from photographs. Blind working, Andy calls it. The customer had declined to pay his airfare to Japan so he could examine the original.

The order called for a replica of a ceramic plaque. The plaque was commissioned by Japan in 1980 to commemorate the bombing of Hiroshima. He thought it odd that a Japanese woman wanted something to remind her of that day. Odder too that the plaque had been created over forty years ago. So, why now? Well, no matter, Mrs. Watanabe's largesse would be the MacCleans' life preserver for this month at least.

The MacCleans' had spent their savings on their sons' college tuition, expecting Melody's six-plus-figure income to quickly fill the breach. Now with Melody no longer working, with their monthly medical insurance premiums and mortgage payments swamping their budget, inflation floated just out of sight waiting to fire the kill shot.

The Spirit of Survival is not a replica of the whole city mushroom clouding into oblivion. It's one man's face, half covered with his hands as if they could protect him. His fingers and face, all in shit-brown and cotton-candy-pink glaze, seemed to fatten the more you looked. You knew he would be dead in seconds.

Through his closed lids and hidden mouth, the man silently badgers, "How could we." It wasn't a question. It put Andy there and Andy really didn't like feeling that uncomfortable. What art was supposed to sometimes do, he'd heard.

Before he had even started to chew wood, he had drawn and painted a dozen drawings each from a different angle. He had examined each under different lighting. He had experimented with a dozen different stains. He had done age-experiments to see how the plaque would look in time with oxidation.

Now Andy overlays his mind's eye image of the original onto the wood, over its grain and almost mindlessly skims off what is not part of *The Spirit of Survival*. He shapes it equally to match the plaque's majesty as to accommodate the cellulose's growth journey into tree. So engaged, Andy can't be taunted by its frozen-in-place-forever closed eyes.

Every wood block is different, and inside differenter still. Until one is split, you can't tell what a slice of it looks like inside, sometimes not even then. Finding a clear trunk chunk was less likely than finding a ripe avocado in the grocery Super Bowl Sunday afternoon. He had spent weeks splitting oak, sycamore, and cherry before finding a walnut block with consistent grain of the proper width-spread and density.

The plaque was forming into wood instead of the other way around, its grain directing his hands. The blinded hero of the plaque wasn't overseeing the work, the wood was. Andy let the grain lead. The feeling of being dethroned as the master is not for the shallow of heart, but when embraced, the wood uncovers its hidden treasure, stalwart, authentic, and slightly adrift.

Two hundred thousand eyes of the Hiroshima deceased were watching him work. See us, feel us, smell us, he hears them say. "Hug the grandchildren we never had." As he works, he responds with sounds of his own that were close to sobs, but neither were they pleas. No, they were applause.

The gravest challenge had been the fingers. Each makes its own statement, and each distinguishes itself from the others as well as the nose, which is not unintentionally the same shape. Cartoon characters were drawn with only four fingers because five just did not work, something about how our eyes take in light.

The original plaque had ten fingers, and so would his copy. The hands have to be perfect. He knows few will notice them, but that is why they have to be perfect. So, the victims, all one hundred thousand of them, will take in the whole, not fragments.

Andy was not one of the big guns like Prestini, Stocksdale, Lindquist, Osolnik and Moulthrop. His pieces were not being auctioned off at Christie's, nor hanging in the Met. Andy had never gone to art school. It had started as doodling. Then as his employers kept getting bought up by Chinese firms which unilaterally laid him off, it had become his mainstay. And it didn't hurt that he lived in a forest with an unending supply of tree trunks.

You'd find his work in bars, restaurants, and home dens. Someday maybe his work would find more prominent establishments. He'd like that but isn't holding his breath. A mortgage payment or two would kick the bucket down the road, was all he was asking for, until he kicked his own.

Melody would assuage his feelings of inferiority by hinting that the other artists pumped up their prices and their prestige by bribing critics. The best his pieces had ever earned at a show was honorable mention. Melody said that an artist would be better off not mentioned at all than fingered as second class.

But he had won this commission. Price! His was the lowest bid.

Andy finds he's chiseled off a sliver too much from where two fingers almost touch. He inhales, examines his gloves for cuts, then switches the lathe off. Fingers, neither wooden nor alive, are in harm's way no longer. He rubs the sawdust away to take a peek.

Yes.

He looks at the clock. Past four o'clock already. He massages the back of his neck with the fingers of both hands. The staining will wait for tomorrow. Besides, he's cold. The only heat in the basement comes from convection off the boiler and the house upstairs must be toasty as right now the boiler is not drumming its customary beat.

Andy feather dusts the wood shavings, looking like children had sprinkled beige Christmas tinsel all over the shelves, to the floor, before he sweeps it. Then he empties the shavings into an oxygen free chamber to prevent spontaneous combustion. He oils lathe bearings, sharpens gouges and then hangs his apron by the glass basement door. This is Benedict Arnold's cue. The dog scampers over to Andy, leash in mouth.

The two look through the glass basement door. The outside thermometer reads thirty. Andy had heard on the radio to expect gusts, but no snow. A gray day, just like yesterday, and the day before that. Winter is here. Benedict Arnold pants, 'Let's go, let's go, let's go,' fogging the glass with his hot breath. Anything outside beats the status quo to a dog who's been inside all day. It doesn't hurt that Benedict Arnold sports a permanent fur coat.

Andy thrusts on his leather jacket, works the leash over Benedict Arnold's head, and walks into the after-the-snow melt scenery. The ground is mushy and half-covered with oak leaves and pine needles. Short mounds of dirt and debris, deposited from the last plowing, rim the roads, looking as if an airliner had jettisoned its bathroom waste from the sky.

They walk down his gravel driveway to the street, which to the right dead ends into a nature preserve, off limits except through the park entrance, two miles away. To the left is a busy street, but it has a bike lane.

To those unfamiliar with the neighborhood, the MacClean home could easily be mistaken for an abandoned chicken coop in the winter. In the summer and spring, it's invisible behind the leaves of a hundred trees.

It isn't much of a house, having been converted from a hunting cabin to a storage shed to a dwelling by generations who had no claim on the land. Melody had found it because actuarial-wise, it was perfect. It sat uphill from the nearest creek and far from any active tectonic plates, so no floods or earthquakes. And the rainfall averaged eighty inches annually, just short of qualifying as a rainforest, so no forest fires. A sump pump kept the basement relatively dry.

It was also hidden in a copse which buffered the roar of Andy's chainsaw and lathe, all while being only a five-minute walk from Elkton's downtown.

They had met their neighbors twice, first at a potluck they were invited to shortly after they had moved in. And then at a picnic that Andy and Melody hosted in their backyard a month later. And then nothing. The MacCleans weren't really entertainers. It might have been their choice to serve lab-grown bison but was, more than likely, Melody and Andy's intolerance for small talk. Talk about ways to change things or put a plug in it.

Ten minutes into their walk, Andy feels icy needles pricking his cheeks. He looks up to see dark gray clouds barreling in. He needs to get back. He eyes the convalescent hospital on the corner. The trusses overhang its walls by at least six feet, creating safe harbor overhead for two souls. He will stand under the overhang until the sleet, which never lasts more than a few minutes, passes. When they make it to the overhang, Benedict Arnold tugs hard for them to keep going. He doesn't understand. This isn't home. Pelting sleet is no impediment to a good walk. Pelting sleet is a pleasant scratching.

Andy, on the other hand, enjoys the respite. Waiting and silence are underrated. He watches the storm clouds darken, enheartened by not hearing any thunder.

He watches as a plump young woman in nurse garb exits the building. She walks briskly into his sightline toward an old van in the parking lot. Before she makes it to the van, a man wearing camo fatigues, intersects her progress.

First the man bearhugs her, then he pushes her not too violently into the van's side. She doesn't call out. He wrangles the keys out of her hand, opens the van's driver door, and shovels her through it, over to the passenger seat, which takes some muscle since she's no lightweight. But he's no shrimp himself, barrel chested and so tall, his head scrapes the car's headliner when he ducks to get in.

With no Melody to tell him what to do, Andy is paralyzed. This can't be happening, he assures himself, as he yells, "Stop! Stop! Stop!" Andy immediately asks himself what he's thinking. He looks around for help. No one is around. His shout is broomed away into a dustpan of unrecorded history by the sleet and the rush hour traffic. Andy curses himself. He used to carry his cell phone, cash, and wallet whenever he took Benedict Arnold for a walk. These days, he leaves without even keys. The automatic garage door opener has a keypad.

"I am an idiot," he says.

But cavalry arrives. Benedict Arnold jerks the leash from Andy's hand, and leaps into the van and onto the abductor's lap, barking at the man and as if to parrot his master's tone, at least: 'Stop! Stop! Stop!' Then, 'I am an idiot.'

Having been pulled forward by Benedict Arnold's tugging, Andy finds himself stumbling within a few feet of the abductor, now settling himself into the driver's seat. The abductor grabs Benedict Arnold by the jaw and throws the ten-pound Lhasa Apso out onto the parking lot macadam. Benedict Arnold decides that maybe now's the time to sniff at a row of bushes he had his eyes on earlier and runs there.

The abductor, laughing at Benedict Arnold's comic rescue attempt, goes to swing the driver's door closed before Andy can intervene. Andy grabs the door handle. He rips the door wide open.

Realizing he has the advantage with the abductor's awkward balancing act, half in and out of the cab, Andy slams the door closed. The abductor manages to duck his head back inside but not his hand. Sensing the feel and sound of metal mangling flesh, Andy backs up. Says to himself, "now you've done it, you stupid moron. Melody!"

Andy can see through the car window and is horrified to see that the girl is mouthing at him, "What do you want?" He's thinking of joining Benedict Arnold's retreat.

In the time it takes for Andy to regain sentience, the abductor has reopened and closed the door, using his other hand. He then makes an exaggerated show of pushing down the van's door lock button with his thumb. The two men exchange macho looks through the door window. Andy starts going over what he'll tell the police when they arrest him for assault.

The abductor starts the van's engine. He backs the van out smartly. But instead of driving out of the parking lot, steers the van straight at Andy. Benedict Arnold reacts to the tires' squeal, returns to save the day, and jumps right up on the van's windshield as if he could bite the van with his teeth. The dog's flattened body claiming half of the windshield obscures the forward vision of the abductor. He accelerates ahead anyway.

Andy races towards the opposite end of the parking lot. The van corrects its course. It's twenty feet behind Andy's heels and closing. Straight ahead are four three-foot high, four-inch-wide bollards, spaced one foot apart. They are there to guard a gas meter from myopic parkers but were installed so long ago, the taxi-cab yellow warning paint had weathered into the color of twenty-year-old used chewing gum. Andy hurdles the bollards, thanking the ten thousand reps of four-hundred-pound leg lifts.

The van can't jump and instead rams and bounces off the bollards. They were not installed for show. Benedict Arnold loses his hold on a wiper blade when the van hits the bollards. Instantaneously, the driver's forehead butts into the windshield, creating in it a small translucent bulge. Benedict Arnold slides off to the asphalt and trots over to ask Andy, "Can we do that again?"

The airbags do not deploy. Old van. The irresistible force meets the immovable object, and in this case, the van's front end and the man's head suffer the consequences. Andy hears a churning of some kind coming from the van. It's not coming from the engine. The engine has conked out. He hopes the driver has too.

Adrenalin pounding, Andy runs to the passenger door, opens it, and finds that the churning sound is from the young woman elbowing the lifeless man in the driver's seat. She stops when she sees Andy, unsnaps her seat belt, and leaps into his arms. Andy runs away from the van with her for about ten feet before he has to put her down. Not enough leg lifts for a long buddy run. Not seeing or hearing anyone else around, he gasps, out of breath, "Give me your cell!"

"It's in my purse, in my van," she says and points at her stalled vehicle, abductor therein.

Andy doesn't want anything to do with the abductor, unconscious, dazed, or dead. Especially if he's dead. The ice-pelting hasn't diminished, and Benedict Arnold is hugging Andy's ankle so tight, you would think Andy's a newly appointed lifeboat distributor on the Titanic. More likely, Benedict Arnold is petitioning Andy not to bring this stray home to share his food ration. She looks like she eats a lot.

"We'll go inside and have someone call for help," says Andy.

"It's locked after five. You need a fob to get inside. My fob…," the young woman starts saying.

"Is in your purse," fills in Andy. Okay, maybe he needed to get back in that van. Better just leave. What did he owe this young woman who for all he knew… What did he know? He asks her, "Tell me, what is going on here?"

"I don't know," she cries. "I'm only seventeen, and this has never happened to me before. I just want to be, you know, independent, free. I'm not hurting anyone."

"What do you want to do right now?"

"Get away from here, as far as I can, as fast as I can."

After suffering through a new heightened onslaught of hail, Andy says, "Let's do that. Follow me."

Andy, the woman, and Benedict Arnold cover the distance to his house in personal bests. Every step signals to Andy that his muscles are strained out before he strides again to prove the signal wrong. Pain intensifies in his calves, hamstrings, and quads, jackhammers his stomach and his chest, but he doesn't slow.

His mom had been determined to make a tennis pro out of him. She figured with his size, height, and especially his large, strong hands, he would be a natural. Her father had been a tennis pro at a small private country club before enlisting. He had become a prisoner of war in Korea, and never picked up a tennis racket after he returned.

His mom played tennis with grace and power. So would her son. He just needed discipline. She refused to see that he was too slow in both meanings of the word. From the time he was three, she strapped him with a thin belt on the back of his calves whenever he lost a match. She would stop only when he stopped crying.

She also insisted he serve left-handed, the coaching trend of the time, even though he was right-handed. She had read that tossing the ball to the perfect spot was more important than the swing, so his dominant hand should toss the ball. He spent hours every day practicing, hitting serves while on his knees to promote the proper technique. He got to be pretty good at tennis, made districts twice but never beyond. His joints couldn't take the rigor. He had spent as much time recovering from surgery as he had on the courts. Now, to ward off midriff bulge, he plays recreationally at a local non-profit club.

He can't afford indoor tennis rates, so when the weather is not conducive to playing outside, he practices in his basement against a Tennis Mate. It's a hard plastic screen, which when you hit a tennis ball into it, drops the ball back to you on a bounce so you can hit it again. The advantage of hitting into a Tennis Mate versus hitting against a wall is that the ball doesn't rocket back even faster into your face or worse, your groin.

CHAPTER FIFTEEN

PORT OF HIGH SCHOOL

Lutz noticed that once the bullies left high school, they began a precipitous decline in social status, and many of the formerly bullied began an ascent, often spectacularly.

When not at work, the bullies spent an incalculable amount of time working on their domestic cars and selfieing these achievements on Facebook. Instead, the formerly bullied selfied themselves in brand new foreign cars, attending sports and theater events, as often out of state as out of the country. The bullies, his friends, assuaged their demotion by jacking themselves up on booze, sex, and amphetamines, bragging about the vengeance they were going to get and investing in bit-coin futures. Their real achievements memorialized in bruised knuckles, bile hangovers, and overnight lockups.

Then came 9/11, a godsend for struggling taverns, embryonic drunks, and military recruitment centers. Taverns extended their happy hours. Drunks flouted the flag along the road to oblivion. And recruiters could finally offer something more than free college tuition to high school dropouts. Kill Arabs and get paid in the bargain.

Every one of Lutz's friends enlisted before September 30, and he had to do the same to keep face. Only Lutz wasn't so sure he wanted to face hordes of Arabs. He had watched Lawrence of Arabia seven times.

So, he drove to the western side of the state, far from the Naval Academy brand of patriotism, and enlisted in the Army Reserves in Cresaptown. This is not a misspelling, though reading a billboard that says, "YOU ARE NOW LEAVING CREAPSTOWN, CHECK YOUR VEHICLE FOR HITCHHIKERS," would seem worth the spell-check.

He was assigned to the 372nd Military Police Company. For an Army division whose primary activity was maneuvering drunken soldiers into the brig, Lutz was made to order—largebodied with three years of high school wrestling.

Through the vagaries of the US military, his unit was sent to Baghdad in support of the Second Persian Gulf War, comically labeled *Iraqi Freedom* by the President at the time. Remember the Vice President's promise that the Iraqis were going to welcome us? It's all fun and games, right? As long as you're not the one obliged to face down a tank.

But the comedy was just starting. The 372nd Military Police was posted to Abu Ghraib. Remember the Abu Ghraib? It doesn't have the cache of "Remember the Alamo" or "Remember the Maine." It never comes up in conversation or on the news anymore.

Abu Ghraib spiked the air waves in 2004, with the President doing the politically required jiu jitsu denial dance. Then, when a cascade of videos showing US soldiers sexually torturing prisoners overran the news outlets, he publicly apologized for it. You knew he was sincere because he did so without once resorting to his hallmark smirk. And a year later, when the names of the convicted soldiers ticker-taped on the bottom of the news screens, not many of us bothered to take out our magnifying glass to speed-read Lutz Delorean.

Abu Ghraib was not the only ugly stain against our country that involved torturing prisoners. Solitary confinement is mental torture. We hold more people behind bars than any other nation. The cost of freedom is high. We flew suspected terrorists to black sites in countries that were non-signatories to the Geneva Convention. There, our dirty work was performed away from watchkeepers' prying eyes. And then, there's Guantanamo. Eventually, reports of torture were flushed down the news-cycle toilet. They weren't new anymore. There is an endless supply of new scandals to harvest. Too many to keep count, too many to remember. That may be the point. With every new conflagration the country starts, we forget about Afghanistan, Iraq, South America, Vietnam.

Some of the prisoners and all of the interrogators survived Abu Ghraib, black sites, and Guantanamo, oblivious of one another's existence except in their nightmares, exchanging ghost cigarettes.

Before Operation Iraqi Freedom, Abu Ghraib was where Saddam Hussein kept those who, in any noticeable way, resisted his authority. Saddam even had the decency to add adjoining cells for the prisoners' family members. "Cultural manners have to be followed when terrorizing everyone alive" is the unmitigated rule of law.

The compound had sat like a turd in the middle of downtown Baghdad, a reminder of where you could end up *if*. When the 372nd arrived, instead of being filled with Saddam Hussein's enemies, it was filled with his soldiers, the ones who had the temerity to surrender before invading US troops. Surrendering beat being killed, they bargained. The CIA field operatives, who had been in from cozy offices, had received only one instruction. Make sure the prisoners lived long enough to regret surrendering, but not too much longer.

The largest building at Abu Ghraib was a two-story compound of Hollywood prison architecture. Its balcony cantilevered so guards could look down on every prisoner since the interior had no walls, only bars. For Saddam's guests, privacy was accomplished via strategically placed clotheslines. America's guests found this strategy unworkable, as they were stripped of all their clothes and weren't issued sheets.

There were also a dozen one-story buildings, spread out with as much organization as oil splatter from a frying pan. They'd been built to accommodate Saddam's ever growing anti-fan base. Now, besides housing some of the prisoners, they served as cafeteria, infirmary, and lodging for the 372nd. The CIA had found better quarters in a commandeered Ritz-Carlton. Saddam had built the infirmary and cafeteria for the guards, not the prisoners. That didn't change with *Iraqi Freedom*.

Each building was connected by barbed wire lanes, divided in the middle by more barbed wire. The wire ensured secure ingress and egress by detainees and detainers and deterred any fraternization between prisoners or guards.

Abu Ghraib also had an exercise yard. Desert scrub surrounded again by barbed and razor wire. Lutz never saw anyone in it. And he was never inclined to break that statistic and venture out there himself. There was one tower, too low to see very far, constructed when the compound was a tenth its current size. Commerce bustled along the roads as if the prison was a factory manufacturing bicycles or lamp shades. Auschwitz residents claimed they had no idea what was going on behind the prison's walls. Anything is possible is the conspiracist's favorite offensive chess play.

The air around the camp smelled of damp sand and rotting flesh. The odor was so strong and unappetizing, Lutz never logged in a good night's sleep. This made him hyper and belligerent, how the 372nd wanted him. The stench did not affect the officers. They knew they had received the winning lottery ticket: a one-year residency at a palm tree resort completely removed from flying armor-piercing bullets.

At Abu Ghraib, Lutz was royalty. And he spent that time in a hazy, alcoholic bliss. He and his squad had absolute control over these prisoners, and no slight went unpunished, even if he could only understand a few words they said. Other than the minimum Arabic words needed to get his prisoners to move or bend over, Lutz learned it was best not to exert any effort to expand this minimal vocabulary. Understanding them would belittle him. Their language was as disgusting as they were. And learning how to read it would be blasphemy. Their alphabet numbered twenty-eight letters instead of English's twenty-six, but when written out on paper, it constituted graffiti.

Nineteen years old, he chugged from a communal never-empty half-gallon bottle of Johnny Walker Black while playing prisoner torture roulette. His commanding officers knew what was really going on. And it wasn't what the mainstream news reported. Lutz didn't remember precisely what supported their conclusions, just that they were confident, they were his leaders, and that while he was posted with them, he was in with the very small number of people who knew the real truth. Everybody else was on the outside. Adult life turned out to be no different than high school. You needed to be on the inside.

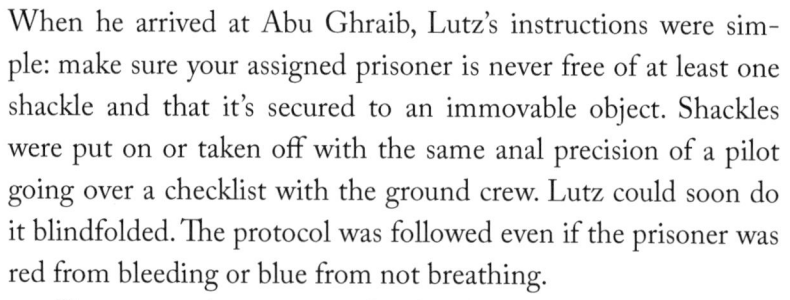

―・―

When he arrived at Abu Ghraib, Lutz's instructions were simple: make sure your assigned prisoner is never free of at least one shackle and that it's secured to an immovable object. Shackles were put on or taken off with the same anal precision of a pilot going over a checklist with the ground crew. Lutz could soon do it blindfolded. The protocol was followed even if the prisoner was red from bleeding or blue from not breathing.

There were three reasons for the shackle obsession. The first was not to embarrass the Commandant by his having to fill out reams of forms if there were ever an unauthorized escape. Authorized escapes were part of doing business.

The second was that every officer knew that the escape report would be front and center if he or she ever came up for promotion or a raise. No exceptions. Letting a prisoner escape was equivalent to a captain crashing a battleship.

The third was that the health and safety of the guards and interrogators was primary, just like it is for the police in the United States.

Still, there were injuries. Some of the members of the 372nd earned purple hearts. A table might collapse during waterboarding. A prisoner would sometimes go feral after his fingernails were ripped out. Amazing how rage strengthens a person despite being fed a diet that couldn't nourish a beetle.

As the prison filled up, more and more officers became casualties of nausea, vertigo, and migraines. As officers' absences increased, Lutz's duties expanded. From shackler to scribe, scribe to interrogator, interrogator to torturer, what we call field promotions.

***

Lieutenant George is a perfect replica of Lieutenant Hoople out of *Beetle Bailey* comics, except for two formidable hillocks snowconing chest high. She shuffles two steps to her left. Her left boot bumps Lutz's right boot, and he takes two steps to his left. The others circling Muhammed follow the chorus line. Ring around the rosie. The rosie is Muhammed.

Muhammed is spread-eagled before them. He's naked except for a hood and a pouch bikini. Muhammed is not going to escape. He's ankle-shackled to chains linked to eyebolts anchored into the concrete floor and handcuffed to the rack behind him, everything over-engineered to put the interrogators out of his strike range.

It's a parlor game. Want to play?

You ask Muhammed a question, and when he doesn't respond responsibly, you inform him of your disappointment physically. Then you take two steps to the left and the next in line repeats the process. A process the administrators had created to keep you fresh and stay focused on how Muhammed reacted. Maybe you'll pick up a tell. Maybe you'll make a friend.

Lieutenant George's progress in the circle has brought her face to face with the terrorist. She says in a strong midwestern drawl, "Muham Med, soldier named after a famous schizophrenic, why were automatic weapons found in your brothers' home?"

Muhammed's eyes swim behind his hood praying for something to look at. When his eyes settle, he says, "My brothers are dead."

"Is that so," continues Lieutenant George. "That's not what it says in your file." She swats the file at an imaginary fly and closes it.

His first thought is "Again with the report you won't show me." His second thought is "You have the wrong Muhammed Cejuna." But he has tried these before. Pain had been the only response. He just wants some sleep, and at this point, even at the expense of being knocked out. Unconsciousness is rest, after all. So, he decides to ask for specifics, what they keep demanding from him, hoping they will get the snub and deliver a knockout blow. Hope springs eternal. "Which brother? I had three."

The Lieutenant is not slow. "You think I care which brother, Muham Med?" She takes a quick step forward, kicks him in the groin, and retreats as fast as she had struck.

Muhammed tries to fall. His knees punch each other but the shackles on his arms aren't having it. They keep him semi-erect and dangling. Not the knockout blow he wanted. He'd vomit if he'd eaten. He'd scream if his throat had swallowed any fluids recently. "It's okay," he reminds himself, "There will be more opportunities. Allah provides."

Lieutenant George looks at Lutz, hands him the file, and two-steps to the left saying, "Your turn, Private." Lutz thanks her for the opportunity then takes his two steps to face the prisoner.

Lutz estimates that if Muhammed weren't so hunched, he'd be over six feet and could easily wrestle in the 165 division. Not a trace of fat on him. Nor is there a trace of fear. Lutz congratulates himself for being on this side of the war.

"Okay, Muhammed," Lutz says, pretending to read from a folder containing mostly penciled-in Sudoku puzzles, "What's your mother's motherfucking last name, or your father's motherfucking last name?"

Muhammed replies with what sounds like an expletive but could be a last name. The appointed scribe writes something on a tablet and shows it to the circle, and they nod that he wrote what they heard.

Under the unwritten rules of torture roulette, Lutz is allowed one follow-up question. He's feeling this is all wrong. He can't even see this guy's eyes. How will they even know if the prisoner understands what he's being punished for? Lutz pulls out a rake from a bucket of farm tools and snaps it prong-side-up on Muhammed's toes. He pulls off Muhammed's blindfold and then skips away.

Muhammed's eyes bulge out like a newborn's, every beam of light a life preserver to a sinking ship. But the pain in his toes overwhelms his knees, and he collapses in the chains again, hanging by his wrists as the chains are too short to let him massage his bleeding toes.

It's hard to tell Muhammed is only twenty-six. He's missing most of his teeth and hair. His facial stubble shows more gray than black. Lutz asks him while he thrashes in his chains, "Muhammed, got three bab.la? Three bab.la and I leave the hood off. Whaddya say?" The seven others standing around the table dutifully laugh in a stale chorus.

It's Captain J.T. Reynolds III's turn. He steps up to Muhammed only long enough to thrust a cottoned tube up Muhammed's nose, and from experience, he knows just where Muhammed will swing his head away from this invasion, allowing Reynolds to competently thrust a second tube in Muhammed's other nostril.

With the hood off, Muhammed can see, but with his nostrils clogged, he struggles to stop hyperventilating. Captain Reynolds asks, "In the Bible, it says an eye for an eye, right Muhammed? You're going to get me after you kill all the Israelis? All I want to know is where Saddam's biological weapons are. I am asking ever so politely. All the other prisoners have confessed. Why are you being the hold out? I think you know something, something terribly lethal, and I'm not going to be satisfied until I know what you know. Understand?"

J.T. Reynolds III wears no insignia as he wears no shirt. It's hot. The malfunctioning air conditioning fans a balmy breeze only. Sweat drips from his bald head and temporarily collects where his glasses reside on his tiny nose before falling onto the table to join the stains of hundreds that had fallen before.

Muhammed mumbles, "*Nawm! Lau samaht, lau samaht.*"

"Begging for sleep, are you, Muhammed?" says Staff Sergeant O'Neill, a wiry specimen, maybe twice as old as Lutz, maybe three times. "Didn't we let you sleep yesterday? Or was it the day before? I can't remember. Captain, do you? But Muhammed, we need to know how you know where they are? Who told you? Unless, of course, you were making them yourself."

"Should we put the hood back on, Muhammed?" asks Captain Reynolds. "That would help you sleep, right?"

Muhammed cries, "*La! La! La!*"

"No hood, huh, Muhammed? Emphatically no." replies Captain Reynolds. "You understand English. Speak it!" And then he says to Lieutenant George, "Arabs don't seem to care. Israelis kill seven for every one of them, and instead of doing the math, they double down."

Lieutenant George, who is now standing behind Muhammed, reaches over and massages Muhammed's penis with her left hand. When he swings around to face her, she pulls down her blouse and exposes her breasts for his review. She pauses and fondles both nipples. "Want a lick, Muhammed? Or are you more of a sucker? How long has it been? Getting hard?"

The first time Lieutenant George had done this, Lutz had practically jumped out of his clothes. Now he just thinks that this is how she gets her jollies. Smoking in the girls' restroom. She positions her breasts back in her bra as nonchalantly as a man straightens his tie, buttons her blouse, and continues, "An eye for an eye makes everyone half blind, Captain. The Jews are outnumbered a million to one. What kind of math is that? Double down will only work in the Arabs' favor."

"Muhammed," says Captain Reynolds. "Just tell us something we can use. Do I need to say please?"

"I don't know," says Muhammed.

"Come on, Muhammed, you know the game," Captain Reynolds says. "Tell us something we can say we learned from you so we might get you out of here." He lowers his voice, "And the same for us."

Lieutenant George signals to Lutz, who leaves and returns with a wheelbarrow filled with water. Muhammed screams when he hears the water sloshing. Reynolds says, "Well, Muhammed, I am not going to see the end of this affair for as long as I, my children, my grandchildren, and their grandchildren breathe. Humans enjoy killing each other. It's Allah's form of birth control, right?"

Lutz and Sergeant O'Neill grab for the scotch at the same time, almost spilling it. O'Neill pulls rank and swigs first. He loses his breath for a moment then says, "Why are we here again? I mean, other than being provided with good hootch."

"Same reason as always," says Reynolds, "to make sure the rich stay rich. And so that the poor stay poor."

"And each's children, grandchildren, and great grandchildren," Lieutenant George adds. "Private Lutz, more water." She takes a swig of scotch.

"Why is everything so fucked up?" asks Lutz.

"It's fucked up because everyone has a different idea of who should be in charge and how to get there. Seven billion and counting, Private," says Reynolds. "Isn't it obvious? The equalizer is force. If you got it, use it. If you don't, expect to be on the wrong end of a pike. Welcome to earth, the land of Oprahtunity. Now China, there's a country that has its act together…"

"If it weren't for the language," says Lieutenant George, "Written or spoken, I'd move there in a heartbeat. How it ever found its way out of the caves is a miracle. Tone beats phonics, kindergarten crazy ass crazy."

"Still, it would be wise for all of us to learn Mandarin," says Reynolds. "It will undoubtedly come in handy. Lieutenant, are you sure your watch is working? My stomach is telling me tee-off time is getting there."

Soon after being posted at Abu Ghraib, Lutz started to have dreams of running downstairs, staircases of stairs, trying to get out, somewhere, anywhere from where he was. Each step looked like the next one, the walls and ceilings harder to tell apart. Sometimes he thought he was running straight into a wall, but each time the wall opened up to expose another staircase. After four or five or fifty flights, he got the feeling he might be running deeper in instead of out. How could he tell? Until claustrophobia would freeze his limbs and he would wake up needing to urinate. Elated that he was now free of it, he would arrogantly forget the dream. But he kept having it.

Sand is the dominant theme and color in Abu Ghraib. The same color as Lutz's khaki uniform and his skin. As he plays his part in torture roulette, he's barely discernible against the white parged cinder block walls and three-foot-thick concrete floors. The only definition on the floors is provided by the scratch marks from heavy and uncomfortable furniture being dragged over it.

Of course, all of this blandness is broken when you enter an interrogation room and see a naked man in fetters. Simple profits were being made here. Someone decided that stripping the prisoners would further humiliate them. Later that it would lower laundry expenses. But laundry expenses were rubber-stamped budgeted, so what to do with the surplus? Cash and perks from the vendors exchanged hands. Opportunities to make money are everywhere if you are observant, in other words, predatory enough to ignore the consequences to others. Meanwhile, the interrogations continue.

"I have told you everything, why won't you believe me?" says Fahad. He doesn't sound very sincere. Perhaps that has something to do with this being the umpteenth time he has heard the same question. Fahad is seated in an iron chair that weighs a half ton. A relic from Saddam's days. His legs are shackled to the chair's legs, his arms to the chair's arms. His head is free to stretch to wherever his neck and torso will allow it. Tony Bennet sings a medley of forgotten tunes in the background, courtesy of the Lieutenant's boombox.

"Because you deceived us before! You didn't tell us you went to Harvard," says Captain Reynolds.

"Why ask me questions if you are not going to believe my answers? Is that not the definition of insanity?"

Captain Reynolds replies, "See how smart you are, Harvard man? You even know America's memes. We need to learn about impending attacks and the location of the weapons of mass destruction. Either or both. Simple, then you can go home."

"I have been here for, for three months," says Fahad. "How could I have learned of an impending attack? I would have had to learn it from you. So, tell me and I'll tell you. I flew here from Boston to serve in the medical corps when the war started. How would I know where WMD was stored? I stitched people up, not blew them apart."

"Listen to that classical use of language," says Captain Reynolds. "Parallelism, I think it's called. But being in the medical corps is the perfect ruse, right? Isn't your second in command a medical doctor?"

"Al Qaeda is not here. Everyone knows that. Americans must just enjoy hurting people." There is a spotlight beaming down on Fahad. The light is so concentrated he can't see more than a few inches from where he sits, so he doesn't see Lutz, who now pours a bucket of leeches over his head. They slosh on his ears and slide down his naked shoulders, some squirming down into his lap.

Fahad is hypnotized in disgust and fright. "What is the matter with you people? Did your TV get jammed on some *Survival* show?"

Captain Reynolds says, "I'm offended, Fahad. You don't think we can come up with anything on our own?" Then he turns to Lutz and says, "Actually, maybe we can't."

Fahad starts to feel a leech getting a sucker hold on his neck. "Ow, ooh, ow, oh my God. Please stop. No? So, I am correct, no? Ooo, mamomo."

"Maybe you need some quiet time to think about it," says Captain Reynolds. Those words turn out to be a signal, and Lutz swirls a quilted hood in the air on his index finger.

"No, not the hood, please," says Fahad. "No hood. I'll tell you; I'll tell you. But what haven't I already told you? Tell me. Tell me. I do not know anything. *Lau samaht.*"

"Quid pro Quo, Fahad," says Captain Reynolds. "Something for something."

Fahad continues in his quiet calm nasally voice, "I have told you everything I know. You Americans are so naive. Raised on TV, you want to believe that one stroke will make everything better. You are stuck in a *Looney Tunes* cartoon. Remember the young man who stood in front of the tanks at Tiananmen Square?"

"A noble bold act."

"And what changed? For him, he became compost under a fifty-ton tank. The weeds may glorify him. Perhaps you can seek comment from the weeds' agent. I think his name is Wile E Coyote."

Lutz was convinced that Fahad had no information to disclose. Actually, Fahad and all of the other prisoners Lutz interrogated never said anything that led anywhere. None of the other interrogators had learned anything significant either. Every piece of information had turned out to be a red herring. Said only to stop the torture.

From scrap two by fours and plywood, the Core of Engineers had fashioned tables two and a half feet high. This was a comfortable height for torturers to work from, being mindful of statistics for officer back strain injuries. Lutz had strapped Fahad to one. It had a fat plumbing pipe latched to its center so the top could see-saw. Lutz would tilt the table, so a prisoner's feet were above his head and then pour water down his mouth and nose. None of the prisoners liked it. Some freaked out so much, they couldn't even talk for days. Lutz performed this ritual to Fahad for seventy-three straight days. At the end of every shift, Lutz reported that he thought Fahad was telling the truth and didn't know anything. The CIA chided Lutz for being too soft. He had to harden himself like they had. But, instead of hardening, he found himself softening before Fahad. After the seventy-fourth treatment, Lutz thought he had killed him. Fahad was unresponsive, and foam only frothed from his mouth.

Lutz went back to his room that evening and cried. But, like the CIA had insisted, Fahad recovered. Everyone back to work. After eleven more sessions, nothing learned still, the CIA released Fahad in just enough clothing to keep him from being arrested for indecent exposure.

A week later Captain Reynolds and Lieutenant George barged into Lutz's quarters, a bleak cubic room that had formerly been a laundry. Captain Reynolds was evidently assigned to do the talking. He yelled down on a reclining Lutz, "What the fuck have you done, Private?"

"I didn't do nothing, Sir!" said Lutz. "I swear it. I've been here all night."

"Haven't you heard?"

"What?"

"The terrorists just blew up Fahad's home."

"Was he killed?"

"You care?"

"Curious is all," said Lutz.

"Everyone inside but one was killed, his twelve-year-old son, also named Fahad. You'd think these people would have more imagination when naming their children. He'll be here as soon as he's released from the hospital. He's missing a leg."

"Why would he be coming here?"

"Think about it, Private. Why do you think Fahad's house was targeted?"

"They thought he squealed?"

"Bingo, Private," said Spencer. "Which means he knew something. And, likely, his son does too. Now, in the future, keep your pedal to the metal. These people kill as indiscriminately as little boys set ants on fire. No mercy, ever. Remember."

Captain Reynolds stomped off. Lieutenant George stayed behind. In cases such as this, the Army must monitor how the chastised take being reprimanded. The infirmary brimmed with pre-suicides.

"Maybe I'm not cut out for this, Lieutenant," said Lutz. "I thought… Maybe I can be reassigned…"

"Nonsense, Private," said Lieutenant George. "First, no one is cut out for this. Second, the CIA sometimes spread rumors. We'll never know."

"Rumors?"

"Such as Fahad was released as a reward because he talked."

"That's murder."

Lieutenant George examined her boots, then the walls, then the ceiling, then her boots again. "The CIA fights war with a different agenda than we do. They're more inside than even we are. But, if you asked me, they are so inside, they're up inside their own butts."

After Fahad's demise, Lutz became bolder. He saw that not only could he get away with practically anything, but also the more outrageous, the more respect he earned from his team members and from the prisoners. He rigged a gibbet with a noose over a slab of ice, made the prisoners put the noose on, and had the prisoner stand on the ice during the interrogation. Everyone knew that if you lied, some part of your body had to respond, and if your hands didn't, your legs would. So, he tied their hands together. The prisoners were quickly hanging themselves. They didn't die. They were carried back to their cots and ordered to do better tomorrow. His process was quickly copycatted by other interrogators. The only drawback was when Captain Reynolds incurred the commandant's wrath for having to drink warm daiquiris.

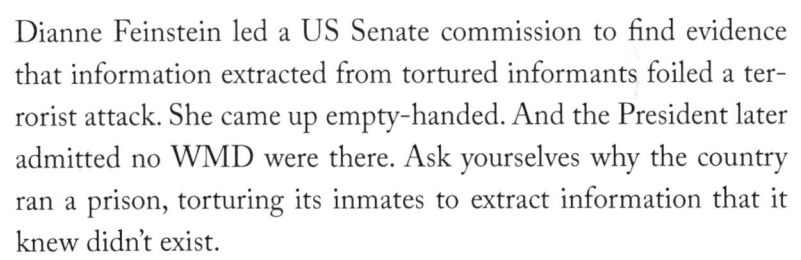

Dianne Feinstein led a US Senate commission to find evidence that information extracted from tortured informants foiled a terrorist attack. She came up empty-handed. And the President later admitted no WMD were there. Ask yourselves why the country ran a prison, torturing its inmates to extract information that it knew didn't exist.

It would seem the US's work at Abu Ghraib was really a psychiatric test run by the US Defense Department. It was measuring the extent of cruelty Americans, grown soft by easy living, could inflict on innocents under the guise of exacting revenge for 9/11, with the inconvenient proviso that Iraq had nothing to do with it. The code name of the operation: *DoubleM* for *Making Monsters*.

Things in the past should stay there, and we really should just forget them. Past sins have been mined enough already. Let's focus on today's past, not yesterday's. It's illegitimate to blame ourselves for what our parents and grandparents did, and we're not paying reparations from the benefits we received from stealing others' property. We're not even going to give the victims a few seconds head start to run from the firing squad we assembled to kill off invading Bigfoots, Loch Ness Monsters, and UFOs. Come on, we know they're out there.

Vietnam was a mistake, right? Thirty years later, we started two new wars. One was initially admired but quickly became a failure, and the other was a failure from the start. That one, named *Operation Iraqi Freedom*, killed from 150,000 to one million people, depending on who counts. The Secretary of Defense said the count of enemy killed is not our concern. Is Israel's categorical mistreatment of Palestinians going to bear fruit in anything but future open murder and mayhem? One death is one too many. The only intelligent and legitimate solution is for all sides to work to see that no one dies. The opposite is what we have. Holy Mary, Mother of God, pray for us sinners, now and at the hour of death. Hallelujah.

When Lutz left Iraq, he was really on the inside—serving time at Fort Dix for prisoner abuse. But this inside wasn't the inside his commanding officers had bragged about being in. His radicalization by the Army against the Iraqis slowly metastasized into a hatred for the Army and the US itself. His fellow inmates at Fort Dix didn't work very hard to dissuade him. Revenge would happen.

Abu Ghraib had taught him he'd better be on the right side of the table when the questioning began. The officers had all skirted imprisonment. The whole adventure made Lutz feel used and stupid, stupider still when he saw his face in the photos taken by his fellow comrades-in-arms, the pictures that broke the Abu Ghraib story. Lutz hadn't taken the pics, and certainly wasn't in many, but he was in one, grinning, a bottle of scotch in his left hand, his right hand pouring water on Fahad's head.

But whenever Lutz had questioned what they were doing, his commanding officers reminded him war didn't make sense, so you do what you're told. And he was told, loud and clear, " We are the aggressors. Bow or get mowed down." The point is to make that point, to etch that into your opponent's psyche, as a fearful enemy is a compliant enemy. This conformed to what he had learned in junior high. It was how boys secured their place in the pecking order. This had felt right then; why shouldn't it still?

In 2007, Lutz was dishonorably discharged from the Army after serving seventeen months of a two-year sentence for prisoner abuse. He was shipped from Fort Dix back home to Maryland. No one came to greet him. No waving conquering hero flags. Instead of beige colored sand everywhere, here there was green farmland, green trees, and long stretches of roads rarely interrupted by a traffic light. There had been no red lights in Abu Ghraib.

Lutz now itched to get even with America, for sending him to Iraq, for ordering him to do disgusting stuff to defenseless men and then imprisoning him for it. He would take America and give it back to the people like him who knew how to get things done, not these bureaucrats who were ruining it for everyone. Without their seeing it, he had put a red tracer on everyone's head, and the day was approaching. He waited for the right moment and the right leader.

Meanwhile, *Operation Iraqi Freedom* is over. Well, not in the no-longer-shooting-each-other kind of over. The US is still at war in Iraq. And, like the Vietnam War, the US is having a devil of a time determining who the enemy is. Are they the Sunnis, the Shia, or the terrorists? It's a hard row when all three hold a large minority of seats in Iraq's newborn legislature that was ushered into existence by the US.

CHAPTER SIXTEEN

359 DEGREES

They met in a bar.
Happy hour would be ending soon, and it was Andy's turn to buy beer as he and his friends from high school sat around a table and boasted about what they were going to do. Melody was holding court to three intern suitors from Walter Reed in a booth kiddie corner to Andy's. Each intern, in turn, was pointing out how much smarter they were than their professors, all four shooting tequila shots. When Andy returned to his table with two pitchers of cheap lager, one of the drunk interns suddenly stepped backwards in exaggerated surprise at another's remark and bumped into him. Fortunately, the floor was open slat for this very purpose, but both precautions did nothing to stop the beer from splashing on their shirts, pants, shoes, and socks. The intern started cussing Andy, who was just as mad, feeling his feet soaking up the suds. He stared at this arm-wringing, loud blur and wanted to smack him but hesitated, as the face looked like it belonged to a twelve-year-old.

Then Andy heard Melody's voice. It was calm, deep, and extraordinarily sexy. "Doctor Charley, in your examination of this patient, did you note the size of his hands? He could strangle you with one and pop a cluster of bananas into his mouth with the other without needing a napkin. Come over here, Java Man. I'll buy you something stronger than beer."

Later, after summarily dismissing the interns, she told him to drive her home. She gave him an address to a neighborhood that had a five-star crime rating. They made love. As soon as they finished, she told him he had to go because she had exams in the morning. You can guess what he thought.

She called him the next day, saying, "Last night was fabulous. We should do that again next Wednesday. Or is that when we are supposed to dine with the Robinsons?"

"I don't know any Robinsons. What are you talking about?"

Melody asked him, "Don't you remember?"

"No, I don't, Melody. When you are around, I'm beginning not to trust myself."

"Andy, trust everyone, just be assured that you'll always be disappointed. That's when the fun begins." Sure enough, he soon found himself with Melody at the Robinsons. They were professional acrobats. And was that not a night to remember?

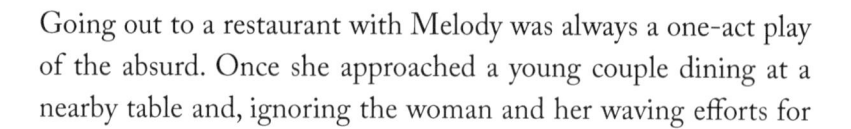

Going out to a restaurant with Melody was always a one-act play of the absurd. Once she approached a young couple dining at a nearby table and, ignoring the woman and her waving efforts for

Melody to desist, sexually talked up the young man to almost the point of ejaculation before asking if he wouldn't mind giving her his girlfriend's phone number, telling him, "She's fucking hot." Another time, Melody witnessed a woman slap a child in the face with the menu. Melody wrestled the menu out of the woman's hand and slapped the kid again, saying to the dumbfounded woman, "It's not fair that only you can enjoy inflicting pain on children. Thank you so much. It's so emotionally freeing. I'm sure your son will now become a respected citizen. May even become a star on a reality show called *Kids, How Much Can You Take?*"

Once, when she thought her shrimp was overcooked, she traipsed into the kitchen and demanded the cook eat the rubbery mess in front of her. When the chef ran away into the street, she started sauteing some fresh shrimp herself until the police arrived.

On the exasperating side of the coin, she had a habit of missing his friends and relatives' weddings and anniversaries then arriving at their homes unannounced and expecting to be fed. She also had a peculiar sense of smell. Like at the movies, patently ignoring their baby's diaper changing needs, yet demanding management evict a patron who wore an offending brand of perfume.

Andy drove a battered pick up the color of milk chocolate and rust. Melody drove a taxi-cab yellow Saab. The only one he had ever seen.

What did she see in him? She didn't keep it a secret. She loved his un-alphaness, his subservience to her. She had always wanted a lady's maid, just not anyone that physically close. And she loved his hands. Palms like loaves of bread, halved, still warm from the oven. Hairy, dark-veined hands, moist from perpetual ointment treatment but calloused from working heavy machinery. Giant carrot-sized fingers that proved to have the dexterity of a blind banjo player in the most sensitive recesses of her vagina.

What did he see in her? Everything. But when Alzheimer's struck, he turned to Donald Trump for direction. Trump's role modeling of doing anything he wanted without guilt warmed Andy's heart if not emboldening him to copycat. And it was so like Melody. Andy never thought through what to do if his two bosses conflicted. Which would he follow? Over his pay grade. He turned wood.

CHAPTER SEVENTEEN

PIZZAS ARE ROUND

My team needed this win to make districts, best of seven matches—three singles and four doubles. Our opponents were the Towson Patriots. Only a sophomore, I would be playing third doubles with Carl. Carl's and my playing styles were complementary in that they were opposite. Carl played aggressive, and I played defensive. Carl jumped up to the net at the first opportunity and stayed there. If he was lobbed, I was to cover the entire back court. I had the legs.

I was no weapon at the net.

I never liked being hit by the ball. Its sting felt like a wasp. So, when the ball was hit right at me, my reflexes manhandled the urge to strike back by telling me to dodge. And that tic, that lost tenth of a second, threw my racket timing off enough so that the best I could do was block the volley back, that is, if I was even able to hit the ball.

The Patriot doubles team had beaten us in the first set, and they were ahead two-one in the second by the time I saw Mom arrive in the stands. On the changeover, she walked up to my chair, kissed me on the cheek, and said, "Surprise."

She introduced me to Wilson, her date and later her husband, my stepdad. He was mid everything: height, weight, color, except for his smile. It was wide, almost kissing his ears. A smile that I learned later he approached every situation with. It gave me the creeps then and still does.

The Patriots coach ran over to Carl and me, yelling at Mom, "No coaching after the match starts."

Wilson laughed at him and said, "Coaching. Why? I do not know the first thing about tennis. Just introducing myself, Sir. We got here late is all, making apologies, only."

The Patriots coach insisted on repeating what he had just said but more fervently. Mom waited until he was spent before she replied, "I know the rules. Wilson insisted we let Andy know we were here. What do you expect me to tell my son anyway, bend your knees, keep your eye on the ball, split-step? Anyway, we're going back to our seats."

She then turned to me and said, "Good luck Andy, remember to bow at the award ceremony." Then she said to Towson's coach, "If that advice isn't a violation? And Coach, wipe your chin. Spittle is all over it. Someone might be hungry and mistake you for a hot dog with onions."

We won the next two games, lost three, but won the next game to stay alive. A game from tying the set up and a game from losing it all. When we changed sides, the crowd yelled out. Magnus had lost, which meant our match would settle which team would go on to districts. A tennis game is decided by four points.

The Patriots served, and Carl's return went very long. I returned deep enough so the server had to half-volley his return, a sitter for Carl who instantly smashed it. The ball hit the net and rolled along its edge before bouncing weakly over on their side. Tie game. Carl hit the next serve, a weak second serve no less, long again. I was so angry. Basics. Carl gave me a look. It wasn't an apology. It was just his, now our, bad luck. The next point was almost a complete repeat of the second, only instead of Carl smashing the ball into the net, he hit the ball wide and long. We and our entire team were one point away from elimination. Our opponents were exuberant, banging rackets and saying, "This is it!" The last point was unremarkable other than I was forced to shag a lob over Carl's head. I spotted a clean down-the-line, but in the middle of my back swing Carl yelled, "Go left," and I took my eye off the ball. Just like that, we weren't going to the district playoffs.

While the Patriots and their fans were setting off fireworks, we sulked. Mom and Wilson walked up to us. He started talking right away, "You guys sure hung in there, good show. I heard that you lost the first go round on lucky shots, yours just out and theirs just in. Tough luck, but you never gave up. True grit. Great job."

"Margaret Lee is hosting the aftergame pizza and pop party," Mom said. "Wilson and I will drop you off there after you shower. You can get a ride home later with Betty Talbott. We are going to visit Wilson's parents. Neither is well."

"Yeah, nor is there much of a chance of their getting any better," said Wilson. "Someday, you'll be visiting your mom like that, praying that she doesn't die on your watch."

"Wilson, the things you say. I'm beginning to wonder why I put up with you," Mom said. They walked away together, bumping into each as if they could be holding hands.

Afterwards, the locker room was a tomb, punctuated by sudden barks when one of us was hit by the handiest missile—jockstrap, shoe, sweatband. No one took offense. Acknowledging being struck with an expletive was answering roll call. Nausea crawled inside me and grew acid hot. I wanted to yell so loud the world would hear me. Coach's wrap up didn't help.

He had assured us we would beat the Patriots. He'd shown us on charts and diagrams how we would win. But that is not what happened. Season done.

Coach blamed himself, praised us, and walked out. My consolation was having to hear the same speech the next year and the one after, when we finally made it to districts but lost there.

At the pizza and pop party, we players quickly let go of our parents' 'tough luck' handshakes and gathered out of their earshot around Todd Predmeyer. He was team captain three years ago when we took home the championship trophy. He now played varsity tennis at Rutgers, a Division II school. Todd dissed the other team's players, one by one. We laughed. It was funny. We were a team again, a defeated team, but one.

Then he started praising Bjorn Borg and Boris Becker, champions of yesterday. "They were the best, the rest detritus."

"Detriwhat?" someone asked.

"Garbage," Todd said. "I'd follow them into hell but would rather follow them into a bordello, even their seconds would be fantastic." I laughed with everyone else as if I knew what a bordello was. Someone yelled cliche, and everyone razzed Todd.

"Bjorn and Boris knew how to kill," Todd went on. "No bush beating, no wimping out, no mercy, no prisoners taken. Every shot was for the kill. No choking ever."

I glanced at Carl. He nodded along like he was in a trance. There was no purpose in just hitting the ball inside the lines like I did. Go for a kill or go home. On ad-out at set point? So, suicide is the mark of a champion. That was why and how I was a loser.

"That's how to play," said Todd. "Your opponents are dirt, make them eat it. They don't even deserve that. You have to feel that way and let them know that's how you feel. That you're better than they are, and nothing they can do will change that. Bjorn and Boris don't walk on the court. They take it."

John Magnus, our team captain and first seed asked, "How do you square that with good sportsmanship?" John had lost today. The bullseye was on him. I looked to where the adults were mingling. I needed a place to set my eyes other than on John's or Carl's. I was a blink away from sobbing.

So, I got up off the bench and walked away the way you do when someone suddenly calls out your name. I said, "I need a slice." It felt good to hear my voice, with only a hint of quiver in it. If there was one thing I wasn't going to do in front of my teammates, it was cry.

I never got strapped again. Wilson and my mom got married. His kids joined ours. Mom stopped giving me tennis lessons. Wilson and she rooted me on at home matches, like all the other parents. Wilson said games teach you about life. I guess that is true. Tennis taught me about losing. The strappings taught me feelings were elective and signal weakness and that if you can't take the pain of losing, you are not really one of the team.

When Mom had divorced Dad, I had become the man of the house at seven years old. Now at sixteen, with Wilson's arrival, I was unceremoniously demoted. I went looking for a new family. I tried my tennis teammates first. Teenage athletes are the last people to feel comfortable sharing your griefs with. So, I never did. As a returning player on our team, I played the part of the stoic non-hero. That role carried me until I left school before graduation and two days after losing my last high school tennis match, second singles, 6-7, 6-7. I moved a hundred miles away to a job at a lumber yard, where my real dad was a foreman. I never missed Mom nor the strappings. I can't say why. As a feeder at a lumber mill, I did come to learn a lot about wood.

Andy never heard Todd's you-guys-have-so-much-to-learn reply to John Magnus's question. "I was telling you how to think before and during the match. After that, it's back to love-love Baby. Drink a pint together. When the match is in the books, thinking about it is a waste. It's in ink. Ink's only good for publishers and coaches. Guys coach when they can't play worth crap anymore, that is, if they ever could in the first place."

CHAPTER EIGHTEEN

FORWARD TO BACK

Andy and Telly make it to Andy's home. Benedict Arnold's proud, short legs keeping up with theirs.

The garage door opener takes forever to roll up and, after they step inside, another forever to roll closed behind them. Andy listens a third forever for the sound of anyone or anything approaching, especially sirens. When his heart and breath return to their normal velocity, Andy opens the door to the kitchen and waves for the woman to follow him in. "I'm going to call 911," he tells her.

"Not a good idea," says the woman.

"Why in the hell not?"

"He's a cop."

"Who's a cop?"

"The man who tried to steal me."

"What? How do you know that?" Andy asks her, thinking "Did I just step in it big time?"

"He's my stepdad."

He had interfered with a father's picking up his own daughter.

She adds, "He's Damascus's Chief of Police, Lutz Delorean."
Can this get any worse? Andy considers running back to the nursing home. Maybe they will take him.

But then he looks her in the face. He recognizes it. He sees her brown eyes in his mirror every morning. He knows what it's like to live with someone who makes your life miserable, seemingly for sport. He guesses how much harder it would be if that someone was the Chief of Police.

He's shivering and soaking wet, standing before her. She's shivering and wet just the same. He's colder now than he was in the garage. Something's wrong. He looks up and notices that the skylight has shattered. A gust had rallied a tree limb into it. Shards of glass lay in ambush all over the floor and the kitchen countertop.

Would stuff just stop for a minute? Let him get his bearings? He wants to ask her, "What should we do?" His glow from the run sheds. No razor-strop strike threatens, but no one is handing out trophies either. What is he supposed to do? He's forty-seven years old. The guy hadn't said he was police. He hadn't said she was his daughter. He had tried to run Andy over. Yeah, there was that.

Andy sorts through the jigsaw puzzle pieces of what he wants versus what he should do. He wants this to be over. He should know what to do. So, he waits. Something will happen. Something always happens. This is all so over his paygrade. Why do dogs need walks anyway?

Melody walks into the kitchen. She's wearing combat boots instead of her usual flip-flops, cradling a phone between one shoulder and ear.

Andy tells her what happened while she eyes the young woman standing in what's quickly becoming a pond on the red quarry tile floor. The young woman is enjoying that no one is frantically running around with a mop.

When Andy concludes his tale, Melody reaches out to shake the woman's hand. Gives her quite a professional businesswoman's handshake. "I'm Melody MacClean. Watch out for broken glass. Glad to meetcha. What's your name?"

"Telly Kind. How do you do?"

"Why isn't your last name Delorean?" asks Andy.

"He's my stepdad, remember?" says the woman.

"Telly," says Melody, "Something tells me you might be hungry."

"Starving."

"But you always are, right?"

"How'd you know?"

"Prader Willi."

"How'd you know?"

"You have the look, honey. It's unmistakable. I am so sorry, that is such a dreadful DNA split." Melody walks closer and hugs Telly. Telly tightens up, fearing a repeat of Donna's. But it's not. It's short and compact and firm and over before she's ready. Telly wants another one. Instead, Melody grabs Telly's hand and lingers for a few seconds before she drops it. Telly thinks she might faint. True unorchestrated emotion without a hint at future obligation. Liberating. Maternal. No one had dispensed that to her since her stepmom had left. It ought to be available in a pill.

Telly turns to Andy and asks, "How did she know that?"

"Melody knows everything, young lady."

"No, I don't, and I know less and less every day. But speaking of today, how about a sandwich?"

"I'd love one," says Telly.

"Andy, would you make her one while I wait on the phone for Ma Bell? I wonder how old Ma Bell is getting to be. Maybe I should be calling her Grandma Bell, she had plenty of children. Remember Mountain Bell, Southern Bell, or was that a lady?"

Andy makes two ham sandwiches. Telly practically drools as she watches him add tomatoes, dill pickles, and Cooper Sharp cheese, then mustard and mayonnaise. Andy places the sandwich on a plate, adds some chips, and puts them on the dining room table. They sit down to eat. When Andy is half-done, he looks up to see her sandwich is gone. So are the chips. When he plastic-wraps the remainder of his sandwich to place it in the fridge, she never takes her eyes from it until he closes the unlocked fridge door.

Melody, who has been pacing all this time with the phone on her shoulder, says to Telly, "You're not my size, but look in our bedroom and select what fits. Andy, collect your and her wets in a hamper and throw them in the washer. Telly, use the master bathroom, it has fantastic mirrors. When you both have on dries, get into our car. Andy, you'll drive. Telly and I will sit in the back and catch up."

"Where are we going?" asks Andy.

"Delaware," says Melody. "A Maryland police chief has zero jurisdiction there. Telly, huh? What's my uncle's name, Andy? I was trying to call him when the skylight blew up, but for some reason the phone wouldn't work."

"His name is Terry. Can't we just call the police to come pick her up, take her home?"

"Sometimes, Handcream," says Melody, "First of all, I am already on the line. Second, are you forgetting that this police chief just tried to kill you? That is, if you have told me the truth and weren't exaggerating."

"I told you the truth. I didn't exaggerate a word. Right, Tuh-Telly?"

"Yeah, I thought you were a goner. If you hadn't cleared those pipes…"

"See, Melody, so what are you doing?" Andy asks.

"Waiting for Grandma Bell to call and tell me she has fixed our phone."

"How can the telephone company call you if you are on the phone?"

"What's your problem? I am the one doing something. Besides, we pay for some never-miss-a-call fail-safe."

"Stay on the line then," Andy says. "Telly, follow me, but steer clear of the glass on the floor."

As they leave, Melody says, "Andy, when we get back, you need to call our insurance company, shop vac the floors, turn on the fans, tarp the skylight, and all that it says in the policy. You should read it sometime. It reads like a novel. It just lacks a climax."

"Like the part that says you should protect your property when you become aware of a hazard?" says Andy. Andy had lobbied Melody to have the tree limbs trimmed back from the house, but Melody had rejected even one live twig's excision. Trees are as valuable as people to her.

Andy and Telly make it to the master bedroom. What he sees there makes him grateful for Melody's OCD. Whenever she had to leave the house, she could spend an hour, sometimes two, sometimes three, sorting through all her clothes. There on the bed is spread weeks' worth of clothes, undies included.

"Take your pick, bathroom's on the left." He opens up one of his bureau drawers, grabs clothes for himself and leaves.

He walks into the foyer and strips. Melody comes in and takes pictures of him with her cell phone. Andy says, "Melody, what are you doing?"

"Turn around Andy, I want your backside as well."

"What the hell."

"Turn around!" says Melody. She takes a few shots of his backside and says, "It's for insurance."

Melody walks out, arranging her pics into a file. Andy finishes dressing and goes into the kitchen. He fishes out his wallet, keys, cell, and cash from a giant yellow Blockbuster popcorn bowl. He's rattled. A few days ago, Melody had refused to get in the car for an infusion that was supposed to prolong her life but now is going to get into the car in order to protect a complete stranger.

When Telly comes out of their bedroom in Melody's clothes, Melody balks. "I'm not going out with another woman who looks just like me."

"I don't think I look anything like you," says Telly. "You're curvy and tall with silver lightning bolts in your hair. I'm round and curveless."

"Your hair has no gray and your face no wrinkles, so I'd switch in a minute," says Melody. "We both do sport a nice waddle. But can't we do this on a sunnier day? It's so cold. Handcream, did you leave a window open?"

Andy has to remind her that this was her idea twice before she's finally sitting in the back seat of their Buick with Telly. But before they leave, she makes him return to the house and bring that half sandwich. He drives out slowly, carefully, expecting police interference at every corner until he merges onto the highway. What if the police chief died?

Andy plans to drive to the first police station the GPS directs him to in Delaware, just a dozen or so miles away. He's going to tell them what, exactly? Someone tried to abduct this large girl, tried to run him over, crashed... No, he'll let Melody do the talking.

Besides, police had access to guns. Andy didn't. He used to. Hunting was manly fun. Melody insisted he get rid of them when their first child was born. She read the number of children killed annually in accidental shootings. Guns were not going to be a furnishing in any residence her babies lived in. But after their sons grew up and moved out, Melody became obsessed with pistols and was upgrading every month until Andy picked up that there were as many intentional shootings in homes as accidental ones, mostly suicides. After her first attempted suicide via sliced wrists, he sold all the guns, told her they had been stolen.

"Don't talk with Miss What's Her Name about what happened." Andy is fine with that. He really doesn't want to know about Telly's life as Chief Delorean's daughter. He switches his GPS to Delaware and keys in 'POLICE STATION.' It directs him to Newport. He's thinking that after he gives his statement, the police will take Telly, he will go home, and things will return to normal, not that that felt like such a cheery thing. He needn't have over thought it.

Melody faces Telly and asks, "Who are you?" And when Telly gives her name again, Melody adds, "How's your day running?" Then before Telly can answer, "I'm so grateful you are here, Andy is such a bore. So, Telly, tell me, exactly where are we going? Do they sell beer?"

CHAPTER NINETEEN

NO PINS NOR NEEDLES

Melody and Telly talk in the back seat. Andy tunes them out. He finds the Ravens game on the radio.

"So that's why you're being so difficult, Handcream?" says Melody. "You're missing the game."

"Yeah, I could be watching the Ravens on TV right now."

"It's not an important game," says Telly, "the Bengals are out of the running."

"Gotta root for my team," says Andy.

"No one can hear you cheer, Handcream," says Melody. "Worship is a strange article, isn't it, Telly?"

"Sounds like a warship to me," says Telly. "Is this about Star Trek?"

"Worship," says Melody, "means acknowledgment of worth. This article is more valuable than that one, maybe enough to die for. We worship idols to keep them in check. Worship requires an underling, AKA us. We sacrifice something of value to our overling to cement our subservient relationship to it. An animal shows his rear end to the stronger animal to let him know he's not a threat but maybe a treat. Screw to your heart's desire, but don't eat me, okay?

"This sacrificing business permeates all the historic epics. In the Iliad, Agamemnon sacrificed his daughter. In the Old Testament, Abraham agreed to sacrifice his son. Both did so to encourage their idol to vanquish their foes. It's the same story, just different names. I've never understood why Homer didn't sue Moses for plagiarism. I would have represented Homer pro boner."

"What does this have to do with watching the Ravens?" asks Andy. "I'm not sacrificing my children."

"Rooting for your home team develops community spirit," says Telly. "My teachers told me."

"You are sacrificing your time, and that is all you have," says Melody.

"The three motivations of life are power, fame, and money. Not time," says Telly.

"Time covers all three," says Melody. "Power, money, and fame are time's currency."

"I don't understand," says Telly.

"If you have power, money, and fame, others do your housekeeping, cooking, laundry, finances, and finding mates. In England, the royal court created a position called the groom of the stool to save King Henry Eighth the time of wiping his ass after he defecated. In the same amount of time it takes to watch football for one season, you could earn three units of college credit and maybe learn something useful."

"Like how many slave women," says Andy, "a revered, now canceled ex-president molested two hundred fifty years ago. I think I know all I need to."

"You are not a sports fan?" Telly asks Melody.

"Oh, I am," says Melody, "but I do not worship it, nor do I idolize its participants."

"Tell her what you idolize, Melody," says Andy.

"Staples and paper clips."

"What?" asks Telly.

"They keep important papers, ergo their ideas, from getting mixed up with other important but different ideas. Paper clips require less effort to release, while licensing the unintentional invasion with other papers not part of the tribe. Staples are more secure, but if you have occasion to pry them apart, you can damage the product, which you were trying to preserve in the first place. But I don't worship either of them. I am grateful for them. And heaven forbid if I should ever sacrifice something for them. Left with neither, I can just fold and pinch the top."

"I'd rather moon over Tyler Huntley," says Telly. "He's my idol."

"Go ahead and moon over Snoop but realize a star athlete is a paperweight next to staples and paperclips. Life could not happen without them. Something had to attach cells together, and some of these attachments had to be transitory via a paperclip and almost forever via a staple."

"Cells aren't made of metal," objects Telly.

"It's the same process. We created paperclips and staples mimicking how biology, chemistry, and physics work. Try to imagine life without some things sticking to us and some things never letting go. Imagine how you would shit and piss. The same can be said for matter. If stuff didn't sometimes clump together and sometimes let go, there couldn't be anything, planets for a starter.

"You are an assembly of parts. Your parts are either paper-clipped or stapled together. Crucial to survival is which. Too much stickum when only a paperclip is needed leads to tragedy, to death. This is the reason why birth defects are so destructive."

"Like Prader-Willi?"

"Exactly," says Melody. "A chromosome that should have been stapled was paperclipped by mistake. A male chromosome by the way, Andy.

"The brain is no different. Some thoughts are paperclipped together and can change hands, some are stapled fast, so separation is impossible. Your left tibia is connected to your kneecap and your femur with staples. Only major surgery can re-attach them if they're torn. Earwax is attached in your ear canal with paperclips; a simple swab with a Q-Tip will clear it. Teardrops, sweat, urine, feces, mucus, and other bodily fluids are similarly attached via paperclips. Imagine what life would be like if we required major surgery for any of these to release its hold?"

"Double ouch!" says Telly.

"Pretty expensive," interjects Andy.

"So, extending this out," says Melody, "Cats are wired to fear an attack when they're eating or defecating because that's when they're most vulnerable. But when they're especially hungry, or the feast is just too tasty, they'll forgo the command. So, the vigilance trigger is paperclipped. Cats' irascibility is an irrevocable proof of its being stapled. After taking a nap on your lap, they'll burst away with a blood-inducing paw strike through your pants when they hear someone crinkling a bag of chips.

"Brain imagery can predict whether your config promotes a liberal, conservative, or libertarian bias. Cool, huh? So, our biases predate the time we were mature enough to make decisions. That is, if we actually make decisions. The evidence of that so far is contraindicating."

"Can we control how many people are born with different biases?" asks Telly.

"We do. In times of war, more conservatives are born, in times of peace, more liberals, and when relative peace has gone on for a while, libertarians sprout."

"Melody, tell Telly what a libertarian is," says Andy.

"Now that I have been given everything, don't tread on me."

"Isn't it a good thing to have an idol to look up to, though?" asks Telly.

"Certainly, but each to her field," says Melody. "I admire Mother Teresa, but I'm not joining a nunnery. I enjoy watching Snoop's scrambling, but I can't translate that to mine. Life is to be faced, not run from."

"What do you like about sports?" asks Telly.

"I marvel at professional players' speed, strength, and athleticism. But I find their shenanigans after a successful play disgusting. It interrupts the story. Commercials are bad enough. It's like when an author speaks to you in the middle of a novel."

Oops.

"So, why do we worship?" asks Telly.

"We are hardwired to," says Melody, "like the cat."

"I thought worship was only for religion," says Telly, "I'm a Methodist."

"Worshiping a religion is no different from worshiping a sports team. A sports fan watches Sunday's game, keeps up on trade rumors, argues with co-fans about ref calls, joins fantasy leagues, and springs for mementos. A religious fan attends Sunday service, reads her local church's organ news, discusses the sermon while commingling outside the church, and pays tithe. The only difference is the Raven's fan gets the summer off."

"I watch baseball too," says Telly.

"You lost the only advantage then," says Melody. "Worship licenses you the opportunity to revile others without condemnation. Worship promotes the unsubstantiated claim that you are the Chosen Ones, which codifies your place in the world. So, if you live in Maryland, you're an Orioles, Ravens, and Wizards fan. That is who you are. You neither have to apologize or explain. Even when sports team owners, coaches, or players commit irredeemable acts and their handlers libel others to cover it up. You worship, ergo you are imprisoned. Forgive me for not sending a congratulations card."

"The team represents us," says Andy.

"That's right," says Telly, "it's our team against everybody else's."

"With trades, drafts, retirements, and injuries, with the biannual firing and hiring of new coaches, sports teams contain no consistent presence," says Melody. "If God, the ultimate idol, is unchanging, a professional sports team is God's antithesis. Game to game, a sports team has as much continuity as your recycled beer bottles."

"Oops, that's my phone," interrupts Andy. He pulls out his cell and says, "Hi, Jeremy. How goes it?"

"Hey Dad, crazy news out of Elkton, right? Police Chief Delorean spoils a carjacking. It happened just a couple of blocks from where you live. There's a BOLO out..."

"For the chief?"

"You can be so dense," says Jeremy. "Not the chief, the two who ran away. A middle-aged male and a teenage female. An arrest warrant is out."

"Let me call you back in a minute or two, Jeremy," says Andy. "I'm running into some heavy traffic." Andy is shaking as much as he did when he slammed the car door on Lutz's hand. He concentrates on slowing his breathing and his driving speed.

After a few minutes he says to Melody, "Jeremy says what happened with Telly and me was a carjacking. The police are looking for us. I've made a mess. I'd better turn around and turn myself in."

"Andy, you will do no such thing," says Melody. "This Mr. Chief tried to run you down, remember?"

"Yes, but there's a warrant out. I'd be breaking the law. I'm driving out of state. That's a crime, I think."

"So is trying to run over someone with a car, Handcream" says Melody. "And filing a false police report is a felony. Call Jeremy back, find out what he knows, but don't tell him anything."

"I don't feel right lying to Jeremy," says Andy. "He's a cop. Why are we doing this? We don't know this girl. I can't run from the law."

"We know her now; she's sitting in the backseat of our car. That is what counts. A person is more valuable than a law. Hand me the phone, Handcream."

"Okay, Melody. Just press redial. But I'm not liking this one tiny bit." He hands his cell to Melody in the back seat. Telly looks like a cartoon fire hydrant before it bursts, but Melody hushes her and dials Jeremy.

"Jeremy, this is Mom. Was anybody hurt during this carjacking?"

"Chief Delorean was," says Jeremy, "possible concussion."

"So, these carjackers are violent."

"Oh, absolutely."

"How did they escape?"

"The perps are on foot," says Jeremy. "You're gonna hear a lot of helicopter chatter until we round them up. Keep that mutt of yours close to home for a few days, and don't open your door to any strangers. By the way, I need a few bucks, a hundred should carry me."

Jeremy and Melody dance the mother-son-money-exchange tango. He sends her an app button to press on Andy's smartphone. She does. He observes, "You guys are out late."

"Yes," says Melody. "Handcream wanted to go for a drive to the ocean. Probably to sightsee the sunbathers at the beach. Can't blame him. I'm not the hot miniskirt cutie I used to be. But he, damn him, looks pretty much the same."

"Mom, it's January not June."

"It really isn't fair how women's looks age so fast. Especially our hair. Your hair still the same color?"

"Black as blue coal, Mom."

"No gray?"

"Not yet."

"Oh, to be Korean."

"I'm not Korean, Mom," says Jeremy. "My blood parents were. I was born here. I'm a full-blooded American."

"Well, tell it to the KKK, not me."

"Mom, there is no KKK."

"Not what the news says."

"Now there's the LuLuxLan," says Jeremy. "This time, they're not comic book characters."

"Do they persecute people because of their hair color?"

"No," says Jeremy. "Mom, are you high?"

"I always thought that if you are going to persecute people why stop at skin color? Why not hair color, shoe color, hat color, and what about car color? Cops drive black cars; doesn't that tell you something? People of color and cars of color. PeeOhCee. CeeOhCee. Sounds close."

"What are you drinking, hair dye? And where do you get your news, Antifa?"

"PBS Newshour."

"That's the same thing," says Jeremy. "I bet it's still saying Trump lost the election."

"I thought he had."

"No, the election was rigged."

"Wow, you are your father," says Melody. "A hundred thousand election officials banded together to mislead three hundred fifty million Americans, when three Americans couldn't keep Monica's hand jobbing Bill Clinton secret for two weeks."

"Strange things happen. Remember the phony Mueller Report, the lying Warren Commission, and the Alfred Dreyfus treason conviction? All lies."

"So, the town of Wilkes-Barre killed Lincoln, the singer Tiny Tim married Frank Sinatra, and Harper Lee's Fairy loved Jackie Onassis, and that's how JFK Jr. was born?"

"That's all nonsense, Mom."

"Well, that's for you to decide."

"Decide what?"

"Whether you want to be a paperclip or a staple. I have to go. We have to drop what's-her-name off. Bye."

CHAPTER TWENTY

BEMUSEMENT RIDE

The Newport police station is one story and brick veneered. Its two neighbors, not quite out of eyesight, are ancient stone farmhouses. The residents of those homes were not pleased to have the station placed next door, but their complaints were beaten back by better-connected nimbys who defended themselves with lawsuits, claiming family heritage while threatening expensive negative outcomes for the cash-strapped municipality.

With more coaxing needed for Melody, the three get out of the car and walk into the front office. They walk into blankness: white painted sheetrock walls with no ornamentation, not even cove moldings to mark where the walls meet the linoleum or the ceiling. But there are plenty of cameras, strapped to black angle iron on the ceilings to record their entry and, hopefully, Andy prayed, their departure. They come to a sign: POLICE, with a red arrow pointing left, and OTHER, with a blue arrow pointing right.

Melody plays bus tour director as they walk left down the hall. "You can appreciate the tax dollars spent to make us feel welcome, even to the point of communicating that you may be staying here a very long time. I'm surprised not to see a spittoon. They could have at least added some *Twilight Zone* music." The hall takes them down another corridor, then another, until it makes a turn, then another, where it dead ends in front of a glass wall, complete with microphone and evidence tray. They detect a strong smell of Vaseline. Melody sings, "The cops invite you in, in order to escort you inner."

Telly says, "Maybe this isn't such a good idea."

They face the glass wall. There's no way to leave except how they came or by a Dutch door to the immediate right. Right now, it's closed tight. The glass wall has a drawer for placing things no bigger than a shoebox through it. No one is behind the glass, and all they can see behind it is another white wall with mail slots and another Dutch door to its left. It's closed too. Some kind of security redundancy that baffles even Melody, but she's not afraid to push the black knob of the ringer. They hear nothing. Andy calls out, "We have an emergency here."

"Just in case you're not too busy dealing with ticketing dangerously parked cars, accepting pecuniary bribes, or herding pedophiliac mosquitos," says Melody. They wait, unsure that anyone is there to listen.

"Hands in your pockets, Handcream," says Melody. "They will use any mark on your hands as proof you were aggressive. For the police, lifting your hands up, even if it is to comb your hair, is classified as a threatening gesture and sanctions a violent response."

"When did you get so anti-cop, Melody?" asks Andy.

"By reading," she answers. One of her non-sequiturs that Andy doesn't get, but it always shuts him up, as he only reads instructions on tools and frozen food boxes.

Relieved that he's on the final lap of this rescue mission, at least, Andy watches it all unravel when Sergeant Barrett walks in behind the glass wall. She takes her time to sit down and get settled, even to the point of twice orbiting her head around her neck as if she were attending a yoga class. Then, grinning like a spider would to a fly, says, "How may I be of service? Are you here to report storm damage?"

Andy starts, noting her name tag, "Sergeant Barrett, I want to report an attempted abduction. I witnessed a man tackling the woman on my left and throwing her into a van."

"That's right," says Melody, who is standing to his right. "This man threw me into my own car and drove off, a flying rat out of Hades, right to this police stand."

Andy flattens his left hand against his head and says, "Melody, this is not about you."

"Can't I make a complaint?" says Melody. "This is the land of equal opportunity. Telly is not so special, you know. I just met her, and I'm practically in my pajamas here. No one can tell me to shut up."

"This man abducted you?" Sergeant Barrett says, pointing the end of her pen at Andy.

"Yes indeed!"

"And you are?"

"Melody MacClean, Esquire."

"You are an attorney?"

"How observant," says Melody.

"And what is your relationship with this man?"

"He's my husband on alternate Thursdays, depending on whether or not this is an odd-numbered year. What is the number of this year?"

Sergeant Barrett turns to Andy, "And you are?"

"Andy MacClean. Let me unravel this."

"Of course he will," interrupts Melody. "I was home, and he forced me into our car with this other woman." She turns to Telly and says, "Hi, again, what did you say your name was?" Telly answers and Melody immediately turns back to Sergeant Barrett and says, "And drives me here. So, you see, this is a clear case of mistaken popularity, and I intend to press charges. By the way, I saw a sign outside that you are hiring. May I have an application form, pretty please?"

Sergeant Barrett turns to Andy. Andy begins again and tells her what he saw in the parking lot, but before he can get close to finishing, she asks, "Why is your wife here?"

"I couldn't leave her alone, she has Alzheimer's."

"But you did, didn't you, when you walked your dog, Benedict Arnold, was it?"

"Yes'm, that's its name, but we were just going for a short walk, not driving to another state."

"This carjacking happened where?"

"In Elkton, Maryland."

"Go back to Maryland Mr. and Mrs. MacClean. Report her abduction there."

"We're in Delaware?" pipes Melody. "You took me across state lines for sex. That's illegal, statutory rape and corpus Christie for Jesus's sake."

"The abductor was the city of Damascus's Police Chief," blurts out Andy.

"Why didn't you tell me that before?" says Sergeant Barrett, pushing buttons on her desk.

"I hadn't gotten that far in the telling," Andy answers. Andy sees three men in uniform walk towards them from the rear of the hallway, blocking any chance they had at exiting. The three do not look like they're part of a festive welcoming committee. Telly places her back to one wall and takes an audible gulp. Sergeant Barrett asks Andy, "How do you know he was a police chief? Been arrested before?"

Andy feels persecuted. He thought he was doing a public service, thought he had been almost heroic, now he's being accused of being a criminal. Jeremy had called him the carjacker. What had Chief Delorean reported? Melody saves his reverie by saying, "It's what this young woman told us. What is your name again?"

"Telly Kind," Telly says.

"And how do you know that it was Damascus's Chief of Police, Miss Kind?" asks Sergeant Barrett.

"He's my stepdad."

A pained sigh runs over every police officer's face. A domestic dispute. Couldn't people deal with their own relationship issues? But the cops quickly stiffen, realizing one of their own is involved, which invokes the code of complete in-transparency, regardless of the consequences to self. "Someday, it might be me." Andy is thinking maybe he and Melody could slink away right now. Leave the girl. Who is she to him? The police might shrug off his misdirected vigilantism. But this isn't an episode on Andy Griffith.

"It makes no difference who was abducting whom," says Sergeant Barrett. "You should have called 911."

"What are you talking about?" says Melody. "How could Handcream have had any idea the police were abducting this girl,

Telly, isn't it? Was he supposed to let a man just drive away with her? How are citizens supposed to identify police chief pedophiles? Unless of course, it's all of them. Handcream, was he wearing a uniform?"

"He was wearing military camouflage pants and shirt," says Andy, "and a COVID mask."

"Who is Handcream?" asks Sergeant Barrett.

"Handcream is Andrew MacClean," says Melody. "He's standing right in front of you. Who did you think you were talking to?"

One of the policemen who is standing behind them, name tag KAVANAUGH, says, "I heard the chief suffered a concussion."

"Isn't that a badge of honor for cops?" says Melody. "Multiple occurrences opportunizing cluster patches and promotions. He hit his head against Telly's—I got her name right this time—windshield when he was trying to run over my husband. You ticket us for not wearing seatbelts but don't use them yourselves. Shame on you. I intend to file a murder charge against Chief Delorean. Maybe, if you offer us something strong to drink, I'll only make it *attempted* murder. Telly, what would you like to drink?"

"A chocolate milkshake. Or strawberry, it doesn't matter."

Melody takes Andy's half-sandwich out of her purse. She gives it to Telly and says, "This should hold you for a few minutes."

Then, she faces Sergeant Barrett and says, "We'd like to add three hamburgers, three milkshakes, and three orders of fries as part of our damages. The first and last medium warm and middle one medium cold, please."

"We are not a fast-food restaurant," says Sergeant Barrett. "And you don't file criminal charges, the DA does."

"Look," interrupts Kavanaugh, "Mrs. MacClean, the chief simply wants to be sure his daughter is safe. He doesn't want any trouble."

Andy asks himself, "How does this guy know that? Are cops all one person?"

"Mr. MacClean," says Sergeant Barret, "may I see some form of ID?"

Andy pulls out his wallet, and when he opens it, twenty or so diagonal pieces of confetti fall out.

Frozen, looking at the pieces falling to the floor, Andy says to Melody, "You cut up my driver's license?"

"Well, you stole mine because you say I can't remember where I am going. The only way you can find your keys and wallet is by always putting them in the yellow Blockbuster popcorn bowl," says Melody. "Who's got the memory problem? One handicap begets another. Equal squeakles."

Telly giggles, and Andy turns to the side and presses his palms against the drywall, as if he could move this room right out of the building. He presses against it hard enough that all seven hear the drywall's stretching complaint. Maybe this is the day he leaves Melody for good. End all his problems. Just walk away and never come back. That is, if the police let him go.

"Don't worry," says Melody. She's on her hands and knees. "I'm a whiz at jigsaw puzzles. Give me a minute, I just need to find one of his noses first."

"Mr. MacClean," says Sergeant Barrett, "am I to understand you operated a motor vehicle without a valid driver's license?"

Melody, still on her knees, kicks Telly's foot and says, "Is that your driver's license hanging from your neck?"

Telly grins and says to the sergeant, "I drove," and waves her driver's license at the sergeant.

Their conversation then slow-mos into exchanging tiny bits of data, as if each is a gem that requires examining by a jeweler's loop and weighing on a jeweler's scale. All the while, Melody sorts through the confetti littering the linoleum on her hands and knees. She gives up and pours them into the evidence drawer. Sergeant Barrett looks at them but does not comment, instead saying, "Mr. MacClean, there is a BOLO out for a man matching your description who assaulted an officer. Since you admit being at the scene of the assault, I am arresting you for leaving the scene of a crime, resisting arrest, and interfering with police actions. Detective Kavanaugh, cuff him. Take him to the interrogation room. Read him his rights."

Andy, who had never been accused of thinking fast on his feet, remains true to form, and silently raises his hands up. Kavanaugh cuffs him. Kavanaugh uses a key to unlock the Dutch door on their right and, not too ungently, pulls Andy through it. Andy thinks of sarcastically thanking Melody for all her help.

Melody, who could speak two hundred words a minute in several languages, and eloquently at that, Usain Bolts, "Handcream happened upon a kidnapping. My client, Telly Kind, confirms that. Sergeant Barrett, kidnapping requires a ransom request. How much are you demanding? We can pay! Telly, do you have five dollars? Ten? Sergeant Barret, would ten dollars cover it? That way we can leave."

Telly doesn't answer. She eyes a chance to run, but the two other officers still block the way out. They do not indicate any interest in clearing a way for her. Sergeant Barrett then says, "Vorsich, take this young lady and get her story."

"No way," says Melody. "You have no right to even touch her. She came here of her free will and is under no obligation to stay if she doesn't want to."

"Let me remind you, you are on police property," says Sergeant Barrett.

"And where in the Constitution does it say that citizens give up their constitutional rights by walking onto police property?" says Melody. "How else can a citizen report a crime? ESP? She's not under arrest, nor have you accused her of breaking any law. If you like, I can recite the penalties for making a false arrest."

Melody links arms with Telly and says, "Miss Telly, as your attorney, I would advise you to say not one word. The man who rescued you is now being charged with the crime that your stepfather committed. This is not a time to respond candidly to law enforcement."

Vorsich yanks Melody's arm from Telly's and escorts Telly back down the hall. Sergeant Barrett says, "Mrs. MacClean, prove to me you're an attorney. Mr. MacClean says you have Alzheimer's. Someone with Alzheimer's shouldn't be able to practice law."

"You'd be surprised how many of us there are," says Melody. "Melody Gurnah MacClean, at your service." She pulls out her business card and places it on the counter. "Miss Telly Kind has come to you for assistance, and instead you arrest the person who came to her defense. I am going to call our insurance broker who will bring in another attorney, and we will file so many briefs you can cancel your lifetime subscription to Fruit of the Loom."

"What?"

"I read it through your pressed white shirt. Inversely, of course. Nice to know Fruit of the Loom has branched out. Dementia doesn't affect eyesight. Look that up at your leisure, which you may soon have more than your share of. The charge of leaving the scene of a crime is based on what evidence? I believe all you have is hearsay filed by my client's stepfather, who is biased, per se." Melody opens her purse, swirls her hand inside it like she was incanting a spell, then turns it upside down on the counter and shakes it. "Why won't my cell phone crash to the floor? It always does that every time I am looking for something else. Ah, a note pad, even better."

CHAPTER TWENTY-ONE

APPLICANT HIGHWAYS

There never was a better time to drive through America without getting a speeding ticket. COVID-19 not only spared all but the most necessary employees the grind of commuting, it also decimated the ranks of law enforcement. Thousands of officers were furloughed for refusing to be vaccinated, and thousands more were suffering through the bug's towpath at home. Every police department was hit, including the D.C. police department.

The Chief of D.C. Police reports to the Capitol Police Board. The Board is made up of the two sergeants-at-arms of Congress and the Architect of the Capitol. Not exactly the gestapo for street peace. Never a more bureaucratic Cheshire Cat was ever created. So, when the number of able-bodied policemen failed to meet the minimum number to keep the Capitol safe, the Chief of D.C. Police did what every business does when cannon fodder runs scarce —lower its recruitment standards. The Capitol Police Board invisibly signed off on it.

Because of his Asian coloring and his build, Jeremy would be a shoo-in if he could pass the interview.

Psychologist Dr. Daniel Abel, Ph. D's handwritten note from before his interview with candidate Jeremy MacClean:

> *He is non-Caucasian, barrel chested, and broad. His biceps and pecs are so large, his shirts must be tailored. He is short, maybe 5'9, but his frame intimidates. His dress is casual but neat. He has a very youthful face. It doesn't show any stubble, but he overdoes the aftershave.*

Typed transcript of interview:

> ABEL: So, Jeremy, why do you want to become a police officer?
>
> MACCLEAN: I don't know. After my fourth speeding ticket landed me in court, I figured the way out of this shit would be to be the issuer instead of the issuee. Plus, would one cop give a ticket to another cop?
>
> ABEL: Anything else?
>
> MACCLEAN: Yeah, I like the uniforms.
>
> ABEL: When have you worn uniforms before?

MACCLEAN: In reform school. Kidding, I was a Cub Scout and a Boy Scout.

ABEL: Earn your eagle badge?

MACCLEAN: No, I didn't make it that far. I think we moved, or something.

ABEL: You have quite a build. Spend a lot of time at the gym?

MACCLEAN: No. I'm not a masochist.

ABEL: You don't work out?

MACCLEAN: I work out, but nothing that's painful. I strut, move the plates around, pump a few then go over and talk to someone. The girls love it.

ABEL: What about the guys?

MACCLEAN: I'm their competition. We talk, but mostly about technique. I listen, do a couple of curl or bench press reps, and move on.

ABEL: What is your major weakness?

MACCLEAN: I cannot hold onto money. Every dollar I get is soon in someone's else's hands. I can't explain it. I guess I'm too generous.

ABEL: Trying to impress others?

MACCLEAN: I do want people to be happy. Let me know I'm cool.

ABEL: What if they're breaking the law?

MACCLEAN: I'll break their heads. Kidding. Naw, that's different.

ABEL: What are you really good at?

MACCLEAN: I'm really quick at figuring out what people really want. It's a gift. Like I can tell you just want to get this over with. You think this is boring, below your intellectual level, but you're going to do the best you can regardless. You're conscientious. I'm also good at not letting people know I'm on to them. I go on acting like I believe everything they put out. At least, they don't act like they know I'm onto them. I would make a great spy. Maybe I could be a narc, though most on TV don't dress well.

ABEL: So, you can tell when someone is lying?

MACCLEAN: Oh yeah, I got that. I'm going to be a good cop. Out there, helping people, making sure they obey the law. You're all going to be proud of me. I'm going to be your officer poster child. You just wait. I'm going to make a difference.

ABEL: Have you ever taken the marshmallow test?

MACCLEAN: I don't really like marshmallows.

ABEL: I mean, could you forgo eating something you really liked if you were promised two of them later if you waited, say, fifteen minutes?

MACCLEAN: How do I know I'm even going to be alive in fifteen minutes? I mean, don't get me going on what I want next week when I can't even imagine what I want beyond the next thirty minutes, unless maybe I'm coming down from a fentanyl parachute ride.

ABEL: You've taken fentanyl?

MACCLEAN: Oh yes, fuck yes.

ABEL: You are an addict?

MACCLEAN: No, I just like it, but I rule, not it. Once or twice a week, that's all. I'm not going to turn into a head. See my teeth?

ABEL: Are you confusing fentanyl with methedrine?

MACCLEAN: Yeah, maybe, it's hard to keep track.

ABEL: Did you take fentanyl during training for help with the physical requirements?

MACCLEAN: Are you crazy? On fentanyl, I can't crack open a peanut. Cocaine works for that.

ABEL: You took cocaine?

MACCLEAN: Yeah, every time my brain said, "get me out of here," I snorted a line. Then I could focus on practically anything, no matter how trivial. Do you know how many handgun manufacturers there are in the US.?

ABEL: No, how many are there?

MACCLEAN: I don't really remember, but that's the kind of stuff they wanted us to repeat back to them. Not too compelling if you happen to be facing one. 'Officer, what was the manufacturer of the pistol that the defendant shot you with?' Mother help us, right?

ABEL: Why do you think you take fentanyl? Does its being illegal attract you?

MACCLEAN: Fentanyl relieves me of never realizing my dreams, you know.

ABEL: What dreams?

MACCLEAN: You know, I'm not really sure. They seem to dissolve like Alka Seltzer tablets in a glass of water when I try to pin them down.

ABEL: I see on your application you attended college. How'd you like that?

MACCLEAN: I'm smarter than they are. I left college early and saved my parents a fortune, if you don't count what the first two terms cost them.

ABEL: Were you ever on academic probation?

MACCLEAN: Yeah, practically from the first day.

ABEL: How did that happen?

MACCLEAN: I don't remember. I think it had something to do with attendance, but I'm not sure. It was a long time ago.

ABEL: Four years?

MACCLEAN: Yeah, way back in the stone age of my life. Gotta emphasize the future. The past is so boring and useless.

ABEL: Unless, back then, you put some savings in the bank, so now you can buy something you want.

MACCLEAN: I guess.

ABEL: Let me ask in a different way. What do you want out of life, Jeremy?

MACCLEAN: For people to look up to me. And give me stuff. That's how it's all supposed to work. So, as a cop, people look up to me, sort of. Then the receiving stuff comes.

ABEL: Why do you think that is the way it is supposed to work?

MACCLEAN: I mean, seriously, doesn't it? No one gives you stuff for nothing, right?

ABEL: As a police officer, you'll be paid a salary.

MACCLEAN: Enough to starve on, I hear. Kidding. Right now, I have to depend on my folks, and they aren't doing too well themselves.

ABEL: Does that humiliate you?

MACCLEAN: No, no, no. That's fun, coming up with reasons why I am broke. Makes me feel like a famous fiction writer. From 'my dog ate my homework' to, I dunno, like 'I tried a new green energy service, and it jacked my electric rates through the roof, and I can't cancel for six months.' Stuff like that."

ABEL: Doesn't fentanyl break your budget?

MACCLEAN: Budget? I'm not a business. I don't have a budget. I just spend what I get. Besides, it's cheap. Ten bucks tops. A good bottle of wine costs five times that, you know.

ABEL: Where do you want to be in, say, five years? Married, children, making sergeant?

MACCLEAN: No, no, and double no.

ABEL: So, where?

MACCLEAN: I don't know, on a beach—no, I don't really like beaches. In a casino, playing poker, betting like crazy, and winning enough to pay all my debts.

ABEL: Why would you want that?

MACCLEAN: Doesn't everyone? Being in the flow, letting everything come to you, raising your pinky and a margarita arrives, glamorous women close by, watching you in adoration.

ABEL: So, you want to be adored

MACCLEAN: Yeah, I want to be an Idol, like on TV. Everybody calling out my name, cheering me on. 'You're fired.' Haha.

ABEL: How do you expect that to happen, I mean, living in a casino with beautiful women all around you?

MACCLEAN: I'm working on it. I'm going to be a good cop, and someday, things will happen. And I want to be tough. I mean the kind of toughness that's immune from feeling bad for what I've done. Like Officer Branhammer, he spoke at my school. He arrested and testified against this guy, got him sent to prison for life, but knew he didn't do it.

ABEL: You talked to Branhammer?

MACCLEAN: Yeah, after the talk was over, I asked him how it felt. He said, 'no worries, the guy had to be guilty of something.'

ABEL: What does moral mean, Jeremy?

MACCLEAN: Is that the color of a horse, maybe?

ABEL: No, it means being ethical. Fair, if you will.

MACCLEAN: I guess obeying the law if others are watching. Hey, you got the time?

ABEL: Actually, we are nearly out of time.

MACCLEAN: What I was thinking...

There is no indication that anyone ever reviewed the transcript. Dr. Abel's notes are not signed. There is no evidence that Dr. Abel passed on concerns to anyone or had any. The box was checked on Jeremy MacClean's application that he had completed his interview.

CHAPTER TWENTY-TWO

TIRE MARKS

Detective Kavanaugh slaps Andy across the face with a pair of leather gloves. Cheek bones have little fat to buffer assaults, and the face is overengineered with nerves. The pain activates Andy's feral defense mechanism, and he lurches at the detective before the handcuffs, chained through a hole in the table and anchored to the floor, throw him off balance and make him crumble over the table like a string toy figure when its tension is released. He is now red-faced, as much for forgetting the manacles as forgetting Melody's admonition not to fight. He is such a dunce.

"You got that bruise on your cheek when you fell, right?"

This is beyond bullying.

"Remember?"

Andy thinks of what Melody would say and asks, "Is this being videotaped?"

"No, consider it a holiday gift. So, remember? If so, no more slapping maybe. No promises though."

"What crime am I being convicted of?" Andy asks.

"You're a big guy," says Kavanaugh. "I could take those handcuffs off, and we could settle this."

"Settle what? I haven't done nothing. I came here to tell you what I saw, that's all."

Andy questions where his fortitude is coming from. Callus peels off, an un-worded recognition of the legions of people he had blamed for being in this very situation. He had always assured himself they deserved it. Now he sees what he might have learned if he read the entire article instead of stopping at the headline. He rubs this recognition against his age-old will to refuse doing whatever he's forced to. A will honed true by a razor strop.

"I'll remember you slapped me with your gloves," says Andy. "You'll remember it too. Nothing can change our memories of what actually happened."

This time with the back of his hand, Kavanaugh slaps Andy across an ear. It feels like being whipped with ball bearings. Flashing in front of Andy is his mother's menacing grin with her tiny blonde whiskers. She had been very pretty. Everyone said so. The beautiful and the uniformed get away with everything. That's just the way it is. He's in pain again, another in a long, seldom uninterrupted streak. He wonders how Melody is making out. He figures she's dealing. They'd better not lay a hand on her. But what can he do?

After a full ten minutes of silence, Kavanaugh asks, "How do you know Telly Kind?"

"Met her in the parking lot."

"When?"

"Today."

"Was she selling drugs? Were you?"

"Drugs?" says Andy. "She was being carjacked. I tried to help her."

"Where do you live, Mr. MacClean?"

"76 Benjamin Franklin Court, Elkton, Maryland."

"Where did this carjacking take place?"

"Corner of Jules and Kale, Elkton."

"Why did you interfere with a lawful arrest?"

"Look, I saw this guy grab this girl," says Andy. "He throws her against the side of a van, grabs her keys, and then throws her into the van. What's a guy supposed to do? Let him drive away with her?"

"You didn't think that you might be interfering with a lawful arrest?"

"I did not," says Andy. "He never said he was police."

"Why do you think that would've made a difference?"

"Huh?"

"Why didn't you just call 911?"

"I didn't have my cell with me."

"Pretty negligent," says Detective Kavanaugh, "don't you think?"

"Yes sir, I do."

"So, while you were driving here," asks Detective Kavanaugh, "did you happen to talk about what happened with the other people in your car?"

"No."

"That seems odd," says Kavanaugh. "What else would you have talked about? Politics? You said you had never seen the girl before."

"On advice of counsel."

"You called an attorney?"

"My wife is one."

"She a lawyer?"

"What I just said," says Andy.

Kavanaugh stops the interrogation and starts pacing around Andy. His face reddens, and white foam appears on the corners of his lips. He's dehydrated, needs something to drink. Andy wonders if he should tell the detective that. Andy calms. He doesn't have to take care of anyone. He thinks, "These officers are children. No wonder we need Trump back in the presidency. He'll clean this mess up." Andy hadn't been aware how bad everything had gone.

His exhilaration of figuring this out has an edge. He's on the wrong side of law and order. It's like standing at a craps table, hearing all the adrenaline-inducing chatter of the croupier calling out the winning throw, but he can't remember which number his chips ride on.

"Look, Detective Kavanaugh," says Andy, "I just want to get out of here in time to attend the Stop the Steal Rally. We have to save this country. You should be for that, right?"

"Of course, we all are," Kavanaugh says as he slowly moves away from the table and stands by the door.

"I don't know what to do. I'm not hurting anyone," Andy says and recognizes that he's copying what Telly had said to him. "You have to listen to me. What am I being accused of? You're a cop, what would you have done if you saw what I did?" Now Andy feels that he's mimicking Melody. Is he just a copycat? She had told him he needed to nurture more original thoughts. Andy didn't think he ever had one. Then Andy says, "If there's a security camera outside that building, it'll confirm what I've been telling you."

"We've checked," says Kavanaugh. "The cameras are for immediate security. They have no film capability."

"Just let Melody and me go home. We aren't causing any trouble."

"And the girl?"

"You're not going to hit her, are you?" says Andy. "She's just a kid, and not a terribly bright one at that."

"So, you want to help us?"

"Of course I do. I'm a law-and-order guy, been all my life. You won't see me destroying public property to make a statement."

Kavanaugh leaves.

Andy waits, rubs his ear, thinks maybe he said something right for a change.

Kavanaugh walks in. He's relaxed now. He has had something to drink.

Andy is thirsty. He smells fresh toner.

Kavanaugh sits down and presses some bright white papers flat down on the table. Then he sighs like he just wanted to be done with all this, with Andy. Andy feels better. "Since," says Kavanaugh, "as you said, we are on the same side, sign this waiver, and you can go home."

Andy looks the papers over. He sees that it's in legalese, as certain parts are in larger and bolder print, just the way the elites require everything these days. If it's not in bold print, the signer may have missed it. What a crock. If you don't know what it says, why'd you sign it in the first place?

Kavanaugh pulls a pen from his shirt pocket and lightly tosses it on the papers as Andy tries to make them out. He sees words about inspections and phone and bank records. Andy remembers the bank and the Watanabes. Then, Kavanaugh reaches over and points to where Andy is to sign. It has one of those yellow Post-its with an arrow pointing to the line.

"What does this do?" asks Andy.

"Corroborates your story."

"How does it do that?"

"Lets us inspect your home, look at your computers and mail. The usual stuff. You don't have anything to hide, right? You want to go home, right?"

Andy balls his hands up into fists and tightens his lips. Andy understands, sign this or miss the rally and see a lot more of Detective Kavanaugh. Andy stares at Kavanaugh's face, trying to remember every crease and wrinkle, like he's examining how a knothole would change the wood's grain deep ahead. He takes a picture of Kavanaugh's face in his head, to be held there the rest of his life, and says, "I need to talk this over with my attorney."

He steals himself.

SLAP.

The whole country is corrupt.

CHAPTER TWENTY-THREE

ROADKILL

Lutz does not know who his co-conspirators are and, as far as he knows, has never met them. That safeguard alone convinces him that the STOPTHECHEAT organization knows what they're doing. STOPTHECHEAT, with his help, is going to take over the reins of this sadly misdirected country. All he has to do is follow their instructions.

When QuoBadass queried in the STOPTHECHEAT darknet chat room about needing a good-sized covered truck, Buffalo Johnniebread texted he had an RV that might meet their needs. Buffalo Johnniebread AKA Sheriff Schuyler of Lackawanna, New York, had been personally upbraided by an alderman just the week before for not clearing out the impound yard. Inadequately secured by a simple chain link fence, the yard overflowed with abandoned motor vehicles and Army handoffs from the Persian Gulf War. One piece of equipment taking up a mountain of space was a fifty-foot RV. The RV was being held as evidence to assist a DA in locking up a small-time drug lord. Unfortunately, at least from the DA's conviction rate point of view, the drug lord had died three days before trial from an overdose of lead.

The RV had operated as a drug dispensary. Customers would insert cash in the drive-in teller drawer and receive the equivalent exchange rate of the dope of their choosing. It's powered by twin Hummer electric motors. Its walls and roof have been reinforced with inch-thick stainless steel. Its windshield and tires are bullet-proof.

Within a few days of BuffaloJohnniebread's reply, a non-profit was created for distributing syringes to strung-out youth. The non-profit bought the RV from Lackawanna for five hundred dollars, and so the logistics began to fill it with weaponry on the way to the Capitol.

When Lutz received the email that he was to drive the RV the final leg to the Capitol on January 6, he tingled. He imagined the selfie. He would be in the dragon's mouth for sure, and as sure would not be omitted when the spoils were meted out.

A short time later, Lutz found in his mailbox a very lightweight football-sized cardboard box. It was from STOPTHECHEAT but had no postage. In bubble wrap were a microchip and a scanner. The instructions explained how to insert the microchip in his hand and how it would self-destruct if he failed to keep it at ninety-eight degrees Fahrenheit within twenty-four hours of receipt. Once the RV arrived in position, the microchip would tell Lutz its location. The instructions also said that the vehicle's driver's door lock had to be picked and that the cargo doors could only be opened with a five-digit passcode. The passcode for the keypad would be delivered in person once the RV was at the Capitol.

Lutz has trypanophobia, fear of needles. But that fear did not deter him from using others. Since his stepdaughter was a nurse-to-be, he had her insert the microchip in her own hand. Why not? All she had to do was stay alive until January 6. That shouldn't be too difficult an ask.

CHAPTER TWENTY-FOUR

HOMELESS POTHOLE

D.C. Training Officer Branhammer figures that the creators of this dark web platform usher his proselytes into a series of lifetime psychological studies. They bill universities and mercilessly print research papers. He doesn't believe anyone actually gets killed. The killing bait is hype to encourage trust and urgency, like asking a potential customer to retrieve your wallet filled with cash from your car because you have to take this call right now. Branhammer is paid one hundred dollars if he can keep the prospect on the line for ten straight minutes and two grand if he can flip him to the next level. Branhammer has three kids and no savings for their college tuition. The creators of the platform promise that filing a 1099 will not be required.

"Yeah, that school propaganda shit, it's mostly communist, Amy," says Branhammer over live chat. "The teachers, our parents, everybody tells us we need to work hard. Meanwhile, the elite stretch out on their designer bean bags, sipping tasteless white wines while scoring endless blowjobs. All I ever got out of school was a sore butt. What did you get out of it, Amy?"

"How long are you going to keep calling me Amy? I don't like it. My name is Jeremy MacClean. Being called names is not what I bargained for."

"Your code name is Amy until you matriculate," says Branhammer. "We use a female name to dig a little, but I like your spunk. I can see that you have real potential. We need men like you. What did you get out of school?"

"Mrs. Hopkins!" says Jeremy. "She got high on dissecting frogs, I swear. Preferred the aroma of formaldehyde to a cinnamon latte. But she was gorge. I sooo wanted her."

"What did she teach you?"

"Nothing. I didn't listen, just jugged and jived for a camel shot. She didn't seem to notice. Wore hot blouses, slinky skirts. Knew she did. Now that I think about it, she probably did it to distract us and keep us from her screwing up her lesson plans. Funny, I didn't figure that out until just now. I'm not too brilliant, am I?"

"How about hot male teachers?" asks Branhammer.

There is a long pause in the conversation.

"Just checking, Amy," Branhammer says. "Any charismatic male teachers?"

"Mr. Krein. Acted so sincere, so concerned about our future, but he was the first teacher out the door and into the parking lot every day."

"Maybe he had a habit. Mrs. Hopkins maybe?"

"They said his son had Down's, so…" Jeremy says.

"Any girls you were interested in?"

"All of the pretty ones, really. Still am, sorta, though I never really had a heart-to-heart talk with any of them. After the first couple of sentences, they would hand me a reason they had to be going. I talk too fast when I'm nervous. You know what it's like when you want so much to impress someone and always do the opposite? After high school graduation, they flew away like geese fly to Florida in the winter."

"Never to be seen again," says Branhammer.

"No, I've seen a few at stores and church services during holidays."

"Get a phone number?"

"No," says Jeremy. "They're really part of a different crowd now. Untouchable. We don't even nod in recognition. Of course, they might give me more respect if I'm wearing a police uniform."

"They'll be respecting you now, won't they?" says Branhammer. "Maybe even be a little afraid of you."

"Nothing wrong with that. I am now licensed to kill."

"You dedicate yourself to protect them, put your life on the line, and they thank you by shutting you out, huh?"

"Sometimes I just want to…"

"Want to kill them?" asks Branhammer.

"Yeah, I do. Fantasize about it. Helps me go to sleep at night."

"Ever kill a person?"

"Almost, once. Well, not really," says Jeremy. "Have you?"

"True."

"How'd you do it?"

"I went poking through a house with the barrel of my jammin jennie and she went off."

"Wow."

"Killed three."

"Who were they?" asks Jeremy.

There's a break in the link, and they have to reconnect before Branhammer says, "It didn't matter. In Iraq, our job was to kill or be killed until we got sent home, preferably not in a box. Capeesh? There's always going to be the winners and the losers. The point is to be on the side of the winners, Amy. If you understand one thing, understand that."

"What's it like, killing someone, I mean?"

"Fills you up," says Branhammer. "Like slowly chugging a gallon of Bud. You start to glow. You think, *these guys're gone, forever, and I can crow about it.*"

"Did it make the papers?"

"It was in Iraq, Amy," says Branhammer. "Killing practice."

"You hear those reports about trials for murder and stuff."

"Amy, that's window dressing for the whistleblowers," says Branhammer. "Hear of anyone getting convicted?"

"No."

"Of course not. Some people just need to die, and some of us are appointed to do the job. The talk of punishing errant soldiery is window dressing just to keep the pacifists quiet."

"So, appoint me. I'm ready. Trust me."

"So, you're in?" asks Branhammer.

"That's why I'm here, but I feel like I'm wasting my time. And being called a girl's name."

"You have to prove yourself first, prove that you're not a plant" says Branhammer. "Unless you have money?"

"Couple of grand, maybe."

"So, you're going to have to kill someone," says Branhammer.

"Anybody in particular?"

"Slurpee Dwayne for starters."

"Your cooker?"

"Yeah," says Jeremy. "I owe him a bunch, can't keep track of it. He keeps needling me."

"You aren't in, you're loco, Amy."

"What?"

"Dwayne is bodyguarded up," says Branhammer. "You'd be signing your death warrant and probably starting a mass shooting. A mass shooting is defined as three or more dead. Mass shootings make headlines and headlines start investigations..."

"What weapon you gonna use?" asks Branhammer in another chat.

"My AK. I want to see him bleed."

"Too much collateral damage," says Branhammer. "Plus, a rifle would be spotted before you could aim. We need stealth here. In and goodbye."

"My Glock then."

"Your service weapon?"

"Yeah."

"Amy, that can be traced," says Branhammer. "You don't have a gun of your own?"

"I have a Cobra Arms Freedom."

"Does it work?"

"Yeah," says Jeremy, "I've test-fired it at the range."

"Is it registered?"

"No."

"Is it traceable?"

"I don't know."

"So, file down the serial number," says Branhammer.

"Okay."

"You'll be leaving it at the scene."

"That's a lot of dough to throw away."

"How much is your life worth?"

"Gotcha."

"What would you wear?" asks Branhammer.

"My high school leather jacket and Tread Bares, just in case I have to run for it."

"Wear something you've never been seen wearing before. You'll be burning them the moment you're free of the scene."

"Why not wear my faves if I'm going to burn them anyway?" asks Jeremy.

"Because some dumb relative, or friend, or cop is going to ask you where your faves are, and they might wonder why you made up such a lame excuse," says Branhammer. "And because some punk might identify the killer by what he's seen you in before!"

"Wow, you've thought this out."

"Invisibility is second nature to us. So, you don't like me calling you Amy?"

"I don't."

"How do you get me to stop calling you Amy?" asks Branhammer.

"Kill somebody?" asks Jeremy.

"Right, and none of us will ever call you that again."

"So, who am I supposed to kill, if I can't kill Dwayne?" asks Jeremy. "Some stupid tourist at the Capitol?"

"Yes and no," says Branhammer. "A homeless. You'll wear gloves and leave your weapon with the corpse so the police can draw the conclusion it was suicide, as the Captains are so antsy to do. They get a bonus for every closed file, and suicides are the easiest to close."

"I get that," says Jeremy. "The captains want glory and an endless supply of Pepto-Bismo. I'm ready. We can leave right now. I'll kill. I'll kill anyone. Just point him out."

"Where are you going to aim?"

"Why would I care?"

"It's important," says Branhammer.

"It's just some random guy."

"You want it to look like a suicide or an accident," says Branhammer. "So, get as close as you can to them and aim for the head. The head. Temple is best. Tomorrow, meet Officer Joe at Twelfth and Rickter at 4 a.m."

"Where the homeless stake out?"

"Exactly."

"That's pretty early in the morning," says Jeremy. And, after a slight pause, "I'm going to plug a homeless guy?"

"Or gal, depending on which is handy."

"That's kinda heartless."

"Killing is cruel, Amy," says Branhammer.

"I got it, okay. Let's do it."

Branhammer says, "By the way…"

"What?"

"Are you keeping up with the STOPTHECHEAT website?"

"I thought it was STOPTHESTEAL?" says Jeremy.

"That's mostly fake," says Branhammer. "It's been created to funnel money into Trump's defense fund. Sign up for STOPTHECHEAT. You'll get an earful."

"Okay?"

"You might be useful."

"You're confusing me," says Jeremy. "I thought this was going to make me useful?"

"Never risk a lot for a little. Rule number one."

"What's rule number two?"

"Never question your leader."

"Why?"

"So much for remembering the second rule. This is real, Amy, not a simulation. Grow up or you die. What's your new code name going to be? Thought that out yet, Amy?"

"Killer."

"Okay. We already have three Killers, but another wouldn't hurt. Maybe we'll start a band, The Four Killers."

An hour before dusk. two men drop out of an unmarked police unit, one wearing a loaded backpack. They separate and slowly walk down opposite sides of K Street. They cross Fourteenth Street Northwest and then over to the JFK overpass, where a homeless encampment stretches out for blocks. Officer Joe, the one without

the backpack, walks along the encampment side. About a quarter of the way up the block, he casually walks back to the sidewalk on the other side of the street. He asks the other man, "Gloves on?"
Jeremy shows blue hands.
"Your blood, Amy."
"Call me Killer."
"Later, maybe."
"It's so dark. Which tent again?" asks Jeremy.
"Either, Fancypants," whispers Officer Joe, but before he walks away, he puts his face in Jeremy's, "If you fuck up or run…" and zips down his jacket revealing a Beretta in his belt then walks back from where they came.

The tent is constructed of a series of blankets duct-taped together, supported by foraged limbs from a tree in nearby Samuel Gompers Park. Jeremy's instructions were to proceed in the opposite direction from where he had come after the killing. But to do that, he had to kill. Jeremy starts hyperventilating but soon says to himself, "What the fuck, everyone's got to die sometime." He throws the tent's flap open and ducks inside.

A homeless encampment is never quiet. There is always at least one intervention in midcourse. Three shots disturb the early morning. An intervention of a different kind is intuited, and all the others are suspended until further notice.

Jeremy rushes out of the tent, away from its former resident, and walks in the direction he was told to before his baptism. His gait is shaky but consistent. He doesn't feel filled up one bit.

He feels empty.

By the time his normal gait returns, a Ford sedan of indiscriminate vintage approaches. The passenger window rolls down, a new voice says, "Weapon?"

Jeremy says, "I dropped it like I was told."

"Gloves?"

Jeremy shows the man his blue gloves are still on.

"Good. Roll the gloves into a ball and put them into this bag." The exchange accomplished, the driver motions for Jeremy to get in the back seat. Jeremy does. There are no other passengers.

"Hi, I'm Killer," says Jeremy. The driver doesn't reply. "I just scored my first kill." Hearing himself say it, Jeremy feels like the next move is for someone to put handcuffs on him or tell him he'd just killed an FBI informant working undercover. That's what happened in a lot of thrillers he'd read. He's planning to bolt.

Instead, the nameless driver takes him to an open barrel fire, hands him the bag with his gloves, orders him out, and drives off. As it's near freezing outside, the barrel fire beckons Jeremy. A man dressed all in black, including welding gloves, stirs the fire with a metal poker. As he raises the poker up, Jeremy can see its end is cherry red.

"Welcome, Jeremy," says the man. "My name is inconsequential. Today was the most important day of your life. It has been forever in coming, no?"

Jeremy thinks not. He visualizes the older woman's face disappearing when he closed his eyes as he fired into it and says, "Absolutely."

"Everything in, the bag first," says the inconsequential man stirring the barrel. Jeremy does as instructed, leaving his underwear on.

HOMELESS POTHOLE

"Don't stop there," says the inconsequential man. Jeremy is naked. He pulls out then starts donning the clothes that were in his backpack. "You can keep the backpack, but don't put on your jacket yet."

As Jeremy dresses, the inconsequential man stirs. Now and then, he squirts in a few ounces of lighter fluid. "I just killed someone," Jeremy says.

The inconsequential man stirs the pot then takes a phone call. Then he turns to Jeremy and says, "So you did. Show me your forearm, Jeremy. Please."

Jeremy rolls up the sleeve on his left arm, and in a blink, the inconsequential man brands Jeremy's forearm with the poker. "Now, you are us."

Jeremy freezes. He thinks being arrested would have been better. But the intense pain fades from ten to five to three after a few seconds.

"It will sting for a while, no worries," says the poker man. He douses Jeremy's forearm with a liquid. "You want the scar so every one of us knows." The scar is in the shape of three Ls for LuLuxLan.

Catching his breath, Jeremy says, "Why not a tattoo?"

"Tattoos are for attention seekers," says the poker man. "We do not seek attention. We seek nothing. We are. Let the sun heal your arm. Wash it only if it gets dirty. Your ride is here."

Jeremy sees a different Ford sedan pull up to where he had been dropped off. A shaken Jeremey keeps his left shirt sleeve rolled up and walks to the car, carrying his jacket in his other arm. This time, the driver gets out of the car and runs around it to open the front passenger door. Puts his hand out. Jeremy shakes hands. It's a tight clasp but not long. The driver says, "So, Jeremy, you are christened Killer Four, welcome to the brotherhood. Where do you want to go?"

"I'm hungry," says Jeremy. The driver takes Jeremy to a McDonalds. McDonalds opens early.

CHAPTER TWENTY-FIVE

FIRST INVENTION WAS THE TRAIL

In a room identical to the one Andy sits in, Detective Vorsicht asks, "Your Christian name, please?"

"What's a Christian name?" asks Telly.

"You've never been told the story of Jesus?"

"Jesus Christ?" asks Telly.

"Yes, of course, Jesus Christ, is there another Christ?"

"Are Jesus Christ and Christian the same thing?" asks Telly. "They don't sound alike."

"Okay, let's try this," says Detective Vorsicht. "What do your parents call you?"

"Which parents?"

"How many do you have?"

Telly counts on her fingers and tells him, "Four."

Vorsicht wipes both of his cheeks with his fingertips, smiles, then asks, "What name does Chief Lutz Delorean call you?"

"Chief calls me Miss Plump Plump, Miss Panty Liner, Miss True Ant, Miss Hangry, Miss…"

"His wife then? Your mother, maybe, what does she call you?"

"She doesn't."

"What does she do, use hand signals?"

"If she's using hand signals, that may be why I can't hear her."

Vorsicht, who had been standing all this time, decides he needs to sit down and does. A big man, Vorsicht has no difficulty sliding a chair over from the table in the middle of the room so he can face Telly. He looks directly away from Telly then directly at her, eye to eye, and asks, "You don't live with your mom?"

After a long pause, Telly says, "No. I don't live with my mom."

"Is she alive?"

"I don't know," says Telly.

"Your last name is Delorean?"

"My last name is Kind."

"Telly Kind is your name?"

"Yes."

"What do your schoolteachers call you?" asks Detective Vorsicht.

"Telly."

"Is that your nickname or your real name?"

"What is an unreal name?"

"A nickname, an alias, a pen name. Perhaps you're too young to understand?"

"If I'm too young, why ask me? My name is Telly. What is your name?"

"Detective Vorsicht."

"You have two names like me. Any chance you can give me something to eat? I'm not feeling so well. I always feel bad when I'm hungry."

Telly stands up abruptly and hurls the remnants of Andy's ham and cheese sandwich over Detective Vorsicht. He jerks up, cursing.

As Detective Vorsicht is slapping Telly's lunch off his slick ironed and pleated slacks, Telly says, "Those are bad words, Detective. Bad Words. You shouldn't say them! Chief said I should not talk to anyone who uses those words."

Detective Vorsicht excuses himself to clean up. When she's alone, Telly asks herself, "Why didn't he just ask to see my driver's license?" She's worried. Melody had told her not to say one word. Did her name count? Maybe Melody was being figurative, that's what adults call it when they don't mean what they say.

Vorsicht returns with a janitor, who sweeps up the mess and leaves without saying a word. Telly tells Vorsicht, "I need something to eat. I faint without food. I just lost my lunch."

Vorsicht waits for her to laugh at the joke. When she doesn't, he says, "Please make this day go away."

"I don't know how to make days go away, Detective Vorsicht. If you want to tell me how to do that, I am willing to learn. But food first, please. Milkshake?"

"So, how long have you known Chief Delorean?" asks Detective Vorsicht.

"Since I was three."

After a slight pause, "Where do you live now?"

"Black's Shelter for Abused Women."
"Prefer not to be with people of your own kind?"
Silence.
He adds, "Aren't there homes for abused white women?"
"The home is owned by Bernadette Black."
"Okay, what's the address?"
"I don't know."
"How are you going to get back there?"
"GPS."
"You have that with you right now?"
"No."
"Where is it?"
"In my van."
Detective Vorsicht is slowly coming to his senses, feeling his way into Telly's mind.
"Why were you at Jules Corner?"
"Work."
"Tell me what happened today."
She does.
"How do you know Mr. MacClean?" asks Detective Vorsicht.
"He saved me."
"You never met Mr. MacClean before?"
"No."
"Virtually?"
"No."
"Have you met Mrs. MacClean before?"
"No. She comes with him, sort of his guide dog. By the way, do you have any food for me? I don't usually go this long without

eating. Everyone I have seen here looks well fed, as do you. Well-fed prisoners make cooperative witnesses."

"Were you hurt?"

She shows him her bruised right temple where Chief Delorean pushed her against the car door window and her blistered fingers where he yanked her keys away.

"Did you talk about this with Mr. and Mrs. MacClean while he drove you here?"

Telly starts to say she drove then pauses. Melody was right. The police are not on her side. She pauses. Feels her scalp, rubs her purple fingers, and says, "I feel that you are trying to trick me. I want to see a lawyer." For the second time today, she feels safe. MacClean safe.

"You don't trust me?"

"Affirmative and even virtually." She giggles.

"Why?"

"That was a leading question," says Telly. "They taught us that in school. When did you stop beating your wife Detective Vorsicht?"

Vorsicht shows his disappointment by walking slowly around the table twice without saying a word. His cell vibrates. He puts it to his ear. Listens without speaking then says, "Miss Kind, come with me."

"It's for food, right? That way I might talk! If I had something to eat, maybe I wouldn't need an attorney. Chicken McNuggets, maybe?"

CHAPTER TWENTY-SIX

LABYRINTH UNFURLED

While writing on her notepad, Melody says to Sergeant Barrett, "I want to see your liability insurance limits. Under Title 18, you are required to disclose them upon demand by the plaintiff. Here is the demand." She tears a sheet out of the notepad and puts it in the exchange drawer.

Sergeant Barrett opens the exchange drawer and reads the note. She knocks on the Dutch door to her left, and a man's head pokes in through the upper half of the door. "Detective Alioto, check out Mrs. MacClean's law license." Alioto takes Melody's business card and crisply extracts head and hand before the door closes on them, as if both are part of a cuckoo clock.

Sergeant Barrett parries, "I'll present this to our attorney for a response. This may take some time. You should go home—oh, I forgot, you don't drive, right?"

"Your limits had better be at least ten mil," says Melody. "By the way, all police have alternate careers ready when they get discharged for mishandling arrests. What's yours, serving warrants on flooded-out pets? Is your personal insurance policy current? Do you have an umbrella? Either way, you should seek legal counsel. Fly there now. We could use a new car, and this will buy us a Cadillac, maybe a Blackwing. I hear Blackwings fly."

"I will not listen to threats," says Sergeant Barrett.

"Applause, but that makes no sense, as you just did. How else would you perceive it as one? Besides, it's only a threat if you're, indeed, falsely imprisoning someone. So, I'll take your attempt at negotiation as an admittance of guilt. Release Handcream and this young girl immediately! Or consequences grave will follow."

Alioto opens the top half of the Dutch door and with a grimace says, "She's licensed. No restrictions."

Sergeant Barrett, a fifteen-year veteran on the force, fifth-senses that quicksand lies underfoot. She's short staffed. Six patrolmen furloughed for refusing COVID-19 vaccinations.

She examines Melody. Her hair resembles the bride of Frankenstein, showing off a few bright patches of pink scalp. Her clothes match the loose blacks women wear to camouflage girth, but her eyes are as clear as a baseball player twirling his bat over his head before sending a fastball into the bleachers. This woman had Alzheimer's, all right, and few disabilities are more dangerous.

Sergeant Barrett had always cottoned Elkton, the town that held the last KKK meeting in Maryland, just a few miles southwest of here. She remembers seeing the pictures of the proud men with their white robes and insignias. They believed in something. Now, nobody believes in anything but getting ahead. And letting this get out of hand would not get her ahead. Time to draw a Get Out of Jail card. She presses a button on her console. Let it be.

First rule of advancement: know when you are in over your head. And she is drowning.

"There is the matter of jurisdiction," continues Melody. "You did, indeed, hear that we are residents of Maryland, right? We have not been charged with any crimes committed in Delaware, right? You have not received any extradition papers filed from Maryland, which means you have no authority here. There is another crime here which is being ignored AKA theft. Title Eleven, chapter five, multiple subchapters, 'being deprived of rightful possession of property thereof,' etcetera. Chief Delorean has taken Telly's purse and car. Stealing something worth more than five hundred dollars is a felony."

Sergeant Barrett is transfixed. This woman is going on and on like the ever-ready battery bunny and speaking authentic-sounding nonsense that resonates with her police training, like a seal pup in search of a life-saving surrogate tit when its own mother is dead.

"The van may only be worth the cost of a tow after the collision, but I believe Telly's cell phone, once I identify its manufacturer, may exceed the five-hundred-dollar threshold. Then, there is the value of the proprietary data contained therein, and in Title Six, chapter five, recently amended, it's an automatic felony to expose someone to identity theft. Her data could be worth millions. Speaking of phones, I just found mine."

Melody brandishes her smart phone out in front of Sergeant Barrett as if it were a lightsaber and yells into it, "I'm coming Handcream!"

"I can never remember how to turn this damn thing on. Did you just hear Handcream scream? I have very good hearing, you know. Or are your fellow officers beating someone else up? Floyd Boy George, maybe? Isn't he on tour?

"Okay, I got it turned on, but before I phone our insurance agent, I am calling Nick Heminger. He's an editor at the Washington Post. Do I have a story for him! The Post loves stories about police snafus. Well, its readers do. Nick owes me a favor, and now he'll owe me another one when this hits the front page. You got any children? They're going to love reading this. I'm a big promoter of reading. Give me your home address, and I'll make sure they get a copy if they don't subscribe to the Post. I hear some children don't."

Nick answers, and Melody says, "Hi, Nick, this is Melody, thanks for calling. Breaking news here, actually pre-breaking. Wow, you're looking buff."

"How'd you know I was on my way back from the beach?" says Nick. "They say this is the best time of year to get a windburn tan."

"But I like your fluorescent lilac skin color. It goes so well with your droopy eyelids and lesioned cheeks. By the way, windburn is a myth. Anyway, my husband caught the police chief of Damascus red-handed trying to kidnap a young woman. Shame on him, right? The Newport police are trying to cover it all up by arresting my husband and demanding ten million in ransom. Would you talk to the desk sergeant for me? Her name is Sergeant Barrett, B-A double R, E, double T, as in what women wear in their hair but spelled without the final E. While you're talking to her, I'll keep busy counting my husband's screams. I've heard three whelps so far. He has a very low threshold for pain."

Melody sticks the cell phone in the pass-through drawer. Sergeant Barrett doesn't move to slide the drawer to get the phone.

She starts to say something before raising her head to see a figure has lined up close behind Melody. He's dressed like he just alighted from a yacht, light blue cap, poplin short sleeve shirt, white pants, and Navy blue deck shoes.

The desk sergeant's Nordic visage, which matches the white wall behind her, pinkens. She says to the man in yacht wear, "Mayor Rrrroberts, glad you could come."

Mayor Roberts doesn't say anything but, with an exaggerated wink, indicates he's listening.

"The Post is on the line," says Sergeant Barrett. "Should I take this call?"

"That's like being told 'I'll be right with you,' when you know it means the opposite," says Melody. Melody then immediately spins around and says, "Hi, Mayor Roberts, how goes the ice fishing?"

Now facing Melody, Mayor Roberts looks over Melody's head and nods to the Sergeant.

With her eyes never leaving the mayor's, Sergeant Barrett pulls back the pass-through drawer, takes out the phone, puts it to her ear, and identifies herself.

Two men in business suits line up behind the mayor. One is short and bald, and he immediately starts whispering out the side of his mouth in the mayor's ear. The man wears that smile which says, "We're this close to stepping in doo-doo big time, Big Daddy."

"Mayor Roberts," says Melody. "When Sergeant Barrett is done using my phone, you might want to look at the pics I took before we left our home today. They are of my husband. Not a mark on him. And don't worry if you accidentally delete them. They have been posted and time-stamped on Facebook, in the cloud, on clockwork orange, blue, and green."

Mayor Roberts smiles at Melody then flicks his hand at the lone uniform left blocking anyone from leaving the hall. He departs, hastily so.

Sergeant Barrett is talking on the phone to Nick in full-blown human resource speak. "I see…We didn't know…Yes, I understand…I think we have the same interests here…Yes, I see the photos on the screen…I'm not sure we have anything here that you want, but yes, you can send a reporter…If you wish…Can you give me ten minutes to…Mrs. MacClean's satisfaction…I'll call you…Thank you for your professional courtesy."

The mayor nods then shakes his head at Sergeant Barrett. She escapes out the Dutch door to her left. No one takes her place. The hallway, though, is getting crowded. Andy and Detective Kavanaugh walk toward them. Andy is growing a shiner and alternates rubbing it and his now unhandcuffed but chafed wrists. When Kavanaugh reaches the mayor and his entourage, he deposits Andy, says, "Mayor," and leaves the way he came. Mayor Roberts deftly pushes the back of the middle of his index finger onto Andy's bruised cheek and says, "You okay, Mr. MacClean?"

Andy looks over at Melody. She scrunches up her lip but nods. Andy answers, "Peachy."

"Good," says Mayor Roberts. "Now go home."

"Yes sir," says Andy.

"We can't leave without the girl," demands Melody.

As if on cue, Telly and Vorsicht join them. Vorsicht keys in a passcode on the Dutch door across from the receiving window and leaves.

"My phone?" asks Melody.

The mayor takes it out of his vest pocket and hands it to Andy.

"How'd you do that?" asks Melody.

"Mr. MacClean," says Mayor Roberts, "as only Telly Kind has a valid driver's license, make sure she's behind the wheel when you leave, or you'll be ticketed for driving without a license before you are a block away. Fair Notice."

As all three walk out of the station Melody says, "Spooky."

CHAPTER TWENTY-SEVEN

HIGHWAY GET-AWAY

Melody race-walks to the car ahead of Andy and Telly. She orders Andy into the back seat. Hands the car keys over to Telly. Andy is fine with this. He still is trying to make sense out of law and order, his go-to, turning on him.

"Telly, adjust the mirrors and the seat to your liking then drive," says Melody. "Once we are far enough away, park the car. There, we'll get our bearings. Maybe you want to tell us something."

Telly is adjusting her judgment about Melody. One minute, Melody's the dotty aunt whom the family hides away on holidays, and the next minute, she's an encyclopedia salesperson with a dirty mouth. "I'll drive us to Black's Shelter for Abused Women," says Telly. "I have caused you enough trouble."

"Sounds like a plan," says Andy.

"Not so fast," says Melody. "A police chief doesn't risk his career because his daughter ran away from home."

"He's been terribly secretive lately," says Telly. "He rushes up and down the basement stairs every few minutes like a nuclear siren went off. Whenever I ask what's going on, he just puts on his wouldn't-you-like-to-know grin."

"The shit-eating one?" asks Melody. "Is that why you left? It had to be more than that, right? Did you refuse to clean up your bathroom, mistake the remote for a nun-chuck, or run up a huge overdue library book bill?"

"I was tired of him always telling me what to do. A girl needs her independence and her privacy."

"And?" says Melody.

"I left to move in with my real mother. Only it turned out she only wanted my Social Security check."

"Okay…" says Melody.

"I didn't like it at Donna's," says Telly. "I had to sleep in the living room with the TV always on. I need peace and quiet. I had the radio removed from my van so I could concentrate on driving."

"I have Alzheimer's, Telly," says Melody. "I had my memory removed from my brain."

"I heard that. I am so sorry."

"Not half as sorry as Andy is," says Melody. "I drive him half-crazy every half hour on the eggshell, and the best part of it is that I don't remember it. The worst part is I've forgotten every role to play but the bitch."

"'Til death do we part," says Andy.

"Don't think I haven't thought of that," says Melody.

"Figured you had," says Andy. "You think of everything."

"You are hereby on notice, Handcream," says Melody. "Don't let me forget either."

As Telly adjusts the mirrors and the car seat from Andy's six-foot two to her five-foot four, she says, "I distract my stomach from feeling empty by drinking a lot. So, well, so, I go to the bathroom really often, and sometimes I can't get there in time."

"You go through a lot of panty liners?" asks Melody.

"Yep, but my stepdad will not let me buy them."

"They should throw him in jail," says Melody.

Andy is entertained until he realizes he doesn't know what pantyliners are. A few more years caring for Melody, and he'll find out. What he's trying to understand is how the police in Delaware knew about Telly's flight from Chief Delorean, like they have ESP or something. It was a conspiracy, but a conspiracy by the people he trusted and believed were being unjustly defunded by the elites and the liberals. Maybe there was something to Melody's mongoose theory. The Hawaiians had imported mongeese to get rid of the rats that had hitchhiked there on English ships. The mongeese ate the rats, but then there was no predator that could get rid of the mongeese, which breed like rabbits. Our police have become Hawaii's mongoose.

Killing a motorist for a blown-out taillight, a husband for a wild night in town, an addict for using a phony twenty-dollar bill to buy cigarettes? The police's trump card, 'you are resisting arrest,' had twisted them into God, the Old Testament version. Who could get rid of the police? Marvel's superheroes are too busy right now cashing in on movie franchises.

When Telly accelerates out of the parking space, Andy shouts, "Let's stay here until we know where we want to go. I'm the one who pays for gas remember, and this car gobbles it."

"Like a five-year-old in front of a bag of potato chips," says Melody. "Telly, you said you had a Caravan. Was it purple?"

"How did you guess that?"

"One purple van with fresh-looking smackings to its bumper and windshield is pulling out six stalls over."

"What," says Andy.

"Is that your car?" asks Melody.

"Oh my god, yes!"

"Drive, she said," says Melody.

"I'm a very good driver," says Telly.

"We should be fine. He doesn't know my car," says Andy, looking through the rear window. And then, he hears the whirr of rubber burning and says, "Uh-Oh."

Andy's Buick LaCrosse has a V-6. The Caravan, on the other hand, a gift from the chief's parents, has a flat4. Telly floors it. Both Melody and Andy are violently thrown forward.

"I'm sorry," says Telly, "but don't worry. Just let me get used to this thing."

"This is crazy," says Andy. "You can't outdrive a policeman. They have years of training."

"Yes, she can," says Melody, "He's driving an old Dodge van with a crashed-in front end."

"Hey," says Telly. I love my car."

"He's not using his siren," says Melody. "He does not want to draw attention. Drive to Highway Forty, Telly, and stay on it."

"Why?"

"For one thing, how much gas is in the van?"

"Quarter tank."

"So, we can't depend on him running out of gas right away, but the van has extensive front-end damage, which will be to our advantage."

In less than a minute, the Buick is only a hundred feet ahead of the van on Highway 40.

"You have to press harder on the gas pedal," says Andy.

"But be propitious," says Melody.

Telly says, "Pro what?"

"When he least expects it. And let Andy pay attention to the peripheral stuff."

"Peripheral?"

"Pedestrians, bicyclists, wheelchairs, and other cops," says Melody. "From the looks of your van's front end, the radiator must be compromised. A cost-benefit design flaw of motor vehicles, putting one of the most fragile car parts where it's first to be disabled in the event of the most common collision—the rear-ender. The radiator is made up of thin aluminum fins to dispose of heat. Sooner or later, the lack of coolant will cause an engine to overheat, and goodbye, Chief."

"My poor van!"

"Don't worry, even if he doesn't crash into us, the collision repair cost will exceed how insurance companies evaluate your car's value. It's over ten years old, barely worth the cost of outfitting it with new tires."

"You sound like my insurance agent."

"Mine's name is Quinn. If I wear especially high heels, he gives me a glorious foot massage." The chief drives ever closer behind the Buick, with Andy keeping Telly advised on where other cars are. Every time the van tries to ram them, Telly accelerates and maneuvers into a different lane. The van falls back every time. On the third ram attempt, Melody says, "No worries. I smell burning metal." A few seconds later, Andy and Telly smell it. A plume of white smoke engulfs the van. Melody slaps Andy's hand and reaches forward into the driver's compartment to slap Telly's. Telly obliges, sniffling a little as she sees her van shrink in the rear-view mirror.

"Well, where are we going to go now?" asks Andy.

"Telly, take the Interstate," says Melody. "Then take the first rest stop. We have to make a plan, and to do that, we need to know what we are running away from."

"How about where we should be running to," says Telly. "Dinner."

―・―

At a Roy Rogers' rest stop on Interstate 95

"What did you tell the Detective when he wanted your address, Telly?" asks Melody.

"Black's," says Telly.

"Then that's the first place Chief Delorean will go," says Melody.

"Cops can't reveal that," says Andy.

"How do you think the chief knew we were in a green Buick?" says Melody. "You've been watching too many cop shows, Handcream. They represent police as Superman-honest in exchange for importing their authentic jargon.

"Telly, Dear, what is Chief Delorean really after? I don't think he wants you. He wants something else, maybe something you took with you when you left?"

"I don't know," says Telly. "If I did, I would have already told you."

"Your mother's wedding ring, T-bonds, your stepdad's signature dental hygiene kit?"

"No, I left everything, even all of my stuffed animals."

"He's on a mission," offers Andy.

"He spends all his free time in the basement," says Telly. "I don't know what he does down there."

"Do you know his password?" asks Melody.

"No," says Telly. "But he keeps repeating the Epiphany, the Epiphany, the Epiphany. I looked it up. It has different meanings. James Joyce thought it was important, but I don't know why."

"It's when the three magi visited baby Christ," says Andy.

"Which, of course, never happened," says Melody, "but the anniversary will be celebrated in four days."

"How do you know it never happened?" asks Telly.

"Only one epistle mentions the three magi. All four epistles portray Jesus as a poor carpenter. So, whatever happened to the gold the third magi brought? Not to mention how much myrrh and frankincense would earn on the spice market. Did the Bible keep secret that Father Joseph had a gambling problem?"

"That's just plain nuts, Melody." says Andy. "And I don't care. I am going to the rally on the sixth. To do that we are going to take this young girl…"

"Young woman, Handcream. Believe whatever you want," Melody says. "Belief is secondary to what you read and experience, but if you ignore the center and only read the edges, you'll spin off sooner or later and never come home."

"Where is home, Melody?" asks Telly.

"Reality," says Melody. "What this police chief is willing to risk his career for. Pass the grenades, hold the tear gas. Drop this rally pilgrimage. Trump lost, end trans. There is no evidence of voting foul play."

"Nah, nah, there's evidence somewhere," says Andy, "they just haven't found it yet. It'll come out."

"The president is the most powerful person on the planet, right?" says Melody. "And after sixty lawsuits, he hasn't persuaded a single judge, some of whom he appointed. If the election was stolen, this only proves that he's impotent and incompetent. So, why keep him when there are so many more stand-up comics looking for work? And most of them are funny."

"The election was stolen," Andy repeats.

"By whom?" asks Melody. "Angels, I guess. Who else could have without leaving a single trace? Now, why angels didn't want the current president back in the White House could be the subject of an interesting debate. I'll buy a ticket to that. Telly, you're invited. And Handcream, while you are at the rally, what am I supposed to do?"

"I haven't thought that far ahead," says Andy. "It's not until Wednesday. It's just a simple protest rally. What is more American than that?"

"Speaking of being American,' says Melody, "Telly, are you pregnant?"

"No. I don't have a boyfriend. Besides, what difference..."

"Are you in line to inherit something?"

"No," says Telly. "My mom's a doper, and I don't even know who my real dad was. I researched, and everything is redacted. Chief had money, he tells me, but no more. I used to have a penny collection, but I sold it on eBay to pay for my speeding tickets."

"Telly are you wearing something?" asks Melody.

"Just the clothes I've got on and three other sets in my van. Chief has my purse with my cell phone. Good thing I keep my driver's license on a chain around my neck. Oh...," Telly blushes and says, "I have a microchip in my hand."

"Some kind of teenage adornment?" asks Andy.

"No. Chief made me inject it."

"Do you always call him Chief?" asks Andy.

"That is what he insists I call him, ever since he made chief two years ago. He said it's more respectful."

"What's it for?" asks Melody. "The microchip, I mean."

"He told me it's experimental. It's supposed to suppress my appetite. I'm a nurse in training. It was easy and didn't hurt much."

"How's it supposed to work?" asks Melody.

"No idea," says Telly.

"Did it suppress your appetite?" asks Melody.

"Not that I have noticed."

"Have you ever done anything like this before?" asks Melody.

"I have had a lot of training giving people shots," says Telly. "But I have no dream of ever being a phlebotomist. Inserting needles in people, gross."

"Have you ever had a microchip inserted in your body before?" asks Melody.

"No."

"Has your stepdad?" asks Melody.

"Not that I know of."

"Is he current with his flu shots, COVID shots?" asks Melody.

"No. He's an anti-vaxxer."

"Does he turn a little gray when you mention getting a shot?"

"We never talk about it."

"He may have trypanophobia," says Melody. "It's the fear of medical needles. So, you inserted the chip in your thumb?"

"Just below it," says Telly. She points to the meaty area below her thumb. "Every few days, he would scan it. Then he'd smile and say everything was hunky-dory."

Melody goes silent and plays with her iPad. Telly wishes this would all go away, as does Andy. Finally, Melody says, "Change of plans. Go back on Highway 95 North, take the Blue Route then 202 to Kennett Square."

"That's in Pennsylvania, Melody," says Andy. "Gas is not cheap, remember."

"It's supposed to be out of the way. We're on the lam, remember? I need time, and we need distance. No telling what Mr. Chief has been up to since we dodged him."

"Melody," says Andy. "Can't Telly just take this microchip out and give it back to him, I mean, if that is all he wants?"

"Not ethically," says Melody.

"Huh?"

"A police chief tries to abduct a woman in broad daylight, tries to run you over, and then files a false police report," says Melody. "He doesn't do that to keep something honest or insignificant from being exposed. He's up to no good. If we turned over the microchip to him, we would be complicit in whatever nefarious scheme he's involved in. The country imprisoned the doctor who treated John Wilkes Booth's broken leg."

"But that was the assassination of the President of the United States," says Andy.

"How do we know this is any different?" asks Melody.

"Someone's going to kill the president?" whispers Telly.

Melody pats Telly on the shoulder and says, "Past, present, or future? I can tell you this, there's research using microchips to alter appetite, but the thumb is too far away from the vagus nerve, and so far, the experiments have only been tested on rodents. Telly, you are not a rat. But right now, I have the feeling we are all guinea pigs in a much more macabre social experiment than weight loss."

CHAPTER TWENTY-EIGHT

ENCIRCLING THE WAGONS

Several times a day, Melody hands Andy a treasure of some kind. The offer usually comes with an admonition to do something with it but not-right-now. Each time she does, Andy waits until she's out of sight then deposits the article in a metal file cabinet in the basement. The drawer is filled with spiral notebooks, photographs of relatives who died before the two were born, ceramic coffee cups, business pens, and magnets. If dementia's progress could be determined from its garbage like a native tribe, the file cabinet would harbor a gold mine.

The articles are safe there. She doesn't go down to the basement often.

Today, she says, "I found you a belt, Handcream. It's perfect for your Trump rally." It's a thin, blue, woven fabric belt with a metal military slide buckle. Glued to the buckle is a sparkling geode that must weigh three pounds.

The belt's strap is like the one his mother used to wield against the back of his calves. He can't guess how this gigantic rock got glued to it. The geode belonged on a shelf on a stand, not at a man's belly button.

"This is a museum piece, Melody," says Andy. "I can't wear this."

"Put it on."

"I'm already wearing a belt, Melody."

"Take it off then," says Melody. "You don't want to wear two belts. You have to dress to stand out at a political rally. Let me see you with it on."

Andy takes off his belt, threads the new gift in his belt loops, and models it for her.

Melody wraps his other belt around her hand like she's going to use it as brass knuckles and says, "You look good in that, Handcream."

"What about my old belt?" Andy asks.

"I'm making plans for that right now," says Melody. "Isn't it time you left to catch your flight?"

Distraction rules political rallies. Everything is bait and switch, but the beautiful part of it is that buyers and sellers are equally in on the grift. First gateway is believing that everyone lies. You win if you bet on the most likable lie. Like Biden's son brought the COVID-19 virus over from China, Laura Bush dated The Joker, or Bill Gates and George Soros were Siamese twins. Look it up, why don't you?

The distractions start right when you buy your ticket. The ticket is free, but before you can secure your seat, hats, pins, and sports jerseys parade before you. Expensive hats, pins, and jerseys. You can't wear last rally's stuff. Be real. Frugality signals you are not one of us.

Then, when you park at the event, you see streams of people flow by. Half are shills, hired to increase the look of the attendance's size. They funnel you inside the arena, sheep to the slaughter. Once inside, only reality is verboten. Everything else, including facts, is on display and for sale.

The cacophony you hear inside codifies that you have left the rule of law, AKA other people's America. Here, you are in mob rule. And you are one with the mob. There are more of us than them. At least right here. Your roar will make up for any deficit you have in actual numbers. We will steamroll anyone and everyone in our path. Hallelujah.

Rallies are also terribly personal. Plastered everywhere are pictures of party members who betrayed the cause. Everywhere posters shout out wedge issues—the Dobbs decision, highway tolls, caravans of immigrants, inheritance taxes, mass killings, sales taxes, fentanyl deaths, school taxes... And everywhere you hear chants at varying crescendos, mimicking the waves and cheers at a ballgame. **Reparations, Where's mine? What would Jesus Do? No Inglaze, Exportay vuself. Feed the Poor, Tax the rich. Biden and his ho have got to go! Stop the killing, Ban assault weapons.** And **no more murdering babies!** Glad to be here.

Loud is the best answer to everything. You know that movie with all the fast action scenes that were impossible, but the speed with which they flew by suspended your skepticism? Political rally organizers took note. A political rally is where everything seems possible, especially the impossible. The constant eardrum-breaking noise makes you forget that nothing is really happening here. It's like you're in a bar at happy hour on a Friday, and to make yourself heard, you try to yell over the emcee barking out that this next singer needs no introduction, when you are just asking for directions to the cleaner restroom.

But it is, after all, hoopla. Exhortations, meant to forgive your letting the other party win in the first place. And it was an inside coup that you didn't see coming. You can't point to a single thing that changed with their winning and your losing, other than the slate of candidates' names.

The arena ceiling seems to swell with all the noise, but the noise has nowhere to escape. So, it rolls up inside itself and rains down on its captives, sprinkling holy water on the anointed, inciting a grand fury to nowhere. The feeling that this is where you belong seeps in. This is where everyone thinks like you do. The conflicts of adulthood, spiked with financial, physical, and psychological cacti, can be forgotten and along with them, your endless series of sixth place finishes.

Your favorite sports team didn't make it to the playoffs again. Your favorite TV show was canceled. Your favorite politician resigned after being caught paying his mistress for an abortion and is healing in a Caribbean detox resort.

And every new court decision erodes what you thought was your standing. The finish line keeps being pushed farther ahead. No one knows how to get the band to slow down. But everyone agrees with the refrain that you are running out of time to make the train that's already leaving the station.

Trump says he'll stop this madness. He's your man.
Biden says he'll stop this madness. He's your man.
'I don't care,' grins in the back alley and shoots up.

———

"This is where we belong, Dad," said Jeremy. The two had just left their cab in Wesaukee. Jeremy, shivering, asked, "Who'd have thought it would be this cold in October?"

"I told you," Andy reminded him, while tugging his pants up. The geode's weight continued to scrimmage with his belt's primary purpose. Andy had tried to pack another belt but couldn't find one. Melody had hidden all of them somewhere.

The two hurried through the front doors to get away from the cold. They stopped to orient themselves to what was inside, others milling around and banners on every wall like at a high school football rally.

While they shook off the shivering, a few of the audience mistake Andy for John Thune. Andy tries to wave them off with, "No, I'm a nobody." But the attendees aren't so easily fooled, so they demand a selfie with him and his belt buckle before they back off.

Having people in expensive clothes, one quite attractive, lean low to photograph your crotch was an action Jeremy wanted a piece of. "Let me wear the geode belt next time, okay, Dad?"

"You can have it right now," says Andy.

The two try to exchange their belts in the hallway. They don't impress anyone with their undressing gymnastics. Especially when the geode belt doesn't fit Jeremy's pants, so they do the re-exchange, loop-by-loop-by-loop. Andy keeps his jacket zipped from then on.

They make it to the collapsible registration table. It's manned by two women. One is old enough to have dated Ronald Reagan. The other is young enough to have been his great granddaughter. Why are they always staffed like that?

Ignoring the older woman, Jeremy hands their tickets over to the young woman. Her name, Averil, is machine-lettered to the name tag in bold, the only thing in the room that looks permanent, nipple high on her red blouse. She candy-eyes Jeremy's overdeveloped chest and biceps.

"I'm Jeremy MacClean, from D.C. We're staying here at The Sheraton." Andy lowers his eyes in meek admiration. There is no Sheraton within hours of Wesaukee. They're staying at the EFront, econo with a capital E, and both of them would have pledged on the Bible the name is honestly earned.

Averil tells them who's going to be here. She's just not very specific about when. Jeremy leans in and gets his face as close to Averil's as he can without their lips actually touching. He repeats his name and flips from a shirt pocket a business card, a handy chit for a DC cop to carry, cell number and email address highlighted in purple. Though the word 'Owner' as his position is a minor overstatement.

Averil reads Jeremy's card, pulls back a smidge, and says, "You both are entitled to a special bonus. Pick a card." She hands Jeremy a deck of cards featuring Confederate Generals. Jeremy riffs through the deck a couple of times like he's expecting Averil to offer him a clue. She doesn't. He turns over General Babcott.

Averil says, "Your prize is a hair from Donald Trump's head and a pill box of Chiclets in the form of his bust. Bon Appetit."

Jeremy says, "I won a hair from Trump before, and when I held it to a match, it melted. Hair does not melt."

"That's the price of burning a sacrament," Averil says. She turns to Andy, "Pick a card Mr. Andrew MacClean."

Andy flips over the top card. It's Stonewall Jackson.

"Mr. MacClean, you're a winner," says Averil. She points down the hall, "You see that black canopy over there? Present your Stonewall Jackson, and they'll let you in. Bill Goat is holding court inside."

"Hey, Dad, you stole my card," Jeremy says.

"Finders, keepers, Jeremy. I'll meetcha later at our assigned seats."

Andy walks away, and Jeremy continues romancing Averil, pecking the air with hand gestures like a randy mosquito. The line backs up and becomes stonily belligerent, buffeted by the cold from the doors opening and closing. Jeremy is oblivious. Averil is amused. She has a space heater under her chair.

Andy heads for the head. He is as enthralled by all this noise as everyone else seems to be. It licks his spirits up. He revels in the showmanship here and credits the grandmaster of clicks, Donald Trump. More than that, the volume reinforces the feeling in him that Trump will win another term in office.

He compares this rally to one the Democrats are having on Zoom. Biden is too afraid of getting COVID-19 to actually meet anyone. He's so old. He stutters and misstates stuff and mispronounces stuff worse than Bush Two, which is really saying something. And the videos that tout that Biden suffers from Parkinson's were dead on. He should be in a hospital. No one in good conscience could vote for a man that ill. What are the Democrats thinking? And his running mate, a woman he couldn't pick out of a lineup of three black women, would take over if he died. Time to update his passport if he had one.

Andy makes his way over to the black canopy. He presents Stonewall, shows his ID, and is patted down and relieved of his cell phone, which is thrown in a bucket of others. When he leaves, he's to tell them his phone number, and they'll call it so his phone rings out. He appreciates the simpleness until he remembers he had turned the ringer off.

It's standing room only, an audience of about two hundred. At the lectern stands Bill Goat, a Trump crony and former soap opera star. He wears a five-thousand-dollar suit and toupee. The attendees are clapping and talking to each other as if they came here to tell each other off and not to listen to Bill Goat. Don't you hate people like that?

Bill stands behind a podium and sips from a Dixie cup.

Andy stays to the rear, cautious before all of this chaotic high energy. He maneuvers his wallet from his back pocket into his front, sticks his hands in his jacket pockets, and holds his elbows akimbo for good measure. Pickpockets don't spare the Chosen. Everyone is crunched in together. Andy understands this is a signature Trump move to give his middle finger to the vaccine crowd. Of course, it might also have been to cut the hall's rental fee. Nothing wrong with Trump being frugal. He's got a campaign to finance.

A man in bright blue overalls nudges Andy's elbow and says, "The election is in the bag. You hear all this noise?"

"What about those fraudulent mail-in ballots," Andy says, not taking his eyes off Bill Goat.

"At least my state is doing something about it," the man says.

"How'd illegals get on the voting rolls in the first place?" Andy asks.

"The Democrats pay them," says the man. "I saw a Korean walk into my precinct, my precinct, voted, and no one said one thing. One thing."

Bill Goat puts his Dixie cup down with the flair appropriate to show that he's not drinking H2O, and says "People of color. Pee Oh Cee. Emphasis on the Pee. I like to call them Pee Oh Tee, for piss on them." An applause peels out.

"POC," Bill continues, "people whose skin color is darker than ours. Any idea what will happen if they take over? Payback time, Whitey. Picture the water fountain for whites out back by the garbage bins. They already started moving them out there under Obama. You saw that, didn't you?"

"I'm now expected to bow down and apologize for their treatment at the hands of my ancestors. Ancestors I never even met. And worse, now they're demanding, *demanding*, reparations for what allegedly happened a million years ago.

"Nonsense. We owe POC nothing. POC owe everything they have to us. More than that, POC need to be showing their gratitude for our letting them in on the most vibrant economy in the world."

Bill stops for another round of applause. While he waits for the cheer's death rattle, he glances at his smartphone. He starts to speed-talk, "And none of this 'Native Americans were here first' business. Both were savages until we taught them capitalism. When are we going to be repaid for training them in the first place? Whipping and corralling the feral isn't for the inexperienced, the lazy, or the fearful. No, siree.

"We have the scars to prove it. Trust me, not all of the POC obeyed willingly. This kind of training took years, not to mention thousands of whips."

Bill takes a sip from his Dixie cup, flashes a licentious grin then continues, "Whips aren't cheap, good ones at least. You see the profits from the whippings every time one of them is courteous to you.

"And don't discount the labor and resources incurred to collect runaways, those who just were not smart enough to appreciate how much better off they had it. It's a human-eat-human world out there. Testimony to that is the number of them who died before being returned to their rightful owners.

"Not paying them taught them frugality. You see them driving by in pretty fancy cars these days. And those aren't just the drug dealers," Bill says as he winks and throws the rest of the cup's liquid down his throat. "So, no harm was done, at least to the living. And the laws to fine and imprison anyone who taught slaves how to read and write, add, and subtract were passed not to punish them, but to protect them from being overcharged. How could they have had any idea of how little we pay teachers?"

Another roar of laughter. Bill talks through it, "Of course, all of these considerations pale to the prospect of having to answer to a POC if one becomes your boss. Having to kiss someone's black ass. Jesus, have mercy on our souls. One became the President of the United States. You know who voted him in. Trump rescued us from not only Obama but also from that white bitch who was most likely his concubine. You may have noticed how much TV time they had together. I sure did. Can't have all that close time together without time close together. White bitch in heat before a dominant black male. Needs no imagination on anybody's part."

More applause. Andy joins in.

"Now TV is telling us that Trump will lose to Lazy Joseph Biden. We Americans are not that stupid. It's not going to happen. Poll workers are being paid again to make us think Trump will lose so we don't show up and vote. As if we were fair weather fans. As if we were stupid.

"No chance in hell of that happening. We're going to win on November third. And if we don't, don't worry. We have a plan, quite a few plans as a matter of fact. Trump will stay in office guaranteed. But we need your help. Fighting corruption costs big-league money. You all have credit cards. You'll have plenty of money to pay the bank back because Trump is going to cut your taxes in half like he did last term, and the economy is going to grow sky high. But what we need is a rallying cry. People used to say 'Remember the Maine' before we invaded Cuba, and 'Remember the Alamo' before we invaded Mexico. The hell with remembering stuff. We're going to give America two rallying cries, not one. And it's not Diversity. It's KME. Kiss my ess.

"And for the children, it's LGB, or Let's Go Brandon. Everyone in the world now knows what that means."

There's a huge roar inside the tents, but it's outstripped by a louder one from outside. Bill looks at his Rolex and says, "I'm overdue to see the Man. Skedaddle now. Vote for Trump this November and every other November." Bill winks, "I mean, if voting is still necessary."

Jeremy loses Averil to a bunch of soldiers in uniform. He should have worn his police uniform. It's taboo off duty, but rules are for chumps. But as Averil air kisses him off, she presses a coin into his hand. He wanders into the aisles, examining the coin. It's plastic and has a phone number on one side. The number is extremely close to the one for the national suicide call center. Not what he was looking for. On the other side is printed, STOP THE CHEAT. He wonders if he can foist it as legal change. Worth a try, except nothing on sale here requires change.

His eyes carom from one customer purchase to another. Every purchaser acting as if something very important is being risked here. Money, the lone ultimate status source. To fend off the vendor leers as he walks, Jeremy buys some Trump popcorn with extra butter and home-brewed water. He raises both in each hand higher than necessary to show the vendors his hands are full and can't possibly buy anything right now. His ruse is immediately busted when vendors bark, "You can rest those down right on this counter young man. You need..." Dodging salespeople is not how a D.C. cop should be acting. Sheepishly, he moves along, reminding himself only he knows that he's a cop.

Jeremy comes upon a clot of people in front of the gate alley to his assigned seat. A camera is suspended above like a giraffe selfie.

ENCIRCLING THE WAGONS

People are angling to get their face before the camera lens while they answer a tall skinny redhead's questions. The thin redhead has the solemn demeanor of a priest raising the host at mass, but he wears khaki pants and a half-buttoned light blue dress shirt. His sweating, freckled chest emits no sex appeal. But it shows he's not wearing a bulletproof vest.

Jeremy pries himself inside the clot. He is experienced in crowd control.

The redhead speaks into a mic, "The polls have Trump down double digits," then swings the mic over to the first who pops in with something to say. Their time to shine.

A young man, shaved impeccably bald, pecks in with, "Polls don't mean nothing. They had him down in 2016 too."

The redhead says, in the same disinterested monotone, "Trump won by seventy thousand votes in 2016. Over three hundred thousand have died from COVID-19 since then. Most were Trump supporters. Worried?"

The balding man pauses and is immediately pushed out as frontrunner by a young brunette waving her hands in the air. The sky will fall if she isn't allowed to speak. "Hear this crowd, we are going to win by seven million votes this time. Our ground game is phenomenal."

"Yeah," the balding man adds, "The polls are biased against Trump."

The redhead says, "The polls are just reporting what people are telling them, so the people polled are lying. Why would they? What are they afraid of?"

A tall man wearing a beret pitches in from the back, "Of course they are. Everyone knows that. The pollsters work for the media, and they know what side their bread is buttered on."

The redhead asks him, "So, which is it? The pollsters are lying, or the people polled are lying?"

The man in back hollers, "How can you not know that?"

The redhead says, "Okay, but which is it?"

"The Democrats have paid the media off."

"You might be right," says the redhead. "Journalism is right behind social services in being the poorest paid. I can be bribed. How much you got?"

A woman dressed in clothes too young for her says, "Another myth the media wants us to believe. We gotta get to Trump's speech, move out of our way. Move."

"Okay, okay. One more question. Every time Trump steps in some doo doo, you back him all the more. Is there anything he could do that would turn you against him? I mean, like, passing our nuclear codes over to Putin kind of stuff?"

"He'd never do that. It's offensive to even suggest."

"I'm just trying to find something, anything, that would cause you to longer support him if he did it, that's all. One thing. How about if a video surfaces showing him ridiculing all of his supporters for being marks? Would that move the needle?" The clot breaks up.

Jeremy lurches toward the mic and says, "One thing…" He pauses to come up with something to say. The redhead looks expectant. He's hoping this Asian looking guy will say something that his producer will actually broadcast. A loud applause erupts from the arena floor. Maybe Trump is coming out. The name Trump bullhorns out. The clot is torn. Here's their chance to tell this guy off, but there's also the chance that Trump is really taking the stage this time. How do you monetize the value of missing a minute of Trump on stage? Many times before, the Trump name had sounded, but they found another rubber-mat politician on the stage making love to the sound of his own voice when they returned to their seats.

The clot coagulates around Jeremy. Its members want to hear what this hearty Asian has to say. It's always great when the least likely-looking person turns the tables and speaks the truth. The cameraperson, a tall blonde, zooms in for a full headshot of Jeremy. Jeremy says, "If he stops eating Big Macs, that's it. I'm done with him."

The clot disassembles in laughter. The redhead smiles wide. But he doesn't give up and asks, "Can you name a specific thing that Trump has done to make America great again?" No one bites. The redhead lowers his head to check his smartphone for the feeds from the camera. The cameraperson telescopes the pole to half mast, her muscles thankful for a recess.

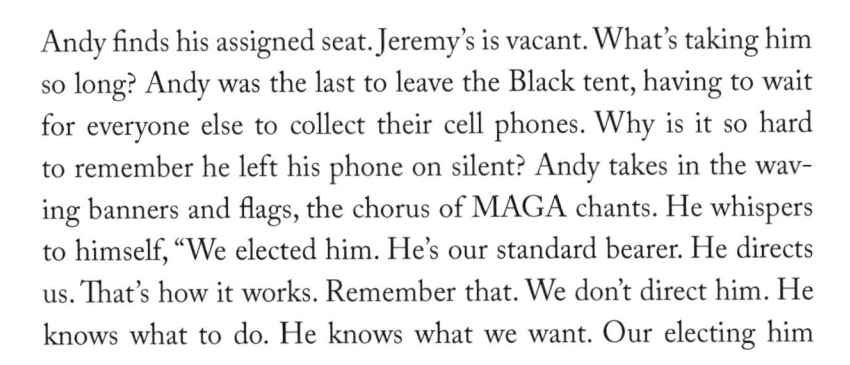

Andy finds his assigned seat. Jeremy's is vacant. What's taking him so long? Andy was the last to leave the Black tent, having to wait for everyone else to collect their cell phones. Why is it so hard to remember he left his phone on silent? Andy takes in the waving banners and flags, the chorus of MAGA chants. He whispers to himself, "We elected him. He's our standard bearer. He directs us. That's how it works. Remember that. We don't direct him. He knows what to do. He knows what we want. Our electing him gives him the authority to do whatever he can get away with. That is what made our country great."

Jeremy joins when Andy is standing and clapping along with everyone else, hoping the next speaker will finally be Trump. Instead, it's John Thune of South Dakota. Now there's a powerful state to pay attention to. A little under one million in population. "He doesn't look much like you, Dad," says Jeremy. "Just his build."

Andy and Jeremy sit back in their seats and join the audience trying to spot celebrities on the speaker platform. Celebrities aren't really human, after all. They live in a zoo somewhere and promenade only on special occasions like the World Series and the Academy Awards.

The feel around them is of a revivalist meeting, which pleases Andy. Even though he had never attended one, he had watched them for years on Sunday morning TV. He appreciated how they played out, mini melodramas of hurt followed by redemption. Their script's similarity to the Jesus story never occurred to him. He had never been religious.

Jeremy is finding the noise as invigorating as running with the bulls in Pamplona, which he had done the year before. He had been eager to spy bulls' horns and red meat *in media res,* so he had flown to Spain to experience it. Red meat is what political rallies promise.

The country had endured eight years under a socialist black president and now was going to reinstate his replacement with a resounding two-peat victory, and if votes are supposed to really matter, a three peat afterward and onward ho. The country would be back on track. Never mind that COVID-19 was knocking off two thousand people a day or Donald Trump's promotion that it was no worse than the flu.

Trump comes on the stage. He's rounder than he looks on TV. He toe-stumbles just a bit getting to the microphone. He shows his fiercest frown, as if he's going to attack someone then sobers up and fakes a laugh, eyes high. "Somebody trying to trip me?" He asks. There is no one on the stage near him. Then someone on the stage lets out an exaggerated laugh. After a ten second pause, everyone is laughing. It's a joke. What could be funnier than making fun of your opponent's prior falls and age?

Donald Trump talks about plumbing and the cost of a haircut. He talks about dumb people, immigrants, and over-educated college graduates. He talks about changing everything. He doesn't ask you to do anything other than vote for him.

He talks until he's tired out and the audience is tired in. Andy and Jeremy get tired too. They equate this semi-nausea with how they would feel if Trump lost, not how they feel being semi-forced to listen to him for four hours.

Trump closes with, "You have to remember what we are fighting for. The Democrats say they fight for the poor. That means they want you to hand over your money to them. The poor are there for a reason. They're losers. I fight so that you can keep what is already yours. Thanks for coming. Come visit me at the White House on rainy days. Otherwise, I'll be golfing. I am a great golfer. And I'm not one to complain, but if I hadn't been so busy making billions, I woulda made the tour."

CHAPTER TWENTY-NINE

PARKING LOT UPPER MOBILITY

Melody directs Telly to a cheesy-looking strip mall that contains a silk screen tee-shirt maker, a tattoo parlor, a 7-11, and a computer repair shop. Melody tells Telly to keep the engine running to stay warm and leaves her with Andy.

Not having a clue what to do or say, Andy collapses in his seat like a ball of cookie dough thrown on a hot pan. Telly unfastens her seatbelt, leans over the front seat, and asks him, "What's it like living with someone as brilliant as Melody?"

"What's it like living with a cop who makes you call him Chief?"

"I asked first," she says and goes back to looking out the windshield.

"It's a living hell, and I'm not far from killing us both. Happy?" Andy says, "I'm sorry, I'm sorry. So unfair I said that. I'm sorry. Fuck me."

"We never use that word at home or at Saved Angels," says Telly, now looking at Andy in the rearview mirror. "I hear a lot of suicide talk, though. Sometimes so loud I'm afraid someone, maybe even me, will call the cops. No one ever does. The nurses tell me I have to develop compassion."

"It feels the opposite," says Andy. "Hard to remember in the midst of it all, it's not her fault. She doesn't mean it. Last week, she scolded the fuel delivery guy for waking her up at noon. Then, instead of apologizing, she says, "I am auditioning for a role in a new TV show called *The Slut Who Straightened Her Hair with Tasers*. How'd I do?" Andy puts his face in his hands.

"You take care of someone who can't take care of herself," Telly says and returns to leaning back and looking at Andy. "That's being a hero. The nurses tell me. I want to be a racecar driver. That's being a hero too, I think. But first I have to grow up."

"You look pretty grown to me."

"Always plenty of food. Chief's big. He's six-two, weighs two-forty."

"I noticed," says Andy. "Do you live in a safe neighborhood?"

"I guess."

"Are you afraid to leave your house?"

"That's why I am here," says Telly. "I left without permission."

"I see all these shootings on TV. Any around your home?"

"Not that I've heard."

"How old did you say you were?"

"I'm eighteen," Telly says and returns to looking at Andy through the rearview mirror. Then, she adds, "Almost."

"Well, how do you two get along otherwise?" asks Andy. "He doesn't hit you, does he?"

"He stopped spanking me when I turned thirteen and started hitting him back."

"I noticed you were giving him quite a pelting in the van."

"That was fun," says Telly, "but I don't think he felt it. He was out."

"Where are your parents?" asks Andy. "I mean your real parents."

"My mom lives in Baltimore. Don't know if my dad even knows he's a father."

"How did you end up with Chief Delorean?"

"He's only been the chief for a few years," says Telly. "Before that, he was just a patrol cop, and before that, he was in the army. Something bad happened there."

"Where is your stepmom, his wife? Will she be looking for you?"

"I haven't seen her since I was nine."

"Where did she go?"

"South America somewhere," says Telly. "There were lawyers and custody hearings and everything. Dozens of strangers interviewed me. I'm a lab specimen for Prader-Willi. Some of the doctors were pretty cute. Mom was the one who wanted to adopt me, but she was ESL, so Chief filled out all the paperwork. Somewhere in the paperwork, the judge had my mom deported."

"Doesn't sound like you've had a good time of it," says Andy. "Growing up isn't for children."

"I don't understand."

"That was a joke."

"Are you making fun of me?" asks Telly.

"No. I meant that it takes a mature person to figure out what to do sometimes, and meanwhile, you're still just a kid." Andy considers just getting out of the car and being done with all this. Just walk away. He's complicit in…what, exactly? He wants to go to the rally, help upend this election fiasco, and here he's nurse-maiding this naive young girl instead, but he's in Pennsylvania.

"I'll be eighteen next month."

"A girl gets pregnant, and her life is ruined before she ever has a chance," says Andy.

"Are you going to get me pregnant?"

Andy looks out the side window. He registers the fabric ripping feel of his jaw drop and thinks how closely this conversation resembles talking with Melody these days. Maybe the chief had only good intentions. He thinks of asking Telly if what she really wants is a cigarette and shakes his head back and forth in loud laughter.

She must be thinking he's making fun of her again. Facing forward, he locks on her eyes looking at his through the rearview mirror and says, "Right now, I miss Melody. And my bet is, you miss your mom."

"I miss Melody too," says Telly. "She's been gone a long time. The Seven Eleven sells food, you know?"

CHAPTER THIRTY

MONITOR CIRCUIT

Lutz jogs down his basement stairs. He's hoping for news. He ignores his monitor lineup of different video links and proceeds to the last six monitors. They contain emails to his different email aliases. He keys in his pass code to the last monitor and is rewarded with a blank screen. He then visits the other five monitors. Every email he opens is a donation request. He fumes a bit and walks back and forth among the screens, deleting the requests to the netherworld.

Lutz walks upstairs. He fills a brandy snifter with Johnnie Walker Black Label, puts a Dave Mathews album on, switches on the speakers to the basement, walks back downstairs, and stands at attention in front of the last monitor. Stands there and waits.

He's near alcohol nirvana when the screen lightens up, gray lettering against black plaid wallpaper. DROPPED CARGO AT 8:38 PM, DONE HERE, GOING HOME. The eagle has landed. Only Telly knows where.

CHAPTER THIRTY-ONE

SPEEDING IN PARK

Melody returns to the Buick. She carries a shoebox and hands it through the car window to Andy. "Handcream, leave this in the back seat and get your ass in the driver's seat. Telly, join me in the 7-11. I need something to read."

The two leave and Andy moves into the driver seat, as confused as he was on their first date.

Within ten minutes, the two emerge from the 7-11. Telly carries a cardboard tray with hot coffee, and Melody carries two large grocery bags. She puts them in the front passenger seat and fastens the seatbelt around them. Telly hands Andy a coffee. Melody and Telly get in the back.

"Thank you, Telly," Andy says, graciously accepting the coffee. He sips it and rifles through the first bag for food but is sorely disappointed. It's filled with magazines, toiletries, a compact space heater, and pantyliners. He peers into the second, and his eyes are rewarded with a junk food extravaganza—Jimmy Dean, Hostess, and Famous Amos are well represented, with three Italian hoagies thrown in to give them company.

"Not for you, Handcream," says Melody.

There is the clink of an aluminum can being punctured then the whoosh of caffeine and sugar wafting up to the car's headliner and hovering there, a non-protesting invisible cloud of humidity seeking release from the car's closed doors and windows. No can do. The windows and doors are closed. The engine hums. The heater is set at 73 degrees. Melody takes a big gulp and pulls from the shoebox a gun, black wiring coiled around it. She unwinds the wiring and plugs one end into the rear console cigarette lighter. She tells Telly to place her hand in her lap and waves the gun over Telly's thumb. The scanner lights up.

"Well, I see numbers and letters," says Telly. "It's encrypted. A lifetime would be needed to unwind that string. This is hopeless."

"Hopelessness is our eternal plight, young lady," says Melody.

"Telly," says Andy, "did you know Melody has an average score of 2.4 on Wordle?"

Melody photographs the string of numbers, letters, and symbols on her iPad. She creates a matrix of nine then multiplies that to eighty-one and says, "It's 2.5 now. I'm losing my juice. This may take me a while. Andy, can you drive?"

"Of course."

"We need to drop Telly off at a safe house. Any suggestions?"

"Why can't she stay with us?"

"The police know we helped her and know where we live."

"How about a hotel?" asks Telly.

"That would be the second place they would look," says Melody. "Credit cards can be traced, and hotels won't rent you a room without one."

"I have a friend at school," says Telly.

"What about my sister, Margaret?" offers Andy.

"Don't either of you ever watch movies, read novels?" says Melody. "Who is the second person to get killed every time? We can't put people in harm's way for our problem."

"How did it become our problem? Isn't it the chief's?" asks Andy.

"Once we become involved, it becomes ours," says Melody. "You can't throw a radioactive smoke detector in the trash because the prior owner of your home installed it."

"Huh?" says Andy.

"It means being in the loop has no less responsibility than starting the loop," says Telly.

"Good girl Telly, I'm going to get you an invite to Mensa before you know it. Andy, didn't you tell me that you once discovered that someone was living at your tennis club? He was having marital discord or something."

"That's right," says Andy. "I kickassed him out. But right now, the club is closed. It's locked up, it has no heat to begin with, and the electricity and water are shut off. No one could live there this time of year."

"Handcream, you're smarter than that."

Taking another mouthful of coffee, Andy says, "Okay, I have keys to get in, and since I was the one who switched the electric and water off, I know how to switch them back on. Still, she will freeze. It's January, you know. Oh shit, you just bought a space heater."

"How fortuitous."

"The club will find out!"

"Too late to matter," says Melody. "*Pronto mi compadre*. Drink your coffee before it gets cold but take your time. We don't need you getting a speeding ticket while driving without a driver's license," says Melody. "And I need some of that time thing to discover what the microchip divines."

CHAPTER THIRTY-TWO

BABBLING EN ROUTE

Melody focuses on her laptop like a horse with blinders. It's the world to her now. Her fingers punch keys Telly had never noticed were even on the keyboard, and in sequences that resemble a banjo-picking maestro suffering an epileptic fit. Telly asks Melody, "Can I interrupt you?"

"No worries, interruptions are welcome. They keep my thoughts in touch with my feelings."

"Melody, is what we are doing dangerous?"

"Life never works out as planned," says Melody. Her eyes never leave the laptop screen, and her fingers never stop their feverish plowing through what looks to Telly like fuzzy labyrinths. "Sometimes unexpected forces influence what happens. For instance, someone in my high school administration office failed to send my transcripts to UC Santa Barbara. UCSB had conditionally accepted me if it received my last marking period's grades. They were, by the way, all A's. I never heard back from Santa Barbara. I ended up at my default, the University of San

Francisco, coincidentally a Roman Catholic college. I was, at the time, attending a Roman Catholic college-prep high school run by Our Ladies of Devout Retribution. Coincidence?

"Now, I'm not complaining here. Life has been okay but certainly different than if I had gone to UCSB. If it was for the best, I'll never know. And if I had the choice to change it, I wouldn't, as only by following a certain Irish history professor who was transferred to D.C., did I move East with him, meet Handcream, and give birth to my son."

"I'm not sure I can get into college," says Telly. "I don't get A's. Words don't stick with me, especially the ones ending in -ist, -ish, or -ism. They all seem to mean the same thing and the opposite at the same time."

"The consequences of going to a different college are massive," says Melody. "Not hearing back from UCSB before I had to commit to USF was one thing. My never hearing back confirmed that it wasn't an accident.

"From that experience, I could have concluded that forces out of sight pull all the strings. We are pattern-hunting berry gatherers at heart, right? If berries show up in the early fall, we will look for them again in the same place at the same time the following year. Agriculture is work. Scavenging fruit is easy pickings."

Having lost Melody's train of reasoning, Telly asks, "How much closer are you getting?"

"A strong simile to, 'Are we there yet?' I actually never know when a code will fall into place. The secret is not to cherry-pick. Look for ways to prove you're off course. When you can't, you know you may be closing in. Always maybe, never sure."

"Chief doesn't agree with you," says Telly. "He says sureness comes first, and if someone tells you your belief is wrong, attack him."

"*Argumentum ad hominem*. And if that doesn't work?"

"Demand proof that's impossible to come up with," says Telly.

"It's certainly a bullet-proof way of never learning the truth," says Melody. "I tie my shoelaces to keep my shoes on and to keep from tripping over them. Any conspiracies going on here? I butter my toast, and the butter melts into the bread, making it delicious. Do you see some conspiracies involving the relationship between bread and butter? Where'd that damn butter go? Why wouldn't there be a conspiracy here? You direct your car by turning the steering wheel appropriately and get to where you want to go. Shouldn't a conspiracy have stopped you? Were conspiracies on strike today? You amass trillions of instances a day when everything happened just as it should have, just as you expected it to have. They rule. So, why believe unseen forces conspired to trip you up if you happen to miss an exit?"

"Maybe it wasn't your fault," says Telly.

"You apply for a job, and you don't get it. Maybe it goes to someone just like you, but you're the one who's getting screwed, right? There must be something in the background you're unaware of, except the most obvious: someone had to *not* get the job if more than one person applied. Duh! If you got the job instead of Debbie, she could rightfully claim that outside forces had a hand in it as well. Both of you can't be wrong. Well, actually, you both can and most likely are. It could be that your face happens to resemble the supervisor's ex-spouse, and there's no way she would want to be seeing that person's image up close and personal every day."

"I got fired," Telly says.

"Another notch in your lifebelt. People who believe in conspiracy theories jiu jitsu through life. Legislators who refuse to extend the statute of limitations for filing suit against pedophiles accuse the proposed legislation writers of being pedophiles themselves. There's a perverted logic to this. No one questions why pedophiles would want to enlarge the pool of claimants against them.

"Telly, here's my cell phone. Google these two strings of three symbols each: Caret, percent, and ampersand, then asterisk, first parents, and dollar sign. I may be onto something. They're recurring more often than happenstance. QAnon has accused the Democratic Party of engaging in child sex trafficking without once naming a single child trafficked, much less an arrest. This is QAnon's genius. If someone points this out, QAnon points out that they can't reveal the identities of minors. No one seems concerned that the democratic leadership must be made up of minors.

"The lure of a conspiracy theory is that it relieves the victim of culpability. I have done nothing wrong. That job you lost, maybe your attendance record is less than stellar, or you once offended the company's best customer, et cetera. Believing in conspiracy theories is, at its core, a defensive mechanism to protect your ego. Letting go of your ego, AKA self, is a prerequisite for learning because learning requires disengaging from former beliefs. Beliefs are what make up the self. You can only appreciate that the earth is round if you thought it was something other than round before, and thinking it was flat is perfectly fine if that's all you've ever experienced."

"I haven't come up with anything on those ciphers," says Telly.

"Excellent, I was hoping that would be the case. In the case of the roundness of earth, in day-to-day activities, it really makes no difference. Even if you're the pilot of a transcontinental aircraft, computers do all the work to make sure you don't fly into space or dive into the sea. And a pilot could still believe that his life was controlled by unseen powers, even if his career and life depended on there not being any.

"Believing that life is completely controlled by conspiracies is fatalistic, while believing there's an opportunity to thwart the conspiracy is comic. Edgar Madison Welch's Pizzagate shooting was consistent with his belief in QAnon, at least. Why do all the other QAnon believers have their hands in their pants? Hopefully, Welch's miscalculation persuaded a few QAnon supporters to ramp up their attendance at AA meetings, perhaps even at a community college course in basic logic."

"How do you know when you're getting closer to de-encrypting?" asks Telly. "It looks to me that you're going around in circles. I'm getting dizzy watching your screen."

"'Close' is an Albert Einstein term. One of the oldest conspiracy theories blames Jews for every bad thing that happens. This is odd on its face but not its trajectory. Jews have suffered at the hands of others more than any other group of people on the planet for as long as we have had recorded history, well, at least of those who have survived. Why the Jews? Why not the Caucasians? Caucasians are much easier to pick out in a lineup, and we're hands down the GOAT for plant, animal, and human murder. The trick is to blame the least able to defend themselves when you're the real culprit.

"You didn't get the boy, job, loan, or bonus, right? Since it wasn't because of anything you did, the only sensible behavior is to not put in any effort at all. When things work out in your favor, it's because even a broken clock is correct twice a day, and being lucky is better than being good. Actually, much better. Being good takes hard work. Conspiracy theories replace cause and effect with a room that has no bottom, ceiling, or walls. It's a drive to a highway with no exit ramps. Watch your mileage, though."

"I know how to remove the microchip from my hand," says Telly.

Melody remains drumming away on her laptop and says, "Take the life extension lobbies. Encouraging people to reduce their ingestion of cigarettes, booze, drugs, and fast foods, especially while driving, is a good thing. And, most likely, that would increase human longevity without a boatload of hard evidence. But the life extension firms advertise that their supplements extend people's lives. How can you prove a person lived longer because he took a supplement before he died from a massive stroke, allergic reaction to melatonin, or a binge streaming hiccup attack?"

"Do you believe in miracles?" asks Telly.

"Until we sent spacecraft to the moon, it was impossible to disprove that the moon was not made of cheese, even though it was pretty hard to explain how the cows got up there in the first place. We know how cheese is made. Why someone would send cows to the moon is a totally different question. Of course, you have to believe the moon is round to begin with, right? How else could it circle around us? So, the flat Mooners haven't increased to intolerable numbers, at least.

"There are still those who believe that the moon landing never happened, that it was all staged in Hollywood. So, for them, the moon will remain cheese forever. I wonder if it's cheddar, mozzarella, or gouda. Of course, that just shows the limits of my imagination. It may just as well be demonici, repubislicker, or liberovich."

"I've never heard of those cheeses," says Telly. "They sound like political parties."

"There are only two real political parties. Conservatives believe everything is fine, so changes are bad. Liberals believe everything is not fine, and changes are good."

"What about the Conspiracists and Independents?" Telly asks.

"They suffer from MCI."

"That's mild cognitive impairment," says Telly. "The doctors say I suffer from that all the time."

"Either party can fall for conspiracy theories. What they want to believe is that the consequences of indiscriminate drinking, speeding, sex, lying, and stealing are not their fault, because even if they hadn't, the results would be the same. An outside force will either smash their dreams or award them a Nobel Prize, eventually. It's not an attitude easily disproved. And it doesn't help when most Nobel Prize Recipients bend over backwards, humbly apologizing for being so lucky, while disingenuously omitting to mention their twenty-year judge trolling campaign.

"Conspiracy theories select facts that explain why what shouldn't have happened, from their point of view, did, and push facts under the bed when what should have happened did. Like trying to support that whites are the superior race. Forgoing that color is cosmetic, that skin is not sentient, why have whites been so diligent in scrubbing out the achievements of non-whites?"

After listening to Melody trashing many of his long-held beliefs, Andy finally pipes in with, "Yeah, well oftentimes, we learn well after all the dust has settled, a secret group was working behind the scenes, pushing things along to their liking. Remember the Pentagon Papers? They showed us that Johnson and McNamara were lying about our progress in the VietNam War."

"You are spot on Andy," says Melody. "The same was done under the Bush and Obama administrations for Afghanistan and Iraq."

"And there were explosives planted in the World Trade Center before the airplanes hit on 9/11," Andy says. "That's why they fell."

"No, there weren't," says Telly. "I watched simulations of what would happen if they were hit by airliners. The towers fell exactly as they did in the model."

"Don't forget, Princess Diana was killed by British Intelligence, subliminal advertising undermines our will, and chemtrails rain down vapors that make our hair fall out," says Melody. "Proof of that is there are no cave drawings of bald men."

"Who's to say?" chimes Andy.

"Andy, then why do you have a full head of brown hair while mine's under attack, follicle by follicle? We live under a different sky? Conspiracy theories are only limited by the imagination of their creators. Have you heard of the magic number Nine-Oh-Five?"

"No Melody," says Andy. "I've never heard of it."

"It just so happens that January 6, 2021, known as the Epiphany, is the 905-month anniversary of the Hiroshima bombing."

"So?" says Andy.

"That's the piece you are working on for the Watanabes, isn't it?"

"There's no connection," says Andy. "I mean, what are you getting at?"

"Did you know that section 905 of Title Eighteen of the PA criminal code makes exceptions for the punishment of treason? And interfering with the peaceful transfer of power would constitute treason."

"I don't like where this is going," says Andy.

"So, it's just a coincidence that Trump selected January 6 for a rally on the appointed day for the peaceful transfer of power in the United States of America, on the anniversary of the mythical magis' visit to the newborn king-god, and the 905-month anniversary of the bombing of Hiroshima, the code number for absolving the new god-king AKA Donald Trump from treason, then. I'm just saying.

"Everything is connected. What's wrong with January 20, the day the newly elected president is supposed to actually move in? We share a zip code with Silver Springs, number 20905. January 20 and 905. Then, there's the year just passed, 2020. Of course, there are flaws to this theory. For one, 90520 is the zip code to Torrance, California. What an awe-inspiring name. Torrance means 'little craggy hills.' Reminds me of our little home. Torrance is farther from D.C. than Canada and similarly known for practically nothing, eh."

Telly, swinging her head around on her neck, interrupts, "January 6 was set as the day of the peaceful transfer of power before World War Two, before the Hiroshima bombing."

"Oops," says Melody.

In the ensuing silence, Andy says, "But we can't rule out that the people that control everything knew World War Two was coming when they set the January 6 date."

"Bingo, Handcream," says Melody.

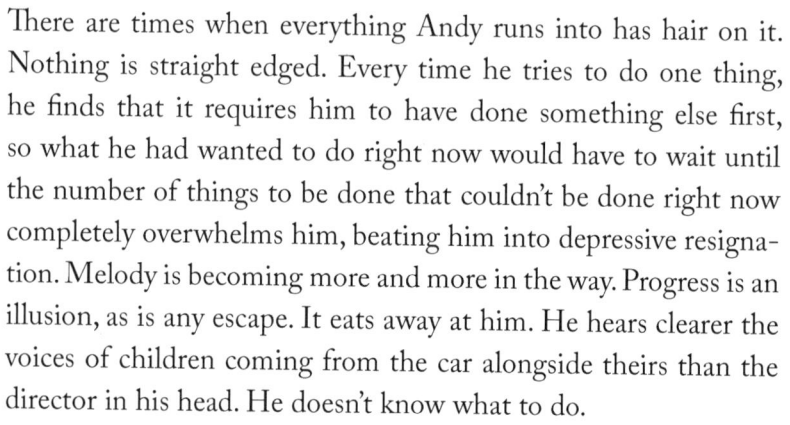

There are times when everything Andy runs into has hair on it. Nothing is straight edged. Every time he tries to do one thing, he finds that it requires him to have done something else first, so what he had wanted to do right now would have to wait until the number of things to be done that couldn't be done right now completely overwhelms him, beating him into depressive resignation. Melody is becoming more and more in the way. Progress is an illusion, as is any escape. It eats away at him. He hears clearer the voices of children coming from the car alongside theirs than the director in his head. He doesn't know what to do.

He's only sure that most everybody is laughing at him. And that he's no more intelligent than this ant climbing up the steering column in search of... He squishes it with his thumb with no more sentience than the ant. So much for purpose. Is he his finger pad or the ant? He turns on the windshield wipers to clear road sludge. He's the finger, at least today, but he feels like the ant. Perhaps, it's time to change their brand of coffee.

CHAPTER THIRTY-THREE

SPLIT-STEP LABYRINTH

The Hurrah Club is two pairs of tennis courts between a one-story cinder block building. The building has just enough space for a kitchen, a living-slash-dining room, and a unisex restroom. It serves the purposes of its thrifty non-profit members during spring, summer, and fall, but it lies dormant in the winter. It's situated in a bit of a gully and surrounded by trees. Most drivers pass it by unnoticed unless the parking lot is full. Today, not one car rests on its gravel driveway. Andy parks the Buick under the pine tree limbs.

"Telly, you only need to stay here a couple of days until this all blows over," says Melody. "No one will look for you here. Handcream, turn the electricity and water back on. We'll bring in the grocery bags, and I'll familiarize Telly with the place."

Andy does as he's told, glowering the whole time like a truant student staying after school, forced to scour the trash cans for the janitor.

Melody takes down the club's drapes, converting them into blankets, and spreads them out on the sofa. She instructs Telly on how to work the TV but tells her to keep the volume as low as possible. She plugs in the space heater and makes sure it's far enough from anything combustible, ordering Telly not to move it under any condition.

"Telly, you keep my cell phone," says Melody. "Don't call us unless the cops are at your door, or you read some juicy gossip about the Bundesliga."

Andy joins them inside and shows Telly where the light switches are. Like most low-bid construction jobs, the switches are where they were easiest for the electrician to install and hardest for the occupants to find.

When Andy and Melody are about to leave, Telly asks, "What about school?"

"School?" asks Melody.

"I'm only seventeen."

"Well, Melody," says Andy. "You didn't figure on that did you? Back to square one."

"Isn't it still Christmas break?" says Melody.

"We start back up on Monday, the fourth."

"That's this morning."

"I know," says Telly. "I've been meaning to tell you, but with all this…"

"So, this has all been for nothing," says Andy. "We better get her to school before there's another warrant out for us."

"We are fine," says Melody. "Notes from parents for absences aren't required until she returns to class. Mr. Chief is unlikely to report she's AWOL. And Telly, you don't mind missing a few days of school, do you?"

CHAPTER THIRTY-FOUR

ANOTHER PARKING LOT

Melody yells down to Andy as he works in the basement, "Handcream, the message on the microchip is an address."

"To what?"

"A commercial parking lot in Bowie," says Melody.

"So?"

"My sentiments exactly."

Andy walks up the basement stairs and says, "Melody, don't you think it's time we dropped this? Telly is safe for now, though she might need restocking. Did you notice how fast she puts down food? The plaque is done, but the Watanabes aren't returning my calls. If they think they're going to weasel out of paying us, they've got another thing coming. Without that check..."

"I've got something, and I've got a couple of things," says Melody.

"Whaddya say, we leave detective work to the police?"

"Of course, that's the answer. I get it," says Melody. "What time is it?"

"Noon."

"Good visibility. I'll get dressed."

Andy looks at Melody and says, "You are dressed."

Melody examines her outfit and heels and says, "So I am. Leave your work clothes on. I'll be in the car. Fill the thermos with coffee."

Andy drives the Buick to the parking lot. It takes up two city blocks. Its signage is ancient and in need of some fresh paint, but the chain-link front roll gate sports a space-age padlock. Thankfully, at one in the afternoon, the lock hangs vainly on its chain. Andy drives in and around a bit before locating block lot 396, a parking space deep in its bowels.

"A beat-up, old RV," says Melody. "I'm not smelling myrrh or frankincense here, and if it has gold inside, Brinks will file a union grievance for negligence."

"It's at least fifty feet long," says Andy. "Its windshield has one-way mirror film, so we can't see inside."

"What's behind it?"

"An empty motorcycle trailer."

"What would that be for?" asks Melody.

"Towing motorcycles?"

"It's large enough for an Oklahoma City fertilizer bomb," says Melody. "But who would trust anything of value in it? Unless its shabby looks are meant to discourage thieves."

"It's leaning pretty bad on the left," says Andy.

"There are very few snow-tire marks around, so it hasn't been here long. It must be mobile, as it's parked too close to the RV in front of it for being towed. Take a look at its undercarriage."

"So that's why you wanted me to keep on my work clothes."

Andy, feeling sheepish but knowing better than, dons his gloves and gets out of the Buick. He looks around to make sure no one is watching then gingerly slides under the RV. He's freezing, but something about all this also intrigues. After thoroughly surveying the undercarriage from front to rear, he gets back to his feet and walks around the vehicle, patting his hands around its tires as if to make sure they're round.

He returns to the steaming Buick after shaking snow and dirt off his gloves. He takes a long swig of coffee and reports, "The undercarriage is clean, no rust. The tires' sidewalls have been professionally roughed up with a sander. I do the same with the bark on some of my bowls. Buyers like the look. Distressed, they call it."

"What does that mean, Handcream?" Melody asks.

"It's camouflaged to look ratty. I quartered the wheel treads, ten thirty-seconds deep. Good as new. The lean is fake too. Two tires need air is all. A minute or two with a pump and she'd sit square."

"Can we get inside?"

"Nope. 100% secured. There are no side windows. The exterior paneling has been reinforced with stainless steel, and the back door can only be unlocked from the inside. No one can get in without a key."

"Can you get inside?"

"I could use an MIG welder and cut through it."

"Would that draw a lot of attention?"

"MIGs burn bright and create a loose electricity sound," says Andy. "Not particularly loud but it's a sound that everyone notices right away. And it would take a while."

"Iffy at best, then. What else?"

"If you could research the lock's manufacture and pick up what type of keys it uses, I could make a series of skeleton keys on my lathe."

"Needle in a stay hack," says Melody, "but so was finding the address. Anything else to report, Corporal?"

"Yeah, I found this in between two frame ribs." Andy hands over what looks like a stopwatch.

"A tracking device," says Melody.

"Yep. Someone knows where it is."

Melody takes it from Andy and looks it over before she says, "I wonder if I can backtrack it, maybe find out where it came from."

"Needle in a haystack,' says Andy.

"My specialty. Let's get back home where I can work on this piece of good news."

"Good news?" asks Andy.

"Neither the RV nor this tracking device is ticking."

CHAPTER THIRTY-FIVE

80-YEAR-OLD CYCLE

America is ripe. The weapons manufacturers, vultures on the power line, lick their chops and await the Eighty Year Cycle. Every eighty years, America suffers an epileptic seizure. We fought in World War II eighty years ago, and eighty years before that we had the Civil War, and eighty years before, we had the Revolution. Notice the use of the word we! Since I wasn't alive two hundred and forty years ago, it's more than a stretch for me to include myself as one of our forefathers who fought and suffered for the country, I now recreate in. But we all do this. Last week, I heard some of us baby boomers taking credit for winning the Second World War. Our parents, 99.9% of them dead and buried, won Doubleyou Doubleyou Two, not us. Our generation's claim to fame was losing the VietNam War.

Essentially, the Eighty Year Cycle is the curse of peace. Eighty years is the span of time it takes a country's citizens to lose its respect for, and memory of, what the prior one endured. Helped along very nicely by scrupulously scrubbing the nation's complicity for its own woes from our school history books.

Eighty years is how long it takes to replace the horrors of war with 'it couldn't have been that bad.' After all, past generations didn't have to deal with spotty Wi-Fi, cyberbullying, constant computer upgrade boondoggles, or the plague of password resets.

And really it can't be helped. Eighty years out from hell, people get bored. Then the demagogues bloom out of the earth like cicadas. It's a shame that demagoguery isn't listed as an exception to the Freedom of Speech. Yelling fire in a crowded theater is. They really are the same.

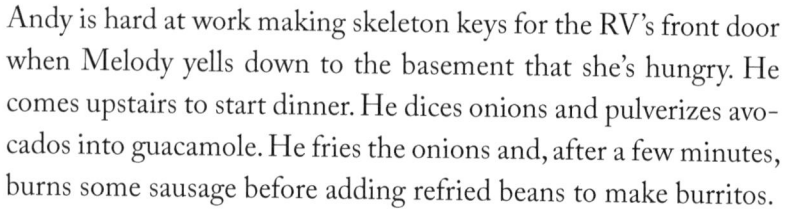

Andy is hard at work making skeleton keys for the RV's front door when Melody yells down to the basement that she's hungry. He comes upstairs to start dinner. He dices onions and pulverizes avocados into guacamole. He fries the onions and, after a few minutes, burns some sausage before adding refried beans to make burritos.

While he cooks, Andy asks, "Melody, why are we doing this again? None of this Telly stuff is getting us any closer to paying the mortgage."

"Nor is it aiding and abetting your attendance at Trump's rally the day after next," says Melody. She pounds away on her laptop keyboard, loud enough to have convinced Benedict Arnold that the master bedroom had the better claim for a place to sleep.

"I'm starting to feel like a recording on a telephone," says Andy. "'Press one if you speak English', press two if you speak hinglish." Melody doesn't bite. "Press three for Trump, four for Biden, five for war and six if nuclear is the first option."

"If you are going to ignore evidence," says Melody, "war is the result. Is that what you are really hungry for? You want a world that is black and white, right? With seven billion people, that's hardly possible. How are the keys coming?"

"Almost done. I'm making them so I can snip them down as I try them. Instead of making a hundred keys, I'm only making a dozen. Ten minutes to plate."

"Leaders today insist on arming up in case a neighbor strikes without warning. This siphons away valuable resources and raises taxes, which keeps the citizenry impoverished and hungry for the red meat it imagines its neighbor is eating at its dinner table."

"We will have to settle for pork sausage burritos," says Andy. "War is the natural state."

"The reason for war is always the same," says Melody. "Someone wants something but doesn't want to pay for it. It works out badly for both parties, always. Do you really want war, Handcream?"

"No, I guess not. They wouldn't take me. I'm too old."

CHAPTER THIRTY-SIX

RV AVENUE

"Hey Dad, where you guys been?" says Jeremy. "I've called you like a dozen times. Put Mom on the phone, will ya?"
Andy turns the burner off and hands the phone over to Melody.
"Hi, Jeremy, so nice to hear your voice. You dropping by this evening? I'm sure Andy could cook up something to eat. He is, as a matter of fact. Do you still like Burritos? And beer. Bring beer."
"Can't make it tonight, Mom, busy, busy, busy these days at the Cap. Listen, Mom, I'm strapped, so could you forward a couple hundred? The rent is past due, and you know us cops have to pay for our equipment. Not cheap."
"How much is that?"
"A couple of hundred."
"Is a couple a pair?"
"Yes, a pair of hundreds."
"Okay, I'll have Andy take me to the bank."
"No need Mom, just Venmo it."
"What? I do not know anyone by that name. Is Venmo Italian?"

"No, Mom, remember that app I gave you on your iPad?"

"Is an app an Italian ice flavor, like vanilla?"

"You don't remember, huh?" says Jeremy. "You know, dealing with you two is getting more and more like watching *Friends* on TV."

"We've always been good friends," says Melody. "Everyone tells us what a fonderfully wun time they have when they come over. That didn't sound right, did it?"

"Mom, you never have anyone over. Okay, I get it. I need to drill down to the source from now on."

"Yes, do that, and give that Italian friend of yours my best."

"Mom, could you put Dad on the phone."

"Okay, I love you too, too da loo."

"So, Jeremy, you coming over to the one-exciting-event-a-minute MacClean household tonight? As Melody said, I'm frying up burritos."

"Dad, look, it's crazy right now. You guys still watch the news, right? We are all working double shifts with the transfer of power Wednesday."

"Yeah, I'll be there too," says Andy.

"Wow, I had forgotten that."

"I could meet you. We could do lunch or something."

"You want to rethink that, Dad."

"You're trained in this kind of stuff, right?" says Andy. "Some are saying it might get rowdy."

"Yes, actually it's guaranteed, Dad. Don't worry about me though. I've got everything sussed. Uh, do you know how to work the Venmo app I put on Mom's iPad?"

"No."

"You are living in the fifteenth century, I swear," says Jeremy.

"Wood doesn't mind. So, you're busy, huh? Well, I've been busy too."

"Turning stumps into children's cereal bowls?"

"No, Big Cop!" says Andy. "Melody and I are protecting a young girl from Police Chief Delorean."

"You are so full of it, Dad. Chief Delorean is true blue. If he's after some girl, you know she's a felon, bona fide."

"What if the girl is his stepdaughter?"

"Dad, is Mom rubbing off on you? This sounds nuts. Chief Delorean is my role model."

"Well, your role model tried to kill me. Then fingered me for carjacking."

"You're the carjacker?"

"Now, you know as well as anyone I never carjacked anyone."

"You sound fine. What did he hit you with, a rubber ducky?"

"He tried to drive over me in a Dodge van," says Andy.

"You know they're 100% aluminum, Dad. Sure, this isn't a lot of trash talk to avoid loaning me a hundred bucks?"

"What happened, Melody said no?"

"No, she said yes, only she's forgotten how to Venmo."

"We're hiding the chief's daughter from him until things blow over."

"Really, she's at your place?"

"No, that would be stupid since the chief knows who we are. I told you, he tried to run me over in a car. Didn't you hear me? We have her out at my tennis club, safe as a filet mignon steak at a vegan wedding."

"Keep her at the tennis club then. I'll drop by tomorrow. You still know how to write out a check."

"That's how I pay my bills. I could mail it out tomorrow."

"You ever hear of… Forget it. On further thought, go ahead and mail it to me. And forget about the rally. It's going to get ugly fast. I won't be able to protect you, okay?"

"Jeremy, you know your mother. I can't predict where I'll be more than five minutes ahead of the minute, I'm in. But don't be surprised if you see me there."

"Reliance, ain't my parents' playing card."

"I heard that," said Melody, the other phone to her ear. "Reliance does not mean 'rely on parents."

"Okay, see you all later. Thanks, Dad. Bye, Mom."

Andy says to Melody as she walks into the kitchen, "Did you hear that, Melody? Jeremy said thanks. Burritos are ready." Andy bites into one, some of the guacamole running down his chin. Melody wipes it off.

"I'm not hungry now, Handcream. You told Jeremy where Telly is."

"So?"

"She has to leave."

"Melody, you said it was the perfect place."

"It was!"

"I don't understand," says Andy.

"Finish your supper," says Melody. "Then let's go."

"Jeremy isn't going to tell anyone."

"Jeremy is a cop. Cops talk all day. Their superpower is gossip. Gossip created civilization. It won't be long before Delorean knows."

"But he's our son, Melody."

"Right now."

"I thought you wanted me to finish these skeleton keys for the RV?"

"Bring the blanks you've made so far. I'm feeling lucky, just not particularly good."

"Okay, okay," says Andy. "I'll call her at the club and let her know we're coming."

"No! Phone calls can be traced."

"Melody, who's paranoid now?"

"Give me a minute to get something out of my car."

"The car we pay insurance on, and you never drive?" asks Andy.

"That's what insurance is for, the accidents you know will happen."

CHAPTER THIRTY-SEVEN

CONVOY TO THE CAPITOL

They pick up Telly at the Hurrach Club then drive to the RV, where one of Andy's skeleton keys fits the driver's door, easy peasy.

All three squeeze hip to hip into the front bench seat, feeling like teenagers stealing their first car. Melody first in shotgun, Telly in the middle, and Andy at the steering wheel. The only thing they can see inside that is not a manufactured part of the vehicle is a lanyard hanging from the rearview mirror. On it is written, *take some weight off,* from a firm called Fitness Doesn't Have to Hurt. It sways to the rhythm of the RV's analog clock, which ticks disproportionately loudly considering its tiny size. They all stare at it. Listen to it. Each wonders when everything, themselves included, will explode.

Melody says, "Don't worry. If a bomb goes off, we'd be dead before we ever felt it."

Comforted, Telly begins searching the cab. She opens the glove box and console. Both are spotless and empty. The door pockets and cupholders are equally empty. "You know, I'm getting thirsty," says Telly.

"Why the lanyard?" asks Melody. "It must be a clue. What driver needs that?"

"It's just some gym promotion," says Andy, pulling it down and examining it before placing it back.

"Is there a hidden door somewhere?" asks Telly. "I don't even see a way to get in the back."

They peel back the carpet under their shoes. Nada.

"Don't RV's have a pathway to the rear?" says Melody. "Pickups often have a truck slider. There's no window here, just a metal panel, the same satin black as everything else is inside."

"Looky here," says Andy, pointing to the panel's corner near Melody's head. They see a numerical keypad below a digital screen with five open spaces.

"There's only five spaces?" says Andy. "We should be able to crack that in short order. Five times five is twenty-five, right?"

"No," says Telly, "it's five times five times five times five times five or three thousand one hundred twenty-five."

"Close" says Melody. "It's ten to the fifth power, or one million." She takes out a silver stopwatch and fiddles with it. "Telly, when I say go, punch in one two three four five and let's see how long it takes for the screen to read the passcode.

"Andy, listen and watch for any signal of something opening."

It takes Telly ten seconds to key in the numbers and for them to show on the screen. Nothing happens.

"So, what is one million divided by six?"

"Why six?" asks Telly.

Melody frowns at Telly and looks over at Andy for support, but she isn't getting any and so says, "Ten seconds to key in one code, six ten-seconds in a minute, et cetera. If we tag team this, and no potty breaks, we can punch in every combination within eight days."

"It looks like they've thought of everything," says Andy.

"What do you mean?" asks Telly.

"Why make it so hard?" says Melody. "It was already impossible."

"I'm hungry and thirsty," said Telly.

"Yeah, let's get in the Buick and get something to eat?" says Andy.

"Why drive the Buick when we can drive this?" asks Melody. "Andy, what's that in the ignition slot?"

Telly blurts, "The key."

Andy tries but no luck. The key doesn't turn.

"Try your skeleton keys, Handcream," says Melody.

No luck either.

The three sit in the cab. No one talks for about twelve and a half minutes.

Melody breaks the silence, "If we were the ones who were supposed to get the RV, we would need a way not only to get inside the RV but also to drive it, right? But we would not necessarily need a way to get inside the cargo hold. Others could provide its passcode when the RV is at the target site."

"And, so far, we only have the microchip that told us where we could find the RV," says Telly. "Maybe I should take it out now?"

"Let's not get ahead of ourselves," says Melody. "We can guess that the encryption code was in the Chief's scanner, the one you said he would read every day. So, his scanner must have come with the microchip.

"Telly, were you there when the microchip was delivered to your stepdad?"

"No, I have no idea where he got it."

"So, you don't know if a door key," says Melody, "or an ignition key was sent along with the microchip?"

Telly shakes her head, no.

"Telly, what are the six factors here?" asks Melody.

"The RV, the RV's location, the key to get inside, the key to start it, and the key to open the back. I don't see what the sixth is."

"The payload."

"The roof is the only other way in," Andy says. "There's no exterior ladder to get up there."

"All the more reason to look."

"It's a cube Melody," says Andy. "I can't climb straight up."

"The Anasazi did," says Melody. "You've hiked Canyon de Chelly."

"Yeah, but the Anasazi had, over centuries, carved in toeholds," says Andy. "We don't have centuries here. We have two days. We could drive it somewhere where I can see the roof, alongside a fire escape on a tall building maybe."

"If we could drive it," says Telly.

"Thanks for reminding me, Telly," says Andy. "Looks like I should be taking advice from you from now on."

"Andy is your door now locked?" asks Melody.

Andy swings it open, closes it back, and swings it open again.

"The passenger door is frozen," says Melody, pushing against it. "It has no button to push or handle to pull. The window doesn't roll down. Andy, go around. See if you can open the door from the other side. See if your skeleton key works."

He does and comes back around the car and says to them, "There is neither a door latch nor a keyhole in that door."

"Handcream, stay outside," says Melody. "Telly, reach over and turn the ignition key and see if this thing will start," says Melody.

She does. The dash panel lights up, and the screen begins its navigation screen.

"Amazing!" says Telly.

Andy laughs.

"Okay, Telly, switch it off, get out of the RV, and take ten steps away," says Melody.

Telly does what she's asked, recognizing both the absurdity as well as the inevitability that Melody is right.

Melody slides over to the driver's seat and turns the key. Nothing happens. She then returns to the shotgun position, turns the key. Nothing happens. Melody motions Telly to come up to the driver's door and turn the key. The RV motor and lights turn on.

Melody explains, "The microchip is a key fob for the RV's ignition. That way the driver doesn't need a key because they have their own microchip. There must be a pressure plate under the driver's ass. Any weight on it short circuits the starter. 'Take Some Weight Off.'

"Handcream, you found one tracking device. There may be another one in the cargo hold, where we can't get at it. Let's see if there's a roof door. Telly, as you have the fob inside you, you drive. I'll ride with Andy. In the meantime, there's something I need to work out."

"Okay," says Telly.

"But take 'er easy, Telly," says Andy. "This is an electric vehicle, and according to the dash light up, it has two Hum-Vee motors. So, it can move."

"I'll give it a chance to do just that," says Telly.

"If you rear end me, I'll sue ya," says Andy.

Telly drives the RV and follows the Buick. On the way out the parking lot, Melody has Andy stop. She gets out and inspects another parked RV. It's about the same size. She walks around it three times.

"Are you a dog preparing to take a nap?" Andy finally asks her.

"What would you think of living in one of these if we lose our home?" asks Melody. "Claims adjusters call them hurricane magnets. I didn't feel a force of any kind, but first things first."

"What's that Melody?"

"We need to put some air in the RV's tires."

With Telly following them in the RV, Andy scouts for a building with an exterior fire escape. He finds a compatible warehouse. Andy climbs its fire escape, and Telly drives the RV under it. No sign of a door on the roof.

"Let's get on the turnpike," says Melody. "We can park at a rest stop and think this through together. There are too many variables for me to dribble without a dunk-slam. Telly, here's the transponder from my car. You can take the EZ-Pass lanes."

"How did you know to bring that?"

CHAPTER THIRTY-EIGHT

FOUR WALL PACE TRACK

In Fort Dix prison, Lutz read Nietzsche, Hegel, and Schopenhauer. Authors who had not been prescribed by his public-school education. He fell under their thrall.

Those who acquired the most power were the truly great men. Lutz saw himself as a fair candidate to join that list. In America, power meant money, so he started to read the Wall Street Journal front to back and invested all in.

However, with unerring precision, he had missed every bull market and social media windfall. He had less money than when he started, and he had had a lot. When he enlisted in the National Guard, his parents gave him a Christmas present of a hundred thousand dollars. In exchange, he was not to embarrass them by, like, actually showing up at their front door. They afforded him annual free refills, that is, until they reached the end of their bonanza. When the hundred-thousand-dollars-a-year earmark trickled to Starbucks gift cards for a half dozen lattes, Lutz had to get a job. He had been born in Maryland and served in the military, in a war zone, just not during the actual fighting. Why would any business have a problem with hiring him? Job placement services pointed out his time at Fort Dix, "Have you thought of sanitation service? They specialize in hiring ex-felons."

As the infamy of the 372nd was stamped in Cresaptown with Cumberland gappers, Lutz moved to the east of the State, home of the US Navy for heaven's sake.

His first job was a purveyor of fake news. Propaganda pays, it's just very slow to. Moses's and Virgil's royalties are still pumping out somewhere in the pipeline for the Bible and the Aeneid. He started reading the news fourteen hours a day. He had to in order to compete with the champion click-baiters.

From all of his reading, Lutz concluded that a large portion of the population was convinced the country was a minute or two away from a Second Civil War. The North prayed that the South would win this time. Nothing had really changed since the first one. As a purveyor of fake news, he intended to incite both sides to keep their powder dry.

Unlike the myth that blacks had it better under slavery, most blacks remember it differently and desired no chance of that ever happening again. Their survival in the States required stealth and persistence, not static riots, and for the most part, this thinking held because most blacks felt the underbelly of racism as a lava so hot, coming within a few feet could incinerate them. Even the mention of past indiscretions would set off a firestorm. There was no calming prejudice with logic, no matter how persuasive. You just got that pinched-lip smile that said, "No worries," which meant, "it's never going to happen on my watch, Baby."

Lutz learned through thousands of rejections that the more bizarre the lie, the more likely a news outlet would publish it.

For instance, he was paid well by his fake-news employer when the Philadelphia Inquirer published his: "We can now cherish Trump's victory lap following his four-year moment in the sun." And what a moment that was. He hired one incompetent cabinet member after another, dismissing each when they disagreed with him or got caught flat-footed with hand in till. He denied there was a pandemic, which has killed a hundred thousand people and is rising. He separated children from their parents at the border, children who have yet to be reunited with their parents. He withdrew from NAFTA and the Iran Agreement and threatened to leave NATO. He instituted tax investigations on his enemies. All hail the Mad Hatter-in-chief.

He was paid even more when the Wall Street Journal published his: "Aren't you tired of bad-mouthing our President?" All you write about are his few vices and never print a single article on his enormous accomplishments. You give no credit to his withstanding withering attacks from the Left, which started before he even took office. He's the first president to challenge the elites' control of our country. History will respond by naming him as our greatest president, greater than Lincoln and Washington combined, and his long-deserved Nobel Prize is minutes away from final approval. He has to be re-elected for the good of the country, for the good of the planet. Amen.

His other pieces argued that defunding the police was surrender, and increasing either police salaries or manpower was bribery. He insisted that police handle mental-health dramas and take drug tests before and after every shift, promoted more mounted police and less-expensive prisons, and justified stricter capital punishment verdicts and looser open-carry restrictions. The dead require no babysitting and cost no tax dollars.

Lutz found minor success in spreading the rumor that Iran was buying up all the LGBTQ bars in order to find work for its dispatriots and that mainstream media had been paid off by Denmark to promote communism. Otherwise, he was a small flame in a supernova of blaming everything on someone else. He didn't have the required imagination to succeed. He went broke paying for tips on scandals that mostly only fooled him.

Eventually, Lutz fell into street cophood, which reintroduced him into the familiar feel of applying personal physical pressure on others. The Damascus police force either hadn't drilled down to learn about his prison sentence or didn't award demerits for abusing Iraqis. They had it coming. Even if the mainstream media insisted Iraq had no part in 9/11, most Americans were confident it had. Why else did we go to war? And let's not get into who had sold the weapons of mass destruction to Saddam in the first place. Focus instead on Saddam's vicious anti-American rhetoric, notwithstanding that rhetoric against the United States is the national pastime of half the countries on the globe, different only in the US's once blaming all the world's ills on Communism in its intensity. When China won the VietNam War, to save face, the US refocused on blaming the USSR for everything. Then, when the USSR imploded, the US switched to blaming street communism AKA labor unions. Evil is always fomented by the workers, never mind George Bailey's speech to Mr. Potter in *It's a Wonderful Life*.

Every leader encourages his supporters to rally against other people, whether a Baptist preacher in a one steeple town or the president of a billion-strong country. The only people we should fear are those who spend their time telling us what to fear, but that is a snake swallowing its own tail. In the background festers the truth. Peace just doesn't pay.

Becoming a cop was invigorating for Lutz. He quickly got the beat and loved being near prison cell walls again. They became his anchor. He figured out that the police, with union help, had become a fifth wall while possessing neither a chain of command nor a wink of responsibility. The first needed fixing. The second needed to be exploited. Lutz intended to do both. Donald Trump would be his ladder.

Once Donald Trump was in office, Lutz recognized that he was ignorant of power's purpose. His failing to woo the military to launder the vote count was utter malfeasance. All Trump ever did was parade his appointees out to fawn over him in public and lash out against everyone who didn't. Even if she was just a teenager.

A second unelected term would end the American experiment. Good Riddance. It had been a sham from the beginning. The only thing united about the US was the word in its name. So, Lutz began to seek out audiences with Donald Trump. It wasn't hard. A hundred-dollar bill bought you a handshake.

The first time was short-lived, with Lutz being shoved aside right after. Still, it gave Lutz the opportunity to watch the President's devotees. They specialized in flattery's harshness, not its substance. The second paid handshake gave Lutz a chance to show Trump his fake news op-eds. Trump said he was impressed, even though he didn't take the time to actually read them, and invited Lutz to join him for lunch. Lutz's hope for a personal chat was short-lived, as the table was overcrowded with sycophants, and before Lutz was halfway through his burger, Trump had finished two and left to watch TV.

Lutz saw why he was making no headway. Flattery worked best with a side of money. Lutz could only flash flattery. His credit was not good enough to impress a self-proclaimed billionaire. He had to find another way in.

STOPTHECHEAT, an Internet start-up formed to fight against mail-in ballots, was now asking for volunteers to help with the recount. It assured everyone that only through its efforts would Trump be able to keep his seat. Lutz volunteered to do anything he could, which turned out to be "PUSH THE DONATE BUTTON." He gave all he could, hoping this might be his gateway to legacy.

It was. The day after the election, he received an email telling him to drive a six-wheel vehicle to the Capitol on January 6.

Lutz would now have an inside track. It would be easy to convince Trump that he needed a Police Tsar when the riots started. All city, county, and state police units would be combined into one department and report to Lutz. The armed forces would necessarily stay in their lane, so he'd have free reign to keep the peace.

Trump would be eager to add another sniveling sycophant to his accordion cabinet. He'd already hired and fired dozens. It wasn't Trump's fault that the ones he fired were inherent vice. Even the Attorney General was floating out to political sea, having signed a tell-all book deal, thereby permanently sealing his fate. Adding another cabinet member would give Donald Trump another photo op, something he never passed up.

There was one glaring stumbling block. Capitalism demands growth. America was in decline, not expansion. At one time, Great Britain, France, Germany, and Spain controlled half the planet. Now, not a single one of them controlled much more than their natural physical borders. America was in queue, having recently lost the Philippines, Panama, and even Cuba. Real leaders expand borders, not shrink them. Xe swallowed Hong Kong whole, despite all of his assurances to the contrary, and now sets sights on Taiwan. Putin annexed parts of Georgia and Ukraine without meaningful pushback and now arranges his army on Ukraine's border, a buzzard surveying its next victim. The Ayatollah threatens every non-Shia country every other day with nuclear teeth. History only notes when borders change.

Donald Trump and Lutz Delorean would take American Exceptionalism to a new scale, replacing America First with America Only. We can and will produce everything we want, right here. If only the Belgians have black Trumpet mushrooms, we will grow them here in abundance and boycott Belgium's. Our wines already surpass France's. We make the best American food on the planet. If you want some, come spend your tourist dollar here.

An alliance with North Korea would start the ball rolling. It almost already had, if North Korea had been more patient, but that was a learning moment. Kim Jong-un could be persuaded with the inducement of increasing his standing in the world order by further cementing North Koreans' allegiance to their leader. Deliver them cheaper fish cake, or something.

South Korea, Japan, and the Philippines, take cover. China, paste on your fake eyelashes and tighten the money belts under your potbellies. But the real move would be to invade and take over Mexico. Mexico, with its huge bank of cheap labor and vacation spots, plus its floppy immigrant panzer movement at the border, made it a ready-made target that many Americans would cheer, "As about time". In one swell swoop, he'd eliminate the immigration mess forever.

Mexico is the perfect acquisition. The US would then be bigger than Canada, becoming the second largest country on the planet. And wouldn't Canada squirm, knowing they shared a four-thousand-mile border with an aggressive country. This is how Ukraine feels about its neighbor Russia, now first place in size. It's good to keep your neighbors nervous. And Canada's security force rated one half-star higher than a 7-11.

Once the Mexican War started, all the other countries would fall into schadenfreude apoplexy. Trump would blame Mexico if the election didn't go his way. You have to blame another country for your own country's problems. It's the natural order. Peace will be extended only if Mexico surrenders right away. Lutz figured he could easily hide out in a beach campsite if it all got too messy.

Lutz's failures at the dating game mimicked his luck on Wall Street. They drove him to buy a wife from Central America, Lydia. He picked her out of a catalog, thankful that her name started with the same letter as his. He'd be mouthing the start of his own name whenever he called her.

She wanted children. He was ambivalent but starved for sex. Lydia wore him out in bed. He found escape and survival from the arduous bedroom ordeals by working overtime, hence his later ascension to chief. If promoted, he would forfeit his accrued overtime pay, and that swamped all the other candidates' qualifications. Lutz and Lydia finally went to a fertility clinic. It concluded they were both infertile. Thence began Lydia's championing of adopting a child, eventually one Theresa Kind.

Telly only gave Lutz one avenue of pleasure. Could she drive! He loved joining her on the grandstands after her junior race victories and looking out at all the cheering, envious faces while she kissed the trophy cup. Otherwise, Telly was more bookmark than joy.

From obstacles like these great men took full advantage. And he was a great man. The word *Lutz*, after all, means light.

CHAPTER THIRTY-NINE

MELODY'S JOY RIDE

When Andy makes it to the Turnpike rest stop, Melody directs him to park with the big rigs. Telly parks the RV right behind. Andy complains about having to walk this far to the food court, so he drives everyone there in the Buick. They drink hot coffee and chow down on re-microwaved wraps. They are suddenly hungry. Melody checks around the eating area to make sure no one will overhear their conversation. Few people are in the building at midnight in January, including staff, who couldn't overhear them anyway. They are all wearing earbuds.

"Something is so important that a police chief tries to kidnap his own stepdaughter," starts Melody, "runs over Andy, and then files a false police report. Each of these is a career-ending move and commands serious jail time. Something is inside this RV, something powerful. Perhaps it identifies those complicit in 9/11 or contains bootleg tickets to a Wizards game. Perhaps it's all one big bomb, set to go off and blow Maryland Mount Fuji sky high.

Jeremy, our son, works at the Capitol. He would be in the bomb's blasting radius. Ideas?"

"Well, I don't think it's filled with panty liners," says Telly.

"Telly, you are getting smarter and smarter as I sit here," says Melody. "Let's see, Christmas is past. When is your birthday?"

"February 16."

"That is close."

"Maybe it's a Trojan Horse, filled with warriors?" says Andy.

"They're awfully quiet for warriors," says Melody, "but they would at least have a bathroom. The cargo has an expiration date, maybe a detonation date, otherwise they wouldn't be so red-hot about getting it."

"We could just leave it here." says Andy.

"If it's a bomb, it would kill a bunch of truck drivers." says Telly.

"Why do we need to do this?" says Andy. "Isn't this FBI business?"

"Did you see that man standing behind the mayor at the police counter?" asks Melody.

"The balding guy?" asks Telly.

"No, the one behind him," says Melody.

Both Telly and Andy look at each other and turn to Melody with the scrunched-up faces that say, "Who?"

"He's FBI! Hodgkins versus Mendolsohn, insider trading case. I was an expert witness. He testified on behalf of the informant."

"I thought witnesses had to testify in person," asks Andy.

"The informant was dead."

"How'd he die?" asks Telly.

"Not relevant but not unscary either," says Melody. "Anyway, FBI is involved. Whether or not it is a bomb, the best solution is to keep it out of reach of the Capitol on January 6. If it's a bomb, we are jeopardizing everyone in its vicinity when it goes off. If the cargo doors can be opened remotely, so can bombs be detonated. Since Alzheimer's has already awarded me a death sentence, I'll drive the RV."

"No, no, no," says Andy, "you can't drive. You haven't in years."

"I'm supposed to die at thirty," says Telly. "Why shouldn't I drive?"

"Telly, you are not going to die at thirty. That number is a statistic, and it includes babies who were born with Prader Willi and died shortly after birth. If it is a bomb, and it goes off with Handcream in it, Telly and I are dead, as there won't be anybody to care for us. If Telly's in it alone, Handcream and I will have failed in our entire reason for being here. But if I'm in it alone, I'll never know it, and you guys are free to live long lives.

"I do not think the RV has a bomb in it. It more than likely holds a high-fidelity broadcast device for the protesters to rally around or Trump trinkets to sell. So, I'm going to play Turnpike shuttle and drive up and down between Virginia and Pennsylvania. What safer place is there? Restrooms, charging stations, and food at the ready. I'll wear a COVID-19 facemask so I can't be recognized, and few men are going to ask me for a date. If I need a nap, the RV bench seat easily allows me to stretch out."

"Where am I going to go?" asks Telly.

"Yeah," says Andy. "Have you figured that out? You driving around on the Turnpike is nuts. I'm not going to let you."

"Well, you have to, and *you* have to take care of Telly. She came to us for help. The police are after her. You alone can protect her, and you're not protecting Telly if you're hauling a bomb around with you. There are no other alternatives. We tried to turn ourselves into the authorities. We tried to hide Telly. With the RV being with me, the target will be off her back. Handcream, your phone is buzzing."

"What could be more important than this?" Andy asks as he opens his cell phone. "It's a text. Seems someone broke into the Hurrah Club. It says they ransacked the place."

"I left it as clean as it was when I got there," says Telly.

"So, someone else must have broken in after," says Andy. "It's not related to us."

"Handcream," barks Melody, "what are the odds that someone breaks into the Hurrah Club within hours of us leaving?"

"Melody, Melody, I don't think I can do this," says Andy.

"Certainly, you can."

"How can you possibly know that, Melody?"

"You've been taking care of a crazy woman for twenty years and a woman with Alzheimer's for two or three or four or… No better training for manhandling the absurd. I wrote an essay on that once, together with a treatise on how reptiles exhibit affection. And no, it's not with their tongues. They're both apropos here."

"Melody, please."

"Besides, Handcream, you seem to be forgetting how we got into this predicament in the first place."

"How was that?" asks Andy.

"Benedict Arnold needs to be walked."

CHAPTER FORTY

HURRAH RUSH

The chief shows up at the Hurrah Club. He sees tell-tale tailings of recent tire marks on the gravel driveway but no cars. The building is dark. He has never been here before and didn't even know it existed. He turns off his unit's inside lights. Draws his Glock out of its holster, finger checks to make sure it's loaded, and switches the safety off. Then eases it back in his holster so the belt lock does not snap in place. He pulls out tape and a flashlight from his glove box and tapes the flashlight to his injured left hand. He moves his fingers around, so they're free enough to turn the flashlight on and, if necessary, pull the Glock's trigger. With his right hand, he pulls out his shotgun, finger checks it, and squeezes himself out of his unit quietly into the open air, a sitting target if he's in someone's crosshairs.

Again, using surprise as a weapon, he runs up to the glass door and smashes it open with the butt of the shotgun. He uses the butt to clear the glass still clinging to the sides of the door frame. He jumps inside and squats low. A hesitant alarm sounds then blares, and a second later the club's exterior lights spring to life. Other than the glass still congratulating itself for being freed, nothing inside the building is applauding his grand entrance. He straightens up, turns on his flashlight, and surveys the interior. No one is in sight, only one other door. It's half-open. He charges inside to meet a toilet and a sink. The ceramics are grateful they're unoccupied and don't become another victim of Lutz's fury.

The place is too warm for being vacant, but there is no other sign of anyone having been here recently. He tries the light switch. Negative. Using the barrel of his shotgun as a prod, he upends everything inside. Even the stove and the trash can are empty. Suspicious. He finds the electrical panel in a closet. Follows the electrical lines to a locked wooden shed attached to the south wall, breaks off the hasp, and locates a secondary electrical panel and a generator. Everything's been shut off, but the generator is warm. He walks to the street and inspects the garbage can. Empty. He's so steamed that he's ready to kill someone. But the first order of business is to call in a burglary. He radios in. He's the first responder.

Lutz goes through the burglary response protocols with the private security guards. He just happened to be driving nearby and heard the alarm. He orders the alarm company personnel to post a sentry, to call a glass outfit to replace the glass door, and to get him the alarm readouts for the last week. They're on it.

He also wants a senior club member out here immediately to make a list of what the burglars took. Nothing a cop likes better than to see a list of what is missing when he knows nothing was taken. It reinforces a cop's innate belief that everyone is a liar and a thief. This exonerates them from taking what they can when they get the chance.

Had Telly even been here? Why did Jeremy MacClean give him this tip? Who'd given it to Jeremy? Wild goose chase except for the warm generator. Maybe someone was there for innocent maintenance purposes. Lutz was sure of two things. His violent entry destroyed all evidence of how the intruder visitor made an egress and ingress, and Telly had never played tennis a day in her life. She couldn't hit a tennis ball. He receives a text. It's from Donna Kind.

CHAPTER FORTY-ONE

ONE RV ON THE LOOSE

"Telly, do you know how to take the microchip out so I can drive the RV?" asks Melody.
"Sure."
"Show me where it is in your hand."
Telly points to the spot below her thumb and Melody finds it. "It's tiny. Feels like a planter's wart. It's small, and it'll pop out if I make a small incision to the side of it and apply pressure underneath like when you squeeze a splinter out. Handcream?"
"Yes."
"Go back to the Buick and bring back a razor blade, a styptic pencil, Band-Aids, plastic gloves, and a bottle of antiseptic."
"We don't have that, Melody."
"Look in the grocery bag that had the space heater in it."
Andy returns with the Hurrah Club Red Cross First Aid Kit that Hurrah club members could truly say is missing.
Melody and Telly excuse themselves for the ladies' restroom. Andy waits outside.

When Melody and Telly return, Melody asks, "Handcream, don't you need to take a leak?"

"I do."

"How do you like my Band-Aid Mr. MacClean?" asks Telly, waving her hand in front of him. "It's a Ren and Stimpy."

"Surprised... Where's yours Melody?" asks Andy.

"Go take your leak," says Melody. "Meet us at the RV, where you can cheer me off on my maiden voyage. See if you can find us some champagne."

Andy senses more is wrong with this than meets the curb. He scratches his head and glances at Melody, who returns it with an angelic pose, the one she uses whenever she does something impossible to correct.

When Andy finishes up in the restroom, he buys three Snickers at the snack shop in lieu of champagne. He walks to the Buick. The girls are not there. He drives to the RV. Melody is standing about ten feet from the RV. She's shaking a little from the cold, her legs tight together, looking at the stars and sipping coffee.

Andy thinks this is crazy. Melody can't drive an RV. He imagines her plowing the RV into the first vehicle that she tries to merge with. And what is he supposed to be doing? Sitting at home and feeding Benedict Arnold and Telly, leaving Melody to nursemaid a bomb?

He looks to where the RV is parked and notices its taillights turn white then red. He looks over at Melody. She sips her coffee, looking indifferent. He walks over to the RV's driver door and tries to open it. It's locked. Telly looks at him through the window. She waves as the RV lurches ahead. He pounds on the door, running alongside it. He can't keep up with it. In seconds, the RV's taillights blend and disappear like the ballplayers did in *Field of Dreams*.

Andy runs over to Melody and yells, "Melody, Telly's taking the RV!" He jumps inside the Buick. Melody makes no move to get in the car when he switches on the ignition. He looks at her through his side window. He waves his hand for her to get in.

"I put too much sugar in this," says Melody, "I'm going back to have them give me another," and walks toward the rest stop. He switches off the ignition and buries his face in his hands, wondering if he should just drive himself to Shepherd Pratt. Is there a waiting list this time of year?

His phone rattles, and he answers, "Andy MacClean here."

"Mr. MacClean, this is Relentless Security, Officer Webster. We have a security contract with the Hurrah Club. It lists you as the maintenance manager and contact. There was a break-in."

"I got the text. What do you need right now? It's late."

"You only live a few miles away from here. The Damascus Chief of Police has some questions that need to be answered immediately."

"Like?"

"Neighbors have reported seeing lights inside and the alarm contact sheet lists two password approved entries in the last few days."

CHAPTER FORTY-TWO

BULLYING ALONG ON THE INTERSTATE

Telly can't help but run through scenarios as she mind-numbingly circuits up and down Interstate 95.

"What's inside? A bomb? How do I find out? Wouldn't Melody be surprised if I figured out the passcode? What would I do then? Getting ahead of myself here. First things first. Stay on the road. Stay in my lane."

To break the monotony of nighttime driving, she listens to the radio. There are very few cooking shows this time of night, so she switches on the CB channel. It has a police monitor. Why not, and how neat? Until she hears a relay of a missing person's report for Theresa Kind. "Oh My God." *She is five foot four, seventeen-years-old, obese, with average facial features except for a pronounced chin and oval brown eyes. She has a short, thick neck and short, chubby arms.*

I am not obese!

"Okay, Telly, don't panic. Don't panic. Drive nice and easy. Cops look for erratic driving behavior. Stay mildly above the speed limit. That shows I'm an American. Stay with the flow. There was no mention of a fifty-foot RV. You're safe.

"I should call Melody. I have her cell phone. But she said to only call if there are cops at my door. I don't see any cops right now. No one knows where I am. No bomb has gone off, as far as I can tell. Melody would tell me to look for the missing pieces. How can I do that if I am blown up? Am I going to be a missing piece?

"I have to be an adult now. I'll turn eighteen in five weeks. I can figure this out. Missing pieces. I know what I need to do. The fifth step. Figure out the passcode. Preferably, as Melody would say, before the bomb goes off. Hee hee."

Telly parks the RV at a charging station, plugs the RV in, and sets it on supercharge. She buys two hamburgers, a strawberry milkshake, and an order of fries. She downs them in the RV while it charges.

"Why would Chief put out a missing person's report for me when all I did was run away from home? Oh, I guess that is what a missing person report is for. But why like this? He's looking to get everyone really excited. Why does he need everyone excited? He's trying to distract everyone from what he really wants—the RV. I have the RV, Chief. So, I have leverage. Gotcha.

"Why did he just now post this when he could have done it day one? Something changed. He learned we read the microchip, Dummy. Who could he have learned that from? Andy must have wimped out and given me up! Melody wouldn't have. Melody's in trouble.

"I can't just drive around until I am eighteen and it comes to me. The panels to the interior are welded shut. The lock is shackleless and requires a pass code, which only someone like Melody could crack. What piece am I missing?

"Me, again.

"It's not going to be hard to figure out the passcode. It's going to be boring."

Melody had said, "Most of life is boring, so make it fun. You might get lucky." Ten by ten by ten by ten by ten...

Telly starts punching in numbers, zero zero zero zero zero; zero zero zero zero one; zero zero zero zero two... Every time, she does it faster.

CHAPTER FORTY-THREE

A MILLION MILES AN HOUR AT HOME

A ndy is relieved when the RV's taillights recede from view. He's tired of all this. Besides, he had seen Telly in action. She was too good a driver, and he just didn't have the muscle nor the interest in risking a speeding ticket, or worse. He could drive halfway to Bangor, Maine, and never catch up to her.

Without discussing where to go, he drives the Buick to the Hurrah Club. He doesn't tell Melody where he's going, not wanting to debate about it. He expects he'll be arrested. A neighbor identified his car or something like that. Besides, he's done with all this running away business. It hasn't helped one single bit. For once, Melody doesn't interfere. She doesn't say a word the whole trip.

When he gets there, the parking lot is empty. The exterior lights are on but not the interior ones. He walks to the clubhouse. No one is there. Yellow tape and particle board are in place of where the front glass door used to be. He walks back to the car. He asks, "Do you think they will come back, Melody? Should I wait for the guy who called me?"

"Did you bring me something to read while you play?" answers Melody.

He's worn out. He's going to the rally tomorrow, and now with Telly out of the picture, why shouldn't he? He will go to bed, get up early, and drive to the rally. He'd damn well be there.

He drives home.

When he opens up their front door, Melody disappears somewhere as is her wont. Benedict Arnold is barking from the basement. He wonders how Benedict Arnold got locked into the basement then remembers that's where he'd left him so the dog wouldn't get cut by all the glass that still lies on the kitchen floor. When Andy opens the basement door, Benedict Arnold nuzzles him, leash in jaws. Despite the hour and Andy's tiredness, he leads the dog down the basement stairs. As Andy descends, he peers at his workshop and despairs. Some of the rainwater had slid through the pine plank floors. No telling how much of his stock and unfinished work has been destroyed. He looks at the Hiroshima plaque. It's sitting in a bed of water. What had he been thinking? He should get to it right away, but no, he has to be fresh for the rally tomorrow. The damage is past. Distressed it will be. The Watanabe's are not going to come through, anyway. He needs to face the music. Benedict Arnold's concern is primary.

Andy is thankful Benedict Arnold doesn't begrudge the quick out-and-in. It's very dark out right now.

Afterwards, Andy gives Benedict Arnold a double helping of dog food and sweeps the glass up in the kitchen and dining room. The water on the floors has already evaporated, leaving white pond circles to mark its retreat. He notices that the voicemail recorder light is blinking. The first message summons him to the Hurrah Club. BEEP. The second squeezes his heart a bit, "Mr. Mac-Clean, this is Linda Watanabe. We are flying out to San Francisco tonight. My parents were beaten up. I'll be back in touch in a few weeks. I apologize for the delay." BEEP.

Andy deletes both. He isn't hungry since he'd gorged himself at the highway rest stop, mostly to avoid interacting with Telly and Melody and talking about fashion and popular culture. He brushes his teeth and puts on his pajamas then goes to say goodnight to Melody and finds Benedict Arnold cuddled up with her on the couch in the TV room. He kisses her forehead as she sleeps sitting up on the couch. The TV shows the trailer for the latest new sequel. He makes his way to bed. They welcome each other.

CHAPTER FORTY-FOUR

BUY THE WAY

"Send 500, I know where she is," reads Donna's text. Lutz Venmos her. She texts, "SAVED ANGELS." He drives there. No sign of an RV. He texts a threat to Donna, puts his flashers on, leaves his engine running, and hammers on the front door. A sleep-deprived guard greets him at the door.

Lutz shows his badge through the glass door and yells, "I'm looking for Theresa Kind. Is she here?"

The guard, eyes rapidly blinking, says, "Uh, I'm not sure. Do you have a warrant? I mean, let me get the director. Wait here."

Lutz ignores the guard's instructions and says, "Take me to him. I do not have a lotta time."

The guard tries shouldering this invader epaulet for epaulet, but Lutz's shoulder is ahead of his before the guard can nudge him back. Lutz says, "What's the director's name?"

"Ruth Schuyler," says the guard and then adds, "Sir."

In a matter of seconds, the two are standing in Director Schuyler's office. Lutz ignores the guard and says, "We're looking for Theresa Kind. She works here."

Schuyler lowers her reading glasses and looks the two over. "Ricardo, you can go back to your station." She waits for his departure before she addresses Lutz, "Have we met?"

"Lutz Delorean, Chief of Police."

"So, those your flashing lights illuminating the night?"

"Flashers on, sirens off."

"I appreciate that," she says, "Our residents and staff complain that loud sounds keep them awake at night." She smiles, pleased with the joke, hoping he might.

"Theresa Kind?"

"I seem to remember the name, but when I check our payroll, the name does not come up. I have only been here a few days."

"Telly Kind!" yells Lutz. "I have dropped her off at this front door half a dozen times."

"Oh, Telly!" says Ruth. "I'm sorry. I remember her. We let her go my first day, the first. She can't be here."

"A few days ago?" says Lutz. "She didn't tell me."

"She a friend of yours, Chief Delorean?"

"She's my stepdaughter, Mrs. Schuyler."

"Oh, so this isn't police business. Please call me Ruth."

"Of course, Ruth. Look, her life is in danger."

"But Chief Delorean, if she isn't answering to you, how can we be of service?" There's a pause. The two measure each other out. Each as strong as the other but one with heavier feet.

"Oh, maybe we can," says Ruth. "I can. A few of our employees have recently found reason to leave. I can offer her her old job back. Bring her in for an interview."

"How would you do that, Ruth?"

"Call or text her."

"She has no phone."

"Oh, well then, email."

"Yeah, that's good. She can get email from anywhere, and I'm sure she keeps up with her friends. I appreciate your help on this. I'll return the favor. Again, her life is in danger."

"Yes, it seems it is."

It's now Monday night. Lutz needs the RV in hand by 10:00 the day after tomorrow.

Out of options, he drives home and types on the keypad connected to STOPTHECHEAT, "HAND INFECTED, MICROCHIP REMOVED, NEED VEHICLE'S ADDRESS!"

The reply is immediate: RETURN THE MICROCHIP.

Lutz had thought of that, which was why he had waited so close to the 6th to contact the website. Fewer options. Anything else he had said would have set off a series of "WE NO LONGER TRUST YOU" questions or, more obviously, no reply at all. He types in, "MICROCHIP FLUSHED, AT HOSPITAL."

Nothing.

After twenty minutes of waiting for nothing, he walks back upstairs and twists off the cap off his Johnny Walker Black Label.

Takes a big gulp and, just as quickly, belches the liquid all over the floor. Not a young man anymore. He sits on the couch and just stares at the alcohol splatter. He checks his cell for a reply from Donna. Negative. He's been taken again.

He's lost. The rally is almost here, and he has no idea where Telly or the RV are. This was to be his in with the President. It was his job to get the RV to the Capitol, and he has failed. All because of Telly. Once again, history and women spit in his face. He hears a chirp and runs downstairs. There it is: 705 Redlea Drive, Damascus, slot 12521.

Lutz is ecstatic. He drives to the parking lot. It's locked up for the night. He bolt cuts the chain on the gate and finds the RV parked in slot 12521. His breath finally slows down as he approaches it. Everything is going to be alright. He'll be remembered after the revolution, just a tiny blemish on his record. Good for a joke maybe. As for Telly, when he gets his two hands on her...

He tries to pick the RV's door lock. Either the lock's tumblers are being stubborn, or his training has aged. In a rage, he breaks the window. Its alarm sounds, loud and moaning. He finds no key in the ignition. No lanyard. He searches around and sees that its insides are motorhome-standard, except for three children's bicycles. He gets an alert of the break-in on his police walkie-talkie. He races back to his car, drives out, and meets another cop car driving up to the gate. Lutz rolls down his window and yells at the cop car that he's headed for the highway to see if he can cut the burglar off.

He drives home. No sense in chasing himself. He's lost. No RV. No Telly. But he has something, doesn't he? Information. He types into the STOPTHECHEAT address, "WRONG VEHICLE, NOTHING INSIDE BUT 3 BIKES, WE'VE BEEN TRICKED." Always use we, never you, never accuse. He's done all he can do. The screen lightens, "CALL OFFICER JEREMY MACCLEAN."

Jeremy again. Jeremy told him about the Hurrah Club, a red herring. Jeremy is just a rookie cop, overanxious for approval and annoying as hell. But...

―・―

Lutz calls Jeremy, "Jeremy, are you an agent or something?"

"It'll all work out in the end, Chief," says Jeremy, "as soon as all Americans realize that the vote count was bogus."

"Jeremy, grow up," says Lutz. "None of this widespread voter fraud business is true, not a word of it. Trump didn't have to make these stories up, either. He grabs them off the Internet, a cat chasing its tail. As soon as the stories get debunked, he tweets that they were absolutely true. What he says is true is no more so than any other myth. Money is nothing but a piece of paper."

"Then, we pay for stuff with a myth?" asks Jeremy.

"Everything's a myth, right?" says Lutz. "Civilization, culture, cause and effect, love, history. Nothing is true. Everything is a story. Everything happens, eventually, even if nothing has. Just give it enough time, and someone will say it did. Just watch."

"That's a lot to watch for."

"You're so young. You haven't seen anything yet."

"I've seen a lot," says Jeremy. "And, so far, it's been no big deal."

"What is true is what you believe. When you get as old as I, you learn to believe in nothing you believe in. And what you think is right today is verboten tomorrow."

"So, what am I supposed to believe?" asks Jeremy.

"What you are told."

"Well, I'm telling you to meet me at the corner of Thomas Jefferson and Alexander Hamilton, as soon as you can get there, but no sirens or no screeching brakes, Old Man. We are about to make history."

"Okay."

"And one more thing, Chief, if you think we don't know your daughter has the guns, you're the one who's naive."

CHAPTER FORTY-FIVE

BATHTUB RING

At about eleven, Benedict Arnold wakes Andy up. The dog is jumping on top of him. Another time, Andy would have thrown something at the dog then grabbed it by the ears and shuffled it out of the bedroom, closed the door, and gone back to sleep. But why are Benedict Arnold's paws wet? Holy Fuck. Andy hears an odd sound. Has a bird flown in? The sound is coming from the bathroom. Nothing ever good comes from that room. He doesn't put on his slippers. He strides with long, committed steps just behind the dog and finds Melody thrashing around in the bath, sudsy water at play all over the floor. She's face down and fully clothed. The plastic bottle of Xanax clearly rides the frenetic activity of the bath water like the Silver Surfer. He has not a clue what to do. Reach inside the tub to push open the plug to drain the water? Turn the water, which is pouring out full blast as these new tubs are designed to do, off? Pull her head out of the water? Let her drown, go back to sleep, and be done with it?

He's surprised not to see a knife, but then, he doesn't put it past her to have one in each hand to stab him in case he tries to interfere. Then Andy sees hope. A little green pill floats on the bathwater. Then he sees another one. She had either not swallowed them all or had vomited them up. Poor, crazy lady. Poor Melody. What hopeless despair surrounds a person who can't remember the minute before. How does anyone know who they even are then?

Andy gets on his knees, lets the water run over the tub, reaches around her body, and pulls her toward him with his large hands, hugging her fast. Holds her. Says to her, "There, there Melody, no reason to worry, no reason. You ain't leaving your Handcream. No, no, no. I need you, remember? Jeremy needs you. Telly needs you. Whatever you forget, don't forget that. Don't forget that. I never will. We never will. Promise me." She's coughing and crying at the same time and weaves her arms around his neck. He's only relieved when he sees her hands aren't holding knives.

Andy accounts for all but eight of the pills. Researches the Internet site *What Overdose Amount Is Fatal*, a website he's familiar with. Eight Xanax is not usually fatal! But he should absolutely call an ambulance and have her hospitalized. She's barely been out a week. What is the hospital going to do? Can pill pushers keep her away from taking too many pills any better than he can? Plus, if she dies. If she dies. He'd just saved her. From what? For what?

The website said she would sleep for a full day after. Not a bad thing, that would give him time to attend the rally. Except Melody never lived up to those drug ablutions. She and drugs were partners in crime.

Andy dries Melody off, puts her in clean pajamas, carries her into the TV room, and lays her down on the sofa where she sleeps at night. She snores the entire time. He jacks the furnace up, takes a shower with Benedict Arnold. Dries the dog off, mops out the bathroom, throws as many wet towels as will fit into the washer without causing it to beat itself into a fifth dimension, gets it going, dries himself off, and climbs back into bed. It's almost three.

She hadn't given any indication that she was going to try this. The doctors were always telling him to be aware of the triggers. Postmortem Monday morning quarterbacks. Damn experts, damn them all. This was a woman, and a woman she was. Her wanting to die was only going to get worse, and nobody could do anything about it. Especially Andy, especially him. He comes out of his reveries, remembers to set the alarm clock, and falls asleep.

CHAPTER FORTY-SIX

JOSE'S BIKE RIDE

Jose had an everyday upbringing and an everyday lack of achievement in the land of plenty. He absorbed what was going on by listening to the radio, never bothering to read anything. Reading was bothersome. In school, his teachers had wanted him tested for dyslexia. His parents refused. "He sees fine when he wants to," they said.

He does what his brain infallibly tells him to do. How to think is known at birth. No one can teach you that. He rose up the escalators of life from TV cartoons to comic books, from cars to girls, and finally, from apartments that stunk to jobs that smelled even worse.

He constantly asked himself, "When do the rewards come?" This was, coincidentally, exactly what Trump asked his fans. Maybe it's because you're having to pay for next door's tornado damage, poor kid's breakfasts, and other countries' wars?

We have our own problems, you know?

Capitalism is based on a mutually agreed upon bargain, no hitches. Contracts are sacred. Caveat Emptor. Read the fine print. Leave me alone.

Being too noble to ask for directions or help, Jose supported his self-esteem by harboring grudges. Somewhere along the line, he had been misled, so he started spending his time looking for who was to blame. The Internet obliged, and visually. So did Donald Trump.

Trump blamed everyone except Jose. Jose wasn't an immigrant; his parents had been. He and they were now American citizens. He wasn't a person of color. Tan is not really a color. He wasn't a rioter, a thief, or a bureaucrat. He certainly wasn't an elite. He was being ripped off.

When the election was called for Biden, Jose was immediately convinced it was stolen. All his friends voted for Trump. Trump signs were everywhere he rode. Trump rallies were very well attended, ignoring that the tickets were free, and the empty seats outnumbered the filled four to one by the time Trump stopped talking. He himself had leaked out of the rally well before Trump was half-done. He just wanted to avoid the parking lot egress. He was smart, after all, and the administrators of the rally parking lots notoriously hadn't a clue how to competently empty one. Imagine them trying to evacuate an airliner that was on fire. Everyone would die. But that wasn't Trump's fault.

When Jose learned that the STOPTHECHEAT lottery ticket Averil gave him at the rally granted him a role, he swooned. He had inserted the microchip in his hand the day he got it. And he scanned his hand every day until an address appeared on the screen.

When it does, he puts on his Converse sneakers, Levi's jeans, and Champion sweatshirt to ride there on his motorcycle. Jose secures his bike on the RV's bike trailer then drives the RV to his appointed rendezvous, Eddie's Guns and Gifts, in Pittsburgh, Pennsylvania.

After shoving the eight-foot by one-foot by one-foot wooden boxes into the one-way slot in the RV, he parks it at the designated parking lot and drives home on his motorcycle. His eternal contribution to the Trump campaign, sealed and delivered. STOPTHESTEAL promised to reimburse him within 60 days. He hadn't been told the boxes were C.O.D. until he got to Eddie's. But it figured, nothing is free in the land of freedom, freedom most especially.

CHAPTER FORTY-SEVEN

KEYPAD RODEO

Telly buys a three-egg cheese omelet and a diet soda. She skips the cinnamon bun this time, needing to show herself some discipline. She carries the food and beverage from the Turnpike rest stop to the RV. She resumes her pose in the captain's chair, her back to the windshield so she faces the cargo doors keypad and starts punching in possibles while downing breakfast. She realizes that this is futile, but that very conclusion tells her that she's doing the right thing. And it feels like it's the first time in her life she has done something without the ulterior purpose of being fed, though the unlimited food at the rest stops might offer a different opinion.

She's getting faster at keying in numbers, so fast she remembers the next in the sequence without fail. "Clever me," she thinks. Hour after hour after hour. This is a no-win lottery, but what had she done in the past that was ever as important?

At 20905, she hears a snickering click. That's her zip code in Silver Springs. 905 is the conspiracy number Melody mentioned. Her eyes widen out of her near-comatose reverie, and she walks around the RV and tries the door. Bingo. Inside are dozens of wooden boxes, the size of coffins for tall bulimic corpses. Names in black block letters are stamped on them: SHELLEY'S SPORTS EQUIPMENT, RODNEY'S RIFLES & TOYS, CARL'S HUNTING. She's only seen boxes this shape before at the police station.

What is she to do? Melody would be so proud of her. She wants to hear Melody's "Atta-girl," but this isn't an emergency. Melody told her not to call unless. Is this one of those times it's best to ignore what she'd been told to do? Maybe so, but she had been keying numbers in for ten-and-a-half hours straight. Her back was aching, and her stomach was saying, "Pizza."

CHAPTER FORTY-EIGHT

BACK FROM THE STORE

Andy wakes up to the alarm, happy to be in his own bed, and says to no one, "And then he died." He doesn't know why he often says this to himself first thing upon rising, just that he did, and never once had he died, as far as he could tell. He looks around his bedroom, his eyes following the wall hangings resting on the carpet. Melody had never decided which one went where after he had painted the room. It had taken her over two years to decide on a sink to replace the one that had rusted out. The dishwasher still functioned, so it wasn't so bad, except for having to clean the dishes too large for the dishwasher in the tub, until Melody had somehow broken its plug. She finally bought an identical sink to one that had rusted out.

Andy goes to the grocery first thing. They are almost out of coffee and milk and completely out of the dill pickles he likes in his sandwiches. Then it will be off to the rally.

When he gets home, he hears someone in the basement. It couldn't be Melody. He goes downstairs and spies Jeremy slamming a ball into the Tennis Mate. Jeremy hits the tennis ball as if killing it were the point.

"Try cocking your elbows out more," says Andy. "Does Melody know you're here?"

"Mom isn't up yet," says Jeremy.

"That tennis thumping'll wake her."

"Has it so far?"

"Give her a minute or two," says Andy. "She had a rough morning. I thought you'd be at work."

"I start at noon."

"So, you're here looking for money then?"

Jeremy keeps hitting the ball into the Tennis Mate. After a dozen or more swings, Jeremy's shot misses the curtain entirely, and the ball ricochets around the basement to who knows where. Jeremy makes no attempt to look for it.

Jeremy does not move away from the squat rack. He stands there and juggles Andy's tennis racket, catching it by its handle. A new revelation is coming. This is Jeremy, melodrama, his opening act. Something about how Jeremy stays in place and flips the racket feels off to Andy. This is not going to be a friendly chat between dad and son. Andy sits on a basement stair tread and waits for Jeremy to tell him what trouble he's got himself into this time.

"So, Dad, what's the core value of life?"

"Making money, Jeremy. Nothing's going to change that."

"Then why waste your time with wooden bowls for the rich elites?" asks Jeremy. "The rich elites you say you hate."

BACK FROM THE STORE

"I love working with wood," says Andy, "can't explain that. And taking money from elites adds somewhat to the joy. They say if you find what you love to do, you'll never work a day in your life."

"Find what you love, and you're eternally screwed is how it looks to me," says Jeremy.

"You're a police officer," says Andy. "Money in that?"

"That could change at any moment. Do a favor for a senator or a congressman, no different from getting a tip on a racehorse, a stock, or a job. I work on the floor where the real deals are made."

"So many corrupt politicians out there," says Andy, "I'm surprised a DC cop lasts a week."

"The competent took the gold and have long ago moved up," says Jeremy. "The ones who are left wouldn't know a legitimate tip if it came in wearing a bikini and holding two margaritas."

"You're not showing much respect for your fellow officers."

"My fellow officers are idiots. My superiors are numbnuts. And the visitors to the Capitol treat us like road construction sign holders. Which is what we are. Slow down, won'cha? Pretty please!"

"So, why are you here crying on my shoulder?"

"What the fuck have you gotten yourself into, Dad? This is so over your head."

Andy feels anxious before his own son. He admits to himself he's not really sure what he's doing or why he's doing it. This feels right, though. A son standing up to his dad, which was probably why he'd always favored Jeremy over Sam. But somehow, it feels wrong too. Had Jeremy fallen for that crypto currency crap or clicked on a, "You're a Winner" email?

"Melody said no?"

"Wrong arena, Dad!"

"Well, what do you say we talk about it while we drive to the rally? I'll buy you a beer when it's all over. We're running out of time to hear Trump speak."

"Well, well, you got the right arena," Jeremy says as he raises left arm for Andy to see.

His left hand is in handcuffs, chained to Andy's weight rack.

Lutz comes out of the shadows and points a gun at Andy's chest.

"What the fuck?" Andy barks.

Lutz says, as calmly as if he were a cashier asking a customer if he wanted to cash in his free Thanksgiving turkey certificate, "Now, Mr. MacClean, I shouldn't need to tell you what is going to happen to your son if you don't give my daughter back." Lutz points the gun at Jeremy, who scrunches up his lips and stares at Andy as if Andy is his only hope and this is an episode of *Rocky and Bullwinkle*.

Andy looks Jeremy over. He looks like his normal, extra excited self. There are no marks on his face. Then Andy hears Melody. She's yelling for Benedict Arnold to sit. Then she closes the kitchen basement door and, still in her slippers, shushes down the stairs. She comes up behind him and kicks his rear off of the tread. He stumbles down to the basement floor, and she makes it there a few seconds later. She glares at the three.

"Chicken again, chicken again, chicken again!" she yells, mimicking Alan Arkin's opening scene in *Little Miss Sunshine*.

"Just get yourself back upstairs, Mrs. MacClean," screams Lutz even louder. "We don't want you to get hurt. Get! Get! Get!"

"Don't be a chicken, Handcream," says Melody. "He wants Telly. We've already talked this through." Andy tries to remember having that conversation. Fails to. Wouldn't he be the one more likely to remember it?

Then she says, "Never give in to a bully, Handcream." That sounds more like him than her.

Lutz points the gun at Melody.

Andy is having a devil of a time weighing his options. Save the woman who spends her better hours tormenting him and just tried to kill herself, his son, or his own hide?

Jeremy pretends to serve an invisible tennis ball with Andy's racket and ends each swing with a violent snap, hitting nothing but air. The sounds from the clinking chains provide background music.

"Mrs. MacClean," says Lutz. "This is a loaded gun I am pointing at you. The safety is off."

"I want to thank you very much for convincing Jeremy to come here instead of the Capitol today," says Melody. "He might have been in harm's way. I didn't think it would require a gun, but champion thinking, Mr. Chief."

"I am pointing the gun at you Mrs. MacClean."

"Why are you saying the obvious? My glasses are on." Melody reaches up and fiddles with her glasses to assure herself that she is, indeed, wearing them.

"I could kill you right this second," says Lutz. "I almost killed your husband once already."

"When you cracked your skull against Telly's windshield," says Melody. "Did you ticket yourself for not buckling up?

"How will killing me or Jeremy show you where Telly is? What am I missing here? Mr. Chief, you haven't thought this through. You should put me in handcuffs since I'm the one who knows where Telly is. That way, I won't run away and call the NBC hot news tip line. What is that number? Something, something, something-7777. Handcream, you remember it, don't you?"

"Tell me where she is!" says Lutz.

"Tell me why she's so important," says Melody. "Maybe we can make a deal."

Lutz mulls this over, but before he can say anything further, Melody blurts out, "But first, you have to show a sign of good faith. This is how bargaining works. Unleash Jeremy. That way I'll know that my son is at least safe. Until then, negotiations can't begin. You can handcuff me if you want."

"I can't let him handcuff you," says Andy.

"So far, you have not can't-ed a single thing," says Melody. "Let me handle this. I'm much better at negotiating than you."

"I know better where Telly is than Melody does," says Andy. "Handcuff me."

All eyes are now on Lutz.

A pin tumbler falls into place to form a shear line so the lock on the minefield of Lutz's brain opens. If it wasn't for Jeremy's continual make-believe tennis services, you would have heard the squishy schlack inside his head. Lutz peeks at his wristwatch. Three hours to get the guns to the Capitol, that is, if the RV is even within reach. His options are slipping away. He has to get closer to the RV, even if it's an inch.

In a matter of seconds, he flings off Jeremy's handcuffs, grabs Andy by the wrists, and slaps the handcuffs on them. Then, in another blink, he pulls a non-resisting Andy over to the weight rack and shackles his ankles to opposite legs of the rack, forcing Andy to a half-squat. "Okay, my article of faith. Now, where's Telly?" says Lutz.

"Can't say you're not agile," says Melody. "The Ravens are looking for a middle linebacker, and you're about the right size. Jeremy, leave."

"Jeremy isn't going anywhere, Mrs. MacClean," says Lutz. "Now tell me, where is my daughter?"

"Don't engage my mom, Chief," says Jeremy. "She's nuts but crafty. She can convince a squirrel to return an acorn to an oak tree and leave a tip. Besides, there is nothing that she knows that Dad doesn't know, so focus on him. Not sure if he'll talk, though. Conversation has never been his strong point."

"Could you please tell me what this is all about?" asks Melody. "We're in our own basement, my husband is handcuffed and shackled, and Mr. Chief is threatening to shoot us unless we reveal the location of his adopted daughter. Your adopted daughter only seems to be in danger from you. So, why would we tell you where she is?"

"None of your business," says Lutz. "I released Jeremy as promised. Now, tell me where she is. Once you do, we are done here, and everyone goes their way."

"Oh, but we can't," says Melody, "not unless we know that she'll be safe. Mr. Chief, you would certainly understand that."

"It's a matter of national defense," says Lutz. "We are saving the country."

"From Telly?" says Melody. "I find that excruciatingly hard to accept. But do explain. I'm putty in the hands of facts and logic."

"The vote was rigged," says Lutz. "We're going to square things."

"Listen, Mr. Chief, Trump increased the national debt by six trillion dollars, incited race riots, applauded the police's murdering of unarmed blacks, separated immigrant children from their parents terminally, and mismanaged a pandemic that's killed half a million Americans. He also promised legislation to ease the border crisis, the medical insurance crisis, and the mass shootings crisis and didn't offer a single sheet of paper. A large number of people would vote against him if he were guilty of just one of those malfeasances. Seven million votes short feels tame."

"When you have a winner, you never abandon him, flaws and all."

"Bullshit! Another lame defense thrown up for the opposition to waste its time trying to shoot down," says Melody. "Winner, leader has nothing to do with anything. I see through you. Again, what does this have to do with Telly? Or should I expose the elephant in the kitchen, what is in the RV?"

"Careful, Chief," says Jeremy.

"Waste of words, Lady," says Lutz. "I have your husband in handcuffs and your son at my command."

"Might is right, huh?" Melody says. "How does that feel right now Jeremy? You are bait. Special status, that."

"See, Chief," says Jeremy. "This is what she can do, turn us against each other."

"Might is always right," says Lutz.

"So, slavery was right," asks Melody, "woman suffrage was wrong, and bananas should be peeled from the top?"

"Misses MacClean," yells Lutz "Okay then, here's a bargain chip. Keep Telly. Tell me where the RV is."

"I know why you're in love with this guy Trump."

"Tell me where the RV is or—"

"Because you're afraid."

"Shut up," says Lutz. "You don't know what you are talking about."

"Did you see the film that was promoted but never released?"

"What?"

"Checkmate, Mr. Chief. Now toddle along. I need a beer, and you need to uncuff Handcream so he can go to the store and buy me some. I like Stella, you want some? Andy buy a case, we have company, but remember to pour slowly or you get too much foam. I can't stand drinking air. Bloats me. Mr. Chief has enough froth around his lips to make Abacus Finch flinch. How about dessert? Handcream, Oreos."

CHAPTER FORTY-NINE

IN AND OUT

Telly charges the RV and takes a nap at a turnpike rest stop. She checks her email when she wakes. She finds an email from Saved Angels, "NEW OPENING, COME IN FOR IMMEDIATE INTERVIEW."

Telly drives over. It's a bit of a hike from where she is right now, but first things first.

She parks in the ambulance lane out back, as that parking space is empty and the RV with its trailer is long. Perfect. She leaves the RV and, not having a fob, walks in the visitor entrance. No one is at the front desk. There is a small sign on the desk stating that the receptionist will be back within twenty minutes. The sign looks as old as her last work instructions. A nurse cruises by. He nods at Telly and scans the waiting room. No one is there besides Telly. He then disappears back to where he came from without saying a word.

Telly walks toward the administration offices. She sees Michael Lewis Reef huffing and puffing. He's playing video darts with all the animus of a bodybuilder. Most of the other residents are watching TV. A few hold large plastic red cups of popcorn and dig down for a kernel or two now and then, looking like those plastic birds on hummingbird feeders. Telly had never seen so many Saved Angel residents in one place at one time. Are they all here to welcome her back? Every TV is on, each with its volume so high, she can't imagine how the patients can understand what is going on. Is that the point?

On the TVs, she sees well dressed and coiffed people standing in Congress, speaking in front of mics while others in combat fatigues frantically wave banners.

She decides the residents are not assembled for her, so she says, "Michael Lewis Reef, have you seen Ruth, the new director?"

"Well, thanks for asking about how I am," says Michael Lewis Reef after launching an errant Nerf dart at the target. "Have you forgotten promising never to leave us and then skedaddling the very same day? You should be on TV with the rest of them."

"Where is the new director, Michael Lewis Reef?" says Telly. "She offered my job back."

"That's better, right to the point, never bandying around," says Michael Lewis Reef. "I think they canned Ruth, but I could be wrong."

"She sent me an email a few hours ago."

"Still don't get it, huh?" says Michael Lewis Reef. "Who cares, you abandoned us, remember?"

"I did not. I was fired!" Telly says this louder than she intended, louder than the TV's speakers. A number of patients turn their heads from the TVs and look at the two of them.

"I came here to get my job back."

"You really think you're the center of the universe, don't you?" says Michael Lewis Reef. "Do you even care that we're watching the violent transfer of power?" Telly scrunches up her face in, huh? The residents, in a wave, turn back to watching TV.

Jane and Sue walk over. Sue asks her, "Why'd they fire you?"

"I broke some rule."

"Getting too close to the patients?" asks Jane.

"No," says Telly. "Getting too close to patient management ratios."

"You know who made that rule, don'tcha?" says Michael Lewis Reef. "Tom Roberts. If it can't be measured, don't count it."

Ruth suddenly appears and, ignoring the others, says, "Telly, so glad to see you. Come with me, we need to talk in private." No one likes to talk in private more than conspirators. Seems like their very DNA forces them to whisper so they can stare at their feet instead of into the eyes of the person they're lying to. They must believe that directing their eyes at shoes thwarts others from listening in on their thoughts.

When they get to Ruth's office, Ruth says, "Wait here. I'll be right back."

"What's going on?" asks Telly. "Your email said to come right away. What am I waiting for? Don't you need me right now?"

"I have to notify others that you're here," replies Ruth. She gives Telly a big phony smile and rushes out. Others, who are others? Why didn't Ruth give their names? Telly knew almost everyone in the building. Identifying everyone by name was a hallmark of Saved Angels.

Telly notices the security monitors behind Ruth's desk. She walks behind and sees security guards assembling at Saved Angels's entrance, swatting batons in their palms. She feels like she did when she was at Donna's.

Telly knows what to do now. It's obvious. The right thing to do is always clear. The wrong thing is always complicated, has many moving parts, and requires perfect timing. A racecar driver doesn't win by waiting. She has to be the fastest without crashing, at least before the finish line. She felt, she felt, she felt unhungry. Curiosity and compassion are sinking in their diabolical hooks. Later always comes after then, then. That's how it works, doesn't it?

Telly leaves Ruth's office and joins the patients watching TV. One screen shows hundreds of people on the Capitol lawn, another focuses on a hotel, another on Congress in session. Everyone on the screens acts excited. None of the residents do. Some are falling asleep on the sofas. The journalists passionately shout out the importance of today but then say it's largely ceremonial. Everyone's waiting for something.

What to do? "Never be afraid to ask for help," Melody had said. The opposite of what Chief had told her, so it must be right. Telly waves for Michael Lewis Reef, Jane, and Sue to form a huddle. They're as happy as guppies watching gold sprinkles fall from above.

"What about my subpoena, Telly Vision?" says Michael Lewis Reef.

"How would you like to bust out of here?" asks Telly.

"As much as I can talk," says Michael Lewis Reef.

"Are we going to shoot our way out?" asks Sue. "You got weaponry?"

"Kalashnikov or Norinco?" asks Jane.

"Maybe both," says Telly. "Who's in?"

"To do what?" asks Michael Lewis Reef. "Kill nurses? Killing is not my beat."

"AK-47s are fine," says Jane. "Used them in Iraq. Secret is to have plenty of ammo. They run through bullets faster than Manny runs through Chevitz."

"How about you Sue?" asks Telly.

"Sure, let's go. I'm tired of this place, including Mr. Know-it-all Three Names."

"You messing with me, Sue?" interrupts Michael Lewis Reef.

"No, we're not," says Telly. "Oh, there's a siren. We have to leave now."

"Where do the AK-47s come in?" asks Jane.

"I have an RV. It's filled with weapons."

"Hahahaha, right." says Michael Lewis Reef, "and I have an armful of gardenias up my ass."

"I'm not looking up your ass, Michael Lewis Reef," says Telly.

The three residents of Saved Angels look everywhere but at each other. Finally, Sue says, "I don't have anything to lose, and if it gets me out of here, even for a minute, it'll be worth it."

"We can all help each other," says Telly. "Like the A Team."

"Wait a minute, wait a minute," says Michael Lewis Reef. "Are the weapons for the guys milling in front of the Capitol right now?"

"I think so," says Telly.

Telly notices that the digital clock clicks out to noon. She thinks she will have to escape alone.

"Wait a minute, wait a minute, will somebody be shooting at us?" says Michael Lewis Reef. "I'm not so interested in getting killed today. There's a Netflix show I want to see play out."

"Bye then, I'm leaving," says Telly. "What about you, Sue, Jane? Will you go with me?"

"If Michael Lewis Reef stays, I'll be free of his BS. Let's go girl, being shot at will be an improvement and liven up my memoir, if I live to write it."

"It was a joke," says Michael Lewis Reef. "Of course I'm coming,"

"I'm still going. No fun in being consistent," says Sue.

"Jane?" They all ask at once.

Everyone looks at Jane. There's no debate in her eyes. Instead, a nervous impatience to get this started, bordering on ferocity. She walks towards the building's entrance.

Telly grabs her shoulder to stop her. Jane caterwauls, "Where's the beef? Where's the beef?" The volume of her scream sets off every sound detector alarm in the building. The patients believe this is a fire drill. They leave the TV and clot toward the main lobby.

"We have to go out the *back*," says Telly.

"There's a back door?" asks Sue.

"Follow me," says Jane, "I'm wearing Saved Angels garb. The new hires still think I'm staff. And most here are new hires."

"And walk like you're not in a hurry," says Telly. "No need to call attention to ourselves."

The four walk to the rear of the building. Saved Angels employees ignore them, hurriedly making their way to the front in order to respond to the alarms. Management had decimated the

IN AND OUT

security guard detail. Every guard was already at the entrance. All three of them.

When they get outside, they hear sirens getting louder. Telly needs to get them on the road.

They all squeeze themselves into the front bench seat of the RV. A police motorcycle drives into the circular front driveway and parks. His bike blocks their egress. He turns his siren off while sirens far off grow louder.

Telly remains sitting at the wheel. The four stare sternly ahead as if they were watching championship point at Wimbledon. The motorcycle cop leaves his bike and walks away from the entrance towards the RV. He bullhorns, "Get out of the RV. Now. You are in a stolen vehicle."

Jane gushes, "Telly, you stole this!" The cop can't hear any sound coming from the RV vehicle. He doesn't know that the electric motor is just waiting for a push on its accelerator pedal to plow ahead, full speed. Telly measures how much room she needs to miss him. Right now, she doesn't see how she can.

———

Director Ruth returns to her office. No Telly. That's even better. Ruth had called the police. The police had appreciated the heads up, assuring her they would be there in a matter of minutes. She had also signaled her security team to hand Telly over to the police as soon as they arrived. So, she's confident she'll watch Telly's arrest on the security monitors in her office. Confidence is fickle.

The motorcycle cop's bullhorn attracts the patients who have clotted up in the entrance. They start pressing on the three guards to let them out. They want to see what's going on out there. They have become convinced that what they were watching on TV is going on immediately outside. "Is that the President? He said he'd be on his way! Can I get an autograph?"

Seniors cooped up in a residential center are more persistent than you might think. That, plus their fragility, makes it terribly hard for guards to exert force against them. The patients make it past the three guards, get outside, and move toward the cop with the bullhorn. When Ruth sees on her security cameras that patients are walking willy-nilly outside, she runs to shoo them back as if they were sheep. This could cost her her job. She just moved here from Seattle. The residents cooperate by thinking this is a game of tag.

The motorcycle cop is flustered. His training on how to handle an elderly mob is too slow getting to his cerebral cortex. The pajamaed patients surround him, impervious to his bull horning out commands, shouting "Where is the President?"

The patients' rush on the cop creates a tiny clearance in the driveway. Telly shoots out without hitting anyone. The motorcycle won't be ridden anytime soon. But that's okay, it's insured.

The three passengers bounce around on the front bench seat like rocks in a tumbler. Jane and Sue giggle while Michael Lewis Reed assumes the role of navigator. When he asks where they're going, Telly says, "Somewhere away from the police."

Michael Lewis Reef directs them along back roads to Jesse Owens Park.

A minute later, police cars converge at Saved Angels. They run into a riot of patients walking helter-skelter and being chased after by staff. It takes a while to sort through. No one has been able to get hold of Chief Delorean, so the second in command powwows with his squad, and they each take a different route to look for the RV. From above, it looks like cat poops circling around in a toilet bowl. That's also law enforcement's technical term for the maneuver.

CHAPTER FIFTY

PARKED IN A PARK

Upon driving through the park entrance, Sue barks out, "Telly, the sign says absolutely no firearms."

"Yeah, maybe we better turn back," says Michael Lewis Reef. "We don't want to break the law."

Everyone laughs except Jane, who says, "Where's the weaponry? Where's the weaponry?" Only she has modulated her voice to an insistent whisper.

"Once I park," says Telly, "you'll have weapons galore."

After she parks, Telly reaches over behind them and keys in the passcode. They all hear a click clank and get out to walk around to the RV's rear. Telly rolls the rear door down. They see twenty-five identical eight-foot-long wooden boxes.

The boxes are heavy. It takes two of them to drag one box out. Telly spots, bungee corded to an inside panel, a crowbar. Sue does the honors of prying the box open.

Michael Lewis Reef pulls out a rifle among six others. He laughs and says, "These are what's between us and freedom?"

"Use your imagination," says Telly. "And only shoot if you have to. I don't want anyone to get hurt. It's us or them. Melody told me guns attract violence, more than even violence does."

"How many are we up against?" asks Jane, fingering the rifle she pulls out.

"You saw them on TV," answers Telly.

"What do these bad guys want anyway, money, drugs, cigarettes?" asks Sue.

"They want the guns," says Telly, "I think."

"They do look a little naked without them," says Michael Lewis Reef.

"What's mine is mine," says Jane. "They ain't getting mine."

CHAPTER FIFTY-ONE

NO HITCHING

When Carl said that he was enlisting in the Army, his parents showed the commensurate false excitement and fake support. They were glad he was starting to do something with his life and, more importantly, maybe finally moving out of their home.

When Warren told his parents he was going to enlist, they were frightened, but for the Army.

Carl and Warren were best friends. They had the same birth date and lived in the same town, White River Junction, Vermont. They held the same passions. One was baseball. If you asked them, they'd tell you playing baseball together had been the best part of their lives. Which was odd, as they had spent the better part of each game dissing the other players from the safety of the bench.

Warren pitched. His inaccuracy was his strength, making batters more frightened of getting hit than striking out. Merely placing one's feet near the batter's box was inviting injury. Carl played every other position on the field but none well enough to entice a coach to insert him very often. Both found themselves playing in games just before one of the coaches invoked the mercy rule.

Their second passion was patriotism, formed from reading used war and western comic books, bought at the local drug store for a quarter a copy. About four years after graduating from high school, they goaded each other into risking their lives for their country, neither mentioning to the other that the starting salary of a non-com competed very favorably with what they made driving forklifts for the local feed store.

Carl and Warren knew they were not getting their fair share of the American square. After all, there were community college graduates. They weren't blind to the immigrant invasion. Every year, more and more winners of the best students of the year, published in the local newspaper, had names that were unpronounceable, last and first.

Both of them were prime specimens for the Army. Marksmen, bagging their deer limit every season and occasionally making the leaderboard at *Street Fighter* and *Grand Theft Auto* tournaments.

They were rejected.

Carl flunked the IQ test, and Warren's blood pressure was close to hemorrhaging. Bogus. They asked each other what intelligence and blood pressure had to do with shooting people.

Cut off from an active military career, the two sought other means of proving their patriotism. They weren't quitters. They became staunch supporters of Donald Trump. He wasn't afraid of having people beat up. They bravely broadcast that allegiance by sticking Trump stickers on their gear and pickup trucks. They just never went as far as actually voting. Bad guys track those kinds of things.

They also front and centered to help STOPTHECHEAT, a website that promised to keep Trump in office. First order of business, after paying a twenty-dollar membership fee, was to troll Trump's enemies. They put all of their *Street Fighter* energy into doing that.

Their intensive trolling of Trump's opponents got noticed. And STOPTHECHEAT assured them that, for an additional two hundred dollars apiece, they would have a chance to help even more. They put their savings together and applied. Here was where they would make their mark and establish their place in the universe.

What they received from STOPTHECHEAT was a voucher for two nights at the Willard Hotel in D.C. One caveat—No guns. Weapons will be provided. Be at the Capitol at noon on January 6. No later. Instructions will be at the hotel. They had to get to the hotel and back on their own. No problem, they each had a pick-up truck, though they'd carpool to save gas money.

If they were going to die for Trump, they wanted to look professional, especially in the event of interview requests from attractive reporters. Plus, if things went screwy, the outfits would keep them from being recognized.

Prior to leaving, Carl starched and ironed his camouflage fatigues and spit-polished his steel-toed combat boots to a fine luster. He pinned two dozen medals to his shirt. The medals had been bought over the years at flea markets from vets and burglars.

Warren chose full-body motorcycle armor, knee and calf pads, touchscreen tactical leather gloves, a synchronized helmet with ear protection, and visor goggles. He completed his accouterments with a standard quick-release police utility belt with requisite gas mask, tear gas, baton, and out-the-front knife. Tomorrow was going to be historic.

When Warren and Carl check into the hotel, the receptionist asks them if they were armed. "Just what we're wearing," says Warren. He hips over his holster for her to see it does not have a gun in it.

"A number of you have been arrested at the border for illegally transporting rifles across state borders," she says.

"Not us, Babe," says Carl. "We're as law-abiding as …" He looks over at Warren.

"Quaker Oats," says Warren. "Quaker Oats. We wouldn't hurt a wounded fly."

"Wouldn't go that far," says Carl.

The STOPTHECHEAT campaign was ahead of the cops once again. Could be because many co-conspirators were cops. Could be because Homeland Security was running interference. Could be that it was all a Russian inspired plot. Probably all three and more. No matter. They would take their country back, and if Russia wanted to help, what could be the matter with that?

That neither of the two had any experience in managing a country was not a deterrent. They worked in small business. They knew how they ran. They had been making their mark in this country by selling cow feed, power tools, and tractor parts to farmers. So, how could running a country be any harder? They'd know what to do, and better, they'd keep it in budget. Regardless, the country would be theirs again. Someone somehow had taken it away from them, its rightful owners, when they weren't looking. All the eyewitnesses to the theft had somehow gone missing behind that expression that the reporters continued to spiel, "Without any evidence," which they interpreted as meaning, "The media was too dumb to figure it out."

CHAPTER FIFTY-TWO

LAST CALL

"I know how to get them to talk, Chief," says Jeremy. Andy looks at Jeremy as if the world has turned upside down. He can't believe it. Jeremy is on the chief's side? Wasn't the reason to keep the RV from making it to the capital to protect Jeremy?

Jeremy picks up a voicemail recorder lying by the phone on a table. He presses the PLAY button.

"Hi, Mom, it's Sam. Know I'm late, but this casting call is taking forever, so—" Jeremy looks first at Melody then at Andy, and presses DELETE with a flourish.

"Who is that coming here?" asks Lutz.

"My brother, Sam," says Jeremy.

"How sweet of him to let us know," says Melody.

"Jeremy, what in the hell are you doing?" says Andy. "Sam killed himself four years ago. This is the only way your mother and I get to hear his voice. It's a tape recorder. Deleting a message is forever."

"So, what's it going to be?" says Jeremy, having swallowed the bird, its trapeze, and its cage whole. "Lose Sam forever or give the Chief what he wants?"

Andy is lost. He has no idea what to do. Swings to his default, "Melody?"

"He'll get here when he gets here," Melody says. "He always does. You're smarter than that, Handcream."

They hear a pinging from not too far away. A trash truck is picking up on the street. Jeremy pushes PLAY again, "Dad, I forgot my lunch, it's in the fridge. It's now yours. I'll bring pizza over for dinner tomorrow. Sausage, pepperoni, onions, and extra cheese. Bye."

"That's my brother, all right," says Jeremy. "Everybody's savior. Maybe I'll save this one, it's so hokey." Jeremy pans the room like a standup comic. "Not!" Jeremy presses DELETE.

"Jeremy, please!" yells Andy.

"Too bad you didn't like me half as much. But then, I wasn't your blood."

"When did I show any favoritism to him over you?" asks Andy.

"In your tone of voice, all day long."

"The last vestiges of a lost argument," offers Melody. "Reality has no standing against what someone wants to believe. The people who are really willing to help you are those who need the most help themselves. Poor Sam. Poor Sam."

"Your mom can certainly sling the nonsense," says Lutz.

Andy looks over his basement. His sanctuary has become his tomb, his lathes are useless, and his woodblock stock will never be finished. Someone will throw it all in the dump. Garbage. His life has been garbage. One son suicided, and the other is bound to an ideal so tight, he enjoys watching a man threaten his own parents. How can everything become so contorted? Andy had just wanted to go to a rally, a rally to support his president. And what about Telly? The chief says he's going to kill her. She's just a child, not a terribly bright one. Why did he have to be so stupid? So naive? He and Telly and Jeremy and the Chief are being used. By whom? For what? He's definitely not smarter than any of this.

"Mom," says Jeremy, "just tell us where the RV or Telly is, and everybody goes home free."

"But Amy, what if these guns are used to shoot your fellow officers," says Melody.

"What did you just call me, Mom?"

"Amy, Jeremy?" says Melody. "I forget. It isn't Terry, is it?"

"FYI, Mom, the officers are in on this. We're going to restore our country to its greatness. We're making a course correction like a ship does when it receives a storm alert. The election was stolen, right, Dad?"

"Then prove it," says Melody. "Why's that so hard? You don't have to kill someone to prove an election was rigged."

"We've proved it enough for us," says Lutz.

"Not to 51% you haven't, that's the line in democracy. You took civics, Jeremy."

"Got a D, if you remember," says Jeremy.

"I remember what a D is," says Melody, "and I remember what democracy is, and what you're advocating is the exact opposite."

"Tough Joe DiMaggios, Mom," says Jeremy. "Where's the RV?"

The chief rushes over to Melody and slaps her face hard. "Where's the RV, old lady? I don't want to hurt you. But, Baby, I can, and I will. There's nobody here to protect you."

"You can't hit a woman like that. What kind of a person are you?" says Andy, shaking in his chains.

"No worries, Handcream," says Melody. "Women know how to deal with pain. It's you, remember, who can't take it. So, Mr. Chief, is sacrificing your daughter worth all this?"

"Stepdaughter, remember," says Lutz. "I'm saving the country. And when it's all over, there will be a place in this new government for Jeremy and me."

"So, it's all about you," says Melody. "You're willing to sacrifice your daughter like Agamemnon in the Iliad. Can't you see the lightbulb going off? It ended badly, remember? Your stepdaughter is more important than the country! The country is not a thing, it's an abstract idea. It doesn't exist. Telly is flesh and blood. She exists! What blinds you to the difference? Where did you go to school, Sociopath Junior High?"

"Maybe I should just tie you up to one of these lathes," says Lutz, "twist you into a pretzel."

"Any idea how fast those lathes spin?" asks Jeremy. "By the time you tried to slow it down, Mom would be bleeding out. Might as well shoot her."

"Want the honors?"

"I can't shoot my mom."

"We're not supposed to kill anyone?" says Lutz. "Seriously, what do you think the guns in the RV are for? Show and tell? Half of Congress is going to be bleeding. Some of the DC cops will fight to the death to protect what they think is their country, their duty, their *constitution*. They have no idea how corrupt it is."

"Does Marvel write your scripts?" asks Melody. "You sound like Doctor Doom in *The Empire Shrieks Back*."

"Enough of this baloney," Lutz looks at his watch. "We're running out of time; the President is scheduled to talk at noon. I'm not going to miss that. The last piece to make all of this work is still out of place. Did I ever tell you, Jeremy, that I served at Abu Ghraib?"

"Only a thousand times, Chief."

"I'll show you how to make people talk. Pain paves the way."

"There's no evidence that any useful information was ever generated from torture," says Melody. "The British concluded that after a detailed scientific investigation. Cheney and you are following a TV script. Jack Bauer learned where the bomb was hidden only after he shot his prisoner and forced him to tell. It only works on TV."

"Mom burned through stubborn before she teethed, Chief," says Jeremy. "She won't tell you even if she could remember, which is doubtful. But she would be more than gleeful to send us on a wild goose chase."

"Just tell me where the RV is, and I'll leave you, your husband, and your son alone," says Lutz.

Melody scrunches up her chin, looks over at Jeremy, and says, "You hear that Jeremy, you're on the chopping block."

"You see, Chief, how soon she can work us against each other?"

"We left it at the park," says Melody.

"Which park?" barks Lutz.

"Camden Yards, the Orioles were playing the Cardinals. It was a bird watcher's extravaganza."

"This is football season not baseball."

"Then you need to tell them that."

Lutz kicks Melody between the legs and she falls without a word in protest.

"Hey," says Andy. "Stop that."

"Sacrifices," says Lutz.

"Why is the sacrifice always somebody else's?" says Melody. She rubs her hip and slowly gets up.

The phone rings, the identifier signaling Wells Fargo. Lutz lets it ring through, and the caller leaves a message in a stern male voice, "Mrs. MacClean, final notice before we begin eviction proceedings. Please call us back immediately. Next week will be too late."

A silence replaces the banker's last words. Funny that life refuses to stop for a breath when you are facing more immediate threats.

"That's so cliche," says Lutz. "I feel like tying you to the railroad tracks."

Silence. No one has anything to say or knows what to do.

Lutz breaks the silence, "Looks like your parents are a couple of deadbeats, Jeremy. Time to stop cutting bait." He extracts a foot-long turning gouge from one of Andy's trays and says, "I hope you keep these clean, Mr. MacClean. I sure wouldn't want anyone to get an infection." Whipping it around in the air above him so that everyone leans away, Lutz walks over and cleaves the voicemail recorder in two.

Andy screams, "You killed Sam! You killed Sam. I'll never, never hear his voice again."

"Handcream, he wasn't in there," says Melody. "I looked."

Lutz shakes his head. He glances down at his watch, curses, and smacks Melody on the head with the flat side of the blade, just above her eyebrows.

Jeremy runs over to Melody. "Mom, you all right? Shit, Chief, I never bargained for this."

"If she doesn't talk now, I'm using the edge. I'll cut her in two. What's not to like? You'll have two moms, or will that make three?"

"This is getting out of hand," says Jeremy. "Mom, Dad, you can't be willing to die for nothing. No matter what, we're going to win. You can't possibly think you'll make a difference. Dad, you're a Trumper. Have been since the beginning. You know we're right. Why are you stopping us from fixing everything? You've never acted this loco before. For Christ's sake, you're acting like Sam."

"This fellow Sam has made quite an impression on you all," says Lutz.

"He killed himself, and you want to know why?" says Jeremy.

"No," says Lutz.

"Because he was ashamed of having helped Trump win the election."

"He was as crazy as your mother is," says Lutz.

"For sure. He was on that escalator cheering Trump on when he announced his run for the presidency. Sam was a paid actor."

"Stupid," says Lutz.

"Imagine having to live with him as your brother," says Jeremy. "He wouldn't even kill an ant if he found it eating his sandwich. He'd tear off a piece of cheese for it to carry away."

"The country was built on compromise, and it already almost broke because it failed in coming to terms with whether a person was human or not," says Melody. "You're making the same exact mistake. Try your hand at reading history or raising ant farms."

The phone rings again. Lutz checks the ID. Its readout identifies the caller as Melody MacClean. Lutz points his gun at Melody, tells her to say "Hi," and puts the phone console on speaker. It still works.

"Hello, so glad I called," says Melody.

"Melody, this is Telly."

"What a surprise, the phone identifies you as me. I was looking forward to the opportunity to talk to myself. That's one too many to's and a thousand miles to Chicago. I'm actually not fine by the way, having sort of an off day. Is today yesterday yet? It will be, maybe."

"You gave me your phone."

"So, what can I do for you? It's early or late or something."

"I got inside the RV."

"Good girl, knew you would."

Lutz, looking like he will piss his pants, whispers, "Ask her where she is."

Melody turns to Lutz and says, "I know where she is Dummy. She's right here. Why would I ask her?"

And then she says to Telly "I told you not to call unless it was an emergency. You seem to confuse your lack of emergency with my present chief one. Are you near a body of water?"

Michael Lewis Reef offers, "Lake Needwood."

"Excellent, Lake Needwood is perfect. Throw my cell in there, and pronto." Melody hangs up.

Jeremy and Lutz look at each other as if they were two adolescents watching the final minutes of a *Three Stooges* movie wherein Curly suddenly starts speaking Chinese. Andy fails to stifle a laugh. Lutz spots a whip hanging against the wall and pulls it down. He sends out a crack near Andy's head. Barely misses. He tries again, aiming at Melody, and misses, but the recoil tags his own ankle. Lutz hops around, walking it off. No one, not even Jeremy, utters a sound.

Lutz goes over to the phone and pushes re-dial, the machine hemorrhages and starts to smoke then statics out. He checks for a dial tone. None. He cusses out a stream. Melody makes a show of rolling her eyes.

"There are always different ways to skin a cat, Mr. and Mrs. MacClean," says Lutz. He thumbs on his walkie-talkie, "Chief Delorean here-Officer down. I repeat. Officer down. Shooter is driving a fifty-foot Craftsman RV, New York license plates 20905 RV. Driver is female, obese, short, brown hair and eyes, no tats, name Theresa Kind. She's armed and extremely dangerous. Again, officer down, proceed with extreme caution. Out."

"I am not obese," says Telly, hearing the BOLO on the RV's CB radio.

"They must mean a different person," says Michael Lewis Reef. "Besides, your name isn't Theresa."

Telly searches on Melody's phone for 'Contacts' and dials one. She says into the phone, "Hello, put me through to Nick, please?"

"Who you calling at a time like this?" asks Sue.

"The President?" asks Michael Lewis Reef.

"Of course, the President," says Jane. "Someone needs to tell him what's going on on TV."

"I'm calling the Washington Post," says Telly.

"You know someone at the Post, Telly?" asks Sue.

"Melody told me to always use the person's first name so the receptionist will think you are friends and not automatically send you into voice mail. I learned a lot from Melody."

"You sure she's not just a tune?" asks Jane.

"Who is this?" comes over the line.

"Melody MacClean." Telly thinks of adding that she has some earth-shaking news, but Melody had told her never to put cinnamon on sugar cookies.

"Nick, hi," says Telly. "Look, Melody's in danger. Remember that business when she called you Sunday? The police have been stalking her ever since. I just called her at home, and the cops are in her home… Yeah, send a camera crew to her home on Aaron Burr Drive in Elkton… I'm on my way with an elect team of warriors to free her… Yes, I think this has everything to do with those people running around the Capitol… Why do I think that? The Melody in me, and because I have what the insurrectionists want… Hundreds of rifles."

"Why are you doing this?" asks Andy. "Nobody is down. How do you know she's anywhere near this RV of yours?"

"Where else would she be? She isn't at home or her mother's or her job's or Black's Shelter for Abused Women. She loves to drive. The RV is not where it's supposed to be, and where else would she have been calling from? You really think I'm dumb.

"Mr. MacClean. I'm going to get Telly, no matter what. She betrayed me, and you can only do that once. If you tell me where she is right now, you might save her from getting killed in a police roadblock."

Andy collapses, closes his eyes, and moans the sound elephants make mourning the death of their mate. How would he know where Telly was? This business of demanding answers to questions from people who you knew couldn't know was new to him. Not to Lutz, and there doesn't seem to be any cure.

Benedict Arnold, on the other side of the kitchen door upstairs, mimics Andy's moaning with a baleful ululation of his own.

"So, Jeremy," says Lutz. "Voicemail charades don't work, pain and threat of more don't work. Where does that leave us?" Lutz's eyes change color to that of a young tick reddening as it serenely munches on your scalp.

Melody looks over at Jeremy, but Jeremy ignores her. His instincts are on high alert. He's recalling the police training on corralling suspects. He sprints to the staircase and sits down on the third step. A look of curiosity and approval takes over as he beams in on Lutz's wavelength. Jeremy has taken in the alert, "Officer down." Is this a prediction? And if so, which of them is going down? He pulls his Glock out of his back pocket and passes it from palm to palm like he's slapping a piece of hamburger into shape.

Lutz charges Melody as he had Telly four days earlier, arms wide, offering little route of escape. But this time, he holds a roll of duct tape in one hand, a foot-long end of it whirly-birding out. He tries to grab her left arm with his free hand, but she grabs the duct tape. His grip is too strong, and she lets go. She breaks for the stairs, but Jeremy's there. She yells at him. Jeremy stands up to block her egress. He's not going to give up his front row seat. She has no place to run to other than the outside basement door. She dashes toward it, but Lutz easily beats her there, forming a five-prong shadow from the sunlight pouring in. Lutz laughs, a cat before his prey.

"What are you doing?" yells Andy. "This is crazy. Go home. If Telly is in an RV, find her there."

Jeremy alternates between fondling his Glock and twirling it around his index finger, thinking to himself, "This is going to be good. Mom and Dad are getting what's coming to them."

Melody runs over to a shelf and pulls out a lathing gouge. It's only six inches long, but the sun through the basement window reveals its lethality. She puts both hands around its handle and, with small jerky movements, lets it speak for her. Lutz gives her an amused look.

"I'll handle this, Chief," says Jeremy. He walks upstairs and opens the kitchen door, and Benedict Arnold scampers down. Benedict Arnold, having pretty much worn himself out growling and scratching at the door, runs around in circles, barking and snapping at everyone in rapid succession, asking in dog language, "Are you throwing a party without me? Is there food?"

"What the hell!" Andy says. Jeremy points his Glock at Benedict Arnold. Melody lowers the blade.

"You treated the dog better than you treated me," says Jeremy. "Making me grovel for every handout. One dead Lhasa Apso coming up."

The bullet misses. Thankfully or not, so does its ricochets. The noise from the bullet is immediately replaced by Benedict Arnold's renewed barking, which registers a longer hang time than the bullet's. The errant shot earns an eye roll from Lutz. But Lutz raises his lips up in a glimmer of gratitude to Jeremy when Melody drops the gouge to the floor. Benedict Arnold's life trumps her own. Lutz kicks the gouge to the other end of the basement then backhands Melody across the mouth. She falls, letting out a mild squeak.

No one can hear much anymore above Andy's yelling and Benedict Arnold's barking. Jeremy sticks earbuds in his ears, calmly repockets his gun, grabs Benedict Arnold's collar, and pulls him into his arms. Jeremy tolerates Benedict Arnold licking his face and neck all his way up to the kitchen landing. Then Jeremy redeposits him behind the kitchen door. Benedict Arnold, all barked out, lays down against the door, his heartbeat thrumming against it. Jeremy resumes his perch on the third stair tread, his feet comfortably resting on the slab. He keeps his weapon in his pocket. He glows from earning his keep.

Lutz steps on Melody's foot, pinning her to the floor. He rips her top off. Her unhaltered breasts fall out, two Jell-O globes reacting to gravity but pulling back to her chest in ever smaller undulations. "Look at these babies. You've been hiding these from us. Fine tits for an old woman."

"You crazy son of a bitch." But it isn't Jeremy who says this. It's Andy, in that this-can't-possibly-be-happening tone people use after accidentally shooting themselves with their own firearm.

Now, laying down on Melody, Lutz slowly unbuttons his shirt, revealing a tattooed chest, hundreds of inked rats scurrying toward the tattoo of a flute pointing up from his midsection. The purple head of his penis peeks out like a mouse at the foot of the stairs, unsure which direction is safe.

Andy can't look. He stares at Jeremy sitting on the stair tread, hoping for an intervention.

Jeremy gloats watching the degradation of his mother in front of his father, the stand-ins for his real parents who so loved him they farmed him out. A personal best fantasy is coming true before him.

Melody jerks her head to bite Lutz, but he's ready and straight arms her neck, winding the duct tape around one wrist. When she tries to claw him, he wraps her other wrist like it was choreographed. Fool's play for a veteran of Abu Ghraib.

But ever the mistress of the situation, Melody shakes her head, lets her curls swing about like coils of snakes, wiggles her hips, and casually, like a topless dancer, which indeed she had been, says, "Okay Mr. Chief, how do you like it, lying or standing, front or back, up or down?"

She pulls down her pants. Then she takes them all the way off. "No sense in getting these soiled, detergent costs money you know." Then she slips off her panties, "These will be in need of a wash anyway." She tosses them in Jeremy's direction. Jeremy is mesmerized, finally getting the chance to see her naked.

"So, Mr. Chief," says Melody. "Let me see what you got, as it seems you've known all along what you were really here for. You're not the first dick who wanted to fuck me." She sways up to Lutz as if this was all part of a script in a porn movie. Her breasts, the size of just ripe peaches, slink toward him, her nipples stiffening as if they were planning to sting.

Lutz looks over at Jeremy.

Jeremy winks back.

Both are sure what will happen is not what the Chief would have predicted.

Melody quickly unfastens Lutz's belt, and a ton of equipment clangs to the floor. She ignores the articles of police entrapment and yanks his pants down to his ankles. "I love bowling-pin calves. Here's hoping your penis isn't cue-stick thin. Your thighs could use some toning, so we might do better on the floor. Raise a foot so I can slide your slacks and briefs off, okay?" While she's saying this, she presses her breasts against Lutz's chest, nudging her nipples against his, delicately roping her taped arms over his neck. She pecks a cheek. Lutz quickly reaches behind his back and traps her hands in his to make sure she doesn't try to topple him. She doesn't.

Lutz eyes his police tools lying on the floor, figuring it will only be a second before she tries something. That will be his excuse to really hit her and finally get Andy's cooperation. But his juices are flowing, his penis is purple red, his scrotum shrunk to the size of a newborn's fist, his legs nearly cramping from the strain of staying half-mast.

Melody, switching her attention to process, says, "Handcream, is there a carpet or pad nearby?" Then she turns her attention to Lutz, "I mean, if you can hold it Mr. Chief. Some men cum so prematurely. There's always re-penising. But that won't work if you're on the clock. We can't forget that, right? What time are you supposed to punch in?"

Lutz is still expecting a last-second sabotage when she pulls down his briefs to join his pants at his ankles. Lutz realizes his feet are lassoed together by his pants, but he figures he doesn't have to run. Jeremy is right there to stop her from going anywhere. She cuddles his scrotum with her fingers and kisses his neck, her chest against his like she really wants it. Then it registers, she does.

She doesn't care that her son and husband are watching. She doesn't care that she's delaying the gun delivery to the Capitol. She doesn't care that she's derailing the coup. Or maybe she'd just forgotten. And everything starts to fall away from him. Like she said, this had been his plan all along. The joy of raping a woman, of being in complete control. The rifles for the Capitol are just a chimera. He just needs a lay. She just wants to be laid.

Andy struggles against the handcuffs. He knows the screws that bolted his weight rack to the slab are ten inches long, ensuring the rack would never tilt, no matter how many pounds he put on it. It could hold an RV. He looks through the glass door, away from Melody's sex dance. But he has been working on an idea. His weight machine needs grease for its central beam to keep the weights from jamming. He has tried to maneuver his hands over to the grease. No luck, but he has been able to stretch a foot far enough out to strip a stripe of grease on the side of his boot. It isn't much, but after multiple failures, he's finally able to transfer some to his fingers. He starts to massage the grease on his wrists, hoping he can slip a hand free. To do what after is yet to be thought out.

Jeremy, on the other hand, is getting hard, fantasizing nexts, a scene he had often imagined during his teenage masturbation rounds. Why not? The country is coming to an end anyway. If the rally succeeds, there will be mayhem. He may or may not have a seat at the table of power. He had trusted the Chief. But right now, Jeremy sees weakness, Lutz's sex urge steering him away from the prize. If the rally fails, Jeremy may be implicated and just might end up in a cement room like this one, but one with a hole for a bathroom, a sink for a shower, and a homosexual or homophobic cellmate. But Jeremy was sure he could get drugs there. There are always drugs in prisons. The guards need them as much as the prisoners.

Something is robbing Lutz of his tumescence, maybe it's Jeremy's overthinking. Lutz's penis shrinks down. Mortified, Lutz pushes Melody away, calls her a whore, and resurrects his underwear, pants, and gear, turning his back to everyone in an absolute incredulous show of modesty. Then he pulls a pistol from his holster and, without a word, shoots Melody in the stomach.

Andy screams, "No! No! No!"

Melody remains standing up and naked. She sees blood dripping down her front and puts a finger to stem its flow. "There's got to be Band-Aids upstairs. Handcream, would you get me two, one for each hole?" Then she slowly slumps to the floor in a perfect imitation of a mime dying.

Lutz yells at Melody, "I'm stuck in a grade-B soap opera. Mrs. MacClean, how you feeling? You need medical care. Ready to tell me where Telly is now?"

Jeremy, his Glock in his lap, looks Lutz right in the eyes. Lutz looks right back at him and offers an apology, "She wasn't your birth mother, just a surrogate. She'll live."

"You're smarter than that, Andy," whispers Melody. She no longer moves. She no longer makes a sound. Her chest neither rises nor falls. All anyone can hear are Andy's futile attempts to slip out from his shackles, which he stops as soon as Lutz approaches him.

"MacClean, for the last time, tell me where the RV is. Look at what you did to my hand." Lutz cuts off his bandage with one of Andy's gouges and exposes the raw, red, swollen skin in its embryonic stage of healing, yellowed by antiseptic.

"After I cut off your right hand, if you still don't tell me, I want you to say goodbye to your left hand. You get that? We're going to make this country great again. Your new nickname will be Handless MacClean! Catchy right?"

"You shot an unarmed woman," spits out Andy. "What is wrong with you? You took an oath. Is this what you want, the US becoming just another monarchy?"

"One with nuclear weapons," says Lutz. "We will all be safe."

"Like Russia, China, North Korea, and Iran?" says Jeremy.

"We're taking back this country," roars Lutz.

"We?" says Andy. "We whites, you mean?"

"And anyone else who wants to follow us."

"So, shooting an unarmed, disabled forty-five-year-old woman is what superiority looks like," says Andy. "There's a mirror down here somewhere, you need to take a look at yourself."

"These are the *sacrifices* we have to make to get our country back, Mr. MacClean. How much more will you sacrifice? How about if we start by taking off your fingers, digit by digit? Only, we don't have enough time for that. We used to just pull the fingernails out. Slower was better. More blood than you would expect, though. Is losing your hand worth telling me where my daughter is? You don't even know her."

"She came to me for help. She helped us back. She's a child, for Christ's sake."

"Keep her. Keep your right hand. I want the RV! I want it now!"

"Those guns are to be used to kill police officers."

"The cops will fall in line with us. The rifles will be used against Congress, the Vice President, and of course, the Speaker."

"Is that supposed to be a bargaining chip?"

"Look, Mr. MacClean, eventually, we're going to find Telly and the RV. If I get to her first, you'll be saving her life."

Andy hangs his head down and crumbles to the floor in his chains. He wasn't made for this. Who is Andrew MacClean, anyway? When Melody was healthy, he was confident. Then Alzheimer's struck. Had he gotten so comfortable shirking leadership he'd lost his sense of self? Melody had called him Andy.

"Aren't we on the same side?" asks Andy. "I'm a Trumper."

"Then tell me where Telly is," says Lutz. Lutz feels that he's being played, a la *Little Big Man* with General Custer. Lutz reminds himself he's the good guy here.

Andy realizes that if Melody is dead, he no longer has to care for her. He no longer has to do what she wants. Except there's Telly now. Telly. So, he talks, "I don't know where Telly is. She took off with the RV on her own. I tried to catch her. She could be in Bangor, Maine, by now."

"On the phone," says Lutz, "a male voice said she was close to Lake Needlewood."

"Go there then," says Andy. "You don't need me. Let me go. I can help you. If I can save Melody. That way they won't charge you with murder."

Lutz looks at his watch.

"Five minutes, Mr. MacClean," says Lutz. "I have to make a call. That's all the time your right hand has. I'd call a priest to give your hand last rites, but there are so few priests around these days, and most of them barely speak English."

Andy listens to his own breathing, marveling at its back and forth, up and down, in and out from lungs to stomach, disinterested in all this. He feels like he's melding with Melody, a bullet hole through their middles.

CHAPTER FIFTY-THREE

CIRCLING DOWN THE DRAIN

Waiting's catharsis is a pinhole leak in an angry balloon, whether it's practicing guitar, watching the Super Bowl, or staging a coup.

Carl and Warren vow to go to bed early and get up earlier, even though the rally doesn't start until the afternoon. Their vow is skinned away like their pickup's brake linings by the fourteen-hour drive, so instead they stay up past dawn playing *Street Fighter* and drinking miniature bottles of hotel liquor. The email said everything would be paid for.

With their wake-up call comes an envelope. They open it and read, "KEYCODE 20905."

A little gray, they make it to the Capitol an hour early and look for the RV. They see a fury of activity. "This is going to be a wonderfuck," Carl says. Then he asks Warren, "What if we don't find the RV? I don't see any RV."

"We think for ourselves," says Warren.

"Right. It's sure going to be awesome when it's over."

"You sound like you wish it was."

"You don't?" asks Carl.

"Absolutely not, this is going to be the major milestone of our lives, Carl. After this, who knows? You think those Antifa fellows aren't going to fight? They don't want what we want."

"Which is what exactly? And where are they?"

"Progress, Man, movement forward, not this constant gridlock bullshit."

"You're damned right," says Carl. "Nothing getting done while everyone else is raking in the money but us."

"Amazing that we haven't already slit each other's throats."

"That's what we're here to do?" asks Carl.

"I need to take a whizz," says Warren.

Five minutes later, Carl says, "I still don't see any signs of Antifa nor a RV. The Proud Boys are represented. The Oath Keepers are here. What do we do when Antifa arrives?"

"That's when the RV shows, Dummy. The guns will be the sign we're free to kill. It'll give us clear authority to wipe the Capitol clean."

"What if the guns don't show up?"

Warren hunches his shoulders.

"Ain't never killed a guy," says Carl.

"Neither have I, but we've killed game, a few giant elk, and brown bears. Huge, you could have ridden them. It won't be any different."

"How do you know that?"

"My granddad did it in World War Two," says Warren. "Though, he always refused to talk about it."

"That counts then. You know, it's colder out here than I thought it would be."

"It's January for friggin' sake," says Warren. "Whaddya expect?"

"The sun is out, and it's freezing."

"Not freezing. Frigging thirty-eight degrees. Thirty-two is freezing, doncha know?"

"Yeah, but freezing in Vermont is warmer for some reason," says Carl. "What are we going to do after? Where are we going to go?"

"There you go again missing the best part, the doing. Ever watch *The Exterminator*?"

"Sure, everybody does."

"It's all there," says Warren.

"What is?"

"One punch, one yank, one head butt, and it's all over. Victory."

"Never did for me."

"Always on the losing side?"

"Yeah, I guess so."

"Well, now you're going to feel the other side of it."

Carl pulls some miniature liquor bottles out of his Kevlar vest and asks, "You want one?"

CHAPTER FIFTY-FOUR

INSURRECTION EPIPHANY

As they wait for Lutz to return, Andy says to Jeremy, "I get it now. I am so slow. But then, so was Melody. She thought you were just being naive. You're not. You idolize Donald Trump because you want to be in on the spoils."

"What's wrong with that, Old Man?"

"Bullying is getting what you want when you don't have a right to it. That's Donald Trump's attraction. You applaud it, you even admire it. But it makes no sense. You lose all empathy for the victim. And then, eventually, you become the victim."

"Mom has taken over your brain," says Jeremy.

"You worship power. And you don't care how you get it."

"Be sure of one thing, Dad, I'm not going to be scraped off of anyone's boot. When Trump gropes a woman, that's a symbol of man's power over the weaker sex. The same goes for stealing. If Trump wants something, he just takes it. No one stops him. We want to be just like him. We are just like him, just too afraid that we might get caught. But with him in power, there will be no one to arrest us. Bonanza time baby."

"So, you don't have to be smart or athletic or educated or even talented?"

"Smash and grab and never let go is my motto," says Jeremy.

"Your brother didn't teach you anything?"

"How do you think the rich got their money in the first place? And Sam, he taught me that nice guys are the first ones to get run over. Like that poor fool in Tiananmen Square. We deserve it because we're willing to grab it."

Andy, while still trying to twist his hands clear of the handcuffs, says more to himself than Jeremy, "You deserve it because you were born to it. You've become the entitled who you say is the problem."

Lutz enters the basement through the glass door. Jeremy asks, "How did your call go, Chief?"

"Telly, my lovely soon-to-be deceased stepdaughter is close. She's in Elkton. She just drove away in the RV from the nursing home my parents used to own. She kidnapped three patients. Every policeman in the state of Maryland is looking for her."

Everything darkens.

The sunlight thief is the RV. Its bulk is blocking the sun from coming through the basement window. Andy, Lutz, and Jeremy see Telly at its wheel. She's pumping the RV's horn to the beat of, "Here I Come to Save the Day." When she stops honking the horn, they hear tires skidding to a stop outside. She has an escort.

Then, in a syncopated Chinese fire drill, four people file out of the RV and three surround it, each holding a rifle. Telly jumps back into the driver's seat. She puts her cell phone to her ear.

"Look at this," says Lutz, "Mr. MacClean. Telly driving to your doorstep. I'm saved. Come to Poppa, Miss Wet Pants."

"You have to let me go now," pleads Andy.

"First, I'm going to kill her," says Lutz. "Then I'll deal with you.

"Jeremy, where do you think you are going? HEEL!"

Jeremy sprints to the basement door and says, "I'm not a dog, Chief. You shoot my mom; I shoot your daughter. You can't have all the fun." He walks out, Glock in his hand.

When Jeremy gets within five feet of the RV he's hit, fired by none other than former soldier, Jane. The dart bounces off his chest and drops to the ground. Jeremy picks it up. He looks over at Telly's posse. Each holds a similar-looking weapon. Jane reloads.

He examines the dart while addressing Telly's posse, "Are these the only type of rifles in the RV?"

"Where do you think we got them, Fort Fox?" says Michael Lewis Reed.

"The RV is filled with them, and they're brand new," says Sue. "Never been fired before."

Jeremy shakes his head and chortles. But the other cops will stand behind him. They always do. The chief will too, right?

Jeremy's police training kicks in—always be the first to deliver the bad news. He yells, "Chief, the rifles are toys. They aren't real. You shot my mom for nothing. We've been stuuung!"

For Lutz, the basement concrete slab floor slips into quicksand. He can identify a non-lethal weapon when he sees one. He sees, through the basement window, toy rifles in three people's arms. His knees work double-time to keep him erect. Cuss words jam his cerebral cortex. "I Be So Glad When the Sun Goes Down," barges in his head. He can't fight the tune off. Shame beyond redemption, defeat beyond perdition. Screwed again. Why was it always him?

Then, Jeremy peers at Telly sitting in the RV driver's seat, "This isn't a toy, Girl. Say cheese."

Jeremy straightens his arm out and aims his Glock at Telly. She's talking to Nick on the phone. The bullets stream out. The RV's bulletproof glass cracks and cackles.

But it holds.

The police, who had trailed the RV to the MacClean's and ducked behind their cars as all good cops do on TV, open up. This is the everyday fantasy that gives heart and soul to their lives. The chance to fire their rifles, oiled every day, at something besides targets on the firing range.

The MacClean basement glass door explodes. Lutz and Andy flatten themselves against the concrete under a thousand glass shards, and blood droplets invade their breathing air. Jeremy loses more meat than a week of buzzard-work on highway roadkill. The three former residents of Saved Angels fare no better.

"A man shot at me, and he just got killed," says Telly to Nick. She can't see her three friends, but she knows. She counts a hundred bullet holes in the MacClean's home siding. "I'm not liking this very much." She isn't hungry. "Is fear what it takes? Can this be marketed in a pill?" She asks, "Nick, is there a process for extending my status as a minor? I'm not ready. Really. Seriously, I'm not ready. Do you know of some paperwork I have to fill out?"

A short burst of self-congratulatory cheer erupts from the cops when their clips run out. Then silence, even the hanging pieces of glass obeying some superior's order to stay in place and shush. Recognition. Police command retinas register Jeremy's uniform. DC police. Optics. The Washington's Post van peels out behind them. Command yells, "Stop them! Stop them." No one moves to.

"The police killed Jeremy!" says Andy. "You killed him. You killed my son!"

"I told him not to go out there," Lutz says.

Lutz pulls out his walkie-talkie, "All Clear, I repeat, All Clear. This is Police Chief Lutz Delorean. All Clear. Weapons down. No one in here is armed but me. Weapons down. Over. Out."

Andy listens. Chief is wrong again. Andy is armed. His two arms are chained temporarily only. He rasps over to Lutz, "Release me. You got your RV. I've got to get Melody to the hospital. That may save your life."

If Melody dies, Andy is finally free. But being so close to the brink doesn't have the feel of freedom. The handcuffs stapled to his weight rack remind him he isn't. The urgency to save Melody reminds him. Melody had made his world.

"Releasing you wouldn't lower my prison sentence much," says Lutz, "but having one less witness might."

"Kill me then," whispers Andy. "You've met your match Chief. You haven't thought this through, just like Melody said. You've taken my wife and my son. Who are you going to threaten next, my parents? Try Manayunk Cemetery, plot number 712."

"You know, you're even starting to sound like her," says Lutz as he slashes off Andy's right hand.

Andy goes into shock. Blood oozes from his stub in heartbeat spurts.

His brain responds to a leak. It isn't able to calculate the extent of the wound. Instead, it dashes out cauterizing white corpuscles to the rescue and shuts his digestive system down flat. Andy sees his hand, lying there, his beautiful hand. On the floor. It trembles. He wants so much to cradle it and just go to sleep with it, hide it from any more pain, thank it, hold it in his… What was that expression? It doesn't get any better than this? No, not that. Instead, he hears Melody's insistent mantra, "Life only gets harder, and you don't want that to change. Easy is boring. Easy is hell." But what about his right hand?

He feels tears coursing down his cheeks, warming them. But his stub, his stub is ablaze, finger synapses firing off into a void denying access. He could just bleed out here, that would put an end to it. No more worries. Wasn't that how these last two weeks started, wishing Melody and he were dead? He's getting his wish. But that isn't why he told the chief to cut off his hand. What is he forgetting? This isn't a dream where he can't get back to where he had just been.

Lutz pulls his gun out of his holster and yells through the broken glass basement door, "Telly, Telly, Mr. MacClean shot Melody. You better get in here to stop her bleeding or she's gonna die."

CHAPTER FIFTY-FIVE

FILM NOIR

In a first take of a speech that was to be released immediately after the Insurrection, we see the President fiddle with a plastic bottle then turn its label away from the camera. He refuses to advertise products he isn't being compensated to.

He says to the cameraman, "Say when." Off screen, someone signals that the film is rolling, so he rolodexes through his different facial expressions until he has a fair mixture of his I-told-you-so smile and his iconic 'Now I've got you, you piece-of-shit' jawline. Then he addresses the microphone:

"You, the voters, have spoken. Thanks to the beautiful people who have risked their lives to defend America. By the way, I salute you. *I think I read that right.* I want to let you know I'll yield to your will. I am taking the presidency back to its rightful owner, Donald Trump. Me.

"First order of business must be deciding what's to be done with those who tried to interfere with your will. Let everyone know I have no ill will for these misguided blanks.

"*Someone was supposed to have filled that in. I think I settled on 'citizens.* I'll get to that in a minute.

"I want to be known as Donald Trump the Tax Killer. For instance, why should you have to pay for legislatures that don't step in to stop a stolen election? I'm firing both houses. I never knew why we needed two nor why we called them houses. No one lives there. They have so failed and given me such a blank. *I think 'stomachache' belongs here, maybe heartache, I don't remember.* Just think how much in taxes this will save you. Donald Trump the Tax Killer, me.

"As for the Supreme Court Justices, who seem to have nothing better to do than prosecute me, 'They're Fired' too. And let's be fair, once Roe v. Wade was overturned, who needs them anymore? But I may keep Barrett on. She's so pretty and very friendly. *Makes me, no, I won't say it. Ever notice that Republicans are all good-looking? Not like…*

"Imagine how much money will be saved with no one prosecuting me anymore. But so, there's no question about that, I am pardoning myself im-meed-dee-ut-lee for all my alleged wrongdoings in per-puh-two-it-tee. *Like the sound of that word? Strong leaders use it all the time, use it in discriminally.*

"The cabinet is dismissed too. Who needs them? I alone know what's right and how to get things done. Why complicate my decisions with other people's opinions? Think of how much money that will save you. Donald Trump the Tax Killer, me.

"On the international front, I am withdrawing the US from the United Nations, NATO, NAFTA, PLATO, PLUTO, and every other alliance that costs us money. I'll keep our alliance with

Israel and will soon extend an offer to ally with Ukraine. If it supplies me with the dirt on Biden's son, *I know they have it.*

"The police will run the courts like they do in most civilized countries. Did you know that before a person can be tried by a jury, the police have to convince a judge someone is guilty? Who needs all that doo-plis-ih-tee? Things will finally start to get done. Lawsuits will no longer delay real estate construction projects, stop the burning of library books, and keep police from shooting suspects. You break the law; you have no rights—goes to show you. There is no reason for these obsolete processes other than to waste your tax dollars. And I am all about saving you money. I'll save you millions, billions, even trillions. I am President Donald Trump the Tax Killer, me.

"Now as for the armed forces, something's got to be done with them, right? They were created to defend us from other countries and are very expensive. Trillions and trillions spent to defend against attacks from Mexico and Canada, which never happened by the way. So, people are telling me, we are paying for all this military equipment that we have no use for. I say, "Use it." I have declared war against Mexico. *I am not sure if that has actually happened yet. Remember, I have only had a few days to write this speech myself.* Details will be forthcoming as soon as we can withdraw all of our military forces from everywhere else, which is really everywhere they were never needed in the first place. I am sure the troops will be thankful for the change of rations to Mexican food. The Mexicans in our services sure will.

"I know, I know. You have questions. That civil case against that guy who rear ended you? Is my job at the tire dealership safe?

Who is going to regulate the quality of gas, food, drugs, air, and baby formula? What about the rising cost of cable and Wi-Fi?

"Here are some answers, and the rest will come later. The post office will now deliver mail once a week. I mean, only advertisers and non-profits use snail mail any more, and as for Aunt Emma Dee's Christmas card, it can be enjoyed and read after as well as before the holidays.

"The police will no longer investigate car accidents. Let the insurance companies do their own investigation. They're the ones who profit. And settling out of court will be the only way to collect. Each side's lawyers will work this out. To make it speedier, the lawyers will lose a percent of their take every month they don't settle. That way, the longer they can't agree, the less they make. No better incentive exists. Brilliant. But you knew that about me anyway.

"Not having to sort out which driver was negligent will free the police up to do important work, like manning drug dispensaries, incarcerating the mentally ill, and regulating what news you get. Drugs will be legal, as long as you buy them from the police. And that profit will overfund the police, another of my administration's slogans. Overfund, Overfund. Remember the Overfund.

"We have single handedly blamed every mass killing on the mentally ill, so if we put them in jail, the only victims will be their cellmates. And what the news is able to report will actually be what I allow them to report. Nothing more needs to be said about that. Alcohol taxes will be tripled. As you know, I do not drink, and I do want to discourage drinking but at the same time pay our bills. Green fees and caddie stipends keep rising.

"I'm also changing our National Anthem to Ben and Jerry's, "I Will Survive." You can purchase the CD at my website. All royalties will go to my campaign. Have a good one, and you can start spending those tax dollars you are not going to have to pay right now, which will begin a new era of pros-per-ih-tee. Remember who finally drained the swamp and don't forget, I hug the flag every day. You should too, and you can also buy a US flag on my website. I'll have that copyright very shortly. I think that is it for now. Good night. This has been the forty-fifth president of the United States, and counting, Donald Trump the Tax Killer. Me."

CHAPTER FIFTY-SIX

SPEED UP IN A TURN

Andy gets that he can't hear or see. He doesn't think he needs to. He feels. He resurrects inside himself the thrum of his lathe skimming off sycamore. The most soothing feeling in the world. He plays it against the continuum of pain spasms fighting over the mastery of his body and mind. Melody had said he needed to rank sensations if he wanted to be more than an animal. The chief is not going to kill Telly.

He recalls his mom's spankings, ranks the pain right up there. Remembers Melody's monologues about pain, that in between spasms and chaos breached life. He waits. Life is action. Pain is waiting. The final out has not been called.

One half of the handcuffs have fallen to the concrete slab, leaving his right hand—well, his right shoulder and arm stub—free to swing. He knows where Lutz was standing in his mind's eye and blindsides Lutz in the kidney with his freshly minted stub.

The Chief is somehow farther away. His brain has not recalibrated the missing eight inches of flesh and bone.

Andy goes lights out, but he can't leave it there. Won't. Every single nerve is aflame and wrestling with the nerve nearest to it. He waits. His hearing returns first.

"Your kid was right; you're a wimp. I barely felt that," says Lutz, still lying face down on the floor and rubbing his side. He fakes laughing, trying to find a reason to rise. Nothing surfaces. He looks up to see if Telly is coming.

Andy's sight blinks back. He feels the shackles tight on his calves. No escape there. His eyes measure the handcuffs dangling from his left hand. No more than ten inches. Too short. He sees his tennis racket. He imagines flattening himself out to reach it. No. He frees his geode belt out of its loops with his left hand. Maybe. Loosens his grip on it to promote whip and delivers the fastest serve the world would have ever seen if the ball was the back of Chief Lutz Delorean's head.

There's a crack of crystal smacking skull bone. Both materials are robust but unrelentingly rigid. Both fail. The geode shatters into a million crystals which shotgun as if in search of Jeremy's tennis ball. The skull smushes in. The brain vacuum exhales. Lutz is beyond feeling, past knowing, afterlife, no meal or movies provided. Lutz feels something is wrong. A nerve triggers an instant of pain, but the absolute invasion of the sacrosanct brain stem immediately floods neuron receptors with an acknowledgement that the memory in the hippocampus has permanently disengaged, along with the software to punish or reward, freeing it of distracting directions. Seconds later, the brain stem loses its link to the nervous system, just like when astronaut Colonel Rick Husband said, "Roger, uh." The last human sound from the Columbia Space Shuttle.

A gray humming blob, obedient to Newton's law of gravity, puddings out on the cement floor. Lutz's fake smile freezes for his final photo op, rigor mortis pushing the shutter button.

Andy lies down. Every nerve, every muscle shakes. The shaking jackhammers him against the unforgiving concrete slab. It doesn't hurt. Everything's so cold. He's expecting his mother's strop now. Instead, he feels warmth against his cheek. Blood? No. It's someone's palm. Melody?

CHAPTER FIFTY-SEVEN

THE STAKES AND CAKE

The defense lawyer that the MacClean's insurance company hired, Ita Branewski, is just assembling all her files and paperwork prior to leaving when Telly bursts into Andy's hospital room. Her hands are full. She's carrying a Wegmans birthday cake, three pints of Ben & Jerry's ice cream, and a six-pack of Reed's ginger ale.

It's February 16, her eighteenth birthday. She's an adult.

Ita nods and smiles at Telly then continues talking to Andy, "Again, Mr. MacClean, capital punishment is not in the cards here. Damascus wants this case pushed underground as soon as possible."

"No police officer wants to see me anywhere above ground."

"The Post's constant barrage of front-page interviews and pictures only cements Damascus's zeal to settle," Ita says. "It's only because of Melody's lawsuits for personal injury and gross negligence that Damascus has agreed to pay Walter Reeds' invoices up front until we settle. Where is Melody, by the way?"

As if on cue, a nurse wheels in, all COVID-19 garbed, and breathlessly says, "Time to have your temperature taken, Mr. MacClean. Turn over on your stomach, please."

"I'd better be going," says Ita.

"Completely unnecessary," says the nurse. "Transparency is our motto here. Shall I strip back the sheets, or will you Mr. MacClean?"

"Melody, where's my coffee?" asks Andy.

"How did you know I was me?" asks Melody. "I'm wearing an N95 mask."

"The wheelchair kinda gave you away, Mrs. MacClean," says Telly.

"Melody," says Ita, "I was just telling Andy how fortunate he was to have you as an attorney and that the Damascus Police Department would settle shortly."

"What about that DA who has his eyes on a run for governor?" asks Melody. "He'd kiss a force-fed goose on a bed of foie gras for another click."

Ita admits, "He's a problem."

"I killed a police chief," says Andy.

"You only know you wanted to," says Ita. "You have no memory of the incident. That's called post traumatic amnesia. A medical diagnosis that's been authenticated so many times, it no longer requires evidence."

"Are you telling me what you want me to say on the stand?" asks Andy.

"I'm telling you what you've already testified to," says Ita.

"What if my memory comes back?"

"Not a problem, everyone assumes you did it anyway. And you had every reason to. Fortunately, no one at the Damascus Police Station liked Chief Delorean." Ita turns to Telly and says, "Sorry Telly."

"He had some good points," Telly says. "He worked hard to keep me from becoming a blimp. But he shot Melody, and for that I could never forgive him."

"And Andy," says Ita, "the only eyewitness is your present dessert deliverer. I keep telling her not to visit you until the grand jury rules, but as we can see, she's not beholden to my advice."

"I make my own decisions," says Telly. "No one is going to tell me what to do."

"Also, we have Donna Kind," continues Ita. "She came forward and testified that Chief Delorean wanted Telly dead, which supports Andy's acting in Telly's defense. There's no more noble act than that."

"Yeah, Handcream," chimes in Melody. "Where were you when I needed you?"

"That doesn't mean I can't be convinced with the proper argument," says Telly. "But why would anyone believe my mom? She's a doper."

"Because everything she said checked out," says Ita. "Her texts, the money transfers, and the cigarette butt with Chief Delorean's DNA. Plus, and I keep hammering the prosecutor on this, how was it physically possible for a man in Andy's condition to have killed Chief Delorean? Andy should have been unconscious. Who is he, Superman? That, and they still haven't been able to find any tool in the basement that matches the impact on the back of Chief Delorean's skull."

All four look from one to the other. Andy is as quiet as any of them. Melody smiles then says, "Have they completely ruled out the possibility that Mr. Chief suicided?"

Melody spins around in her wheelchair to face Andy and says, "Handcream, you would enjoy prison, though. You wouldn't have to cook anymore, and your cellmates would crown you Chief of Police Killer. Plus, you would no longer have to obey my demands. I mean commands. But, not to worry, the Steep Date will see to it that we are never separated. They know better than to get between me and my beer distributor. By the way, how did Andy cut his hand off again? Was it a lathe accident in the basement? It happened in the basement, didn't it?"

Ita, Telly, and Andy ignore the impulse to go over the events again. They look at each other. Telly and Andy's eyes hand the ball to Ita. She knows how to summarize. "A couple of teenagers hacked the former president's campaign. They inserted a link to a fake website, promoted as helping the former president stay in office. They were really siphoning off money meant for themselves. Things got out of hand."

"Trump had nothing to do with it," says Andy. "How about some of that cake, Telly?"

"Ita, cake and ice cream?" asks Telly.

"No, thanks, have to watch my waist. Besides, I have another appointment."

"All work and no play, Counselor," says Melody, "turns you into John Foster Dulles."

"Okay, I'll have a Reed's. They make the best ginger ale."

"Oh, I forgot," says Telly, "I wrote a poem. Got an A. Here it is."

Melody reads it out loud, "*Melody Says*

> *A real man is unreal.*
> *An idle man is clueless,*
> *Idolizing is cluelust.*
> *Believing is slavery,*
> *Doubt is freedom.*
> *Loyalty benefits royalty*
> *and only hurts everyone.*
> *Idolatry attracts lies,*
> *Frugality swats flies,*
> *Liberalism fuels tries.*
> *A closed mind wastes the most time;*
> *A lime rime makes the margarita.*
> *What are you waiting for,*
> *When all there ever can be is more?*"

"I don't remember saying those things, but I do remember thinking them."

"Where's your stapler, Melody?" says Telly. "I want to add it to my other poems."

After his arrest and hospitalization, Andy figured a life sentence would be too stiff a price to pay, and capital punishment would be a welcome mat. But then living in the hospital with Melody this last month taught him that his anger over caring for her never trumped the joy he got from having her around.

So, now he's anxious to return home. Finding the TV remote in the refrigerator, no washcloths in the bathroom when he placed a dozen therein the day before, and Benedict Arnold rubbing his side against his leg for a walk. Living with Melody was like playing tennis, you never knew where your shot would go nor your opponent's. But it was fun. Melody had been the one person in the world he wanted out of his life, and now he finds that without her, he'd have no press to continue.

Donna was assigned by the court as Telly's housekeeper. She moved into Telly's home, Benedict Arnold in tow. No longer having to live day by day, she started detoxing. A government grant to assist recovering addicts was paying her tuition for a nursing license. Her mother had been a nurse. Her daughter is a nurse-to-be. You're either caring for someone or being cared for by someone, so what the hell? Besides all that, Benedict Arnold and she had bonded.

What's important to Andy is that Melody is with him, even if she's in a wheelchair. Lutz's bullet severed her spinal cord at L6. Andy's content. She keeps him a little crazy. The way he likes it. She throws shit at everything he brings up. He never wanted a cheerleader, never credits anyone who praises him anyway. He had forgotten that about himself.

THE STAKES AND CAKE

"Thanks for the Reed's," says Ita. "I'll just take it with me, Good byya."

Ita leaves with her files. The three stare at Andy's reattached hand. Its color reminds them of the plaque.

"Let's see you move those fingers, Mr. MacClean," Telly says. "I know you can do it."

"I'm never going to use my right hand again, except as a paperweight, Telly."

"Of course you will, Mr. MacClean," says Telly.

"Shut up. These doctors make a living peddling nonsense."

"Telly, he doesn't mean that," says Melody. "He forgets you saved our lives by getting us to the hospital in record time. No one drives faster than Telly Kind."

"I'm sorry Telly" says Andy. "I'm just stupid and ungrateful and even more stupid. Forgive me, please."

"Handcream, you have to get back the use of your right hand," says Melody. "You have three dozen orders to fill. Ever since Mrs. Watanabe presented your plaque to Japan, and Japan installed it adjacent to the original ceramic piece in the Hiroshima Museum of Art, a day doesn't go by without a new commission request."

"It wasn't me," Andy says into his lap. "It was the water damage from the storm that gave it that look. The rain damage I blamed on you for not letting me trim the trees."

"Mr. MacClean, you did 99% of the work," says Telly, "but you won't take any of the credit? I think that's a mental illness, I just can't remember its name."

"You know what he did?" asks Melody.

Andy and Telly wait to hear a fantasy of what didn't happen for the umpteenth time.

"Mrs. Watanabe called for the plaque. Andy told her it was damaged in the storm, and he would have to redo it. She wanted it anyway, so Andy retrieved it from the garbage persons as they were pulling away from the curb. The rest is geography."

"Wonderful," they say in unison.

Of course, that is not what happened. The bank started eviction proceedings. Mrs. Watanabe read in the Post about the MacCleans when she returned from San Francisco. She sent the bank a check covering all the back-due mortgage payments, asking the bank when it would be opportune to request her plaque. The bank demanded the plaque from Andy the day her check cleared. When Andy realized she had paid for something he no longer had, he tried to get back in the house to get it, but the cops wouldn't let him. It was still a crime scene.

Melody filed a Motion of Return of Property to no effect. Telly asked Donna to help her burglarize the place. Donna said, "I'll take care of it." It pays to know local law enforcement, even when they will never admit knowing you.

When Donna presented the plaque to Mrs. Watanabe, she remarked on its cracking and coloring. Donna sold her, "You wanted it to look forty years old, didn't you? Anyone can make something look brand new. If you want new, go to Walmart." The result sits in a museum six thousand miles away.

Andy, nursing a Reed's in his good hand, watches Melody and Telly compete to polish off a pint of ice cream each. He says to no one in particular, "I'm going to return those commission checks. I'll see if my equipment is still in working order as soon as Walter Reed releases me. Right now, my heart's not in it. Ita says losing a hand qualifies you for 75% disability. 75% of what?"

"Handcream," says Melody, wiping ice cream from her nose with her sleeve, "you're starting to sound more like me every day. You just need to practice. Practice right now by giving me the finger! How could you get along if you couldn't give me the finger?"

Andy raises his right hand for her to see. He imagines giving her the finger, but his carrot fingers follow gravity's pull and flop down like a wilted flower. He flips his palm up. His fingers stay in a semi-fetal position. He says, "How's that?"

"Then who's going to eat this Ben and Jerry's," says Telly as she plops a pint of ice cream onto his open right palm. He looks at it as if it's a dog turd. His reflexes instruct his left hand to catch it, but he's still holding the bottle of ginger ale. He doesn't want to spill that. His right thumb pokes the pint container, half-pinning it to his palm. His pinkie stretches, a thick pink worm righting the sweet concoction, to crown the save.

"I thought you didn't like ice cream, Handcream," clucks Melody.

Andy watches his pinky wave again. Feels a connection, a shadowy tumbler fits into its homebase. The pint of ice cream cradles safely in his palm.

"I told you. I told you Mr. MacClean," yells Telly. "Never give up. You just have to keep trying. Woohoo!"

His pinky straightens, steadies the load. Tearing up, Andy says, "How about that?"

"No reason to cry, Andy," says Melody. "Telly, how about some privacy?"

"Huh?" says Andy.

As Telly scoots, Melody says, "Andy, let's run a trial and see if your other equipment has returned to working order."

William Francis Kirk was a Navy Brat, made and born in Japan; shuttered between Hawaii and California for a bit, until nesting in Alabama, before optioned back to California and receiving a degree in philosophy and a wife in extraordinary behavior from the University of San Francisco. Later moved across the Bay to Oakland, then to Phoenix, rebounded to Thousand Oaks before the last sprint to Doylestown. The author spent his working years dropping down into the latest and greatest catastrophe, an insurance claim checkbook serving for a parachute. He worked with people who had lost everything, guiding their rebuilding lives and beliefs from scratch. He has two grown sons, who have never disgraced him, at least as far as he can tell, which is as far as a father needs to know.

Melody and Handcream MacClean learn of a suspicious delivery bound for the Capitol on January 6th, the day of the 'peaceful' transfer of power. Their son works at the Capitol. He's a D.C. cop. Melody, a polymath, now suffers from early-onset Alzheimer's. Andrew, a wood turner, is certain the election was stolen and fully intends to do his part.

Anjanette Delgado: Editor of *Home in Florida: Latinx Writers and the Literature of Uprootedness* "William Kirk's debut novel is refreshingly quirky, hilarious and heartbreaking. Set against the backdrop of a divided America, it's a story of overcoming aging's challenges, of humor inspiring us to find connection, and of meaning amid the political chaos we live in."

"Once you start laughing, then tearing up, between taking deep breaths after every page, you'll hardly be the same, or samely be that hard, or something like that." Tony Norristown, author of *Second Shooter* and *Paper Clips Beat Scissors and Rocks Nine to Five*

Made in the USA
Middletown, DE
24 July 2024